THE CONSPIRATORS

THE CONSPIRATORS

G. W. Shaw

riverrun

First published in Great Britain in 2023 by

riverrun

an imprint of

Quercus Editions Limited
Carmelite House
50 Victoria Embankment
London EC4Y 0DZ

An Hachette UK company

A CIP catalogue record for this book is available
from the British Library.

Hardback 978 1 52942 007 4
TradePaperback 978 1 52942 008 1
Ebook 978 1 52942 009 8

10 9 8 7 6 5 4 3 2 1

Typeset by CC Book Production
Printed and bound in Great Britain by Clays Ltd, Elcograf S.p.A.

Papers used by riverrun are from well-managed forests and other responsible sources.

To Adrian and Polly

The cloth says to the weaver,
Do not weave me, for tomorrow, or the day after,
I will be your shroud.

Traditional Indian poem

ONE

The rich were careless about their wealth.

They deserved to be ripped off. The concierge at the Arcadia Shard Hotel was an old hand at this. He recognised an abandoned suitcase as an opportunity.

Mr Rakesh Garg's pale grey Samsonite case sat on the shelf in the left-luggage locker. The concierge glanced up at the CCTV camera that kept an eye on it.

Mr Garg had been in Room 2004. Nobody in the hotel really remembered Mr Garg or what he looked like. Guests came and went. Like Rakesh Garg, many didn't check out at the reception desk. If they settled their bill online, there was no need for them to talk to anybody.

The housekeeper remembered cleaning Mr Garg's room, the day before yesterday, after the first night of his stay. Room 2004 was particularly spectacular. High above the city, its north-facing wall was made entirely of glass. From the desk, or from the luxury free-standing bath, a guest could gaze out over the Thames. Tower Bridge and the Tower of London were below, small and unimpressive from this height, dwarfed by the new, brightly lit skyscrapers of the City of London.

The two nights had been paid for in advance. After the first, the housekeeper had tidied the room, vacuumed, made the bed, replaced two Johnnie Walker miniatures in the minibar and put new soaps onto the dishes in the bathroom.

This morning, after the second night, reception called up to his room but nobody answered.

Assuming he had gone, the way many guests do, without returning their key cards, the housekeeper knocked on the door at 11.15 a.m., called out, 'Housekeeping,' as she always did, then opened it with a key card.

She peered into Room 2004 and saw that, though tidy, it still appeared to be occupied. There was a jacket hanging on the back of a chair.

'Hello?' she called again, then backed out of the door. The front desk tried the mobile number Mr Garg had left with the booking, but that went straight through to voicemail.

'Mr Garg. This is the Arcadia Hotel. We've been trying to reach you. You don't appear to have checked out. However, we need to prepare the room for another guest. I hope you understand.'

Shortly after eleven thirty the duty manager arrived. Together they knocked again, twice, then let themselves in with the key card.

The housekeeper could see right away that something was not right, for the room remained exactly as she had left it the day before. It appeared that nobody had slept in the bed last night. Mr Garg's suits were still hanging in the wardrobe, his toothbrush still sat in the glass by the sink. The new miniatures of whisky were untouched.

But the room was booked for another guest, flying in from Abu Dhabi, so there was no time to stand around wondering what had happened to Mr Garg. The duty manager ordered the housekeeper to pack up Mr Garg's belongings. There was no passport – no belongings had been stored in the safe. If he had a briefcase, that must have been with him too, wherever he was.

Everything else – a couple of suits, shirts, underwear and shoes, some personal belongings – fitted neatly into Mr Garg's single Samsonite suitcase, which the duty manager took down to the concierge's office.

That Sunday afternoon, the passenger check-in officer at Heathrow Airport offered seat 8B on Air India 128 to a standby passenger.

The passenger who had originally booked the flight to Mumbai, a Mr Rakesh Garg, had not materialised.

Again, nobody thought much of it at the time because the rich are sometimes careless about such things. If they can afford one first class air ticket, they can probably afford another.

The concierge eyed the Samsonite case.

The trick to remaining unobserved was to arrange the other left luggage in such a way that it obscured the view of the camera.

The opportunity came when a film crew arrived to stay at the hotel. The concierge went out of his way to help them stack their outsize bags of lights and stands, until the pile blocked the camera's angle completely.

For all his work, the contents of the case were disappointing. No watches, no money, just a thin gold chain which he slipped into his tucked-in shirt, feeling it slither down his belly until it lay along the top of his belt. The only other items of interest were several packets of some kind of medication he didn't recognise, so he pocketed those and closed the case up.

In the gents' he untucked his shirt, retrieved the chain and looked at the packet of drugs. According to the name on the packet, they were called Lutinol.

'Never heard of it,' he said aloud to the empty room.

Taking out a vial, he examined it. Its contents were clear. Cracking the top, he sniffed it, then allowed a drop to fall onto his tongue. As far as he could tell, it tasted of nothing at all, so he tried a few more drops. By the time his shift ended, whatever it was had done nothing for him at all, so he threw the rest into the bin.

TWO

If Jacob Meaney had known from the start what accepting the job would get him into, he would never have taken it.

He was smart. He read the news. He knew that there were bad people out there.

But Carla had said, 'If you can't raise twenty thousand pounds, there's no point in our relationship. I'm over it.'

At the time twenty thousand pounds had seemed like such an absurd amount of money to a man who earned such a slender living translating books and poetry. There was no way a man like him could ever raise it.

It was Monday, Carla's lunch break. She had taken time from her job at the office.

Carla had a proper job. She was a marketing executive. She and Jacob sat together, knee to knee at the cafe table.

On the same day that Rakesh Garg had been checking into the Arcadia Hotel, Carla had removed her belongings from the dingy London Road flat she had shared with Jacob for a year. She said she couldn't live there any more.

'We'll never get a chance like this,' she told Jacob. 'The new apartment is perfect. Twenty thousand pounds. That's all.'

'I'm trying,' he said, pushing his fringe away from his eyes. 'I'm really trying. I just don't have the money right now.'

She was right. The flat was perfect. The estate agent had assured them of it. They had visited a show apartment for the third time just a week ago. Theirs was to be built in Phase 2 of the development, but the layout was identical. A living room with a fully fitted luxury kitchen, a deluxe marble bathroom and a second bedroom which was big enough to fit a desk in. Their balcony would look out over the rooftops of Brighton. 'You will have the most amazing sunset,' the estate agent had said. 'We have a crazy amount of interest in Phase Two. Especially the west-facing ones like yours.'

The agent looked serious, sympathetic, impatient all at once.

'I'll be frank. They're going fast. If you want one with the view, you'll need to let us know as soon as you can.'

The east-facing ones only looked out towards Phase 1, which was where the show apartment was. Phase 2 would block Phase 1's view completely.

'I'm putting in forty thousand,' said Carla. 'All you need is twenty. Then we have enough for the deposit.' In reality she was only putting in ten. Her wealthy Mallorcan parents were giving her the extra thirty.

Jacob reached his hands over the small table towards hers and laid them on top. 'I'll get it, somehow, I promise.' His own parents had died when he was twelve – he had no relations to borrow from.

6

'We need this if we're going move forward in life,' she said. 'Otherwise, as far as I'm concerned, it's over.'

Carla was the most beautiful woman he had ever gone out with. He had never expected to be in a relationship like this. He had always suspected that women like her were way out of his class. They had met four years ago when he had been teaching at a language school. She had been his student, wanting to improve her English so she could get on in business. Her English was now excellent and her career in digital marketing impressive.

'I just don't know how soon I'll be able to raise it, that's all,' he said.

'You don't even have a proper job any more, Jacob.'

'I do,' he protested. 'I'm a translator.'

'That's not a job,' she said. 'It's a hobby. Find the money, Jacob. For once, please show some commitment to our relation-ship. I'm thirty-five. My clock is ticking. If I'm going to have a baby, I need us to be secure, to have somewhere decent to live. Or I need us to end it.'

For five years, Jacob Meaney had been a teacher at the Regency Haplern, a private language school in Brighton. It is where he had first met Carla.

Jacob loved language. He believed that to speak many lan-guages was to be a citizen of the world.

Carla was classy, clever and ambitious, both for herself and for him. She had always told him he was so good at teaching, he should set up his own language school. He had loved her for her faith in him. She had made him spreadsheets to show

7

how much money they could make, and searched the city for properties they could rent to start the school in. She designed a logo, talked about a website and social media marketing, and bought him smart, businesslike clothes for his birthday. 'There are so many opportunities out there, Jacob. For once just reach out and take something. Quit the job. Start your own school.'

In the end, his reluctance turned out to be a blessing. Covid would have swallowed their new business whole. When the virus hit, the Regency Halpern Language School furloughed him for six months – as long as it could – before making him redundant. The foreign students had vanished. At the time he had relished the chance to spend more time translating, however little income it produced. The world seemed to be descending into chaos. His refuge was language – and Carla.

Finding any money at all would not be easy, but he had to if he was going to keep her.

He was owed a little for a Russian book he had finished work on in the spring – but that money would probably never come through, now Russia had been sanctioned – and he was midway through translating a young British poet for a Portuguese pub-lisher. Pay for this kind of work was a pittance, and saving anything was impossible. Much as he loved translating and the delicate task of trying to carry meaning from one language to another, it was never going to provide a deposit on a flat. He needed another plan.

Carla regularly bought magazines like *Wallpaper* and *Vogue Living* and left them lying around his little flat on the London Road, hoping that her aspirations were infectious. He studied them dutifully.

'Is there nobody you can ask?' Carla said. 'If we don't put our offer in soon, it'll be gone.' She pulled her hands away from his and picked up her cup of coffee. 'You must know someone.'

He thought about his friend Tariq. Tariq was rich. 'I can't just ask a friend to give me twenty thousand pounds,' said Jacob. 'It doesn't work like that. A hundred pounds, maybe. But twenty thousand . . .'

Tariq was another former student, one of those with rich parents who sent him to Brighton to learn a language.

'I love you, Jacob. You're funny. You're clever. You're kind. You would be a good father,' Carla said. 'But I don't want to live in a dump like a fucking tramp any more. I hate your flat. It stinks of mushrooms. I need a fresh start, with or without you.'

Her idiomatic English was excellent. He was proud of her and everything she had achieved.

She had packed a bag at the weekend. She told him it was a break, but it was more than that. It was an ultimatum.

'The estate agent says we need to put the deposit down by the end of September,' she said. She raised her cup and drained it. 'At the latest.' She stood. 'I am sorry, Jacob. I have to get back to work.'

Leaning across the cafe table, she gave him the lightest kiss on the cheek. Out of the front door, she turned right, past the window where he was still sitting. He raised his hand to wave her goodbye, but she had already marched on up the hill.

The moment she was gone, the waiter swept up her cup. 'Anything else for you?' he asked chillily. 'Or is that all for today?'

Jacob didn't answer.

Carla loved the flat in Phase 2. If only he had some way of earning that kind of money.

Just then, his phone rang. He peered at the screen, frowning.

It was not a number he recognised. Normally he dismissed numbers he didn't recognise, but now, the voice in his head was repeating, *There are so many opportunities out there, Jacob. For once just reach out and take something.* He answered the call.

'Hello?'

THREE

'Hello?'

'Is that Mr Jacob Meaney?'

In the busy cafe, Jacob held the phone to his ear. 'I'm sorry. It's quite loud in here. Why are you calling me?'

'I'm calling from the Windows Service Centre,' a voice said.

'The what? Is it about a job?' he demanded.

'We've detected that your computer has been infected by a virus,' said a man with a South Asian accent. 'I'm calling as a courtesy to help you fix the problem.'

Jacob was still laughing as he paid the bill. Stupid of him to imagine that some miracle might arrive out of the blue to save his relationship.

It was a question of biology. He understood that.

She wanted children while she could still have them.

In the flat above the charity shop that he had shared until recently with Carla, he poured himself a glass of cheap rosé and switched off his phone so that he could work uninterrupted. He picked up the volume of poetry he was translating into Portuguese.

He enjoyed the challenge of poetry. One language did not sit on another one like a red Lego brick on top of a yellow one. In poetry especially, everything was in play. Usually it felt like an adventure. Not today, though.

After lunch, he took a break and flipped through one of the design magazines Carla had bought for him. That made him worry that Carla might have been trying to get in touch, so he switched on his phone again and a voicemail symbol appeared on its small screen. Another unrecognised number. This time he ignored it.

He was on the verge of calling Carla. Instead, he dialled Tariq, his former student.

'Jacob,' his friend said, picking up immediately. 'Been ages. How are you?'

'So-so, being honest.'

'Still no work?' He could tell from the clatter and clink that Tariq was in his kitchen. There was music playing in the background.

'Carla has moved out. Temporarily, obviously. It's kind of a thing,' Jacob said.

There was a pause. 'Yeah. I heard. Sorry, mate,' Tariq answered. 'How many years was it?'

'It's not over. It's just a break.'

'Right, mate.'

'She has her heart fixed on getting on the housing ladder. The problem is, I don't really have the wherewithal.'

Tariq laughed. 'Give me a sentence using the word *where-withal*.' A joke from when Jacob had been Tariq's teacher.

Jacob smiled. Tariq was a good friend. He wouldn't mind him asking for a loan, at least. 'Listen, mate. I've got a favour to ask you . . .'

'Go for it. Anything.'

Jacob took a breath. He wasn't sure if he was making a fool of himself, but Tariq's family was wealthy. Maybe it wasn't such a ludicrous thing to do.

'What did you want?' his friend said. 'Go on.'

'Who is it, Tariq?'

There was somebody else in Tariq's kitchen. Jacob recognised the voice immediately. For a second, he was too shocked to speak. 'Is that Carla?' he said eventually.

'Yeah. It is,' said Tariq awkwardly, keeping his own voice low. 'She's staying around here for a bit.'

Jacob pulled the phone away from his ear, looked at it for a second. 'I thought you were my friend.'

'Mate. It's nothing like that. Listen. She just needed a place to get her head together.'

Jacob ended the call and laid his head onto the open poetry book in front of him.

Immediately his phone rang again.

Jacob answered it and blurted, 'Are you two sleeping together?'

'I beg your pardon?' A woman with a hint of an Australian accent was speaking to him.

'Who is this?'

'I'm just after a minute of your time, Mr Meaney.'

Angrily, Jacob ended the call and switched off the phone. If

13

he was going to earn money, he had to work. He returned to his desk and settled back into the slow task of translation.

But it was hard to concentrate. Life was slipping away from him. In his twenties, when his friends went clubbing, or wind-surfing, he had mostly lived in a world of books and languages. They had mocked him for being old before his time, but he had been, for the most part, content. He had imagined that would be enough for him, until he had met Carla. He had thought they had been on a journey of discovery together. It had changed him, but he understood that he had not changed fast enough to keep up with her needs and desires.

'You're not a man of action,' she had complained, and that was still very obviously true.

He was still at his desk just after four in the afternoon when the doorbell rang. When he looked down from the first-floor window he saw a smart black Lexus with tinted windows, parked illegally in the bus stop outside his house.

The doorbell rang again.

There was no entryphone, so he descended the narrow stairs to the front door next to the British Heart Foundation charity shop. When he opened it, a woman stood there. She was tall, with straight dirty blonde hair and had a Burberry messenger bag slung over one shoulder. She lowered her dark glasses and peered at him.

'Jacob Meaney?' she said.

'Yes.'

'*The* Jacob Meaney?'

'I'm sorry?'

'That was a little rude,' she said. 'Putting the phone down on me.'

'Did I?'

'Mr Meaney,' she said. 'I have a proposal for you. One that I think you're going to find very interesting.'

FOUR

The woman took off her dark glasses, folded them, and put them into her shoulder bag. She was in her late thirties, he guessed, a little older than him. 'Know what?' she said. 'I have been trying to get in touch with you for bloody hours.'

'Me?'

'First. You are the Jacob Meaney – the one who speaks Hindi, Russian and Portuguese?'

He blinked. 'How did you know that?'

She grinned. 'Oh my God. I've been looking for you all over.' She moved forward, hugged him. He stood, startled, until she stepped back again, looked him up and down. 'Do you have anything else to wear, Jacob? I've booked tea for us at the Grand.' She looked at her watch. 'And we're running a little late.'

'The Grand?' The big, cream-white Victorian layer-cake of a hotel, decked out in ironwork balconies and fluttering Union Jacks, that stood above the beach.

'Five minutes,' she declared. 'I'll wait in the car.' The car's driver was sitting in the front seat, playing a game on his phone.

'You didn't tell me your name. Or what any of this is all about.'

'Eloise,' she said. 'My name's Eloise. Very pleased to meet you.'

Back in the flat he peered out of the window again and watched Eloise lean back against the illegally parked car. She dug into her handbag and pulled out a packet of Marlboro Lites and a lighter, then looked up and smiled at him, as if she had known all along he was watching her.

He had a tweed jacket which he wore when the language school hosted formal events. Carla had always said it made him look like an old man. He chose the least crumpled of his shirts and the cleaner of his three pairs of shoes.

When he opened his front door she dropped the last of her cigarette into the gutter and trod on it. 'I guess you'll do,' she said and leaned forward to brush lint from his shoulder. Close up, she smelled expensive. 'Let's go.'

Walking around to the other side, she got in beside him and the car pulled out into slow traffic.

'Can I call you Jacob? Are you working right now?' she asked. 'I mean. Of course a man like you is working. I wondered if you have availability. I represent an elite European company. We are are in urgent need of an interpreter. We would like to offer you a few weeks' work.'

'I'm sorry,' he said. 'I don't really—'

'You probably won't have heard of us. However, we can offer a generous rate of pay. Are you available right away?'

Jacob Meaney wasn't an interpreter. He had never done interpreting. Interpreting was a very different skill to translating. 'How did you find my number? How did you find me?'

As the car descended down a narrow street towards the sea, she mentioned the name of a website on which interpreters and translators offered their services. Now she said it, he dimly remembered signing up to it years ago when he was younger, before he had taken a job with Regency Halpern. Nobody had ever contacted him using it.

'My phone number was on a website?'

'Not on the website. I had to dig around a little more to find you, but fortunately there are not many Jacob Meaneys in the world.'

'You found out where I lived too?'

'Listen,' she said. 'Let me get to the point. Our company has a problem. I came to London for an important meeting with our suppliers. Unfortunately the person I was supposed to meet didn't show up. Instead another gentleman contacted me. He appears to have taken over the business at short—'

She stopped because house music was blaring from her bag. She pulled out her phone and answered: '*Myroslav. Ya nashla yego. Ya seychas s nim razgovarivayu.*'

She was speaking Russian. *I've found him,* she was saying to a man named Myroslav. *I'm talking to him now.*

She ended the call and turned to him. 'So anyway. We have an urgent business deal to complete and it turns out that our new business partner speaks Hindi, but very little English. Which seems a bit unusual.'

'Not really,' said Jacob.

'Really? OK. Well, our company is run by a Ukrainian who speaks mostly Russian. The business operates out of Brazil, so we need Portuguese. You have no idea how hard it is to find an interpreter with that combination of languages – let alone at short notice. So how much do you charge a day?'

He hesitated. 'It depends.' He was not used to job interviews in black limousines.

'You must have a day rate, Jacob.'

He realised he should try to explain to her he was not, formally at least, an interpreter. He was simply a translator. The jobs were very different.

'Come on. You probably realise I'm desperate. Who else would drive down from London on the off chance? How much do you charge a day? Name a figure.'

This woman was offering him money. An opportunity to do something different. An opportunity to change. He was not a man of action, but perhaps he should become one.

'Three hundred pounds?' he said, and kicked himself for starting with such a high figure. 'Obviously that includes evenings.'

The woman didn't even miss a beat. 'And you have a valid British passport?'

The car pulled up outside the hotel. A doorman in a bowler hat and checked trousers opened Jacob's door.

'This way,' beckoned Eloise, marching up the stairs to the hotel lobby, where she stopped and spun around, looking up at the ornate plasterwork. 'I adore this place. Don't you?'

'You've been here before?'

'God, no. I could never have afforded it,' she said. 'Come.'

She had reserved a table. 'Tea will be with you shortly,' said a waiter.

'I don't really have any specialist vocabulary,' said Jacob. 'I might have to spend a week or so getting up to speed.'

'We need someone who can start straight away. It's extremely urgent. We're halfway through this mega deal.'

He hesitated. 'I don't even know who you are. What kind of work is it?'

She picked up a starched napkin and shook it out. 'Simple interpreting, that's all. At business meetings. We will pay four hundred a day, plus we'll pay a weekend bonus of a hundred a day. There's a minimum of three weeks' work, including week-ends.'

The waiter approached to offer a choice of Breakfast, Darjeeling or Earl Grey. 'Three weeks' work?'

'At least. I can guarantee you three, but almost certainly if we like your work, this will total up to six weeks. You will stay with us and be paid whether we require your services or not. We just need you to be on hand.'

He hesitated. 'How much?'

She repeated the sum: four hundred pounds a day, five hundred at weekends. 'Plus,' she said, 'you would be staying in the most amazing place you've ever been in. You won't believe it. Like, the swankiest house you've ever seen. Jesus, you will die when you see it, Jacob. There's a pool, a gym, tennis courts, a boat on the lake. Everything. You get your own apartment. Food. All included. Anything you want. To be honest, you will only be needed for an hour or two at a time and maybe only two or three days a week. I'm sure you're a busy man but there would be time to do your own work out there too. We will cover travel, naturally. Think about it. Nine thousand pounds for the first three weeks. It's a doddle.'

He opened his mouth to speak but nothing came out.

'Please, Mr Meaney. Say something.'

'Well . . .'

'Starting tomorrow.'

'And I can do my own translating work in my free time?'

'Naturally.'

A woman brought two cake stands, each tier loaded with pastries, sandwiches, scones and cocktail sausages. 'Isn't this just gorgeous?' said Eloise. She reached out and picked up a tiny ham sandwich and popped it whole into her mouth.

An unexpected job offer that could solve all his problems. He thought about Carla, and about how she would handle this situation. 'Fifty per cent of the first three weeks in advance?'

'Why the hell not?' That rich, full-throated laugh again, crumbs on the corners of her mouth.

And when he was back home in the flat, he checked his account and the promised money was already in there, as if by magic. Four and a half thousand pounds. He logged out of his bank account, then logged back in, just to check. There it was. Paid from a PayPal account.

As instructed by Eloise, he scanned his passport. She had asked him to send her a copy of the main page to a Gmail address. There was no hint at all of the name of the company he would be working for.

Many thanks for the payment. Passport scan attached as requested. Will I need to revise any specialist vocabulary?

The reply – it wasn't exactly an answer – arrived in his inbox a few minutes later.

Pick up at 6 a.m. tomorrow.

He sat at his desk, a little stunned. He should call Carla and let her know the good news. He would have the money within a month – most of it, at least.

He was on the verge of dialling her number when he stopped. If he called her now, right after finding out that she was with Tariq, she probably wouldn't even believe him. He wasn't entirely sure he believed all this himself. He would call her when he was there. He imagined the conversation – how impressed she would be, how happy he would make her.

That night he slept badly, waking from strange dreams to wonder if he should have found out more about the job before committing himself to it.

The next morning, Jacob woke before his alarm went off, shaved and dressed and stood at the window.

At twenty to six in the morning, the black Lexus was on the street outside again, parked at the bus stop. Its windows were dark, making it impossible to see inside.

My dearest, dearest Tymko

As always, I miss you. I hope you are with your Baba. I hope she is keeping you safe. I miss the smell of your skin. I miss that laugh of yours, the one that sounds like a sink emptying of water. I miss the way you cry and run to me when you fall off your scooter. I worry that you will have grown so much by the next time I see you, I will not recognise you at all.

Today I pickled watermelon in horseradish, cinnamon, garlic and chilli, and Japanese cider vinegar. I cut the watermelon into slices that are about 1.5cm thick. That way there is still a good crunch to it. Be careful when you cut watermelon. The best way is to cut a centimetre from one end and stand it on the flat area, then slice it down the middle.

I am surrounded by knives. I dream of stabbing people with them. I dream of it every night.

Please understand that I love nothing in this world more than I love you.

FIVE

The Lexus pulled up outside a small square building.

'Here?' asked Jacob, peering out of the window. They were somewhere in north Kent. The car had driven through a barrier and onto the grounds of a small private airport.

'Just inside,' the driver said.

Eloise was standing at a glass door, waiting. She waved.

'I don't know how to thank you,' she said. 'You've saved my bloody life. Is that your bag? I'll have it put on board.'

He looked around the terminal. It looked more like an office reception area. 'You never said where I'm actually going.'

'How careless of me, Jacob. We're going to Vienna. Do you have your passport?'

'I'll need German as well then?'

'Maybe,' she said vaguely. That hint of an Australian accent again. 'The passport, please.'

Jacob pulled it from his jacket pocket.

'Anything at all you need, just ask me, Jacob. I'm here to help.'

She took his passport, flicked through it briefly, then, instead of returning it to him, placed it into her leather shoulder bag. 'So you speak German too? How many languages altogether?'

'Six professionally, including English. A few more passably. My mother was Portuguese. I taught in India for a year. The rest I sort of picked up along the way, and then added a few more.'

'Freaking amazing.' Her eyes were wide. 'You are a god.'

'In Africa, it can be perfectly normal to speak six or seven languages.'

She raised her eyebrows. 'Well, isn't that fantastic? You are a mountain of information.' It might have been the Australian inflection in her voice, but he was not sure whether she was mocking him or praising him. 'Sit down. Relax. Have a cup of coffee.'

'Do I need a boarding pass?'

She smiled. 'Oh no, Jacob. It's a private jet. Everything is taken care of.'

'A private jet?'

Within a minute a woman in a red suit approached to offer him coffee, which came on a tray with a small plate of madeleines.

If he had owned a smartphone with a camera, he would have messaged Carla now: *Guess where I am.* She would have loved this. She who had doubted he would ever earn anything. Over the next few weeks he'd be earning more than she did, if things went well. It was a long shot, but for the first time he was starting to think he could win Carla back. They would settle down. She could have babies. He would provide for her. He had always worked hard. Now, finally, it was paying off.

There was a table full of newspapers. The *Standard* had a

gory story about an unidentified torso being discovered in the Thames. The man had been beheaded and his hands and feet cut off. A South Asian, probably around forty years old, police said. Nobody had come forward to report a man of that description missing, so the police were appealing to the public for help. He picked up a copy of the Norwegian tabloid *VG* instead. He read the headline. *Uhyggelig oppdagelse i Themsen*. They had gone one step further and printed a fuzzy photo of the corpse being dragged from the water.

Up until the age of twelve, Jacob had had a perfect upbringing. Jacob's father had been a lieutenant in the British Army, stationed in places like Belfast and Osnabrück. His mother had been a Portuguese viola player. For a small child, life on army bases was idyllic. Father Christmas came every year by helicopter. When invited to the officers' mess, he was given chocolates and spoiled by the soldiers. Life was perfect.

Then, one New Year, returning from a party in Gesmold, his parents' car was hit by a petrol tanker. The driver, police said later, probably had a heart attack at the wheel. His mother and father had not been killed instantaneously but when he had asked to see them, the grown-ups became awkward and evasive. 'Soon, soon,' they said. His mother died first, his father a day later. Their injuries had been too severe to survive.

They had held a ceremony on the base, lines of soldiers, saluting his mother and father's coffins as they were loaded onto the plane. Jacob travelled back to England with them.

His aunt was at the airbase, waiting for him. His father's sister was a woman who had never wanted children. After two weeks in her big dark house in Bexhill-on-Sea, his aunt sent him on to public school where the food was recognisably military.

What he had found harder to cope with was the complete absence of love. He missed his parents. It wasn't just the petty cruelty of a minor public school regime. He had arrived halfway through the academic year. *This is Jacob. He's had some very bad news. You must be nice to him.* The other children had already made friends. Bereavement had already marked him as different. He accepted that he was an outsider.

The other thing that would mark him out as different from the other boys was language. Jacob had grown up bilingual, speaking Portuguese with his mother and English when his parents were together. By the time he arrived at the school in England, he had learned German because that was what they spoke where he lived, and because the family had spent their summers in Brittany, he had picked up French too.

It didn't surprise him how bad his fellow schoolchildren were at languages; what did was that they didn't seem to care. Language lessons were baffling to him. The French teacher was called Mrs Hardwick and her pronunciation was so wayward Jacob sometimes struggled to understand what she was saying. On his third week at the school, Jacob made the mistake of trying to correct her when she uttered the word *écureuil* – squirrel – pronouncing it as *eck-oo-real,* instead of *ec-cue-roy.* Instead of thanking him, Mrs Hardwick gave him a detention.

After his first half-term holiday, Mrs Hardwick asked each pupil in turn what they had done during the break. *Pendant les vacances.* Mostly they had been playing *au football dans le parc* or watching *la télévision.* When it came to Jacob's turn he said that he had stayed with his aunt in Bexhill-on-Sea, but that his aunt had not wanted him there because she was having an affair with a veterinary nurse who was a married woman.

The following week Mrs Hardwick approached his desk, pulled a yellow hardback book out of her bag and said, 'If you're so clever, work your way through that. Silently, please.'

It was an old yellow hardback with a frayed dust jacket called *Teach Yourself Norwegian* by A. Sommerfelt and I. Marm.

Uhyggelig oppdagelse i Themsen. Everyone these days seemed to know the Norwegian word '*hyggelig*', a kind of sentiment of cosiness. *Uhyggelig* was the opposite. In this case he would have translated it with the word 'grisly'. 'Grisly discovery in the Thames.' *VG* speculated that the killing was the result of a gangland execution.

'Poor guy.' He looked round. Eloise was standing behind him with a pastry in her hand.

'Do you speak Norwegian?'

She laughed. 'No! But he's obviously dead, isn't he? You don't need to speak Norwegian to see that.'

The plane was small. The seats were large and upholstered in white leather, the table and walls were shiny polished walnut and mahogany. On his table there was a small white vase with a single white lily in it. The vase remained upright as they rose steeply into the sky. It was, he discovered, secured by Velcro.

Jacob Meaney had never been in anything like this in his life. He was impressed. Carla would have been even more so.

Airborne, a woman appeared from the rear of the plane with glasses of champagne.

'Go for it,' said Eloise. 'I won't tell if you won't.'

The woman appeared again soon afterwards with smoked salmon and cheese. Somewhere over France they refilled glasses. 'To an exciting life,' said Eloise, raising hers.

Immigration at Vienna was swift. A single official checked their documents and bags. A private minibus with tinted windows was waiting in a nearby car park to take them across another expanse of tarmac towards half a dozen helicopters. They pulled up by a small, bright green one. A broad-shouldered man lowered himself from the pilot seat and approached the minibus.

'Hi, Iosef,' said Eloise. 'This is Jacob. Iosef works for Mr Bondarenko.'

Iosef nodded and grabbed Jacob's bag. 'We fly in this?' Jacob nodded towards the helicopter. He thought of the big machines that had brought Father Christmas. This looked too small, too flimsy.

'Five minutes, Iosef, OK? I need a cigarette.' Eloise turned to Jacob. 'I bet you don't smoke, do you?'

Jacob shook his head. 'Are you even allowed to here?' But there was nobody to stop her. Jacob watched her, phone held in her left hand, answering messages with her thumb, placing the cigarette in her mouth with her other hand and then blowing smoke out into the warm air.

'When do I actually begin work?' he asked.

'Soon, soon,' she answered, still looking at her screen. She flicked the half-smoked cigarette across the tarmac. 'Come on. Let's go. You first.'

He pulled himself up into the aircraft's small interior, took the seat furthest from the door and set about buckling himself in. She followed him in, eyes still glued to her phone screen.

'It's been a while since I did this kind of work, you know? I'm mostly a translator. It's a little different, interpreting.'

She stopped tapping and looked him in the eye, frowning. 'Don't say you're not up to this, Jacob. I've just paid you four and a half thousand pounds.'

'No, no,' he said as the rotors began to turn above them. 'I'll be fine.'

SIX

They rose above the tarmac of Vienna Airport, then the heli-copter tilted and began speeding over thin suburbs, out over neatly farmed countryside and small villages.

'Where are we going?' Jacob mouthed.

'Carinthia,' Eloise shouted above the noise. 'The Alps,' she explained. 'Close to the Slovenian border. It's stunning. You will love it. Less than two hours and we're there.'

Jacob pressed his head back against the perspex of the window and watched as the flat farmland gave way to woods and then hills.

The hills became mountains and the mountains became steeper. They passed a trio of hang-gliders, playing in the rising evening air. As they rode over peaks, the helicopter was buffeted by warm updraughts.

Eventually the deafening noise of the rotors softened.

Eloise leaned right across him. 'There,' she said, pointing past him.

They had emerged into a lush valley above a long, thin alpine lake, the water a deep, dark greeny-blue. Properties dotted parts of the north shore. They dropped down above the water, heading for what looked like a much less populated slope on the south side.

There, straight ahead, was a clearing in the trees, about half a kilometre above the waterline.

'That's it,' she said, squeezing against him to show him. 'It's the most fabulous place in the world.'

'Which one?' As they approached, several dazzling white rectangles were visible, cut into the slope of the hillside, surrounded by lush gardens.

'All of them. The whole place is his.'

'Jesus,' he said. The estate was huge. Whoever owned this must be worth a fortune.

As if she had understood his thoughts, Eloise laughed. 'Right?'

And now they were descending fast onto a square of tarmac a little way down the grassy slope from the cluster of buildings, dropping below the treeline, then landing with a gentle bump.

They waited for the rotors to slow, then a tall, good-looking man in a black bomber jacket and jeans appeared at the passenger door, opening it for them.

'Hello, Webb,' said Eloise.

'Hiya, Eloise. All good?' Webb spoke English.

'Mission accomplished. This is our man.'

'Pleased to meet you.' Webb led the way up the slope towards the buildings. 'Welcome to the organisation.'

The garden was magnificent. Huge exotic pines shaded the lawns. As they neared the building the pathway was fringed by rich, lush flowerbeds, leading to a huge paved terrace in front of the house.

'Well,' smiled Eloise. 'Here we are.'

'My God,' said Jacob.

The large, graceful mid-century modern building sat in the natural slope of the hillside. Its white-painted concrete and grey steel frame seemed to defy gravity, spreading itself thinly over the curve of the hill. To the front, the building lifted clear of the land, as if the whole structure were just balancing there. The building's lines were clean and uncomplicated, its horizontal geometry punctuated by bamboos and Japanese maples.

'He lives here?'

'And so do you for the next few weeks, Jacob.' Eloise put her arm through his and pulled him forward.

The horizontal expanse of glass reflected the world the building had been placed into.

'He must be rich.'

'Oh, very.' Eloise smiled. 'Very, very rich. Come on.' She led him up open stone steps towards a platform a couple of metres above ground. She pulled open a large glass front door. 'Let me show you round.' She stopped, shouted, 'Tamara! Come here.'

Jacob turned to see an immense brown and black dog padding towards them over the polished concrete floor of a huge open plan living area. The room was dotted with carefully placed furniture. Eloise let go of Jacob's hand, squatted down on her heels and pushed her face into the dog's. 'Tamara, this is Jacob. You're not to bite him, OK?'

'Bite?'

'Joke. Tamara is a pussycat. She's the love of Myroslav's life. Big, isn't she?'

It was the first time she had mentioned her boss by his first name, Jacob realised.

'Immense,' he said. 'What is she?'

'She's a pure-breed Leonberger. Myroslav named her after a famous Ukrainian weight lifter. Tamara is the only girl he ever loved.' She stood up again and said, 'This way.'

They emerged into the living area, which was huge and filled with sunlight. Jacob's footsteps seemed unusually loud on the hard floor. He paused and gaped at the room.

'My girlfriend would love this,' he said.

'You have a girlfriend?' Her eyebrows raised slightly.

Ahead of him stretched a plain, dark wood floor. A pair of orange chairs had been carefully placed next to a glass-topped coffee table, on which lay three art magazines, none of which looked like they had been touched.

'Arne Jacobsen Swan chairs,' he said, surprised at himself.

'Yes. Originals apparently. Myroslav spent a lot of money on them. You are a fan?'

He had seen them in one of the magazines Carla had given him. He turned slowly, taking in the huge living area. Positioned to look out over the front garden on the other side of the room, a perspex bubble chair with a big yellow cushion in it hung from a chain. To his left there seemed to be an indoor pond. Lush green plants grew from white cubes artfully placed around it. And to the right was a second sitting area – this one sunken into the floor, grey upholstered sofas placed in front of a giant TV screen.

'Eloise?' A man's voice boomed across the room.

Jacob swung round. Two people were sitting at a big glass dining table to the right. One of them was a large, well-groomed man in a crisp shirt. He got up and approached her, grasping her by the arm, kissing her on the cheek.

He pointed at Jacob. '*Eto on?*'

'*Da.*'

Myroslav was speaking Russian, he realised, and so was Eloise. *Is this him?*

The man looked around sixty, in good shape. Thinning hair was swept back over his head. He offered a hand. 'Hello,' he said in hesitant English. 'I am Myroslav. Welcome to my house. You are my guest.' He switched to Russian, obviously more comfortable in the language. 'I'm very glad Eloise found you. She says you are a genius.'

Jacob laughed, nervous. 'Well, I wouldn't—'

'You are sent by God, Mr Meaney.'

'This place . . .' said Jacob, still looking around him. Beyond the dining table the dining-room area opened onto a huge garden, with lush lawns to the west side of the pathway they'd walked up. Light dappled the grass below a false acacia tree. 'It's incredible.'

'You like it?' Myroslav seemed genuinely thrilled.

'Is that a Florence Knoll sofa?'

Myroslav clapped his hands in delight. 'You recognise it? You know about classic furniture?'

'That's a Noguchi table, too?' Jacob pointed.

'A 1948 original. I paid a fortune for it. You are a connoisseur.' He beamed. 'Eloise, you have excelled yourself.'

'I just picked a few things up . . . from magazines.'

There was another man sitting at the table, much younger,

wearing a white T-shirt and jeans. He didn't stand, but he looked round briefly as if to acknowledge Jacob's presence. Eloise grabbed Jacob's arm again, this time almost possessively, and marched him over. 'That is Draper,' said Eloise. 'He is our head of IT.'

'Hi, man,' Draper said in English.

'Draper is from Florida, has a tattoo of his mother on his ass, and he has terrible taste in music,' said Eloise.

'Actually it's a tattoo of you, Eloise,' said Draper.

'Children, children,' said Myroslav. 'What about Rakesh Garg?'

'Like I said,' said Eloise. 'I went to the restaurant. He never showed up. I called his phone. Nothing. I called the company, they told me we had to talk to this guy Nazim instead.'

'Nazim? Nazim who?'

'Just Nazim. That's all I know. They said he would be in touch, but warned me that he didn't speak English.'

'Unprofessional,' said Myroslav.

'It's what it is.'

'It's fucked up,' muttered Myroslav. 'We had a deal.'

'It will be fine,' Eloise said. 'I promise. And look.' She held out her hand. 'Now we have an interpreter.'

'Yes. We do.' He turned and stared at Jacob for a second, then broke into a smile. 'Welcome to the team,' he said in loud, accented English.

SEVEN

'Eloise says you are a genius with languages.' Jacob's new boss, Myroslav Bondarenko, addressed him in Russian. 'You know the importance of language in any business deal? It can be absolutely crucial. Any misunderstanding can cost a fortune. You know why the Honda Jazz is called the Honda Jazz?' Myroslav didn't wait for an answer. 'Originally it was called the Honda Fitta. They had a big campaign planned. Until someone pointed out *Fitta* means pussy in Italian.'

He laughed uproariously, looking around him, as if expecting everyone else to laugh too.

'Is that the one about the Honda Fitta?' asked Draper, speaking in English. 'He tells that story a lot. He just likes saying rude words like pussy.'

Jacob turned to Myroslav. 'Norwegian,' he said. 'Or Swedish. Or Danish.'

'What?' Myroslav frowned.

'It wasn't Italian. *Fitta* is slang for the female genitals in Norwegian, Swedish and Danish.'

For a second, Myroslav glared, angry at being contradicted. 'Is that so?'

'Be nice, Slava,' warned Eloise.

Myroslav broke into a grin. 'Well, we are obviously in most excellent hands. I hope you enjoy the house. We have a swimming pool and an excellent gymnasium. There is a spa and a jacuzzi. There is a maid who is an excellent cook and will prepare excellent food any time of day. We also have a speedboat.' He paused. 'Do you play tennis?'

'A little.'

'Excellent. We can play together.' He grasped Jacob by both shoulders. 'Well . . . anything at all, please don't hesitate to ask. I want you to feel absolutely comfortable here. Eloise will show you to your apartment.'

'"When do I start?" would be the first question,' said Jacob.

Myroslav spread his hands wide. 'Soon. Soon. Whatever you need, Eloise will provide.'

'Within reason obviously,' said Eloise, switching to English.

And then Myroslav turned away, returning to the table next to Draper, opening up his laptop and lapsing into silence.

'This way,' said Eloise.

'You speak Russian?' asked Jacob.

'It's why I got to know Myroslav in the first place. I met a Russian man in a bar in Vienna. I told him I was looking for a backer for a business idea. He put me in touch with Myroslav.'

Eloise led him down a corridor, past a door with a round window.

'My parents were born in Russia. They emigrated after the end of the Soviet Union. Myroslav grew up in a Russian-speaking family in Ukraine. He made a lot of money there, fifteen, twenty years ago. I mean a lot of money, understand?'

'So what is your job?'

'Finding you, apparently, though I'm supposed to be head of development and marketing.' Jacob caught sight of a kitchen. A thin woman was slicing meat with a large knife.

At the rear of the building was a door. It opened onto the gardens that Jacob had seen from the dining room.

'Marketing for what?' he asked, but was immediately distracted by the view ahead of him. 'Wow.'

'Isn't it?'

The way they had approached the house from the helicopter landing pad, the view back across the valley had been sheltered by the surrounding trees. From the terrace at the rear of the house the view down to the lake below was stunning.

'You will be on call. Whenever he needs someone to translate, I will contact you. As he said, we have a difficult situation. We have lost contact with our supplier. Because we're working across an eight-and-a-half-hour time-zone difference on this project, you might be called on at any time, day or night. Do you understand?'

Jacob stopped and said, 'But nobody's told me what this project is.'

'Pharmaceuticals,' she answered.

He looked back at the luxury mansion; he thought of the tinted glass of the vehicles parked outside and his skin felt cold. 'Drugs?'

She laughed. 'Your face, sweetie.'

'What?'

'Not *that* kind of drugs. Medicines. Good drugs. Not bad drugs. Myroslav Bondarenko is a businessman,' she said simply. 'He uses his finance to leverage business deals. Big, big deals. Right now, there are a lot of interesting opportunities in pharma, and I came up with one and together we are going for it.'

'What kind of opportunities?'

She didn't seem to have heard the question. 'There's the gym and behind it there is a pool and a hot tub.' She pointed to a grey rectangular building with small high windows to the left of the path. 'And that's your accommodation.' Behind another acacia tree was a small block, more modest than the house, but built in the same dazzling style. 'Come on.'

'You're on the first floor,' she said, leading him up an external staircase. 'Draper's below you. If he starts playing metalcore at two in the morning, you are welcome to kill him. You're right here.'

She pushed open the unlocked door onto a large living room with a settee, armchairs, a desk and a huge TV. 'That's an Eames chair,' he said.

'Is it? Bully for it.' She led him through to a bedroom with a gigantic double bed, with an en-suite bathroom with bath, shower and bidet. A large glass window looked out over dark woods to the east. There was a pile of thick white towels stacked up on a table. A white towelling dressing gown hung next to them, with matching white slippers.

'Is it OK?' she asked.

'OK? It's amazing.'

At the back of the living room was a kitchen with a hob, a microwave, a kettle and a fridge.

'This is your home for the next few weeks,' she said.

He gazed around. The place was immaculate. 'Dial five if you want food or anything at all. The kitchens are open twenty-four hours. The maid will deal with any dietary requirements.'

There was a knock at the door. Webb appeared with his suitcase and, without waiting for instructions, took it to the bedroom.

'One more thing,' she said. 'Obviously your work is confidential. You do understand that?'

'Of course,' he said. As he spoke the words, he realised he didn't understand very much at all.

'Good. Because Myroslav is a very private man. The conversations you will be part of may be commercially sensitive. We have a very unique business opportunity. In a matter of a few weeks we can make a great deal of money if everything goes to plan.'

'It might be easier to understand if I knew what the business was.'

'For now, we would prefer if you didn't discuss our business with any of your friends or colleagues. They don't need to know where you are, or what you are working on. Do you have a phone?'

'Well, yes, but I don't think it works out here.'

'Can we have it all the same?'

'My phone?'

'You said it doesn't work. We'll keep it for you anyway. It's just standard business security.'

'Really?'

'You'll get it back.'

41

He hesitated.

'It's standard, Jacob. You've nothing to worry about. It's part of the deal. We pay you well but it's our terms and conditions.'

She held out her hand. Slowly he reached into his pocket and pulled out his device.

She looked at it, amused. 'Old school.'

'I'm not a big believer in smartphones. They know a bit too much about you. What about wi-fi?'

'Wi-fi is not available, I'm afraid. If you need to get in touch with anyone, you can do that through me. I live in the main house. If you need to do a web search, or need a printer or something, contact Draper. Oh, Draper has some web pages Myroslav wants you to look at to check the Portuguese translation's good. There are also some Spanish pages and French pages on the website. You speak those?'

'Fairly well. Website?'

'Marketing stuff. Nothing crazy. Just cast your eyes over them tomorrow. Just hang out today. Relax.'

'Wait. No wi-fi?'

'Is that going to be a problem?'

He frowned. 'How do I stay in touch with my girlfriend?'

'Can't she survive a few weeks without you?' Eloise looked amused.

'We're about to buy a flat together. I may need to be in touch.'

'No problem.' She smiled. 'I can send messages for you. Just write them down and give them to me.' She turned to go.

'Also I'm translating some poems. I'm supposed to send them to my editor.'

She swung back around, her smile thin. 'Of course. Give them to me and I'll send them. It's the rules round here. We have to be super-secure. You do understand, don't you?'

'Not really. Because you haven't told me anything about the business.'

'Relax,' she said. 'Enjoy the sexy furniture. We'll call you if we need you.'

'What if I want to go for a hike?'

That small smile again. 'Come on, Jacob. A few weeks of your life, that's all we ask. Then you can go as wild as you like. We've got Netflix and Prime and all that. There's a gym and there's an amazing pool. You got swimming shorts? No? I'll get some sent round.' She leaned forward and grabbed hold of his forearm. 'Just give into it, OK? This place is heaven. I just want you to enjoy yourself.'

Only after she'd gone did he remember that she hadn't given him his passport back. That was when he first felt uneasy, realising that something had begun to close around him.

EIGHT

That afternoon Eloise returned with a pair of swimming trunks for Jacob.

'For you,' she said. 'Ralph Lauren.' She smirked, showing him the label, as if he needed to check. 'Pretty cool, huh?'

'While you're there, I have a message I'd like you to send.'

He picked up a notebook from the desk. It was a beautiful desk – polished walnut, on thin silver legs with a white laminate surface. He tore a hand-written page out, folded it in half and handed it to her. 'The email address is at the top.'

Eloise took the paper, unfolded it and read it aloud. '*Dearest Carla. Everything is going to be all right.*'

'It's private.'

She looked up from the paper. 'I have to read it if I'm going to send it. That's the point, isn't it?' She continued: '*I have taken a well-paid job in Austria and I'm sure I will have the twenty thousand pounds soon, if things carry on well, perhaps just a few weeks.*'

'It's personal,' he protested.

'*I know that we're very different people, but that's a good thing, right? I really want to make this work. I love you and miss you. Kiss kiss kiss. J.*' She turned the paper over in her hands as if wanting there to be more. 'This is the girlfriend?'

'Obviously.'

'And your relationship is going through some stuff.'

'Not that it's your business,' he said.

'Is she very beautiful?'

'You're not really allowed to ask stuff like that, are you?'

She looked back down at the paper. 'I'm going to have to take out the bit about you being in Austria.'

'Fine. But will you send it? As soon as you can?'

She folded the paper in half. 'So what's the twenty thousand pounds for? Please tell me it's something exotic like a gambling debt with the mob. Or reconstructive surgery.'

'It's a deposit on a flat.'

'Disappointing.' Putting it in her back pocket, her face lit up. 'Oh. I get it. She doesn't think a translator can raise that kind of money? And you feel you have to prove it to her. Is she a gold digger?'

He leaned forward to take the paper back off her, but she pulled it away. 'I'm sorry,' she said. 'I'm Australian. I over-stepped.'

'Can you just send it? Please.'

She thought for a while. 'So it's twenty thousand you actually need? And we've agreed nine, with an option for eighteen?'

'Yes.'

'Interesting. And now you've looked around a bit, you're wondering how much you should really be charging us, aren't you?'

'Is that all?'

She laughed, backing out of the room. 'Sorry. Don't mind me, Jacob. I'm sure your girlfriend is absolutely fucking gorgeous.'

Jacob donned the trunks, found a towel and wandered down to find the pool.

Eloise had said it was behind the gym. He found a pathway and some steps that rose up a slope. It was there, surrounded by slender Italian cypress trees.

'Wow,' he said, though there was no one to hear. It was built into a terracotta terrace and the tiles that lined the pool were metallic gold. The water sparkled. At the far end there was a seating area of armchairs and grey woven cane recliners, with thick sage green cushions.

He dipped a toe. The water was warm.

He swam leisurely lengths, first breaststroke, then front crawl. For a private pool, it was remarkably big. Then he turned over and did a couple of lengths of backstroke.

Reaching the end, he paused and looked up.

A shadow appeared over him. He twisted in the water to see Myroslav standing by the pool edge in a white towelling gown.

'Sorry,' he said in Russian. 'I'll get out.'

'No. Stay. You swim well.' Myroslav untied his gown and dropped it onto the tiles. He was broad-chested, a little squat. There were old tattoos across his chest, hiding under a thick mat of curled black hair. The letters 'VM' and a large open eye. 'Would you like to race?'

'I'm not sure I . . .'

He smiled. 'Come on, Jacob. A little bit of sport.'

46

'OK.' Jacob pulled himself out of the pool to stand at the pool edge next to him, ready to go.

'Ten lengths. What about a wager?' Myroslav turned to Jacob. 'If you win, I double your fee. If I win, I halve it.'

Jacob looked back. Myroslav seemed fit. He obviously used his own gym. 'I haven't seen you swim. You might be an Olympic athlete.'

'I might be,' said Myroslav, with a grin. 'Come on. Take a risk.'

'I don't think so.'

'I am disappointed. Go,' shouted Myroslav, and dived in, stealing the advantage.

Jacob followed him into the water and swam the first length as fast as he could, reached the end and turned. He was halfway through the second length when he realised that Myroslav was still on his first.

Jacob moved to breaststroke so he could see more clearly. Myroslav's stroke was more of a doggy paddle. Even swimming more slowly, Jacob was on his third length by the time the Ukrainian finished his first, his face determined, splashing as he moved in the water.

On his fifth length, Jacob said, 'Do I win?'

'Not until the end. Go on. Go on.'

So he carried on until he'd finished, then got out and watched the rich man going up and down until he'd finally finished his ten.

Myroslav got out and laughed. 'You wish you had taken my bet now.'

'I do.'

'What about a game of tennis? Just one set. Same rules. If you win, I double your fee. If you lose . . .'

'Pass,' said Jacob.

'Disappointing. This is why I am rich and you are not.' He put his right arm around Jacob and, with his other hand, sucker punched him in the stomach, hard enough to knock the wind out of him. 'What about boxing? Do you like to box?'

Eloise appeared in a one-piece swimming suit and a black straw sun-hat, a straw bag in her hand. 'Boys, boys, boys,' she said.

'Let's eat by the pool,' said Myroslav, clapping his hands. 'Will you join us?'

Eloise said, 'He's heterosexual, Myroslav. He has a girlfriend. They're buying a flat together.'

'I'm just being friendly,' said the millionaire. 'I'm trying to teach him that to survive in this world, you have to compete.'

'Did she send any reply?' Jacob asked Eloise.

'Your girlfriend? Do you miss her?'

'Did she?'

'No,' Eloise said. 'Not yet. Don't worry. I promise you I will tell you the moment she does.'

A little way off there was a small square cabin – a changing room, Jacob guessed. Eloise went over to it and he could hear her speaking into a phone, ordering food from the kitchen. A few minutes later, a maid appeared with tablecloths and cutlery, trays of glasses and bottles of wine and water, and started setting up a table at the far end of the pool.

Jacob watched her. The maid was tall and awkwardly thin, and was dressed in a black Lycra mini-dress. In it, she might have fitted perfectly into the designer ambience of her environment but for her hair.

Her hair was a mess. Someone had cut it roughly. Uneven tufts sprouted from her scalp. Above the nape of her neck there was a patch that was almost bald.

It looked absurd.

The woman finished laying the table and disappeared again.

Eloise sat sideways on a lounger, pulled one of the smaller tables up towards her and sat, legs wide, rolling a joint.

'So you're a Russian Ukrainian, living in Austria. How did you end up here?' Jacob asked.

'I just like it here,' said Myroslav. 'It's nice, don't you think?' He grinned.

When she'd finished rolling the joint, Eloise lit it, lay back and blew a cloud of smoke into the blue Austrian sky. Myroslav ambled over, took the joint from her and took a couple of pulls on it, then held it out towards Jacob.

He shook his head. 'No thanks.'

'If he won't, I will.' Draper was walking towards them in a pair of Hawaiian shorts. 'Are we having dinner?'

They sat around the table in the evening light, candles on the table. The maid brought them salads and borscht. The borscht was particularly good. After that she brought them fresh lobster ravioli.

Jacob watched the maid across the table as she spooned the pasta onto Draper's plate. As if knowing she was being watched, she looked up, straight back at him. Her eyes were dark, and the skin beneath them dark too. They were filled with contempt. It was unnerving.

'The borscht was delicious,' Jacob said, trying to make conversation.

'Borsch,' she muttered, irritatedly correcting him with what he assumed was the Ukrainian pronunciation, before moving on to serve Eloise.

'I need to know what's going on,' said Jacob, a little drunk. 'I don't really know what I'm doing here.'

Draper was stoned. He raised his glass, answered in English. 'That's the best way. Know nothing. I'm working hard on it.'

Eloise shot him a look.

'What is Jacob saying?' asked Myroslav.

'He says he doesn't really know what he's doing here,' explained Eloise.

'You have a great talent,' said Myroslav, in stilted English. 'You are sharing it with us.'

'Though pretty soon we'll just use Google Translate,' said Draper. The entire conversation switched back to Russian. Draper seemed to be fairly proficient in it too.

'Do you think that's true?' Myroslav asked. 'Am I wasting my money on you?'

'Interpreting is not just about words,' said Jacob. 'It's about the whole meaning. It's about context. And it's about trusting people.'

'There you are,' said Myroslav to Draper.

'Whatever,' said Draper.

'Draper is scared of any face-to-face encounters. He prefers everything virtual. Including his sex life,' Eloise said.

'Fuck you, Eloise.'

'I speak Ukrainian. Russian obviously. Maybe a little English,' said Myroslav. 'To speak another person's language is to under-stand their mind.'

Everybody seemed to be looking at Jacob to say something, so he did. 'I believe that's true. There's a language in Australia which gave us the word for kangaroo. It's spoken by a people called the Guugu Yimithirr. You ever heard of them, Eloise?'

She shook her head. 'I grew up in a shitty little place in New South Wales which nobody had ever heard of.'

'The interesting thing about these people, the Guugu Yimithirr, is that they have no word that's a simple translation for left and right.'

'So I guess they get lost all the time,' said Draper.

'The opposite. They don't use left and right. They use geo-graphical directions, using their own cardinal directions. Like, north, south, east, west. They wouldn't say you're sitting to the left of me. They would say you're to the north of me.'

Draper found this hilarious. 'They carry a compass with them all the time?'

'No. Because their language doesn't have egocentric notions of position, left or right and so on, which depend on only where you are, they are always making a map of their world in their heads. They always know where north is.'

Myroslav still looked interested. He sat, eyebrows raised.

Jacob continued. 'So even if they're watching TV and they want to describe how a car moved on the screen, they would say, well, it drove from east to west. But if they moved the TV to the other side of the room, they might say it had gone from west to east, or south to north.'

'That's insane.' Draper shook his head.

'Or maybe it's just important for them, living in a desert, where resources are scarce, to always have a very precise map in their heads,' said Jacob. 'Their language enforces that. So what Myroslav says is right in a way: if you understand someone's language, you understand their world.'

'I was right,' said Myroslav loudly.

'But they still ended up in a shitty bit of desert with a bunch of kangaroos for company.'

'Go to bed, Draper. You're drunk,' said Eloise.

'You're pretty, Eloise. Anybody ever tell you that? In a kind of MILF-y way.'

'Bed,' said Eloise. Obediently Draper stood and wove his way into the darkness.

'Why am I here?' asked Jacob.

Myroslav leaned forward, put his hand on Jacob's knee. 'You said it's all about trust. Do you trust us, Jacob?'

Myroslav dug his fingers in and squeezed until it started to hurt. Jacob sat, trying not to flinch. 'My parents grew up in a world where order was the most important thing and they were happy together. Then the world changed. Now the world is chaos, Jacob. Understand that. You cannot stop the chaos. If you want to prosper in this world, you have to understand chaos. You have to create it, and be part of it.'

'Strap in for the ride,' said Eloise, raising her glass.

'I don't know what you're talking about. I don't know who you are. I don't know what I'm supposed to be translating. I haven't done any work yet.'

'Where did I put my cigarettes?' Eloise looked around.

'Is it going to be like this every day?' asked Jacob.

'No,' said Myroslav, still laughing. 'Some days it's going to rain.'

Jacob walked back to his apartment, woozy from drink. Draper was in the apartment below, playing some kind of shoot-'em-up on his computer, volume up loud.

My dearest, dearest Tymko

As always, I miss you. I hope you are with Baba. I pray she is keeping you safe. I miss the dimples in the small of your back. I miss the snot on your sleeve. I miss your crying in the night.

Today I made borsch. Beetroot is excellent at this time of year. Always make sure you use the best pork sausages. Tinned tomatoes work just as well as fresh. What is more important is that the chicken broth is fresh, not from a packet, and you should never, never be afraid to add too much garlic.

I know, when you are older, you will find this funny, but today I also added my own piss to the dish. My own special recipe. They ate it all.

An Englishman has arrived too. Another stupid mouth to feed. Another bed to make. Another man's dirty laundry.

I am so tired.

I love you always. Kiss Baba for me.

NINE

Jacob sat up late, watching Hindi films on Netflix. It was partly for fun, partly to refresh himself in the language. He had found learning Hindi a challenge. He had started picking it up on an undergraduate year out, living in a hostel in Faridabad while teaching English to ten-year-olds there. There was always some kind of way in with a new language. In most languages, he had learned his first sentences by speaking them; with Hindi it had been through reading. Devanagari was a simple script to learn, the forty-seven shapes and swirls hanging like clothes from a horizontal washing line. Unlike unruly English letters, they were reliable, spelling out the same sounds, providing a simple gateway into Hindi. He had spent months wandering around stations and markets, spelling out words, absorbing the vocabulary, trying them out on stallholders and on his students.

It took him six months to be understood, but another year to master the syntax accurately enough not to be patronised or laughed at when he spoke. Syntax was the uniformed border guard of a language; it was the barbed-wire fence. Being understood in a language was one thing. Being accepted was another. Good grammar was there largely not to help create meaning, but to prove that you were one of them.

He woke early. Summer flooded through big glass windows.

He put on his own white towelling gown and walked to the front of the apartment. The big house looked dark. A gardener was spraying a hose over beds beneath his window.

The desk was set a metre back from the window that looked out onto the gardens. He sat at it and opened the slim volume of love poetry he was supposed to translate into Portuguese and struggled for a while, finding it hard to concentrate. In the middle of the lawn the gardener was using a shovel to pick something up from the grass. Dog shit, perhaps.

At around seven, the maid carried a tray with a domed silver cloche on it across the lawn and disappeared into the apartment below, emerging a minute later.

A couple of minutes later he picked up the phone. 'What did Draper have?'

'Pancakes.'

He thought for a second. 'Can you do eggs Benedict?'

'If you want,' replied the voice flatly. He remembered the angry look on the woman's face yesterday at the poolside.

Twenty minutes later she arrived carrying a tray crammed with fruit, a pot of fresh coffee, freshly squeezed orange juice, and in the centre, under his own silver cloche, the eggs Benedict.

'You're Russian?' he asked.

'No,' she answered brusquely, then closed the door behind him, leaving him with his breakfast.

He ate the eggs at his desk, toying half-heartedly with the love poem. He was just finishing a second cup of coffee when he saw Draper sauntering across the lawn. Showered and dressed, he followed Draper into the main house. By the time he reached it, Draper was at the table with a MacBook open in front of him, working on something.

'Eloise said I should check the language on some pages.'

Draper nodded. 'There's not much. Mostly the Brazilian pages. They need to sound . . . Brazilian, I guess.'

'Not much of what?'

'Our website,' said Draper. 'I'll print them off. Hey. Language Man. You ever heard of a guy called Doctor Dee?'

Jacob looked up. 'John Dee? The court astronomer?'

'Elizabeth the First. I read that he tried to discover the language of the angels. Do you speak that one?'

'I do. Apparently the language John Dee discovered turned out to be remarkably similar to English.'

This seemed to satisfy Draper. 'There you go. If my mom ever tells me I swear too much, I'll tell her I'm speaking the language of the angels.'

They sat next to each other at the big dining table. At around nine, Myroslav emerged in a yellow silk dressing gown. '*Dobroye utro*, Mister *Poliglot*.' Good morning, Mr Polyglot. 'I am going for a swim. Work hard.'

It was the first decent chance he had had to try and figure out what he had been hired to do. The website was a pharmaceutical sales website for a company called Kolophant which was apparently based in Brazil. It sold a variety of drugs. From the menu it appeared that there was an English language version, a French, a Portuguese and a Spanish one.

The pages he had been given were FAQs, notices about delivery times, disclaimers and the usual stuff you find on any website. There was also a section for customers to upload their prescriptions to the website. Jacob spent an hour going through the pages but there was nothing in particular he could spot that was wrong – just a couple of phrases that were a little ungrammatical. Machine translation was getting better all the time, but it was never elegant. He marked them and suggested alternatives and handed them back to Draper.

The screen in front of Draper was filled with dense code. 'How come you need me?' asked Jacob. 'You could send that out to an agency.'

'Believe me, you'll be earning your money soon enough.' He lowered his voice. 'There's some shit going on.'

'What kind of shit?'

'They didn't tell you?'

'Nothing.'

Draper smiled. 'Oh boy. You really are just an interpreter, aren't you?'

'What is going on?' Jacob asked.

Draper zipped his finger across his lips.

Jacob had learned a little by looking at the pages. 'The website is based in Brazil?'

'Kind of.' Draper didn't take his eyes off his screen. 'That's what it looks like, right?'

'But payments are accepted in Singapore?'

Draper dragged his eyes off the screen and said, 'Yeah. Exactly.'

'So people buy pharmaceuticals from us. The money goes to Singapore but the products are shipped from Brazil? Where are the pharmaceuticals coming from?'

'Well. Right now that's the problem. They've actually been coming from India. That's why you're here.' He lowered his voice again. 'There's some kind of fuck-up in the supply chain.'

'What kind of fuck-up?'

'You some kind of industrial spy, Jacob?'

'I'm just trying to find out what I'm supposed to be doing. Whether I've made a big mistake taking this work. I'm beginning to think I have.'

Draper turned his eyes back to his screen and he started tapping at the keyboard. He muttered, 'Seriously, man. I have to work. I'm just the code monkey.'

Myroslav came back, dripping water across the immaculate floor. 'You two boys enjoying yourselves?'

Just before he reached the door he had emerged from an hour earlier he stopped and turned. 'Don't mind Draper,' he said, speaking English. 'He's an asshole.' He laughed, then closed the door behind him.

'You remember I actually understand English, don't you?' Draper called after him.

Five minutes later, the maid with the badly cut hair emerged with a mop and swept it over the wet footprints that Myroslav had left. She caught Jacob looking at her. Very deliberately she turned her back and continued her work.

★

59

At around midday, Jacob emerged from the front door to take a look at the front of the house. The gravel was white marble. It was blinding in the summer sunshine.

Two vehicles stood on it. One was the minivan, the other was the SUV. Tucked away down the slope, there was a garage, built half underground. Above it, another block of apartments.

At the front of the house was a large elaborate classical fountain, playing water into the pool that surrounded it. It looked as if it had been lifted from some Roman piazza and placed here. It probably had, Jacob decided. In the centre, a stone cherub sat next to a skull. An oddly mawkish sentiment, at odds with the modernism of the house. The huge dog emerged from the house and watched him walk around it, tongue out, panting from the heat.

Beyond the fountain was the front gate, a single sheet of plain white metal set into a white painted wall. The wall was huge, over three metres high, and imposing. He followed the wall one way and then the other. It seemed to surround the entire estate. Looking up, he could see there were security cameras, placed discreetly, looking along the walls. It would be hard to break in without being seen. Or get out.

Back in the house, Draper was still tapping at the keyboard.

If he didn't work, would they ask for his money back? He called the kitchen on the house phone to order lunch.

It rang for a while, then the woman answered in Russian.

'What can I have for lunch?'

'What do you want?'

'I don't know. What is there?'

'I'll bring you a salmon salad,' she answered, and ended the call without giving him a chance to order anything else.

Again she knocked, brought it into the room and set it on his dining table. Jacob watched her unloading the plates and cutlery. 'You seem to be on call all the time. Do you ever get time off?'

'Are you hitting on me?' She looked up from the table, straight at him, though her face remained expressionless.

'No.' He held up his palms.

'Good.'

'I was just curious. You seem to work so hard, I mean. I wouldn't mind hanging out with someone sane for a change.'

She paused in her work, then picked up a knife from the table. She took a single step forward and held it towards him, and said in a flat voice, 'You think I'm fucking sane?'

'I'm sorry,' he said hastily. Right now, with the knife in her hand, this woman with the strangely cut hair looked far from sane. 'I didn't mean anything. I really didn't. I was just trying to make conversation.'

She replaced the knife and left without saying another word. He picked at the salmon, but didn't finish it.

In the afternoon, Jacob pushed open the door of the gym.

It was brightly lit and shiny. An internet radio station was playing enthusiastic pop music. There were running and cycling machines he thought he could probably try. If he was going to be trapped here, he would need to find some way of keeping fit.

Punchbags hung from the ceiling. At the far end of the room, Iosef was squatting at a rack, preparing to lift an enormous set of black weights.

'Hello,' said Jacob.

'Hello,' Iosef answered politely, then braced and slowly lifted the weights off the rack. He grunted, then flexed his limbs and, in a single motion, raised the bar up above his head. He held it up, legs apart, sweat breaking out on his forehead while Jacob watched.

After what seemed like an age, the man grunted, exhaled, then dropped them back onto the rack with a clang.

'How long have you been working for Mr Bondarenko?'

'Many, many years. Since I left the military.'

'You're from Ukraine too?'

He didn't answer.

'How come he lives here in Austria?'

'Some bullshit with the tax people. I don't ask.' And he picked up the weights again.

'What kind of bullshit?'

'I do not ask. You should not ask either.' Iosef was straining at the weights again.

On the way out he noticed Iosef's jacket hanging from a peg. There was a holster hanging behind it, weighted by a pistol.

'Everything OK?'

Jacob looked round. A towel round his shoulders, Iosef was glaring at him.

Jacob drifted back to his room but couldn't concentrate on work. At six a pan-fried steak arrived with sautéed spinach and garlic. This time, unasked, the maid brought a bottle of Pinot. He was on his second glass when the phone rang.

It was Eloise. 'You are needed in the conference room in ten minutes.'

'Where is the conference room?'

'I'll come and get you. Just be ready.'

He went to the bathroom to clean his teeth and get rid of the smell of wine. When Eloise knocked at his door he was tucking a shirt into his trousers. 'Hurry,' she said.

'Any reply to the email? From my girlfriend?'

'Not yet. Hurry.'

She led him across the lawn into the main house, then opened a door that had stairs that went down to a small windowless room with plain office furniture in it, a round table and three chairs. Against one wall there was a bank of servers in a cabinet, LEDs blinking gently.

'You'll be translating between Hindi and Russian.'

'Interpreting,' he said.

'Sorry?'

'Not translating. Interpreting is a two-way process. It requires fluency in both languages.'

Eloise gave that little smile. 'Has everything been OK?'

'Perfect,' he answered.

'The food? The apartment? The house? The pool?'

'Again, perfect.'

'Good,' she said, unsmiling. 'Now it's your turn to earn your keep.' From a bag, she produced a large iPhone and set it in the middle of the table.

TEN

'Sit there,' Eloise ordered Jacob, pointing at a chair in front of the iPhone screen.

In a crisp white shirt and chinos, Myroslav entered the windowless room, his big dog padding behind him. The dog approached Jacob and laid his huge head in his lap. 'She likes you,' said Myroslav.

'She likes everybody,' scoffed Eloise. The huge dog snuffled, then headed under the table and curled up next to Jacob's feet.

'Who the hell does this guy think he is?' Myroslav complained.

Eloise said, 'Let's start by being polite, OK? This is the man who contacted me on Telegram when Rakesh Garg didn't turn up.'

Myroslav held up his hands. 'It's my money, remember? All of this. It's my money.'

'Of course,' said Eloise. 'Don't worry. Everything is under control.'

Jacob looked from one to the other, apprehensively.

'Ready?' She looked around the room. Jacob nodded.

Myroslav said, 'Fine. Let's find out what this turd wants.'

The room was suddenly quiet. Eloise leaned forward, opened up the Signal app, then scrolled through contacts.

Myroslav sat in front of the camera, his face on the screen. He adjusted his hair. 'Go,' he said.

Eloise pressed the CALL button. It took a little while, then a man answered. He was thin, with a neatly clipped dark beard and was dressed in a crisp white shirt. He seemed to be sitting at some kind of office desk in a large black leather chair. 'Mr Bondarenko?'

Off screen, Jacob interjected in Hindi straight away. 'Hello, sir. I am Jacob. I shall be interpreting for you.'

'An interpreter? Like we are the United Nations now?' The man smiled. 'Very good. Please begin by sending my greetings to Mr Bondarenko. Tell him I am very pleased to be working with him. I have heard a lot about him.'

'And who the hell is he?' said Myroslav. 'Ask him what happened to Mr Garg?'

'Mr Bondarenko wants to know who you are and he wants to know what happened to Mr Garg.'

'My name is Nazim,' said the man on the phone.

'Just Nazim?'

'All you need to know, *bhai*.' Despite his knowledge of the language, Nazim spoke in a kind of Hindi slang Jacob found hard to grasp. Hesitantly, Jacob spoke his words in more formal Hindi.

'We should celebrate our new business partnership,' said Nazim. Jacob interpreted slowly, finding he was struggling.

Myroslav and Eloise exchanged a worried glance. 'So what happened to Rakesh?' Myroslav demanded.

'What do you mean, our new business partnership?' asked Eloise.

'I am pleased to tell you that I have taken over the business from Rakesh. He is no longer an interested party.'

Again, another look between Myroslav and Eloise. Myroslav spoke. 'Our agreement was with Rakesh Garg. Not with you.'

'And now, because I have taken over Rakesh's business, your agreement is with me. You have sold the entire order you received from Mr Garg in a week, I understand. That is cause for us to celebrate, I think.'

Myroslav was twitchy. 'How do you know that? How do you know how much we have sold?'

Nazim just laughed. 'I know everything about your business. We have eyes everywhere.'

Jacob rendered this back into Russian. The phrase was as ambiguous and vague in another tongue as it had been in Hindi.

'What does he mean, "We have eyes everywhere"?' whispered Eloise.

'You have already made a great deal of money.'

'Yes,' Myroslav said cautiously.

'We need to discuss where we go from here. So let us celebrate our success. You. Me. The Australian woman named Eloise.'

'What the fuck is going on?' muttered Myroslav.

'Yours is a very beautiful house,' said Nazim. 'You have a big golden swimming pool. One day, I would very much like a house just like yours.' Nazim's Hindi was closer to the Bollywood

66

slang Jacob heard in movies than the language he had learned living in Delhi.

'Thank you,' said Myroslav, at a loss.

'Moving on, let us discuss the cut.'

'The cut? What do you mean?'

'The cut. The split. What you get. What I get. How much of the profit you keep. How much I keep.'

'The split?' Myroslav seemed at a loss once again.

Nazim had stood and was holding his phone in front of him. Jacob could see now that Nazim was in a high-rise apartment. The lights of a city below him showed on the screen. 'Of the profits. Rakesh Garg was simply selling you a product. I calculate that Rakesh Garg was making considerably less than ten per cent of your total revenue. Going forward, we would like a partnership and we would like to increase our proportion of income.'

'Going forward? If you continue to supply the products on behalf of Mr Garg's organisation, we can discuss this, of course.'

'Next time it will be fifty per cent.'

Jacob repeated this in Russian. Myroslav turned to him. 'Did you translate that figure correctly?'

'Fifty per cent,' said Jacob.

Myroslav's eyes widened. He banged the table. 'Fuck him. End the call. Now.'

'No,' said Eloise hurriedly, muting the phone.

'What?'

Eloise reached out and put a hand on top of Myroslav's. 'Think for a second. We don't understand what has happened to Rakesh Garg. We need to find out why this man thinks he's worth that much. Tell him that we are sorry but that is not possible.'

She unmuted the device. Jacob delivered Eloise's reply in Hindi.

Nazim's voice remained even. He answered, 'Of course it is possible. You will make money. I will make money too. It is a more equal relationship now.'

Eloise spread her hands. 'You must understand the market, Nazim.'

'I understand that the market pays five thousand dollars for each treatment of Lutinol.'

'Of what?' Jacob spoke directly to Nazim. 'I'm sorry. I am not a specialist. What is Lutinol?'

'You don't know?' Nazim spoke. 'Lutinol is the brand name of a fertility medication. Tell Myroslav that I understand that the market pays around five thousand dollars for each vial of it.'

Jacob translated.

'And I understand that if we sell only a thousand of those, that is five million dollars in turnover and you have already sold a great deal more than that.'

Myroslav's voice was suddenly distant. 'There are other manufacturers we can use.'

'I would advise you against that,' Nazim said.

'And it is our sales network,' said Eloise.

'It's a very good network. That's why I want my cut from it,' said Nazim.

'Who does this man think he is?' Myroslav complained.

'Your name is Jacob?' Nazim addressed Jacob directly. 'It is good to meet you and thank you for your work today. Your accent is good. Tell Mr Bondarenko that in two days I will call again at the same time. I think that he will accept my offer then.

In the meantime, madam, I am sending you a photograph. Perhaps that will convince you that I am not a joke.'

And the screen turned blue.

'What the hell was that?' demanded Eloise, her face pale. 'What was the last thing he told you?'

Jacob explained. 'He said he was sending you a message.'

'A message?' Eloise frowned.

Myroslav looked dark. 'He's some small-time Mumbai gangster and he wants to sweat us. He thinks we are idiots. We need to find another manufacturer,' he said.

Jacob looked around. Sitting in his chair, he said, 'I don't want anything to do with this. I want to go home.' What he had heard made him convinced that he had stumbled into something bad. 'I'll be flying home tomorrow.'

But before anyone could answer, Eloise's phone gave a faint ping. She looked down at her screen, then gasped, dropping her phone on the floor as if it were on fire.

'What is it?' demanded Myroslav, rattled. 'What are you looking at?'

She dropped to the floor, scrabbling to pick it up.

'What was the message? Was it from him?'

She lifted the phone and held it up towards Myroslav. The screen was spiderwebbed with cracks.

'What happened?' said Myroslav. 'Where did that picture go? Bring it back. I didn't see it properly.'

Still on her knees, Eloise turned the screen back towards her and stabbed at it a few times. 'It's gone,' she said. 'Fucking phone.'

'What do you mean, it's gone?'

'It's Signal,' said Eloise, still staring at the blank screen of her broken phone. 'The sender can make the photo be displayed for thirty seconds or whatever they want and then it's gone.'

'It's from him? The Indian? Who was it? What was the picture?'

She looked up. 'He's trying to scare us, isn't he?'

'How? What was the picture?' Jacob demanded.

'I'm not sure. It looked like a picture of a dead man.'

'What dead man?'

'You,' Myroslav told him. 'Mind your own business. Go.'

Sitting at the desk, Jacob held his ground. 'What is going on here? What did you see in that photograph?'

Eloise looked at Jacob. 'Nothing,' she said hastily. 'I didn't get a chance to see it properly.' Jacob noticed that her hands were shaking, though.

'What is going on?' insisted Jacob.

Eloise stood finally. 'Don't,' she said, quietly, in English. 'Just leave it alone, Jacob. This isn't the time to confront Myroslav.'

'I've been brought here under false pretences.' He switched to Russian. 'If this is anything illegal, as I suspect it is, I don't want to be part of it. Give me my passport back. I am going home.'

The underground room suddenly seemed very small.

'You are staying here,' said Myroslav, with a small, lopsided smile. 'You leave when I say you can leave.'

'You can't hold me against my will.'

'Can't I?'

'No. This is not what I do. Thank you for the opportunity, but I would like to go home now.'

'Do you box?' asked Myroslav, looking down at him in his chair.

Jacob was confused. 'Sorry. What?'

'Please, Jacob. Just leave it,' Eloise said. 'Just leave and go to your room. We will talk later.'

Myroslav asked, 'Do you box? Do you fight?' He stood, with fists up, one higher than the other.

'No,' said Jacob. 'I don't box. I just want to get out of here.'

'Come,' said Myroslav, grabbing the shoulder of Jacob's shirt and lifting him from the chair. 'I'm going to teach you Russian boxing.'

And before Jacob could stand properly, Myroslav was pulling him up the stairs, and out through the back of the house.

ELEVEN

Iosef and Webb followed Myroslav as he dragged Jacob across the terrace, down the steps and out into the garden.

'Give us some space to fight, please,' ordered Myroslav. 'In Russian boxing, we take turns. First you hit me, then I hit you back.'

'Don't be stupid,' said Jacob. 'I'm not a boxer. Leave me alone.'

'Hit me.'

'I'm a translator. I don't want any part of all this. I'm going to my room and I'm going to pack a bag.' He looked around, searching for anyone who might support him, who might back him up. Through the big glass doors above, Jacob could see Eloise standing in the living room, hand up to her mouth, watching him, scared – but she was keeping her distance.

'Put up your fists. You are right-handed, yes? Spread your legs like this.' Myroslav took a pugilist's pose, left foot forward, right arm back, ready to punch.

Jacob stood defiantly, arms by his side.

'Come on,' said Myroslav, leaning his chin closer as a target. 'We fight. Bare knuckles – in the traditional way. If you beat me, I'll double your fee.'

'I'm not fighting you. I don't want a fee. I want to leave.' He turned, but realised that Webb was already walking behind him to block his way should he decide to make a run for it.

'It's not your choice,' said Myroslav. 'Fight me.'

Webb crossed his arms, gave him a little nod, as if to say, *Go on*. The Austrian evening was muggy. Jacob turned back towards Myroslav. 'Please,' he said. 'This is not me. This is not who I am.'

'Because I challenged you to the fight, you must hit me first. That is the rule. It is your turn.'

Jacob didn't move.

'But if you don't punch me, you forfeit your turn. I will strike you instead.'

His father had been a soldier. His father must have known how to box, but Jacob had never inherited a love of fighting from him. 'This is crazy.'

'OK,' said Myroslav. 'My turn then.' The bare-knuckle punch came suddenly and hit Jacob squarely on the cheekbone. It was not particularly hard, but he had not been ready for it. Jacob was suddenly on damp summer grass, looking up at Myroslav.

Behind him, Webb stepped forward, put a hand under each armpit and lifted him back onto his feet.

Jacob raised his hand to feel his face. The punch hadn't hurt at the time, but now he felt the skin it stung. There was no blood. Though it had taken him by surprise, the blow had not been particularly hard. Myroslav was taunting him.

'Your turn,' said Webb quietly in English. 'Go on. Hit him. Get it over with.'

'No,' answered Jacob.

'Your choice, obviously.' Webb looked at his face, as if checking for damage. 'It won't help you none, just letting him hit you. He'll fuck you up more if you don't fight back.'

'No?' Myroslav was saying. 'My turn again then.'

Webb stood back. This time Jacob tried to jerk his head back as the blow came. Instead the fist struck him on the other cheek, much harder this time, spinning his head around to the right. He felt blood in his mouth, but this time he stood his ground. He blinked, trying to shake off the force of the blow.

'Now yours.' Myroslav again offered his chin, leaning for-wards.

Jacob shook his head. 'This is insane.'

'You're just going to let me punch you, yes?'

'I'm not any part of this,' he said. The inside of his mouth stung as he spoke, torn gum moving against his teeth.

'Yes you are. You work for me. You took my money. You eat my food. You sleep in my bed. You accepted my hospitality. And now you're insulting me by telling me you want to leave.'

Jacob didn't move.

Myroslav shook his head. 'My go again then. Number three.' This time Myroslav feinted with his right. As Jacob flinched back the Ukrainian brought his left up and smacked him squarely in the middle of the gut. Jacob doubled up in pain, gasping for air.

From the living room he heard Eloise call, 'Stop, that's enough, Slava. You've made your point.'

Myroslav ignored her. 'Your turn,' he said quietly.

Jacob was winded. Each of Myroslav's assaults was harder than the last. If Myroslav kept this up, he would not survive.

'Come on, mate,' said Webb. 'He's not going to stop until you hit him back at least once.'

Jacob tried to straighten.

'Take a second,' said Webb. 'Breathe.'

Myroslav said, 'Iosef told me you were asking him questions. Is that right?'

'I just wanted to know what's going on.'

Jacob was upright enough to look Myroslav in the eye again.

'You don't need to know anything. I do the knowing. You do the work. That's all. Come on,' taunted Myroslav. He was clearly annoyed by Jacob's lack of reaction. 'Hit me.'

Jacob took a breath, reached his fist back and punched straight at Myroslav's face. It was a lousy effort. Myroslav yanked his head back out of the way and Jacob's fist only found air.

Before Jacob had even had time to register his mistake, Myroslav had smacked Jacob with an uppercut, snapping his head back, sending him staggering backwards into Webb's arms. Webb pushed him forwards. Myroslav was laughing now, enjoying himself. 'Four.'

Jacob spat blood again. 'You said he'd stop if I hit him back.'

Webb said, 'You never actually got him, though, did you?'

Next time Myroslav punched him exactly where he'd hit him the first time, only harder. 'Five.'

The first time it had not hurt much, but this time it did. Jacob saw stars but managed to stay standing. 'You win. I surrender.'

'You can't. It's not your rules,' said Myroslav.

'I'm not fighting,' said Jacob.

'Bad luck,' called Myroslav, back at him. 'It's my turn again.'

He had been punched five times. He couldn't last many more. Jacob backed away. Webb had been right. He had no alternative but to fight, but he had never had to do anything like this before. He was not equipped for this.

As Myroslav moved forward into the space he had left for him, he put his head down and lunged. Taken by surprise, Myroslav was still moving towards him as Jacob's shoulder hit him square in the chest.

He heard Myroslav grunt. 'Oof.'

Jacob was already jerking his head up, deliberately catching the Ukrainian on the chin with the crown of his head. In the same movement he swung his left round and up, and felt it connect hard with something soft.

When he pulled away, Myroslav was clutching his nose. Blood dripped onto the Ukrainian's white shirt.

He had stopped laughing, at least.

Jacob surprised himself as much as he had surprised Myroslav, who was gingerly touching his face, then examining the blood on his fingers. He looked furious.

Before Jacob could react, Myroslav punched him hard, a fast jab connecting with his skull just above his eyes.

Jacob went down fast. When he finally opened his eyes, laid out on the grass, his right socket was filled with blood.

His head rang. He tried to open his eyes – his right seemed to be gummed shut – but when he squinted through his left, he saw Webb leaning over him. 'He'll live,' he announced.

Wiping blood away with the back of his hand, Jacob felt Webb taking an arm and lifting him to his unsteady feet. 'Look.'

With his good eye, Jacob looked around. Myroslav was no longer there. He had gone back into the house, satisfied he had won the competition.

Jacob could see him in the living room by the dining table, head back, fingers squeezing the bridge of his nose to stop the blood. Webb put Jacob's arm around his shoulder and led him away. 'He always has to have the last word. Don't worry. You did good. Nice move, the headbutt. Bit dirty, but no harm. If you hadn't hit him back good, he'd have bloody killed you.' He called over to Eloise. 'Tell the maid to bring the first-aid kit.'

Webb marched the dazed Jacob across the lawn, then up to his apartment. 'Just do what he says, next time, right?' said Webb.

'I'm a prisoner here, aren't I?'

'You're an employee.'

'No. I'm a prisoner. Eloise took my passport.'

'Look on the positives. At the end of your contract you can go home and you'll have money in the bank. Until then, just shut up, if you know what's good for you.'

Webb dropped him onto the couch and disappeared into his bedroom. He returned with a white towel he had taken from the bathroom. 'Hold that there.'

'You're ex-army.'

'Don't ask questions.'

'I could tell,' said Jacob. 'The way you hold yourself. My dad was Fourth Armoured Brigade.' He was trying to make an ally of Webb, trying to find common ground. 'I grew up in Osnabrück. I'm guessing you're Marines, or something like that.'

'Something like that.'

'So how come you're working for Myroslav?'

'Thought I told you not to ask questions.' He leaned over and looked at him in the light. 'There's a cut above your eyebrow, but you'll live. That punch you gave him wasn't very pretty, but I bet it hurt. He wasn't expecting that.'

'Special Ops?'

'Maybe.'

'So why does Myroslav need armed guards?'

There was a soft knock at the door. The strange maid with the badly cut hair arrived and handed a green first-aid kit to Webb, then picked up the bloodied towel and left without saying anything.

'He has your passport too, doesn't he?'

Webb cleaned him up and put a small bandage above his eye. At the door, Webb said, 'I work for him because it's a job, and it's very well paid. There are terms and conditions. End of story. I'll go home rich. I keep my head down.' Gently he secured the bandage with a sticking plaster. 'And so should you.'

TWELVE

Jacob lay on his bed all night not sleeping. His head was bruised and his neck was stiff, sore from the pummelling it had received.

He was an idiot for coming here. He should have asked more questions first. The menace in Nazim's tone last night was obvious. Whatever Eloise had seen on her phone had terrified her. Plus, Iosef carried a gun, and if Webb was an ex-Marine, he probably did too.

He got up around four and turned up the air conditioning, then lay on his bed again. It was only when he was woken by someone knocking on his door that he realised that he must have dozed off.

When he opened it in a white dressing gown and slippers, the maid was asking him, 'Would you like breakfast in the garden?'

It was the first time she had spoken to him in anything other than a monotone. He was a little taken aback. Last time she had spoken to him she had been holding a knife in her hand.

'OK,' he said. Looking past her, he saw a white table set up in the middle of the lawn.

This time she brought him coffee, orange juice and pastries.

'Why are you doing this?' he asked.

'Because you broke Myroslav's nose,' she said.

'I broke it?'

'He's gone into Villach to see a doctor.'

'Jesus. Did I hit him that hard?'

For the first time, she laughed. 'I don't think it's very bad. But he is vain. He is worried it will spoil his good looks.' She pointed to the small bandage above his eye. 'Did it hurt?'

'Yes.'

'Iosef said you told Myroslav you wanted to leave the house.'

'I did. Apparently I can't.'

'No. You can't.'

'Can you?'

She looked at him like he was stupid. 'You think I stay here making your beds and cleaning your toilets for pleasure?'

'I'm sorry.'

'I watched you. You fought like a baby. You should have punched him harder.'

He laughed. 'It's true. Would you like to share this coffee?' he asked. 'I can get another cup from my room.'

She shook her head. There was still that darkness under her eyes he had noticed, as if she didn't sleep enough. Her limbs were long and bony, as if she were undernourished, despite working in a kitchen full of rich food.

'You're Ukrainian, aren't you, like Mr Bondarenko?'

She glared at him. 'I am not like Mr Bondarenko at all.'

'And I suppose Mr Bondarenko is keeping your passport safe for you too?'

She looked around her. 'You people. You all get what you deserve. You come here because you think you're going to get rich.'

'That's not why you came here?'

'I don't give a shit about the money. All I want is to get away from here.'

'You're never allowed to leave here?'

'What do you think?' She spoke softly but with profound bitterness.

'It must drive you crazy.'

'It drives me crazy having to look after people like you –' she tugged at her black uniform – 'having to wear this stupid dress. It drives me crazy trying to be polite to people I want to kill.'

'You often threaten them with knives?'

'Sure,' she said. 'If I think they might want to have sex with me.'

'I wasn't trying to have sex with you. I just wanted to talk.'

'Sure. You were just trying to talk. What is the name of that plant?' She was pointing to a shrub at the edge of the lawn. It had big yellow flowers that hung down floppily, like witches' hats.

'I don't know.'

'My mother used to grow it. She always told me never to touch it.'

The sudden turns in her conversation left Jacob on edge.

'I have to go,' she said abruptly. 'I have to do the bedrooms.'

'Wait. What about your hair? What happened?'

'Do you like it?' She smiled again. 'Mr Bondarenko told me

I should grow it long. He wants everything to look like it's from a magazine. So I said fuck him.' She ran her hand through her uneven tufts, making it as messy as she could. 'You don't even know who he really is, do you?'

'Who? Myroslav Bondarenko?'

'That's not even his name,' she said.

'What is his name, then?'

'It's right there on his chest. If you knew who he really was, you would not be here.' She turned to go.

'Tell me. Please. Do you understand what is going on here?'

'He didn't actually kill you last night. You should be thankful for that. It means he believes he has a use for you, like he has for me. For now you are safe. When you are of no more use to him, then you should worry.'

'When is Mr Bondarenko back?' he asked. The food lay on the table untouched.

'How long does it take to fix a broken nose?'

'And Eloise?'

'She's gone away with Myroslav, anyway. I don't know when they will be back.' She checked her watch. 'I have to go and clean the house.'

'I'm sorry. I didn't ask your name,' he said.

'No,' she said. 'You didn't.'

Jacob stared at the uneaten breakfast in front of him. The maid was not working here of her own free will any more than he was. She had said that Myroslav Bondarenko was not his real name. He remembered the initials on his chest, 'VM'.

The luxury of the house turned darker. Eventually he gathered up the plates and set off across the lawn with them. He entered by the kitchen door. The kitchen was empty. He wanted to try and understand what the maid had just told him, but she must be somewhere else, doing her chores.

He scraped the food off into the bins, washed the plates, and stacked them by the sink, then went back into Myroslav's empty living room.

The architect had placed the house cleverly into the landscape. Windows framed perfect vistas of the Alps on the far side of the lake. Light bounced off polished floors. He stood in the middle of the huge living room and turned slowly around.

Though the abstract art on the walls looked expensive, he noticed there were no photographs of Myroslav's family or friends, no indication of who he really was. There were no books, just a few magazines on art and design.

Passing through the house, he found himself in the front garden, with its immense white wall facing the world outside. He crunched his way over the white gravel towards the huge metal gate. It was firmly shut, of course, but to its right there was a pedestrian doorway. It looked more like a sentry box, a covered steel grille. Beyond the grille was a second metal door. It was like a castle keep, he realised. You needed to get through both doors to get in – or out.

Next to the grille was a simple keypad. A red LED showed. He tapped some buttons randomly. The keypad beeped, but the light stayed red.

As Eloise had warned him, he was locked in. They all were, unless they had the codes to these doors.

He was about to turn back when he heard the noise of a vehicle outside the main gate, tyres crunching on loose stone. Thinking it must be Myroslav or Eloise returning, he waited for the gate to roll back but it didn't.

Instead the door buzzed. The first steel door opened and a man in jeans and T-shirt pushed it open. He stood behind the grille, unable to go any further. 'Hello?' he called. 'Anyone there?'

Jacob ducked down behind the fountain, just as Iosef emerged from the main house. 'What is it?' Iosef's German was poor.

'Phone,' said the man, holding a parcel. A replacement for the one Eloise had broken last night, Jacob guessed. 'Give it to me,' demanded Iosef.

'You have to sign for it.'

Iosef pressed numbers on the keypad and there was another buzz. He pulled open the grille and the delivery driver stepped forward onto the gravel. Still in his white dressing gown and slippers, Jacob peered out from his hiding place behind the marble fountain. Iosef was still standing on the steps, examining the box in his hands.

The man stood halfway out of the open grille, looking round. 'Cool house,' he said. Behind him, through the open door, Jacob saw trees. The world beyond the wall.

'Now go,' said Iosef.

The grille door closed slowly. Then the gate behind it. The tantalising glimpse of the outside world disappeared again.

Jacob crouched behind the fountain until he heard Iosef retreat back into the house.

There are so many opportunities out there, Carla had scolded. That had been one. He should have taken the chance to run out of the gate before it locked again, begged the delivery man to take him. Instead he had hesitated.

THIRTEEN

He waited a while, then emerged from his hiding place.

Back in his apartment he sat for a while, head in hands. Then he dressed, went to the desk, picked up the house phone and called the kitchen. It rang for a while before the maid answered.

'I can order whatever I want, right?'

'Within reason,' she answered. 'But you didn't touch the breakfast.'

'Do you have caviar?'

'Would you like some?'

'No.'

'Why did you ask then? Don't fuck me around.'

'What about lobster?'

'No. We don't have lobster. If you're hungry, I can make you wild mushroom ravioli. I can make it fresh.'

'You were a cook in Ukraine?'

'I was a chef, not a cook.'

'How did you end up here, then?'

'What did you want? I am busy.'

'Eloise said I could order anything I wanted. What if I want lobster?'

'Eloise is full of shit. I have to finish the beds. You want the ravioli?'

'I would like lobster.'

'It will take a couple of days, though. There is nothing like that locally.'

'What about fresh fish?'

'We have cod, zander, catfish, perch.'

'Fresh?'

'Frozen. If you want fresh fish, I can order it from the fishmonger in Feld am See. They do fresh trout.'

'How long would it take them to deliver it?'

'An hour maybe? Two if they are busy.'

'Then I want fresh trout. A big one. The biggest they have.'

She was quiet for a while. 'I have to ask Iosef first. He has to sign for it. I have to go.'

After that, he went and sat at his desk and waited.

When almost an hour had passed, he left the apartment and walked back towards the house. The groundskeeper was mowing the grass. His name was Fedor, Jacob had learned. Like Iosef, he appeared to be ex-military too. Iosef stood at the doorway to the gym, watching Jacob as he approached. 'Where are you going?'

'Maybe shopping,' said Jacob. 'Or hang-gliding. I'm not sure.'

'Hilarious.'

'I'm going for a walk. Want to come?'

Iosef didn't move, just watched him as he walked past the groundskeeper's shed, towards the copse that lay to the west of Myroslav's compound, as if he were just going for a stroll to pass the time.

Then, when he was out of sight, he cut back towards the front of the house and took up position behind the fountain again. There were cameras above the gate, one pointing out to face approaching vehicles, another facing the house, to watch whoever arrived. The fountain's pool was an elaborate hexagon, with large corbels at each corner supporting absurd decorative carved scallops. They jutted out far enough to offer a space to hide behind if he pulled his legs in close.

Time passed. The day was warm. From the house came the sound of a vacuum cleaner. The maid had said it might take an hour or two for the fish to be delivered, but the second hour passed and he began to wonder if she had placed the order at all.

To make sure he was not visible from the house he had to press up against the fountain base. His legs started to ache. He waited in the hot summer sun and was about to stand and go back to his apartment when he heard the sound of a motorbike making its way down the hill.

He crouched lower. The bike stopped. The engine cut.

There was a buzz at the door. Next thing, a man in a red bandana was standing behind the grille holding a white plastic carrier bag, repeatedly ringing the bell.

Again, Iosef appeared.

Jacob squatted, preparing to sprint the moment the grille was unlocked. If he made it out before Iosef could stop him, he would throw himself on the delivery man's mercy, perhaps jump on the back of his bike, or at least beg the use of his phone.

But this time Iosef didn't unlock the door. The delivery man simply passed the bag with the fish in it through the grille, then turned away.

He thought about shouting a message, but the encounter was over in a few seconds. The front gate was already closing behind the delivery man.

'Shit, shit, shit.'

Tucked behind the fountain, he felt like screaming out loud in frustration, but that would give his position away and there might be a better chance another day. The motorbike's engine kicked back into life.

Then, the sound of another vehicle approaching, coming down the same hill.

Jacob stayed exactly where he was, crouched down behind the corner of the fountain. With a soft rumble, the main gate started to move back, revealing the lane beyond – the delivery man sitting on his motorbike directly in front of the entrance.

Next thing, a black Mercedes SUV was outside, waiting for the gate to open wide enough for it. Jacob could see that Webb was behind the wheel, Myroslav next to him, Eloise in the back.

Surely they must have seen him, crouching there, he thought, but Webb's eyes were on the motorbike. He pressed the horn, urging the driver to get out of his way, giving Jacob the chance to creep round to the back of the fountain – the side that would be visible from the house.

But Iosef had already gone back inside, presumably to take the fresh fish to the kitchen.

He watched the car drive past the fountain. Instead of stopping at the house, it carried on towards the garage, whose automatic door was already opening as the other one, the main gate, began to close.

He stood, stiff from crouching, and walked calmly through the big gate a second before the door closed behind him.

It was simpler than he could have hoped. The gate had been open, unobserved, for just a few seconds and he had walked out. Now he was free.

He could not believe his luck. He wanted to shout for joy, but he needed to get far away from this place. Once outside he sped up his pace, taking the track to the right heading straight into the dark pine woods beyond the house.

Behind the house, the slope of the mountainside rose more steeply, thickly wooded by pine trees. There were no neighbours, no other houses.

He imagined that somewhere above him, up the slope, there would be a bigger road and that there would be passing traffic. He wondered how far he would have to walk around here before he met another person, or came across another house where he could beg to use a phone. He tried to remember what he had seen from the helicopter. As far as he could recall, he had not seen any other buildings on this part of the hillside. The nearest neighbour might be several kilometres away.

When he was far enough into the woods from the house to be safe, he realised he needed to find the track again. He set off eastwards along the contour of the slope.

He laughed out loud. It felt good. He was free. He had a plan. He had wanted to earn twenty thousand pounds. When Eloise's offer had come along, he had taken it without much thought. It was clear from last night's phone call with Nazim, the brutality of Myroslav's fight, and from this morning's conversation with the maid, that he had stumbled into something very dark. But the nightmare was behind him.

He needed to get back to the real world, to contact the local police to get them to investigate what was really going on behind Myroslav Bondarenko's tall white walls. Whatever it was, it was not good.

The hill was steep. He had gone only a hundred metres when a shadow crossed his feet and he looked up to see a huge bird of prey circling in the blue sky above him, wings wide. He marched on, and was rounding a slow bend fringed with brown grass when he became conscious of another noise besides his own feet.

He stopped. Listened.

Somewhere behind him, he could hear a car grinding up the steep slope. He ducked back into the woods, in case it was one of Myroslav's men.

A grey Audi emerged from behind the trees, inching uphill.

Jacob waited for it to catch him up, ready to leap out and wave his arms to flag it down.

But instead of coming up the hill, the car stopped a little way off, close enough for him to see that the driver was a man in dark glasses.

Jacob took a step further back. The man seemed to be searching the woods. He wasn't just someone who happened to be driving up this remote track.

He waited. The car didn't move.

Something was wrong. This wasn't just an ordinary driver on his way to work or a tourist exploring the woods.

He jolted back into the woods, away from the track.

The car's wheels spurted gravel and it accelerated fast up the hill to where he had been standing. The driver must have spotted him.

Jacob was crashing through the undergrowth now, trying to get deep into the trees again.

Behind him, he could hear that the man in the car had got out and was chasing him too, his footfalls heavy on the debris of the woodland floor.

FOURTEEN

'Stop!' The man called out first in German, then Russian. Then he tried one last time in English. 'Wait!'

Jacob kept on running.

'I saw you,' the man behind him shouted. 'I saw you coming out of the house.'

Jacob stumbled on uneven ground but kept moving forwards.

The man tried again in German. 'I want to help you.'

Mindful of how he had already been tricked into coming here in the first place, he ignored the man, and pushed on.

'OK. I'll wait here,' the man shouted. 'When you're ready, come and talk to me.'

The footsteps behind him stopped. Out of breath now, Jacob slowed, then looked around.

The man in dark glasses stood in a shaft of sunlight, arms crossed in front of him.

'Who are you?' called Jacob in English, panting.

'I've been watching the house. I saw you coming out of it.

93

From the way you were sneaking out into the trees, I'm hazarding a guess you were hoping no one else in the house was going to stop you. Right?'

Jacob didn't answer.

'Look. I'm a friend. I'm not here to do you any harm. You American? English?'

Jacob rested, hands on his thighs, leaning down, listening to the thump of his own heart. 'Why?' he asked. 'Why have you been watching the house? What do you know about Myroslav Bondarenko?'

The man laughed. 'Yeah. I heard that's what he's calling himself these days.'

'Who are you?'

'Come on. I have coffee in the car,' he said, speaking in an American accent – in perfect English. 'We need to talk.'

When they reached the Audi, the man opened the boot and pulled out a backpack, out of which he removed a flask. 'Get in.'

Jacob got into the passenger seat beside him and the man handed him a cup of warm coffee.

'My name is Murphy,' he said. He reached inside his jacket pocket and pulled out a small black wallet. On the right-hand side there was a metal badge, on the left, the letters 'CIA', the man's photograph.

It took Jacob a second to process what he'd just seen. 'You are CIA?'

'That's right.' He snapped the badge shut and returned it to the inside pocket.

Jacob folded forwards, leaning his head onto the black dash-board in front of him.

'You OK?'

'Just relieved. I thought I was going mad. So the CIA are watching Bondarenko?'

Murphy pushed up his dark glasses and rubbed one eye with his finger. 'I can't exactly comment on that. I just want to talk. That's all.'

'If you're CIA, what the hell have I got myself into?'

'Drink your coffee,' said Murphy, and poured himself one. 'Take a breath. Calm down. You were looking pretty scared back then.'

'No shit. You were chasing me.'

'You asked what have you got yourself into? Truth is, that's what I'm over here to find out.' He took a sip, then laid the cup on the dashboard above the steering wheel. Steam obscured the glass. 'I haven't seen you around before. Where did you get those bruises?' Murphy's hand circled around his own eyes. 'On your face?'

'You should have seen the other guy,' said Jacob with a small laugh.

'Wait. Was it you who arrived in the helicopter two days ago?'

Jacob straightened, nodded. They really had been watching the house. This was even bigger than he had imagined. He took a sip from his cup. The man next to him was lean, around forty years old, balding with a dark stubbled chin. Now he had pushed the dark glasses up onto the top of his head, Jacob could see the CIA man had pale blue eyes.

'What's your business in there?' Murphy asked. 'What are you doing?'

95

'Tell me first. Why are you watching the house?'

The man considered. 'OK. I can let you have a few details if it helps, but no specifics. What did you call him? Bondarenko? The Ukrainian? He's had a few identities in the last few years.'

'So that's not his name?'

'Let's just say he's someone we've been interested in for a while. I can't go into it much. So? What are you? Whose side are you on?'

'My name is Jacob Meaney. I'm a translator and language teacher.'

'No shit.' Murphy took out a small notebook and asked for his full name and date of birth. 'You're a translator? What in Jesus are you doing mixed up in this?'

Jacob told Murphy everything he knew. He told him about Rakesh Garg and Nazim, and about the drug called Lutinol. He told him how they had kept his passport and were intending to force him to work for them.

'Interesting,' said Murphy. 'Very interesting. Thank you, Jacob. I am grateful.'

'So who is he really?'

Murphy seemed to take a while to decide how much he was going to tell Jacob, but eventually he spoke. 'Like I said, I can't tell you too much. You heard of the Russian mafia? He was involved, if you know what I mean. Made a lot of money.'

Jacob said, 'I'm glad I'm out of it.'

Murphy stopped talking and looked at him. 'Right,' he said, quietly. 'Thing is, that's not all that was going on. Even then there were whispers this Bondarenko guy was really just a Russian stooge propped up by the Kremlin. People thought he was likely funnelling a lot of Russian money into Ukrainian politics to tip the system in Russia's favour. Following this?'

'Yes. So why is the CIA interested?'

'Because it wasn't just about Ukrainian politics. We know Bondarenko bought a bunch of property in the US in the 2000s, and we believe that he was a hundred per cent funnelling Russian money into American politics too. Can't go into details, but we're trying to get the evidence to prosecute everyone who was involved. Right now the stability of American politics is kind of in the balance, and there are people out there who are standing to profit from it.'

'What's he doing here in Austria then?'

'Sitting pretty on a big pile of cash, because unless we can prove he's involved in illegal activities, we can't extradite him and prove that he was part of a Russian plan to corrupt the American political system. Which he one hundred per cent was.'

'Jesus.'

'I know. The thing about this guy is his glory days are gone. That makes him vulnerable. Vulnerable to us, sure. We finally get the chance to find out what he was up to. But vulnerable to other sharks just like himself too. The big money from Russia doesn't exist any more. But if we can get Bondarenko, we are hoping we can get to the bottom of a substantial network of people – some very senior figures in our own political establishment – in a conspiracy to destabilise US elections.'

'I had no idea what I was getting into.'

'No, sir. I don't expect you did. Despite his cool house and shit, he's just an old-school thug who has been implicated in multiple murders. And he's backed into a corner and that's why he's dangerous. He's lost his Russian allies in the Moscow regime. He tried to get a foothold in the US but we shut it down. All that money that paid for this luxury lifestyle of his has started to dry up. We figure that in the last eight years he's been having to make his living in other ways. Question is, what? There's an ongoing case against him in India for bribing officials to get his hands on mining contracts there. We think he's also rebuilt his old links to the Russian mafia, and we suspect he's up to something new. If we can figure it out, that's our leverage. Maybe drug smuggling or people trafficking.'

'People trafficking?'

'Maybe.'

'Russian mafia?'

'He's connected, that's for sure. We can only speculate as to the rest. Right now the US is trying to extradite him to face charges of fraud on some of those property deals so we can interrogate him properly, but the Austrian legal system isn't playing the game. If we can get him prosecuted on a charge of something that's illegal here, then we know we can get to him. That's the prize, Jacob.'

'So he's stuck here?'

'Pretty much. He can't leave the country without us having an arrest warrant ready for him somewhere else. That's why he's locked up behind these walls. We just don't know what he's doing in there.'

Jacob blinked. 'So, what do you do next?'

'So we wait. And we watch.'

'You wait?'

'Exactly. Until we have enough information to persuade the Austrian government to let us get our hands on him.'

'I've just told you. They were holding me against my will. I can give a statement. Anything you need.'

Murphy removed his dark glasses from the top of his head and rubbed his scalp.

'I understand what you're saying. Except it's not enough.'

There was a concerned look in Murphy's pale eyes that he didn't like the look of. 'You see, I don't think you're going to like this.'

'Like what?'

'Right now the best thing you could do for us is go right back in there.'

FIFTEEN

'You want me to go back in there?' Jacob said, shocked.

'Being honest, Jacob, what you've told me so far . . . that's not enough for us to act on. This man is a monster. From the outside, he looks all shiny. Collects art. Pays a licence fee to have a boat down on the lake. Probably sponsors the local opera. Beautiful house. If we tell the Austrian authorities what you've said, yes, they'll get a warrant, go in there and what do you think they'll find? You claim you were being held against your will? He'll deny it. What actual evidence is there?'

'He stole my passport.'

'Big deal. Police come knocking on his door and when they search the place it'll turn up lying in a drawer in your room.'

Jacob racked his brains. 'What about the website that the American man, Draper, built? I don't know what they're up to with it, but the evidence will be in there somewhere.'

'A website? Probably hosted somewhere like Sweden or China. Almost certainly containing nothing to link it back to Bondarenko.'

'You're kidding me? You're out here observing them. Surely you have something?'

'For sure we do. But nothing we'd be prepared to share with the Austrian police at this stage because it'll compromise our investigation. And what we have relates mostly to offences on American soil anyway. Right now we can't touch him. But with your help . . .'

Jacob gazed at the patches of light flickering on the bark of the trees ahead of them. 'Wait a minute. You said people trafficking? There's a Ukrainian maid in there. I'd think she's been trafficked. What about that?'

Murphy flipped his notebook open again. 'OK. Good. What's her name? Age?'

'I don't know her name. She didn't tell me. Aged late twenties, early thirties.'

'Do you have any pictures of her?'

'I don't have a phone. She seemed to be in danger, though.'

'What kind of danger?'

'She's held there against her will. If Myroslav used violence on me, he'd almost certainly use it on her.'

'You don't have her name or any of her details?'

'No. No, I don't. I mean, she is a chef . . .'

'OK,' said Murphy cautiously. 'We'll look into it. But we'd need a name, at least, if that's going to be useful to us right away. And what about the Australian woman you mentioned? Does she have a last name? Is she here under duress as well?'

'Eloise? No. She never told me her last name. She's Bondarenko's right hand. It's the Ukrainian woman who we need to get out of there. I think she's in real trouble.'

Murphy closed the notebook slowly. 'So the Australian woman is in there entirely of her own free will?'

'Yes.'

'Shame, because an Australian national held prisoner would be useful.' He looked back up at Jacob. 'To be brutal, it's not enough. The real danger is that we notify the Austrians, they rush in there. They're not going to find anything. Bondarenko is an old hand at this game.' Murphy looked at Jacob. 'More coffee?'

Jacob shook his head.

'Look. I would totally understand it if you just want to go straight home and pretend none of this happened. I would be tempted to do the same myself, honest to God.' Murphy pulled on his ear, rubbed his chin.

'What?' asked Jacob.

'None of this is your responsibility. None of this is your fault. But you have to know something that will happen as a consequence of you leaving there now.'

'What?'

'They're going to start to panic. Like I said, they're going to start to cover things up.'

'That's a good thing, though. They'll have to stop whatever they're doing.'

'This Ukrainian woman you think has been trafficked? By the time the police come to the door, she'll have gone. They'll want to make sure she can't tell her story. They'll want to make sure there's no trace of her ever having been there.'

'You mean, they'll kill her?'

'Of course, you have to think about yourself too. That's understandable.'

Jacob turned round to look back down the hill towards the house. 'I can't go back in there. It's a madhouse. I've already been assaulted. I need to get back to England.'

Murphy looked at his watch. 'What time did you leave the house?'

It felt like a lifetime ago, but Jacob realised it had only been about forty minutes. 'About twenty to two.'

'How long before they notice you're gone?'

'I don't know. At best another hour?'

Murphy sighed. He drummed his fingers on the wheel. 'Whether we tell the Austrian authorities or not, if you stay out here, they'll assume you've gone to them yourself. They'll probably disappear from view now and eliminate any evidence there might be – if there was any in the first place.' Murphy let that hang there for a second.

'You're trying to say that me escaping puts the life of another person in danger?'

'Obviously you weren't to know that. If you want to walk away now and go back home to England, it's your right to do so. I'm not going to persuade you otherwise. It's just you need to be aware of the consequences.'

Jacob laid his head back on the dashboard. 'You think I should go back in there, don't you?'

'It's a hundred per cent your call. Look. It may only be a few hours before we can get some clarity on this. I'll be looking into everything you have just told me. I swear I'll do all I can. A day or two at most. And in the meantime any further details you can get out of there for us is going to speed things up.'

Jacob stared straight ahead. 'Will you contact the British Embassy for me and let them know I'm here, at least?'

'Naturally.'

'And I need to write a letter to my girlfriend. Will you send it to her?'

'That too – as long as you don't give any operational details.' He tore a page from his notebook and handed Jacob the pen. 'I appreciate what you're doing. It's not easy.' He added, 'Better make it quick, though. We haven't got much time.'

Jacob took the pen and looked up. Above them the bird was still revolving slowly in the hot summer air.

SIXTEEN

Jacob approached the house slowly. None of this was his fault, or his responsibility. But Murphy had been right. He could not leave.

To the right of the main gate was the visitor bell. He pressed it.

It seemed like a long time before the door finally buzzed, and when it did, Iosef was standing on the other side of the grille with a gun in his hands, pointing it at Jacob. Myroslav was standing right behind him. Jacob had grown up around guns, but he had never had one pointed right at him. He stared at the barrel. 'Where the fuck have you been?' Myroslav demanded.

The anxiety on the Ukrainian's face pleased him a little. It made coming back here worth it. If he had stayed away, they would have known he had talked to the authorities. 'It was a nice day,' Jacob said calmly. 'I went for a walk. How is your nose?'

'Better than your face.' A hint of a smile. 'I thought you wanted to leave?'

Jacob looked at him in the eye and said, 'Obviously I had the option. I just wanted to show you that.'

Iosef squinted, sighting his pistol on Jacob's head.

'I could have gone home, but I thought about it and decided not to.'

Myroslav narrowed his eyes. 'Why?'

'I figured if you risked taking a beating from me, you probably wanted me to stay.'

Myroslav laughed out loud. 'I could fight you again, if you like.'

Jacob was trying his hardest to remain calm. 'Maybe another time,' he said. 'I don't want to have to break your nose a second time. But if you want me to stay that much, you probably think I'm worth something. So if you pay me properly, I'll stay.'

Myroslav frowned, and for a second, Jacob thought he was going to hit him again. Instead he smiled. 'I didn't take any risks, believe me. Next time I'll kill you with my first punch. You want more money? How much?'

Jacob named a sum.

'Let him in.'

Iosef pressed the code and the grille opened. 'You believe him? You think he just went for a walk?' Iosef muttered.

'It's a nice day. I was bored. I wanted to see the world.'

'How did you get out?' demanded Iosef.

Jacob pointed to the gate. 'It was open. So I walked through it. Why? Oh dear. Were you supposed to be the one watching it?' He tutted. 'You really need to smarten up your operation a little here, Mr Bondarenko.'

Myroslav put his hand on top of Iosef's gun and pushed the

barrel down. Iosef glared at Jacob as he walked past, towards the house. Jacob knew exactly what Bondarenko was thinking: that it was better to have him inside than outside.

'Did you see anyone out there?' Iosef called out after him.

Jacob carried on walking as calmly as he could. 'Was I supposed to?'

And he was back inside his own prison again, wondering if he had made a terrible mistake.

The rest of the afternoon was hotter. He lay on his bed, with the air conditioning on, thinking about everything Murphy had said.

'But I'm not a spy,' he had told Murphy. 'I'm a translator.'

'Who better?' Murphy had answered.

At around four, Eloise came and knocked on his door. 'Naughty boy. You went out,' she said, like a disappointed mother.

'I just wanted to go for a walk.'

She pushed past him and closed the door behind her. 'Iosef says he thinks you were meeting someone.'

'Iosef is a bit embarrassed because he was the one who was supposed to be keeping his eyes on me.'

She laughed. 'It's true. Myroslav called him an idiot. I wouldn't make an enemy of Iosef, though. He's a piece of work. He'll try and get his own back.'

'I was making a point. I hid when the car came in, and before th gate closed, I walked out. I just walked half a mile up the road and felt better for it.'

'But you came back? Why?'

Jacob poured two glasses of cold water from the fridge and handed her one. 'Did Myroslav send you to talk to me?'

'As a matter of fact he did,' she said.

'I thought so. I came back because, like I told him, I figured you need me.'

'Yes we do.'

'Nazim said he is calling again tomorrow. If you want me to interpret, I told him you're going to have to pay me more.'

'Wow, Jacob.' She grinned at him. 'I didn't know you had it in you. It's oddly sexy. But I knew I was right about you, first time I saw you. How much are you asking for?'

Walking back to the house, Jacob had realised that was the only explanation that would make any sense to them. They were all greedy. It was what they understood. 'He said he'd double my pay if I beat him in a fight. I said I wanted ten times as much.'

She grinned. 'And getting sexier by the minute. You're getting the hang of this. I knew you would.' She dropped onto his sofa, looking down at him. 'It's just not safe for you to go out there on your own, honey, OK?'

'Seriously? It's not safe out there? It's not exactly safe in here.' He pointed to the cut on his face. He thought about what Murphy had said. None of them were safe in here, really.

'I don't want you to be unhappy, Jacob. You and me, we're colleagues. Next time you want to go out, just ask.'

'Deal.' She was halfway back out of the door when he said, 'Wait. I am curious. What was that photograph Nazim sent you yesterday?'

She stiffened. Her eyes became expressionless. 'I didn't get much of a chance to see it before I dropped my phone.'

'It shocked you. I could see that from your face.'

She shrugged, trying to make light of it.

'I don't know. Just something to scare me, I guess.'

'And you've had nothing from Carla?'

'Who?'

'My girlfriend, remember?'

'Oh, *her*,' she said, laughing, and closed the door behind her. It would be in her inbox. She would have read it too. Or maybe she had never even sent Carla the message in the first place. Everything here was a lie.

Draper was sitting at the edge of the pool, a glass of beer in one hand. 'I heard you pissed Iosef off.'

'Word gets around.'

'You hit Myroslav in the face and he hasn't killed you and dumped your body in the woods, so you are not the man I thought you were.'

Everything appeared to be a joke to Draper but Jacob suspected that underneath, Draper was as frightened about all this as he was.

'When you took this job, was it what they told you it was going to be?'

'I don't even know what it is now,' said Draper.

Jacob kicked off his sandals and sat next to him, legs dangling over the edge of the pool.

'Hey! Mr Meaney.'

Jacob turned at the sound of another voice. Myroslav was striding towards the pool, Eloise following behind him and the big dog padding after them both. The man squatted down next to Jacob and said, 'He definitely said the pool was golden?'

'Sorry?'

'Yesterday. That shit-stain Nazim. He used the word *golden*?'

Jacob looked down towards his feet, paddling slowly in the water. The tiles under him were all gold. 'Yes.' *Aapake pass ek kone ka swimming pool hai.* You have a big golden swimming pool.'

'How did he know the fucking pool was gold?' said Myroslav, standing again.

Eloise had a cigarette in her hand. 'Probably he'd just seen a photograph.'

Myroslav was turning around slowly, as if he expected to see Nazim in one of the acacia trees or in the tall firs beyond the white wall.

Darling Tymko

As always, I miss you. Nobody warned me that having a child would mean so much pain.

You were born in pain. In the end, they had to cut you from my belly. I remember being in the hospital, waiting for the man to give me an injection so they could start the operation, but he wouldn't give me it until he had finished the story he was telling all the doctors and nurses who were standing around me in the room.

The story was about a fish he had caught in the Dnipro River. It was a long story. He went on and on and on, and I was just lying there groaning in pain.

The fish he had been trying to catch was a karas – a special type of carp. I remember this very well. This particular one on his hook was the biggest of its kind he had ever caught. But just as he was trying to land it, the fish escaped and jumped back into the water, and when he looked down his own hook was stuck into his thumb instead.

Not just stuck, but the hook went in one side and out of the other. Impossible, he said, for the hook to come out of the fish's mouth and appear in my thumb like that. He had had to get his knife and cut his own flesh to remove it. He swore that the karas must have been a magic fish, and he lifted up his hand to show everyone the sticking plaster on his thumb.

And all the time I was just lying there screaming, thinking this is a man who has just blamed his own clumsiness on a fish, and he is about to spike me.

Men are dicks. Not all men. Not you.

One day I shall cook you karas from the Dnipro. If you score the flesh in a criss-cross pattern, then dip the fish in finely chopped ginger and crushed garlic, you can then put it in very hot sesame oil and cook each side for five minutes and the skin will become crisp. Squeeze a little lime juice on it and it is delicious hot or cold.

To score the flesh, make sure you use the sharpest knife you have.

I never minded the pain, my darling. I never mind it still. Kiss Baba if she is there.

SEVENTEEN

Myroslav stood by the swimming pool, slowly turning, peering into the woodland around his house.

'Let me take Jacob out on the launch, Slava. He said he wanted to go out.' Eloise turned to Jacob. 'I think he deserves a treat. Would you like that, Jacob? You want to look around, you want to leave the house, all you have to do is ask. It's just you can't go wandering off on your own.'

'What about me?' said Draper. 'You want to take me out on the boat too?'

'No, Draper. I'm not asking you.'

'Bitch.' He smirked at her, then flopped into the pool with an ungainly splash.

'You wouldn't like it out there, Draper. You only like sitting in your room watching underage porn and playing *Call of Duty*.'

'Actually not *Call of Duty*.' Draper paddled back to the edge of the pool and took his beer. 'It's *Fallout*.'

'Come on, Myroslav,' Eloise said. 'He's on our side. He's proved it.'

Myroslav went back to peering into the trees.

'It's very beautiful,' said Eloise. 'The lake is really warm this time of year. We could swim.'

The gardener, Fedor, was waiting in the minivan that had been parked at the front of the house. Eloise was already sitting in the back. 'Get in,' she called.

'You're here to make sure I don't try and run away?' Jacob said to Fedor. Fedor didn't answer, just pushed back his black bomber jacket far enough for Jacob to see the gun that nestled under it.

The gate opened. Turning left, they drove around the tall white wall, taking a private road that headed south, towards the lake. Out of the right-hand window Jacob looked at the forest around them. The trees were tall and dark.

It was a short ride. At the bottom they were suddenly at the waterfront. Fedor unlocked a gate and there, at the end of a track, was a boathouse. It must have been built at the same time as the house, designed by the same architect. It was modern and white, made of concrete and glass, with a black wood jetty that extended out over the dark water.

From the back of the van Eloise produced a large wicker hamper and led the way down to the boathouse.

It was the kind of speedboat you might see on an Italian lake, built on classic lines, a blue fibreglass hull and dark wood deck.

'Are you any good with boats?' she asked. 'I can't even drive a car.'

'No.'

'Fedor, you will drive the boat then.'

Fedor stepped onto the rear of the classic boat and sat down in the cockpit where he started the engine. A low, throaty hum filled the boathouse.

Jacob followed Fedor aboard, feeling the boat dip a little as he stepped onto it. Eloise handed him the hamper, then joined him on the stern. Fedor unhitched the lines and eased the boat into the open water. 'Ready?' he asked.

'Ready for what?'

'I think you better sit down' said Eloise.

Next thing, the boat was roaring and Jacob was thrown back onto the brown leather upholstery.

'Wooooo!' Eloise cried out above the noise of the huge engines that were pushing them through the dark blue water. He looked back. The boat left a big V of white behind them, breaking up the reflection of the beautiful boathouse. He turned forward again, felt the warm wind that blew in their faces. 'Special, isn't it?'

Leaning forward, she unbuckled the straps on the hamper and pulled out a chilled bottle of Riesling, a corkscrew and two glasses. 'Hold these,' she said, offering him the two glasses. She opened the bottle, then filled them both. 'To a life of luxury.' She raised his glass to his. 'My parents were born in Moscow,' she shouted above the roar of the engines. 'My dad was a scientist. He emigrated to Australia when the Soviet Union collapsed, worked like a dog as a taxi driver in Melbourne until he had a stroke when I was sixteen. Never recovered.'

Spray shot from the bows, catching Jacob in the face. Eloise laughed at him as he wiped it away.

'My mum ended up cleaning offices, but it didn't bring in much. Every time I went shopping with her, we'd take stuff to the checkout and then have to empty out half the basket again because we couldn't afford it. I always swore I'd never be poor. This is what I have been aiming for all my life.'

She swept her hand around the lake, like all of it was hers.

'Went to business school and did marketing. Ended up as a PA, first in tech, then advertising, and a bit in international financial services. Working for men who couldn't wipe their asses, but they earned ten, twenty times more than me. I even went out with one, but he turned out to be a bigger loser than the rest.'

A V of geese flew high overhead.

'He was an older man from Canberra who told me he was a multimillionaire, but I wasn't just after his money. I really thought I loved him. I was totally bowled over by him. Turned out he was just a con artist, a scammer who made his money selling people investments that didn't exist. He was wanted by the police. Sweet guy, but it was all a big story. Police froze our bank accounts and everything I'd put into them. That bastard ended up costing me money.' She laughed and drained the glass. 'Live and learn.' She stopped suddenly and looked at him. 'I don't know why I'm telling you all this.'

'Who else are you going to tell?' He looked around the big empty lake. 'So how did you hook up with Myroslav?'

The speedboat slowed. The noise of the engines became quieter.

'After my millionaire husband, I went back to being a PA in pharmaceutical start-ups for a while. I spent two more years watching other people get rich. You can be ugly, you can be stupid, you can be hated, but the fact is, if you're rich, none of it matters. Just never be poor. Two years learning, looking for an angle . . . Last year I was at a conference in Vienna and I met that guy I told you about at a bar. I spoke Russian. No one else in the bar did. He wrote down a phone number for me. Told me this guy was looking for a PA. It turned out to be Myroslav. I told him I wanted to work for him.'

'What did he say that made you quit your job and come out here?' asked Jacob, fishing for information.

'Oh, that he'd made a bunch of money in gas contracts and minerals. He was looking for ideas for something new. I figured working for him was going to be much better than working for another start-up run by someone who thinks he's Jesus. Back in the day, in Ukraine, he was the big boss, apparently – that right, Fedor?' She switched into Russian.

Fedor looked like he had been listening in. 'Pretty big,' he said, in the same language.

'Back in the day he was sitting on billions, but then they booted him out and he's been looking for an angle. So I gave him one.'

He and Eloise had been speaking in English. As far as Jacob knew, Fedor only spoke Russian, but he was beginning to wonder if that was true.

'I want to swim,' he said.

'Here?'

'Why not? Don't you?'

She leaned forward and tapped Fedor on the shoulder. 'Stop the boat,' she said.

The boat slowed to a stop, but still bobbed gently on the lake.

Eloise pulled off her shirt, unbuttoned her skirt, and dropped it onto the deck. She stepped up onto the back of the boat. 'Coming in?' And she dived into the blue water.

He calculated how long it would take to swim to the shore. They were far out now. The speedboat would have caught him easily if he had wanted to escape. When he plunged in after her, the lake was bathwater warm, black and deep beneath his feet.

EIGHTEEN

Fedor stayed in the driving seat, ready to start up the engines. Like Iosef, he didn't like Jacob, or trust him, that much was clear. In the water, they could talk more freely.

He swam close to her, so he didn't have to raise his voice to talk. 'So what was the angle?'

'It was to game the pharmaceutical industry. I could see a way for a great deal of money to be made.'

Eloise was a strong swimmer, Jacob judged. She moved through the water with ease.

'I figured Myroslav must have been a big deal once. I mean, look at his place. He must have earned a ton of money, right?'

'You ever ask yourself how, exactly?'

'So here I was, giving him his chance to get back to being the kind of man he wants to be. This thing, it can make millions, I promise you. Me, I'm walking away from this rich. You can too, you know. Just accept what's happening. It's a blessing.'

'You took my passport.'

'It's necessary. You may need visas. We may have to travel to Brazil or Singapore at the drop of a hat at the end of this deal. You can have it back when we're done.'

'And I can't go anywhere until you give it back to me.'

'Well, yeah, obviously. It was Myroslav's idea. He likes to make sure he's in charge. It'll all work out, don't worry.' She dived deep into the water and came up brushing his legs, then his chest, her head emerging right next to his. 'You've just got to have the right perspective. Right now, life is good, isn't it?' She twisted in the water, looking around. 'Do you like your apartment? No rent to pay. No outgoings. It's all money in the bank. And the food. It's to die for.'

'To die for,' said Jacob.

Eloise missed the irony in his voice. 'You just need to trust me.'

'I still don't understand.' Eyeing Fedor, he swam a little further away from the boat. She followed.

'I'll explain. You know about all the big drug companies, right? Johnson and Johnson, Roche, Novartis, AstraZeneca, GlaxoSmithKline. They develop new drugs all the time. You know what's tragic? Sometimes drugs fail certification because they're not good enough. But sometimes they are great drugs that can save lives and it still takes them years just to jump through all the hurdles. Just think of all the people that could have been helped in that time.'

She stopped swimming and lay on her back, arms stretched out in the water, looking up at the sky.

'Hundreds. Thousands. Tens of thousands. As a business, we just find territories in which a particular drug has been certified ahead of others and sell those particular new drugs, the ones people really need, from there. It's a little window of opportunity.'

'Brazil.'

'Exactly. Well. That's the thing. Notoriously, Brazil has been really slow on certifying new drugs, but their president has pushed hard to make them speed that up. And there's one particular drug—'

'Lutinol.' Jacob remembered the name from the conversation with Nazim.

'Right. It's like a miracle cure for female infertility. It's a hormone which encourages women to ovulate. It stimulates the better eggs, or extra ones. Results are amazing. It's transforming lives. Some women, especially older women, are desperate. And older women often have a lot of money.'

'And it's legal in Brazil?'

'It's one of a raft of drugs that certain pharmaceutical companies – start-up companies – have managed to get certified in Brazil since their president intervened personally. Six months and it will be available in Europe and America, but think of all the women around the world who can have babies between now and then. Especially the older ones for whom time is running out. Not me, I hasten to add.' And she rolled in the water over to face him. 'Fuck that. I am never having children.'

She came so close they were practically touching.

'So basically we are finding opportunities for new drugs in those months when they're approved in country X, but not yet in country Y. That's all you need to know.'

'Is that legal?'

'You tell me if it's right that a government can stop someone from buying a drug which is perfectly safe because they haven't done the paperwork yet.'

'But the drug is being shipped from India, right? Not Brazil at all.'

'Come on. I need a drink.'

She swam with an easy front crawl back to the boat and pulled herself up onto the small deck at the rear. Grabbing a towel, she dried herself quickly and stood, legs slightly apart to steady herself on the bobbing deck, smiling down at him.

'I like you, Jacob. You have . . . depth. This is an opportunity like nothing else you've ever seen in your life. If you work hard and play your cards right, you'll find you're a very lucky man. You asked for the money. I promise you, he'll pay it. When it comes to money, he plays a straight hand.' She reached out to him, pulled him up out of the water and handed him a towel.

'What about my girlfriend? Still nothing from her?'

Eloise handed him his glass, shook her head. 'Poor baby.' She smiled at him. 'Maybe she doesn't love you any more?'

'You did send her the email, didn't you?'

'Jesus, Jacob,' she said. 'A little trust, please.' She reached in her bag and pulled out a pack of cigarettes.

The water around them looked black now, as the sunlight paled.

'Nazim is trying to scare you. That's why he sent that photograph.'

She scowled. 'He's trying to scare us into doing a deal with him, that's all. He wants a part of all this.'

'But what was it?'

'I didn't get a proper look at it. I don't even know if it was real. Listen. Nazim's in Mumbai. We're here. He can't touch us. Besides, we have Fedor here to protect us.'

'That's why you have a gun, Fedor. To protect me?'

Fedor didn't answer. Either he didn't understand or was pretending not to.

Eloise walked to the cockpit where the hamper lay, and pulled out cheeses and fresh figs and a loaf of bread, and a freshly cooked cold trout. 'Apparently you ordered this from the kitchen.'

'Yes. I did.'

She lifted some onto a plate and tasted it.

'Good call. It's frickin' delicious. You really are getting into this, aren't you?'

'I guess I am.'

'You should order more stuff. Myroslav always asks the maid for borscht and dumplings, given the chance. If I ate what he ordered, I'd never put on a swimming suit again.'

'What about the maid?'

'What about her?'

'What's in it for her?'

'She's a bitch. She pretty much hates everybody.'

He put the fish in his mouth and chewed. It was soft and delicious, with a tang of garlic, ginger and lime. 'Why does Myroslav keep her then?'

'I guess because she cooks good borscht.'

'Borsch. She called it borsch.'

'Who cares?'

'Do you even know her name?'

'What? Why are you so interested in her?'

123

'She cut her hair, apparently, because Myroslav wanted her to grow it long.'

'Like I said. Crazy bitch. Her name is Vladyslava apparently.' She spoke in a deep, mock-Ukrainian voice: 'I hate everybody and my name is Vladyslava.'

They ate as light left the sky. Eloise offered Fedor wine, which he refused, and by then the bottle was empty anyway. The back of the boat formed a sunbed. They lay on it side by side in the middle of the big lake on a perfectly still night, looking up at the stars above them and the lights of houses fringing the north side of the lake.

She rolled onto her side, so close he could feel her breath. Reaching out, she brushed his hair back from his eyes. 'It'll all be fine,' she said quietly. 'Come on. Live a little. Relax. Forget your preconceptions. You're an intellectual. You think too much. All this will be over soon. It will all be a little story you can tell your grandkids.' She ran her finger down his forehead, along the ridge of his nose. 'It's OK to want more than you have. I'm going to buy a house somewhere and do all the things I've never had a chance to do,' she said quietly. 'Grow apples. Maybe read some poetry. I never really got poetry. Will you teach me about it?' she asked.

That night, when they were back in the compound, on the main steps to the house, she said, 'Fancy a nightcap? Myroslav keeps a very good brandy.'

'I've drunk too much already,' said Jacob.

She leaned forward, took both sides of his face and kissed

him, slipped her tongue inside his lips. He didn't respond. She laughed. 'Oh. I remember. You've got a girlfriend.'

She left Fedor to silently escort him back to his apartment. Fedor stopped at the bottom of the stairs and raised two fingers of his right hand, pointed them first at his own eyes, and then at Jacob. *I am watching you.* Then he turned and walked silently back to the main house.

NINETEEN

The light was on in Draper's room. Jacob heard the sound of gunfire from his TV and knocked at the door.

Draper muted the movie. 'Who is it?' he shouted.

'Me. You're still awake?'

The first thing he said when he opened the door was, 'Did you just fuck Eloise?'

'You know that I have a girlfriend back in England?' said Jacob.

Draper threw himself back onto the sofa which faced the big screen and picked up his controller. 'I would have. And,' he said in a sing-song voice, 'I think she likes you. Come on in. Want a drink?'

Draper's living room was a mess. The cushions from the sofa had been put on the floor and there was an Xbox controller and a broken iPhone lying on them. The TV screen was frozen – a man was about to shoot a gun. Draper walked over to his fridge and pulled out a couple of red cans.

'There's this local version of Coke they call *Almdudler* which tastes pretty rank if you have it on its own, but it makes a passable mixer with white rum. Try it?'

'Was it Eloise who recruited you for this job?'

'Of course it was. Myroslav is just money and muscle.'

'And you knew what you were getting into?' If he was a spy, his job was to gather as much information as he could.

Draper picked up the rum from the floor and added a few fingers to a glass, then handed it over. 'Why you asking?'

'If I'm staying, and it looks like I don't get a great say in that, I want to know who I am really working for. Did you have any idea what the set-up was?'

'Yes and no. I was pretty sure I wasn't signing up to work for the Children's Cancer Foundation. I could tell she was up to something. But I just do what I'm told.'

'And you didn't have a problem with that?'

'Eloise told me that no one was going to get hurt, and I'd walk away with a half mil and probably a bit more on top.'

'Half a million? Dollars?'

Draper held up his glass. 'Chin-chin. You should have asked for more, Language Man.'

Jacob pulled out one of the dining chairs and sat on it. Draper returned to his cushions and pressed PLAY on the remote. He was watching some subtitled South Korean movie on Netflix. Men in suits were fighting each other with guns and swords. 'I'd tell you what was going on but I don't really have any idea.'

It took Jacob a second to realise that he was talking about the film.

He noticed the iPhone on the floor again. 'Is that Eloise's phone?' Jacob asked.

'Yeah. She smashed the screen. Bought a new one. She was asking me to get some stuff off it.'

Jacob stared at the phone. 'Someone sent her a photo on Signal the day she broke it. It was only on her screen for a few seconds, then it disappeared. There wouldn't be any way of recovering it, would there?'

'She asked me the same thing, as it happens. And the answer is no. Questions, questions. Why are you so interested?'

'Because whatever it was she saw seemed to scare her. That's why she dropped the phone. Do you have access to the internet?'

'You really like to ask questions, don't you?'

'Do you?'

Draper laughed. 'I do because I need to access our servers. But I was told to make sure you don't. So don't ask me. When Eloise said no one was going to get hurt, apparently she meant except anyone who crosses Myroslav. Iosef would probably kill me if they found out I let you use the internet, so I'm not going to.' He took a sip from his drink. 'Why? What do you want?'

'I just wanted to find out more about Lutinol,' he lied. 'Never mind.'

'I already looked. You'll just get a bunch of stuff about how it stimulates the luteinising hormone and shit like that, but how, unlike other drugs, it runs less of a risk of producing ovarian hyperstimulation syndrome. It's pretty cool if you're a woman who wants babies.'

He remembered how on his second day at the house, Draper had asked him about Dr Dee. 'You put a lot of work into pretending you understand less than you do, don't you, Draper?'

Draper seemed momentarily embarrassed and looked at him strangely for a second. Then his goofy smile returned. 'Listen, I'm dumb enough to wind up here. But then you are too, aren't you?'

'Fair play,' said Jacob, and he took a sip from his sickly sweet drink. If he had thought Draper might be an easy ally, he was mistaken. There was something off about him.

'You ever googled Myroslav Bondarenko?' Jacob asked, as casually as he could.

'Sure I did. Funny thing. There's nothing at all on him out there. He doesn't actually exist.'

'Really?' Jacob tried to sound surprised.

'Seriously. You'd have thought a gazillionaire like Myroslav might have a little more chat going on, wouldn't you?'

'There's no mention of Myroslav Bondarenko?'

'There are a bunch of Myroslav Bondarenkos, sure.' He lowered his voice. 'But none of them are our guy. It's like he doesn't even exist. You know why?'

'No.'

'Because I don't think that's actually his real name.'

'Really? Interesting.'

There was a bang on the door. Draper jerked his head round towards it, looking as if he'd been caught out doing something he shouldn't. 'Who is it?'

Webb's voice came through the door. 'You're needed in the conference room.'

Jacob stood and went to the door. 'I'd better go, then. Thanks for the drink.'

Webb was standing outside. 'Myroslav wants Draper there. And you too.'

Sitting cross-legged on the cushions in the middle of the floor, Draper looked up, puzzled. 'Me?'

'He's a little drunk,' said Jacob.

'What's new? Come on.' Webb entered the room, took the glass from Draper's hand, put it on a nearby table, then leaned down and lifted him off the floor.

'I'm coming. I'm coming.'

'Call the maid,' Webb ordered Jacob. 'Tell her to put some coffee on for him. Then join us there.'

Watching Webb lead Draper across the lawn, Jacob found Draper's house phone by tracing the lead to a pile of discarded clothes on the floor. 'It's Jacob,' he said.

The woman sounded tired. 'What?'

'Your name is Vladyslava. Eloise told me that.'

'You woke me up to tell me my own name?'

'I woke you up because Myroslav wants coffee in the conference room. Draper's drunk and he needs him sober on the conference call.'

'Fine,' she said, and slammed down the phone.

By the time Jacob made it down the stairs, Draper was sitting in a chair next to Eloise, blinking in the harsh light. Webb had remained in the room, standing by the door, as if on guard.

Myroslav was wearing a pair of white silk pyjamas, suggesting that he had been woken for the meeting too.

On the screen of Eloise's new phone, there was a man with neat black hair and a Southeast Asian face. He was speaking in perfect English. 'I am sorry to tell you that there has been an unfortunate breach in security,' said the man.

TWENTY

'Around six this morning we became aware of something unusual happening on our computer system,' said the man.

'Who is this guy?' demanded Draper.

Myroslav glared at him, but Eloise said, 'His name is Cheong Young Zu. He is calling from Singapore.'

Vladyslava arrived with a tray of coffee. She poured it silently, moving around the table as Cheong Young Zu continued talking. 'The system was running too slowly. When our IT department checked, it noticed a surge in our DNS traffic.'

'What does that mean?' Myroslav asked in Russian, turning to Draper for an explanation.

'It could mean all kinds of things,' Draper spoke hesitantly. 'Which computer system is he talking about? I can't start to ask the questions unless I know why his computer system is so important.'

Eloise stepped in. 'He's the nominated director of Kolophant Limited. He's a lawyer who fronts companies for other people.'

'Oh shit', Draper lapsed into English. 'This guy runs the shell company?' Even drunk, Draper seemed to understand more of this than Jacob did. Vladyslava was pouring Jacob's cup now. He tried to catch her eye, but she ignored him, finished pouring the coffee and left the room.

'That's right,' Eloise answered him. 'Effectively Kolophant is an offshore company operating out of Singapore.'

'So he's the guy handling our company data and he's been hacked? Jesus,' Draper said.

'Exactly,' said Eloise. 'So what precisely is he saying?'

'A surge in DNS traffic could mean a few things,' said Draper, reverting to Russian. 'Could mean that the domain is hosting malicious content. If someone deployed an exploit kit on the site—'

'Talk in a language I understand,' muttered Myroslav.

Draper cradled his cup. 'Someone – a hostile agent – may have inserted software into his servers and is using it to send out information from its databases.'

'What kind of stuff?' asked Eloise.

Myroslav turned to Jacob. 'Ask the little shit if our money is safe.'

Cheong Young Zu answered. 'I can reassure Mr Bondarenko that his bank accounts are perfectly secure. That is an entirely separate situation.'

Draper leaned forward. 'Have you looked at the logs?'

Cheong Young Zu nodded. 'Our IT guys are looking at them now.'

'And?' Draper said.

'It is too early to know for sure, but yes, we believe there was mass data export.'

'What is going on?' demanded Eloise.

'From which server? Like some kind of Panama Papers shit?'

'Maybe,' said Cheong Young Zu. 'Except . . . it appears to be more targeted.'

Jacob was struggling to understand the conversation. The Panama Papers, he dimly remembered, was a massive hack of a database holding details of thousands upon thousands of secret – and often dubious – offshore companies. The hack produced a massive data export which exposed how dictators, oligarchs, politicians and criminal networks all around the world hoarded and laundered their fortunes.

'Except what?' Draper was asking. 'What do you mean, it appears to be more targeted?'

Jacob needed to understand all this so he could pass it back to Murphy. If Cheong Young Zu was the nominated director of the company Kolophant Ltd, then Kolophant was an offshore company based in Singapore, presumably designed to conceal Myroslav's activities and protect its income from the prying eyes of authorities. Trying to memorise all this information while translating it was making it hard to concentrate.

'Except, one hour ago,' Cheong Young Zu was saying, 'we started receiving emails to our inboxes. Which is why we thought we should get in touch with you directly.'

'And?'

'The emails were all the same. The IP address shows that the messages came from within our own system.'

'So the malware created a data export, but it also triggered your servers to send an email out?' Draper was in his element here. 'What did it say?'

'I think you need to see it.' Cheong Young Zu held a sheet of paper up to the camera. It was a print out from an email and it was short. It read: यूरोस्लव् को नमस्ते कहो

They all turned to Jacob.

'It's Hindi. It says, *Say hello to Myroslav,*' he told them.

There was a second's silence in the room. Jacob glanced at Myroslav, sitting on a chair next to him. The Ukrainian's oddly expressionless face was a volcano crust.

Draper was the first to speak. 'Actually pretty clever. Letting you know like that, I mean. It could only be that Indian guy, right?'

'Shut up, Draper,' said Eloise quietly, who Jacob guessed had also picked up on Myroslav's simmering rage.

'Understood.' Draper nodded.

'I offer our sincere apologies,' said Cheong Young Zu. 'After the Pandora and Panama leaks we upgraded all our systems to make sure this could never happen to us. But it has. We do not understand how. We are conducting an immediate internal examination of our security systems. I will obviously keep you up to date with any further developments.'

When the call ended, Myroslav said, 'I will kill him, the little shitter.'

The hack was Nazim's doing. He was making that obvious.

They returned to their rooms, supposedly to sleep.

Jacob stayed awake, watching as the lights went out in the big beautiful house, one by one. He spent a little time at his desk, writing. Then, when it had been dark for a while, he crept out of his apartment.

135

Murphy's plan had been a simple one. 'Paper planes,' he had said.

Jacob had imagined that the CIA would have something more sophisticated up their sleeve, but it made sense in a way. Paper planes were simple. There was no special equipment that might give Jacob away. If Jacob wanted to send Murphy a message, he was to write it on a sheet of paper and send it over the walls. 'There are cameras everywhere but they'll be set to human detection,' Murphy had told him, 'else the birds would trigger them all the time. Make a paper plane and send it to me, over the wall. Drop it anywhere on the east side, preferably near that clump of trees by the wall. I'll check that lane every morning at dawn.'

'And what if you need to contact me?'

'I'll find a way,' Murphy had said. 'Don't you worry.'

Jacob noted the name of the company and the name of the company's nominal director, Cheong Young Zu. He was not sure of the spelling, but it should be enough for Murphy to be able to track him down. Jacob figured that the more information he could get to Murphy, the sooner the authorities could make their move on Myroslav's operation, and the sooner he could go home to England and to Carla. He gave the maid's first name, Vladyslava. Though it was a common name, it might mean something to someone.

Jacob had folded the note carefully into the shape of a plane, the kind a child would make. He had stepped out of the door with it in his hand, so as not to crumple it. After a couple of steps he stopped and carefully placed it inside the leg pocket of his trousers. It was fortunate he had done, because when he was

136

halfway across the lawn, moving as quietly as he could on the soft grass, the lights glared on.

Murphy had been right. There were motion sensors everywhere, presumably attached to cameras. Jacob remained stationary for a while, standing on the grass, wondering what would happen next. After a few minutes, the lights snapped off again, leaving the place darker than it had been before.

Another foot forward and the same lights came back on again. There was no way he could cross the lawn at night without making his presence known.

Defeated, he walked back to the apartment and waited for the lights to turn off again.

The next time, instead of heading straight across the lawn towards the main house, he turned left and walked slowly alongside the apartment block, towards the copse of pines. After twenty metres in the darkness he became more confident.

He was almost at the trees when the lights came on again. This time they illuminated something strange. Standing right in front of him, a young fox, orange in the light, was gazing back at him, utterly unperturbed.

He waited again for the timer to switch off the lights, but this time they stayed on, blinding him.

Hearing footsteps coming towards him, he raised his forearm to try and shield his eyes. Out of the glare emerged a man. Jacob was already pretty sure who he was.

Iosef was holding a gun. 'Going for a walk again?'

'Yes.'

'At this time of night?'

'I like to walk.'

The fox had had enough. It had vanished as Iosef arrived.

'Did you see the fox?'

'Little bastards trigger the lights all the time.' Iosef held the gun on him for a while. 'I've been watching you. I think you are up to something.'

So there were security cameras that were now recording what they were doing too.

Jacob shrugged. 'I don't care if you do or if you don't.'

Iosef considered him for a second. 'Empty your pockets,' he said.

'What?' Jacob blinked at him through the light.

'I said empty your pockets now. Turn them inside out.'

'What do you think I'm carrying?' But dutifully Jacob turned the top pockets of his trousers inside out. There was nothing in them.

'And the others.'

Jacob giggled. 'They don't turn out. You'll have to check them yourself.' It was a bluff. There were two more pockets on the back of his trousers, another further down each leg.

He stepped forward, towards Iosef, as if inviting him to check for himself, knowing that the letter was in one of them.

Iosef stood there for a second, gun in his hand. 'Myroslav thinks you're OK,' said Iosef. 'I don't. And pretty soon I'm going to catch you out.'

Jacob turned and headed for the dark copse.

TWENTY-ONE

Jacob calculated that it would be too risky to try and fly his message over the wall while Iosef had his eyes on him. Murphy was out there somewhere. He had said that rescue might come within hours – or days.

The more information Murphy had, the sooner he would be able to make his move. He wondered if it would be less dangerous in the morning. Iosef was suspicious and determined to catch him out. Instead he just paced around the garden, pretending he was just walking.

He crossed to the dark woods. At night, the smell of pinewood seemed twice as strong. There was a bird somewhere in the woods – an owl probably. It made a low, hooting noise, like it was laughing at him.

Crossing back towards the house, he approached the gardener's shed. The door at the side had been left open. Moonlight shone inside. No artificial lights came on this time, though. He continued, wondering if Iosef had switched them off, but ten paces later the lights came on again.

Which meant that there were places that the sensors didn't reach.

He walked for another hour, up and down the garden, arms behind his back, sometimes ambushed by the lights, other times not. He started to treat it as a game. Each time the lights came on, he saw new, bright, visions of Myroslav's garden. Each time they didn't, he had discovered a place where it seemed like he could walk unobserved. In his head, he was starting to build a map of the grounds, and the routes through it.

He stopped, shortly before dawn, exhausted. But he had the satisfaction of knowing that if he wasn't sleeping, Iosef was unlikely to be too.

He was woken early by a knock on the door.

'Who is it?' he demanded groggily.

'Breakfast,' came a voice.

He got up, went to open the door. Vladyslava stood with a tray with coffee on. 'Would you like breakfast in the garden again this morning?'

The morning's sunlight seemed twice as bright.

'Jesus Vladyslava,' he said. 'What time is it?'

'Eight o'clock.'

He sighed, tired from last night's escapades. 'I'll take it inside.' He backed away to let her into his room.

'Wouldn't you prefer the garden, sir?' she asked.

'No. I need to get some more sleep.'

She didn't move.

'It's a very beautiful day. The garden is very lovely today.'

He was still inside this prison to save this woman's

life – supposedly – and here she was, demanding he follow her out into the garden. He was about to lose his temper with her when he clocked the determination in her eyes. She was not asking him, she was telling him.

'OK. I'll be a minute.'

By the time he had splashed water on his face and put on his white dressing gown, she had set up the table again on the lawn. She was nowhere to be seen, but the coffee was down there, waiting for him.

He poured himself a freshly squeezed orange juice and then a coffee. The coffee was excellent as always. She returned with a tray.

'You mustn't trust Myroslav,' she said as she lifted the plate of salmon and eggs onto his table.

'I don't,' he muttered. 'I'm not an idiot, Vladyslava.'

She was keeping her face perfectly still as she talked, as if she feared being watched. 'I need to get out of this place. You need to, too. You can take me.'

He looked around. They seemed to be alone together in this big garden. It was an absurd scene. Him in a dressing gown, her standing beside this table. 'You brought me out here because you think my room is bugged?'

'Maybe. I don't know. I heard him talking with Iosef this morning. Iosef said he thinks you are some kind of spy. Fedor told Myroslav you were asking Eloise things yesterday, on the boat.' Without being asked, she reached over and poured the rest of his coffee into his cup. 'Myroslav told him he needed you still, so you were to come to no harm yet.'

'Yet?'

'Vlada.'

He looked up at her. 'What?'

'My friends call me Vlada.'

He grinned. 'Oh. I'm your friend now?'

She nodded. A bee hovered around his orange juice, landed on the rim of the glass.

'Thank you,' he said.

'You are welcome.' She hesitated. 'Are you a spy?'

There was no one you could trust in this house. 'I'm a translator,' he said.

'Fuck you then, if you're still working for Myroslav.'

Upstairs in the big house, the blinds rose in one of the bedrooms. Myroslav, in white silk pyjamas, was standing at the big glass window, looking down on them, dark against the whiteness of the room. Jacob and Vladyslava would be clearly visible, him in white, her in black against the green lawn. Without another word, Vladyslava inclined her head and set off across the lawn back to the kitchen.

Jacob looked down. The bee had fallen into the orange juice and was swimming around in circles.

Back in his apartment, he glanced around. If there was a chance there were microphones hidden here, were there also cameras? Nothing was safe.

He was just an ordinary man from a small city in England. He was not supposed to be here. Paranoid now, he looked up at the light fittings and the smoke alarms as he dressed, then returned to the living room and pushed the desk forward so that it was closer to the window.

He had flushed his first letter down the toilet when he had returned to his apartment last night as a precaution in case Iosef searched his room.

Hunched over the table, his back to the rest of the room, he re-wrote it, signing it off: *Please hurry. It is becoming very dangerous here.* He folded it carefully, then emerged back into the sunshine.

'Where you going, honey?'

He turned. Eloise was approaching him across the lawn.

'Nowhere – of course,' he said.

She slipped her arm into his. 'Bored?'

Every time he tried to approach the wall it seemed as if someone was watching him, or getting in his way.

'We're just waiting,' he said. 'It's exhausting.'

'Until we sort out our supply chain issues, all we can do is wait. It's Myroslav's fault, basically. He was never convinced that Lutinol would be as profitable as it is, but then he doesn't really understand women and their needs at all.' She laughed throatily. 'I told him we should order more, but he didn't believe me. And then, of course, Rakesh Garg, our supplier, just disappeared. We were supposed to meet at the The Shard – my choice because I love that place – only he never showed up. I waited. I messaged. I waited some more. And then I got a text telling me that someone had taken over Rakesh's organisation.'

'Nazim? That was the day you hired me.'

She tugged him a little closer. 'Does that make you uncomfortable?'

Jacob shook his head. 'No.'

'You're safe. I'm a married woman.' She laughed hollowly. 'Didn't I tell you that?'

'The con man from Canberra?'

'Oh yeah. Him. I'm still married to him, believe it or not. Asshole. Nazim is going to call later today. He will want to do a deal. Myroslav will refuse.'

'How do you know that?'

'Because he's stubborn. But just be nice. Do your best not to make Myroslav sound so angry. We need this deal, OK?'

She leaned in, kissed him on the cheek and left him standing alone in the middle of the lawn. Interpreters were supposed to be neutral, but that was not what she had employed him to be, he realised.

After lunch by the pool, he wandered the garden with apparent aimlessness, trying to pick his moment. He circled the helicopter that sat on a flat landing pad behind the pool, found a new path that led to an area he had never discovered before, where rattan furniture sat neglected underneath a pergola, then headed back up the slope towards the copse again. He was about to enter it when Fedor emerged from the trees, a bow saw in one hand.

'Looking for something?' Fedor asked.

Frustrated, Jacob turned away and headed back to the apartment. Eloise was waiting on the steps. The smiles were gone. 'Where the hell have you been?' she demanded. 'Conference room. Now.'

TWENTY-TWO

'I hope you have had time to reconsider the deal I suggested,' said Nazim from the screen of Eloise's big new iPhone. Nazim was holding a phone himself, apparently sitting in the back seat of a car, listening on earbuds. 'Fifty-fifty.'

'We have no shitting deal,' answered Myroslav.

The interior of the car Nazim was sitting in was entirely black. To Nazim's right, a woman's bare arm showed on the screen.

'Let me explain again,' said Myroslav. He spoke carefully. 'There. Will. Be No. Deal. You sell us the stuff. That's it.'

'Unfortunate,' said Nazim.

Eloise leaned forward. 'The hack in Singapore. That was you, I presume.'

Nazim smiled. 'I was able to access the database to assure myself of your project's income—'

'You are bluffing,' Myroslav interrupted.

Nazim continued: 'It would obviously be difficult for you if I was to share that database with anyone else. I should imagine the American law enforcement would be very interested in any details I can pass to them.'

'You're trying to blackmail us?'

Nazim's face remained bland. 'It's simple. If we reach an agreement, we will keep that data private. If we fail to reach an agreement, we can share that data with the financial authorities and there will be consequences for you.'

Translating the words was easy, but the casual tone behind them contained menace. Whether it was because of his own loathing of Myroslav, or because he was taking on the interpreter's role more successfully than he had anticipated, Jacob found himself becoming Nazim as he spoke, with all the complicity that implied.

'I don't like to be threatened.'

'All the more reason why we need to come to a deal,' said Nazim.

'Impossible.' Myroslav raised his voice. 'We have invested in offices, in staff, in computer systems, in a distribution network. Giving you half the money makes no sense.'

The car Nazim was in stopped. Someone opened Nazim's door and he got out. It was night. Jacob could see the lights of the Indian shops and nightclubs. It reminded him of being there himself – the hustle and charm of the place.

'You invested. But you still thought it was OK to pay an Indian company a pittance for a product and then make millions from them?' said Nazim.

Myroslav yawned ostentatiously. 'My heart is bleeding. It's the market.'

'That's what you think? We're just a country that makes cheap shirts for you?'

'I wouldn't know,' said Myroslav. 'I never buy cheap shirts.'

'This time around, we want you to pay a fair amount. That is all.'

Nazim entered a building of some kind, crossed a lobby. 'We have the product. You have the system. We have strengths. You have weaknesses. You are old, Myroslav, we are young.' People stepped forward to greet him as he walked.

'Fuck you,' said Myroslav.

Eloise attempted to be more diplomatic. 'It simply isn't profitable for us to pay you fifty per cent.'

Nazim paused, smiled back at her. 'She is the one with brains, Mr Bondarenko. She is negotiating now. If it is not profitable, then we will have to make it profitable for you. To do that, we need to increase the volume of sales.'

'No, no, no. That's not the plan!' said Eloise, horrified. 'I worked it all out at the start of this. There's a point where, if we sell too much, we'll attract attention. People will notice. There's a limit to the volume we can do.'

Nazim said, 'Obviously they will notice. It's a question of how much money we can make before they do.'

'Notice what?' Jacob interrupted.

'Just translate,' hissed Eloise.

'Notice what?' he repeated.

Nazim was in a lift now, looking down at his watch as if time was limited. 'Instead of five hundred units a time, sell five thousand.'

Eloise gasped. 'You are crazy. That kind of volume and people are going to ask questions.'

As he pressed a button in the lift, Nazim let the phone camera wander. The woman with him was beautiful – in an Instagrammy way. She had long black hair and studs that glittered expensively in her ears. 'I've looked at your figures. You will have no trouble selling it.'

'It's already risky enough. Too much attention and they will start looking at the Singapore connection.'

'Cash out too early and you miss your chance to make a lot more money,' said Nazim. 'I say we take it to the brink.'

'Ridiculous,' snapped Myroslav.

Jacob was struggling to keep up. As soon as he'd translated Nazim's sentences as well as he could, Eloise was asking the question: 'What do you mean, take it to the brink?'

'I like this scheme of yours,' Nazim was saying. 'Do you want to run it for a few more days and then take the money and leave, or find out how much money it can really make?'

The lift reached its floor. Nazim got out and walked across the lobby, making them wait while he opened the door. It looked like a penthouse apartment. Nazim was in a living room now. He walked through it and out to a balcony. 'Besides, it is not an offer you are in any position to refuse.'

Jacob was struggling to think. Interpreting used so much brain power it was sometimes hard to stop for a second and process the words. But something wasn't making sense.

'Well, I do refuse,' Myroslav was saying. 'We'll find another manufacturer.'

Nazim shook his head. 'Inadvisable.'

There was a heavy silence in the room. It gave Jacob a second to gather his thoughts. Things that he had been translating didn't add up. Pharmaceuticals were not just something you arranged another manufacturer for. Eloise had also said that it was only a matter of time before people started to notice.

'Fuck you,' said Myroslav. 'Share the data if you want,' he said, with a shrug.

'You're calling his bluff?' said Eloise, speaking Russian.

'Of course I am. If he exposes us, he gets nothing. He looks all smart in his limousine, but I know men like him. Five years ago he was running around in rags in the slums. He called me old. How dare he? He is a child. He will take what we give him.'

'What are they saying?' Nazim demanded in Hindi.

'End the call,' said Myroslav. 'I have had enough of this shit.'

Nazim's balcony was high above some city. They could see the lights below him until he held up the phone close to his face and said, 'I'm very disappointed to hear that. Mr Translator. Do you think he means what he said?'

Jacob realised he was being addressed himself. 'Yes,' he said. 'He is not interested in making a deal. The woman, however, is more interested.'

'Interesting,' said Nazim. 'Thank you for sharing that.'

'What is the little shitter saying?' Myroslav blurted.

'Talk to the woman now,' ordered Nazim. 'Ask her if she remembers the photograph I sent her.'

Warily, Jacob translated.

'I didn't see it properly,' answered Eloise.

'You didn't recognise the face in the photograph, Eloise? That was the last man who said no to me.'

'What is the little shitter talking about?' Myroslav demanded.

'Tell me, Mr Translator, do they look worried? Just nod or shake your head.'

Jacob held his head steady.

Being an interpreter meant deciding how you took people's thoughts and put them into other people's minds. He had crossed one line by speaking on behalf of Eloise. He had no reason to cross another by becoming Nazim's mouthpiece.

Nazim laughed. 'Think about what side you're on. I can pay more than they can. Much, much more. Listen to this. Next time we talk I will ask you again, do they look worried? And I want to know what you think.'

And then the screen went blue. Nazim had ended the call.

TWENTY-THREE

'What was that?' demanded Myroslav, staring hard at Jacob. 'You were talking directly to him. You stopped interpreting.'

The Italians have a saying, '*Traduttore, traditore*'. Translator, traitor. People don't trust people who speak foreign languages. They live in too many different worlds. An interpreter was a kind of conspirator. He was suspect; neither one side, nor the other. By speaking directly to him, Nazim had very deliberately lit that suspicion.

They were still sitting around the table in the conference room. Jacob looked Myroslav in the face. 'He offered to pay me more money than you do.'

Myroslav's face was cold. He was staring right at him. 'Is that all you talked about?'

He could feel Eloise's eyes on him too. It was not all he had talked about. He had told Nazim that Eloise was ready to negotiate, even if Myroslav wasn't. And Nazim had warned that something would happen in the next two days that would make Myroslav even more worried than he might be now.

'Yes,' Jacob lied. 'That was all he talked about.'

Traduttore, traditore. Jacob's job, he realised, was to get as much information as he could so that when Murphy finally arrived, all this would be over. That meant trying to be all things to everyone.

Myroslav stood, as if trying to make up his mind whether he believed Jacob or not. 'Mind games,' he said. 'It's just his stupid mind games. He wants us not to trust each other.'

He looked around the table. The truth was, none of them trusted each other. Myroslav had secretly given permission to Iosef to kill him when all this was over. Eloise appeared to be trying to cut a side deal with Nazim. Jacob himself was pretending to be in on the conspiracy so he could feed information to Murphy. Myroslav had guns and security devices, but Jacob had language. He alone knew what everyone in the room had been saying.

'But we all trust each other, right?' said Myroslav, with a smile. 'We are a team. Aren't we?'

'Of course, Slava,' said Eloise. Everything was a lie.

Myroslav stood, clapped his hands. 'So we wait. A day or maybe two. When the Indian sees we are not moving, he will come back with a better deal. OK?' He looked around at the other two. 'Don't look so unhappy. Everything will be great. I am going to go to the gym. I need to punch something. This time it is not you!' He laughed loudly and slapped Jacob so hard on the back that it stung.

Alone with Eloise, Jacob looked down at the table. 'It's counterfeit, isn't it? The Lutinol. It's not real.'

Eloise said nothing.

'You strung me along. It's the only thing that makes sense. You couldn't just get another company to manufacture it if it was the real thing. If it's counterfeit, the profits must be huge.'

'I didn't know how far I could trust you,' she said.

'Rakesh Garg wasn't a legitimate businessman. He was a counterfeiter. So it's hardly surprising that another organised crime gang wanted to muscle in on his business.'

She put her hand on top of his. 'I really mean it. I'm sorry.'

'What did he mean, Eloise,' asked Jacob, 'when he said you should have recognised the man in the photograph?'

'I have no idea,' she said. She took her hand away, lifted it to her mouth and chewed on the skin on the edge of the thumb. 'I don't know what he was talking about.'

She was lying, though. Jacob knew that. He understood. The dead man she had seen was Rakesh Garg.

There was not much of the afternoon light left. Nights here came suddenly at this time of year. Soon the security lights would be active again.

To throw off anyone who might be watching, he didn't head straight for the pine copse; instead he headed downhill first, passing the apartments, then making his way back up the hill.

Once he was finally in the small stand of trees he felt safer. He looked around, peering up into the trees for any signs of hidden cameras.

Everything felt like an enormous risk now.

Seeing nothing suspicious, he pulled the letter from his pocket. Since he had written it he had discovered even more about how Myroslav's operation worked – the fact that the whole thing was a fraud – but that would have to wait for his next chance. He didn't have time to write a new letter right now. Every piece of information he could get out of here would speed up the end.

The letter was crumpled. He squatted down, flattening it on his thigh, then folded it into a dart before looking up.

The wall was a little over three metres high, he judged. The first time he threw the paper plane it shot into the air, decelerated and fell straight back towards his feet.

Jacob realised it was harder than it looked to make a paper plane rise that far into the air. He tried a second time, and the results were just as bad. It flew high but changed direction and turned away, leaving him to scrabble for it among fallen branches. The third time, the paper flew higher, but became caught in the needles of the pine tree above his head. He jumped, hoping to catch one of the lower branches, but they too were out of reach.

Looking around, he found a long branch. Carefully raising it, he knocked the plane out of the tree.

This was never going to work. Instead he looked around, found a small stone and wrapped the message around it instead.

He was just drawing back to throw it when he heard what sounded like the soft crack of a stick. Heart thumping, he looked around, but in the dimming light could see no one. He stood absolutely still, barely breathing.

He must have imagined it, he decided finally.

Taking a breath, he lobbed the message over the wall and heard it land with a soft and satisfying thump on the other side.

It was a start. He had communicated with the outside world. Things felt better already.

Murphy was looking for a dart that would show up easily on the verge on the other side of the wall. If the ball of paper had rolled beneath old vegetation, he might never find it. Jacob wouldn't know until the authorities came and broke down the doors. Hopefully that would not be long now.

The evening light was deep lilac through the tree trunks. When he turned and took a step forwards he thought he saw something move ahead of him.

He froze, hoping that he would be less visible against the wall.

The shape moved again. A figure was silhouetted against the white of the house behind them. There was someone watching him.

TWENTY-FOUR

If it was Iosef or Webb who had been watching him, the best he could do was pretend he had just been walking, so he set off deliberately heading in the direction of the figure he'd seen, not trying to avoid his watcher. Only when he got close did he realise who it was.

'So,' said Vladyslava. 'You are a spy, like I said.'

'I don't know what you mean.'

'I saw you. Who are you sending your message to?' She must have seen him trying to propel the paper over the wall.

You could trust no one here, he thought. 'I was just messing around.'

'You didn't look like you were messing around.'

He breathed.

'So you are a spy? Who for?'

'I'm trying to help you. I promise. Please. It's very important that you tell no one what you saw me do.'

She looked at him with hostile eyes. 'You think I would tell Mr Bondarenko?'

It was possible. Everyone inside these walls was out for themselves.

'If you are a spy, then I want you to send a message for me.'

'Sorry?'

'Is there someone there receiving your messages?'

He didn't answer.

She glared at him angrily. 'Why else would you be sending it over the wall? You have someone on the outside.'

'Who do you want to send a message to?'

'To my mother. And my son.'

Something flitted above his head. A moth, he supposed. 'Myroslav won't let you do that?'

Abruptly she laughed. 'You think I'm here because I want to be here?'

'OK. Do you have an address for them?'

She shook her head. 'No.'

'A number?'

'I think she is in Hungary. Or Poland.'

'So how do I get a message to them if you don't know where they live?'

She looked around, to see if anyone was coming from the house, he supposed. Then she lowered herself onto the bare earth. 'Sit with me,' she said. 'I need to tell you a story.'

He lowered himself onto the ground beside her.

She leaned back against one of the fir trunks. 'You know I'm Ukrainian, yes?'

He nodded.

She traced a circle in the dry earth next to where she was sitting. 'When the Russians invaded Ukraine in 2022, my mother left the country and took my boy with her to Poland to keep him safe. Millions of people left in those first terrible weeks. I was working still. I had to stay to earn money. I didn't hear from her for a few days after she crossed the border, and I was sick with worry, but I knew there was a lot of confusion in those days.'

The evening was still. Jacob heard the *thuck* of a tennis ball from somewhere on the other side of the gardens. Myroslav had probably finished his boxing practice and had found someone to play against.

'And then, when I was going crazy with worry, my mother finally called me and told me everything was going to be OK. She had met a man at the border who said he was helping refugees, she said. They were travelling with him to Hungary. I told her to be careful. That was the last I heard of her for a week. I didn't worry too much, because in those early days of the war, everything was chaos. People couldn't get phones, or SIM cards. But then I had a message on my phone from a number I did not recognise. There was a picture of my mother and Tymko. My mother looked frightened. A few minutes later, I had a message from the same number. It said that they were both somewhere safe, but I must pay ten thousand dollars to the people who were looking after them, to cover documents, rent, food, bills and so on.'

Inside the copse it was dark now. He could barely make out her face. 'They are holding your mother and son as hostages?'

'I called the number but the phone was already dead. They had deactivated it. I tried to find people to help me, but everything was madness in those days. Russian invaders were close to Kyiv.

There were battles going on every day. Everyone was busy. The police said they would try to help me but they could not.'

In the evening, the thick scent of the pine trees seemed to become overpowering.

'The message contained the details of a bank account. So I paid them what I had. I worked in a good restaurant, but business had collapsed when the Russians arrived. All the same, I gave them all the money I could find. It came to less than three thousand dollars. Next day, another message from a different phone. The amount I owed now was fifteen thousand dollars, even after the money I had paid them. Costs had risen, they said. I had not given them the money on time. I messaged back straight away to tell them I didn't have any more money. I was desperate.'

They had sat side by side completely still in the woods for minutes now, it seemed.

'The next message said that in that case they would not be able to care for my mother and son any longer.' She lowered her head.

Jacob wanted to reach out and take her hand, but he didn't dare. 'What did that mean?'

Looking up again, she said, 'What do you think it meant?' In the evening gloom he couldn't see the expression on her face. 'They sent what they said was a helpful suggestion.' She gave a small snort. 'They told me if I couldn't pay, I would have to work for them to pay off the debt instead. They gave me a phone number and told me to meet them at an address in Kyiv.'

'And you did?'

She nodded.

'And they brought you here?'

'Eventually. I got into a minivan with three other women in Kyiv. We were blindfolded. I don't know what happened to the others. Maybe they were luckier. Maybe they weren't. Probably not. They were younger than me.'

'How long have you been here?'

'Too long. I have been here eight months.'

'That's awful.'

'Sometimes they send me letters written by my mother. She always begs me to work to earn money to free her and Tymko. It is her handwriting, but the letters are dictated. She would not write to me like that. My mother would never beg. She is a proud woman.'

'I'm sorry.'

Before he could offer her any support or comfort, she said simply, 'I must go now,' and pushed herself up off the ground. 'I must prepare dinner.'

'I need your mother's name,' he said. 'Her home address in Ukraine. Anything like that.'

'Why?'

'Because I want to help you.'

She looked at him for a second more, then headed off without another word.

When Jacob finally reached the edge of the woods, Tamara was standing on the grass, as if she had been waiting for him. Jacob stepped forward, to try and walk to the right of her, but the dog moved the same way, lowered her head and growled. When he tried the other side she blocked him there too.

On the third attempt, the dog began barking.

'She thinks you are an intruder.'

Jacob looked up. Iosef was sitting on the steps that led up to Jacob's apartment.

'I think she's right. I think you are an intruder too,' said Iosef. As he spoke, his hands were in motion, working on something that Jacob could not make out.

Tamara took a pace closer to Jacob and barked again, teeth bare.

'Call her off.'

'She's Myroslav's dog. She wouldn't pay any attention to me.'

The giant dog drooled, eyes on Jacob. 'I can't get past her,' said Jacob.

'Yes. She doesn't like it when guests act suspiciously.'

Jacob raised his arms, tried to look bigger than he was. 'Shoo.' The dog barked again, and then again and again.

'What's wrong?' Jacob looked round to see Myroslav and Webb walking up the slope towards them, both in shorts, tennis rackets in their hands.

'For some reason, your dog doesn't like the Englishman,' explained Iosef, still sitting on the steps, working with his hands.

'What was he doing this time?' asked Myroslav.

'He was coming out of the woods, there.' Iosef stopped what he was doing and pointed. Jacob saw he was holding a knife.

Myroslav gave a soft whistle. The dog abandoned her post at the edge of the woods and ran towards her master.

Myroslav strolled on, dog at his side. Only when Jacob got closer to Iosef did he see what he had been doing with his hands all that time. He had been whittling a stick with the large, sharp knife. 'Goodnight, Jacob,' Iosef said, as he curled another shaving off and dropped it onto the stairs.

TWENTY-FIVE

Draper's door was half open. He knocked.

'Hey, Language Man. I've given up on the Bacardi. Today I have bourbon. Want some?' The room was dark. 'I asked the maid to get me Knob Creek Kentucky Bourbon 'cause I like the name. She gets everything you ask for.'

'I know.'

'Want to get fucked up?'

Jacob walked into the darkness of his room. 'I fucked up quite enough already, thank you.'

'Preach.'

Draper picked up his TV remote and switched it on. From the dim light, Jacob could see that Draper's room looked even more like a student's than it had last time he had visited. There were discarded underpants on the floor, half-finished bowls of cereal on the table. He flicked off the news and found a porn channel and turned up the volume. The room was full of the noise of sighing and groaning.

'Don't blame yourself,' said Draper. 'I just wanted money, like you.'

Draper pulled two glasses from a shelf in his kitchen, picked a half-drunk bottle out of a cupboard and walked towards the settee with them, making space on the table by pushing a half-eaten bag of cheese popcorn onto the floor.

'Can we turn down the TV?'

He poured two enormous glasses of the dark bourbon. 'If Iosef didn't hear the sound of delicious sexy porn coming from my room, he might think I was having a conversation with you.' He handed one of the glasses to Jacob. 'Ask me, this is a grade one fuck-up. Myroslav is in way too deep.'

Jacob looked down at the glass. 'You always knew they were counterfeiters?'

'It took me a while to figure it out. I built the website for Adolf and Eva out there and it can sell hundreds of different drugs. Everything from Thalidomide to Tamoxifen. It's kind of cool. On the first day I put in a few test orders and they all came back saying the items weren't in stock. I told Eloise and she said, *Oh baby, don't worry. We are just having a few problems with our supply chain.*'

On the screen behind him someone was fake squealing.

'So I kept doing it but kept coming up with an empty shopping basket. I thought the whole thing was a joke. Except, after the first week I checked the database and I noticed we had made over half a million dollars. In one week. But we hadn't sold a single vial of Thalodomide or Tamoxifen.'

Jacob took a sip from his glass and listened.

'So I checked all the other drugs, and you know what? We had no stock of any drugs at all. All except for one.'

'Lutinol.'

'Right. This whole operation is designed to look like a respectable online pharmacy, but in reality it only sells one drug, Lutinol. It's a big illusion. You know, like those plants that look like flowers and then eat bugs.'

Jacob's eyes were trying to avoid the huge TV screen, which was filled by flesh, pumping mechanically, sweatily.

'And every rich career woman with a ticking clock wants a baby and leaves it too late. You have any idea how rich these people are?'

'What if they're not rich people? What if they're just people who want babies?'

'Whatever. Go anywhere you like on the internet and someone's talking about how great Lutinol is and wouldn't it be great if you could actually buy it? Eloise does the digital marketing. She's pretty shitting good at it, as it turns out.'

'Except it's not Lutinol at all.'

'There you go.' He turned to the screen. 'I've seen this one a million times before. The guy has a dick like a firehose.'

Jacob looked at his glass. He felt sick. 'So that's why this is so absurdly profitable. I couldn't figure it out. They are selling a drug that retails at thousands of dollars per dose and it costs us . . .'

'Pretty much nothing. Maybe a hundred bucks.'

'So five hundred vials at five thousand dollars a throw . . .'

'Two-point-five million.'

'And five thousand would be twenty-five million.'

'Easy money,' said Draper.

'We're cheating people out of millions.'

'Rich people, mostly, to be fair.'

On the screen a young-looking woman in a school uniform had taken her shirt off and was sitting in a chair in front of a bearded man.

'From what I can figure out, this was Eloise's plan to make millions, and Myroslav's plan to get back into the game.'

With such a lucrative operation, it was not surprising that other organised crime syndicates wanted to muscle in on it. Eloise was a con artist, just like her husband. She'd taken Jacob for a ride. She had seen how naive he was, wrapped up in his world of poetry, telling them all facts about language and how many tongues he could speak in to show them how clever he was. 'When you first met Eloise, she told you how awesome your code skills are?'

'Oh yeah. She was right, obviously, though I'm not immune to a hot woman telling me that. I like her. She's just greedy, and I can get along with that. Myroslav is just an old-fashioned psycho.'

Jacob tasted the sweet whisky. 'Doesn't it trouble you?'

'Of course it does. But not enough. This scene coming up. In a minute this other girl comes in and she's even younger-looking than that one there. Like, really young-looking. Not just done up in pigtails and shit. That troubles me. But, if I'm honest, not enough.' He sighed. 'The world is a bad place. Want another drink?'

Jacob took a mouthful, held up his glass. 'Still got some.'

'You get used to it,' said Draper. At first, Jacob thought he was talking about the whisky.

★

Back in his room, lying on his bed and staring up at the white ceiling, he could still hear the groaning and squealing of the women on the screen in Draper's room, pretending they were having a great time. It seemed to go on for ever.

He got up and stared out of the window. Lit by the glare from Draper's room, the fox, beautiful and slender, emerged from the back of the gardener's utility shed. Halfway across the lawn it stopped. As if it knew it was being watched, it glanced up at Jacob's window. The white fur under its muzzle seemed to glow in the dark. Jacob could have sworn it was looking straight at him.

My sweet Tymko

Oh God. I miss you. I am not sure how much more of this I can take.

Keep your knives sharp. It's the best way to protect yourself. It's the truth. In the kitchen, it's the blunt knives that cause the most injuries.

The trick to keeping a knife sharp is to hone it, regularly. You have to understand what the blade of a knife is. The blade of a good knife makes a fine point, so sharp you cannot even see it with the naked eye. The finer the point, the more vulnerable the blade is to becoming dull. Every time you use it, that point gets blunted a little, bent to one side. So after every two or three times you have used a knife, you should hone it. For this you need a good steel. All you are doing is rubbing steel along the side of the knife and pushing that sharp point back into shape so it can slice through anything.

TWENTY-SIX

That night Jacob dreamed he was in a castle full of corridors, some broad and lined with dark paintings, others so narrow he wasn't sure he would fit down them. Each corridor led to different rooms. In one room, people dressed formally were eating dinner. When he opened the door, they looked round at him. 'Sorry,' he said, 'I was looking for the way out.'

When they answered him, they spoke in a language he didn't understand. He backed out of the room and tried another door. Behind this one, a man was strapped in a chair; another man was methodically beating him. Again, they looked round at Jacob. The man who was being beaten shouted angrily at him, but again, Jacob didn't comprehend a word.

In a third room a couple were making love.

In the next an old woman lay dying. All looked at him angrily, spoke to him in languages he didn't know.

When finally he reached a guard, standing at a gate, he begged him to let him out. When the guard answered, Jacob understood him perfectly, though he didn't recognise the language, but when he tried to answer, his own words remained trapped inside his mouth.

He woke to a knocking at the door, disturbed at the half-memory of the dream.

'Vlada?'

He put on a dressing gown and answered the door. Instead of Vlada, Eloise was standing there in a towelling robe, dark glasses perched on the end of her nose.

'Oh,' he said.

'You sound disappointed.'

He tried not to look it.

'Breakfast by the pool. What do you say? Ten minutes?'

Eloise had a new swimsuit on – an expensive-looking asymmetrical one in a black-and-white design.

She lay on a sun lounger, under a large parasol. 'I think we should drink champagne,' she said.

It was as if nothing was wrong.

'I mean, why not? We have nothing else to do until the boys have stopped squabbling and done their deal.'

Vladyslava threw a white tablecloth over the table and laid out pastries and juice.

'And an ice bucket,' Eloise shouted after her, as she returned to the kitchen.

'So you lied to me,' he said, 'about pretty much everything. About the drugs. About what I was doing here.'

'*Mea maxima culpa*. I knew you'd figure it out in the end. But you wouldn't have taken the job if I'd told you what it really was.

169

If it helps, Myroslav has just paid the money into your account,' she said. 'I asked him to.'

'Do you think Myroslav is right? That Nazim will negotiate?'

'Either he will crack or Myroslav will. There's too much money to be made. We just need to wait.'

That's what was happening. Everyone was waiting for something, but nobody knew what it would be. Jacob was waiting for the front gate to be burst open and a SWAT team to swing in on ropes. Vlada returned with a silver ice bucket and a bottle of Cristal, and two glasses.

'God,' Eloise said. 'Doesn't she ever smile?'

Vlada's face remained bland.

'She's such a misery.'

If Vladyslava understood English, she was pretending not to.

'I've been thinking,' Jacob said. 'What happened to the interpreter you had before?'

She laughed. 'Oh my God. You think they're somewhere buried in the garden?' She picked the bottle up and went to pour him a glass. 'We didn't need one before Rakesh Garg disappeared. Rakesh spoke perfect English.'

Her hand shook. Champagne darkened the white cloth.

'Spoke,' he said. 'You used the past tense.'

'Figure of speech,' she said, avoiding his eye as she picked up her own glass to take a large gulp. 'Let's get drunk.'

He took a sip from his own glass. 'So what will happen to me afterwards then?'

'That's up to you. I'll be pretty rich when all this is done. You could be too if it works out. I've always wanted to go to St Kitts. It's a pretty cool place.'

'If Myroslav lets me go, doesn't he worry I'll expose him?'

'Not if you're well enough paid.' Again she laughed. 'It's amazing how money works.' She lifted a Danish and took a bite, then licked the flakes from her lips. 'We're just trying to make a shitload of money. What you choose to do after you're finished, that's up to you. You could come to St Kitts too. It might be fun.'

After breakfast, he swam a few lengths and then dozed under a shade. The champagne and lack of sleep had left him exhausted.

The morning heated up. Draper emerged from the main house at around eleven. 'God, is that champagne? Gimme. I drank way too much bourbon last night.' He took the bottle out of the ice bucket and poured himself a glass.

Jacob sat up on his elbows, blinking in the light.

'I am so bored,' said Draper.

From somewhere above came a faint insect-like whirring. Jacob held his hand over his eyes, looking upwards. 'Is that a drone?' Jacob asked.

'Hate those things,' said Draper. 'They are everywhere.' He lifted a finger skywards.

Eloise lay down again and stared upwards. 'I can't see it.'

Jacob wondered if the drone was Murphy, looking in on them. He hoped so. Maybe Murphy had found the message and was checking in, preparing to storm the building. He took a breath, tried to stay calm.

'What are you going to do with all your money, Draper?' Jacob asked.

'I want to live in Japan.'

'Seriously?' Eloise lowered her glasses on her nose.

'Sure. I want to live in one of those cool neighbourhoods in

Tokyo like Akihabara where it's all neon lights and pachinko parlours and manga cafes where you get these cosplay waitresses serving you bubble tea and shit. I would love that.'

Eloise said, 'Do you even speak Japanese, Draper?'

'I don't want to speak to anyone. I just want to live there. Did you know that in Japan, there are islands where there are more cats than people? That would be so cool. Maybe I'd live on one of those, instead. Cats are way better than people.'

They were still discussing cat islands when a cry went up from the garden. '*Moya sobaka!* My dog!'

Then a roar. 'Who did this?'

Eloise sat up, startled. 'What happened?'

She stood, wrapped a towel around her and marched out to where the shouting was coming from. Jacob followed her.

Myroslav was kneeling in the middle of the green lawn, cradling Tamara.

'What's wrong?' demanded Eloise, champagne glass in her hand.

Myroslav looked up, miserable. 'She's dead.' The immense dog lay lifeless. Myroslav held her head in his arms. He glared past her at Jacob. 'Was it you?'

'Don't be stupid. Jacob was with me,' said Eloise. 'How would he kill a dog anyway?'

'What happened?' Draper had arrived too.

'Some shitter poisoned her.' There were tears in Myroslav's eyes.

Eloise was a little tipsy. 'Why would anybody do that, Slava?'

'Could it have been a heart attack?' Jacob asked.

Myroslav straightened. Draper blurted, 'What's up with your shirt?'

Eloise gave out a short squeal, dropped her champagne glass onto the grass, and pointed. Myroslav looked down. A red circle of blood darkened the white cotton.

TWENTY-SEVEN

It was a bullet wound, deep in the fur. Myroslav had parted the dog's hair to reveal a neat red hole in the dog's skull. Tamara had been shot. Myroslav stood, looked around, as if expecting to see someone in the trees beyond the walls, someone with a gun.

'How?' asked Jacob, turning slowly. The garden seemed oddly quiet. The sky above was a rich blue, crossed only by contrails.

'Fucking fuckers,' said Myroslav, switching to English for profanity.

Jacob was rattled. Guns had been on display, but no one had actually fired one around him. 'Could it have been a mistake? A hunter somewhere?'

'She was shot right between the eyes. It was no mistake,' said Myroslav.

Jacob tried to see a vantage point outside the property from which the dog could have been shot. Dark trees surrounded the perimeter.

'It had to be someone in here,' said Myroslav, glaring at Jacob.

'Jacob was with me, Myroslav.'

Jacob stared at the dead animal. 'I don't have a gun,' he said. 'Nobody has guns except Webb and Iosef and Fedor. Who would do this to a dog?'

Neither Eloise nor Myroslav answered.

Draper shrugged. 'I mean, I didn't like her much . . .'

Myroslav walked over towards him and slapped him hard.

'You hurt me,' he said, shocked. 'What did you go and do that for?'

Eloise shrugged. 'To be fair, I've wanted to do that for a while.'

'Fuck all of you,' said Draper.

Myroslav stepped forward again but Eloise took his arm. 'That's enough, Myroslav. It wasn't him. The only gun he's ever fired is in a video game. Besides, he was at the pool with us too.'

'Jacob saw a drone,' said Draper.

Myroslav stopped. 'Did you?'

'I didn't really see it. I just heard what sounded like one.'

And then they were all looking up into the hot sky.

In his apartment, Draper looked around at the mess and said, 'I should get the maid to tidy this place up.'

'You should do it yourself,' said Jacob. 'What do you know about her?'

'She's a witch. What else am I supposed to know?'

'Why do you think she works for Myroslav?'

'For the money? Like everyone else around here.'

'You ever actually asked her anything about herself?'

'Don't start on me, Jacob. You're getting to be as bad as Myroslav. She's the maid.'

There was a shadow on the floor. Jacob looked up and Eloise was standing at the door of the apartment.

'What about the maid?' she demanded. 'Why are you so interested?'

'Myroslav hit me,' Draper whined. 'He's insane.'

'What happened to Carla?' Eloise asked Jacob. 'Aren't you in love with her any more?'

Draper peered out of the window. Myroslav was hunched over Tamara's body. 'Somebody actually shot Myroslav's dog? Jesus. How did they even do that? What if it was a sniper?' he suggested. 'A sniper can shoot from a mile away. It couldn't have been any of us, could it?'

Jacob had been shocked by the violence of someone killing a dog, but Murphy was out there somewhere.

Jacob looked up. If the CIA had been flying drones over the house, perhaps they had seen Jacob's confrontation with the dog yesterday evening. Maybe they were trying to make it easier for him to move around Myroslav's estate. In that case it made sense that Murphy had shot the dog to protect him. It was disturbing, perhaps, the lengths they would go to, if he was right, but also reassuring. Murphy was looking after him.

What was happening was terrifying, but for the first time he realised it was thrilling too. If it was what he thought, he wasn't acting alone.

'Have you got any weed, Eloise?' Draper demanded. 'I'm seriously cracking up here. There's a sniper out there shooting dogs.'

'You don't know that, Draper,' scolded Eloise. 'You don't know what actually happened.'

'Nothing good, for sure.'

Jacob left them to it and went upstairs. The first thing he noticed was that somebody had been in and vacuumed the room. It must have been Vlada.

In particular, the pile of books on his desk had been tidied. The book of poetry he had left open was now closed, but he noticed there was a slip of paper tucked into it, as if it were marking the page. Perhaps Vlada had closed the book and had wanted to keep his place.

He went to the fridge and poured himself a glass of water, then returned to the pile of books.

Looking around, he wondered again if there really were cameras hidden in his room. Taking the water over to his desk, he spent a little while shuffling papers, making it look as casual as he could, then took the book and opened it.

It was a small sheet of paper. Written on it in blue ink was the name *Iryna Yershova, 17 May 1969, Vakhivka 072311*. Vlada's mother's name, her date of birth and her postcode.

If Murphy had found Jacob's first message, he would be back in the morning. Jacob needed to get a new one over the wall before it got dark. There was a lot to share. He had composed his first note before Nazim's call. Now he was more convinced than ever that Nazim was somehow implicated in the disappearance of Rakesh Garg. He had proof that Myroslav was selling counterfeit pharmaceuticals. Plus he had the details of Vladyslava's mother, Iryna. If Murphy could prove people trafficking and slavery were

177

taking place within these walls, he would have to act. Jacob's ordeal would be over – soon – and so would Vladyslava's.

When he'd finished the note he headed out again. To the right of the main lawn, Webb and the gardener were digging a hole. Beside them was a shape, covered by a blanket now. It was going to have to be a big hole.

Without the dog, it was simpler this time. Again, he found a stone and lobbed the paper over the high wall for Murphy to find in the morning.

Eloise was sitting on the terrace behind Myroslav's house when he casually ambled back. He went and sat with her, looking out over the treetops towards the huge lake and the mountains on the far side.

She stubbed out her cigarette and said, 'I never wanted anyone to get hurt. Or any dog. I just want it all to be over now. But I know Myroslav. If you threaten him, he just digs in deeper.'

'This isn't going to get any better, Eloise. We all need to get out of here before it's too late.'

'We?' She raised her eyebrows.

'Maybe.' Webb had apparently abandoned the digging, leaving it to Fedor, who was knee deep in the hole now. 'Do you think it was a sniper, then?' Jacob asked.

'I don't know. Myroslav is getting Iosef and Webb to search the perimeter, to try and figure out if the gun was fired from out there. They're going out there now.'

'Now?'

'Yes.'

Jacob realised how stupid he had been. Just a few minutes

earlier he had tossed a note, wrapped in a stone, onto the verge outside the wall, hoping that it would be easy for Murphy to spot. It would be just as easy for them to find it.

'What's wrong, honey?' said Eloise, looking at him with concern.

He stood, turned and faced the house. Through the glass of the big rear windows, he could see to the front doors, where Myroslav, Webb and Iosef were standing. Webb wore binoculars around his neck. Myroslav appeared to be checking a handgun, removing the magazine and replacing it, working the slide back and forward. Iosef had donned military fatigues.

Jacob watched, thinking that he might have just ruined everything.

TWENTY-EIGHT

'Where are you going?' demanded Eloise.

Jacob didn't answer. He strode through the house and caught up with Myroslav just as he and his men were leaving through the front door.

'Can I help?'

They stopped and turned towards him.

'Go back to the swimming pool,' said Iosef.

Jacob thought fast. 'If we're going to find who shot Tamara, there's a lot of ground to cover out there.' He turned to Myroslav. 'What are we looking for? Shell casings? Footprints? Signs of someone getting a vantage point in the woods? Tyre tracks?'

Iosef stood with a walkie-talkie in one hand. He laughed. 'What are you now? A Boy Scout?'

Jacob said, 'You are going to need as many eyes as you can get. There are a few hours of daylight and there's a lot of woodland out there. Just a suggestion.'

'We can handle it, little boy.' Iosef adjusted the walkie-talkie on his belt.

Jacob ignored him and addressed Myroslav instead. 'You're the one who's paying me to sit around and do nothing. I'm just offering to help find out who killed your dog.'

Myroslav looked him up and down, then grunted. 'You go with Webb.'

Iosef pulled Myroslav to one side. 'What if he's working with the people outside?'

'He goes with Webb,' said Myroslav. 'Webb will keep a close eye on him. Won't you, Mr Webb?'

Standing in military boots, cargo trousers, a white T-shirt and a small backpack, Webb nodded. 'This way,' he said. He approached the keypad at the double gate. Jacob stayed as close as he could, hoping to see the numbers he was punching in, but Webb shielded his hand with his body. There was a click and the first gate opened.

Outside, Jacob stepped forward and turned immediately left and started marching west.

'Where do you think you're going?' demanded Webb.

Jacob was thinking fast. 'If there was a gunman in the trees, he must have been able to get clear sight of the lawn, right?'

'Obviously.' Webb caught up with him and laid a hand on his shoulder to stop him.

'So the likelihood is that the gunman would have been on the east or the west side of the estate, because those are the closest trees. The trees to the north are obscured by the rise of the hill and by the house. From the south it's a longer shot.' He had to persuade Webb to let him search to the west. 'The apartments obscure part of the sight line, plus there are a lot of trees on the grounds that would get in the way. So best chance is either east – or this way.' He shook off Webb's hand and set off again determinedly until he reached the corner.

The track to the boathouse ran alongside the wall. From the corner, he could see down to the treetops of the copse where he had hidden when he had thrown the two messages over. The paper missile would be lying somewhere in the grass between the wall and the track, about forty metres down the hill.

'So we start from here,' he said, hoping that Webb would disappear into the woods to commence the search, leaving him to retrieve the message.

Webb didn't move.

'Maybe you take the woods and I'll do the track?'

Webb looked at him, suspicious. 'We stay together,' said Webb.

'Right. Good plan.'

The green helicopter rose from behind the walls, close enough for Jacob to see that it was Myroslav hunched at the controls.

Webb led the way about ten metres down the track and then turned west, into the woods. He walked slowly and methodically, pausing every now and then to look up into the trees. He stopped. 'I thought you wanted to help,' he said.

'I do, but—'

'You're not bird spotting. You're supposed to be looking for signs that a gunman has been in the area. Walk six foot to my left. Scan the ground in both directions. That'll be quicker.' He set off, then said, 'Five paces, look for footprints, any rubbish that might have been discarded. Then look up. Check for any sign of damaged bark, of anyone having climbed a tree. Then move forwards again.'

Webb seemed to know what he was doing, acting like a policeman searching a crime scene. The woods around him were untouched, as far as Jacob could see. The only footprints were the ones they left themselves. They walked about thirty metres into the woods, then turned in a U, moving a little lower down the hill and returning towards the road.

On the third pass, Jacob found a cigarette packet, but it was old and faded and must have been there for months, if not years. At this rate it was going to take them twenty or thirty minutes before they reached the wall by the copse, which was where he needed to be if he was going to find the message before Webb did.

This time, when they reached the westernmost limit of their search Webb stopped and raised a finger and very quietly hissed, '*Shh.*'

The pair of them stood statue still for a whole minute, until Webb said, 'Did you hear anything?'

Jacob shook his head. 'Just the helicopter.' Myroslav was high above them now, scanning the woods.

'Not sure,' said Webb. 'I thought I heard a branch break.'

Jacob peered into the darkness below the trees around them and wondered if they were being watched by Murphy or one of his colleagues.

Webb started walking again, feet cracking sticks. Each time they reached the track, Jacob tried to look down the verge without attracting attention. Wherever the message was, they would be on it soon.

'What are you going to do with your money?' asked Jacob.

'Mind your own business,' said Webb.

'Just making conversation. I'm buying a flat with my girl-friend,' he said.

'I hope it makes you happy,' said Webb.

'You married? Girlfriend?'

'Nope,' said Webb.

They had been patiently walking up and down for almost half an hour now. Webb paused, slipped off the backpack and took out a metal flask. He unscrewed the top and drank from it, then offered it to Jacob.

Jacob took it and sipped the water. In Webb's backpack, a walkie-talkie crackled. Webb took it out and spoke into it in Russian. 'Anything?'

'Nothing. What about you?'

'Nothing,' said Webb. 'We shall keep looking.' He returned it to the backpack.

'Where did you learn Russian?' Webb's Russian was clunky, but he got by.

'Evening class. Useful for bodyguarding. Got me a few jobs. Rich clientele. Including this one.'

He started walking again.

'They like that I'm British military,' Webb said. 'They pay for it.'

He walked a little further, looked up, walked on.

'I got a kid. Twenty now. She's about to go to college to study English and Philosophy.'

'Good for her.'

Webb started talking slowly, his voice soft and even. 'Her mum didn't like me much. Understandable really. So I missed out on being a dad.' He spoke while looking away into the woods, never meeting Jacob's gaze. 'So I'm saving up some money for her to see her through university and things.'

'That's good,' said Jacob.

Webb took the flask back and replaced it in the small backpack, then took a few more steps forward.

Jacob followed his line of sight. There, in amongst the grass and ferns on the far side of the track just under the wall, was a rolled-up ball of paper.

Webb was several paces ahead of him, and moving more quickly now towards it. Jacob had no chance of catching him up.

'Wait!' Jacob shouted.

TWENTY-NINE

'Wait!' Jacob shouted again, looking around desperately. 'There's something here.'

What was strange – amazing – was that as he spoke, he realised there was indeed something there.

There at the base of the track he was next to, the ground had been trodden down. There were the imprints of boots that belonged to neither of them. And when he looked up into the tree, he saw, dangling three metres in the air, a length of blue climbing rope, and attached to it, a dull metal carabiner clip.

'I've found it!' Jacob pointed upwards, then swung round to look at Webb, who was in full sunlight, halfway across the road.

'This is where they fired the gun from. Right here.' Jacob was practically screaming now to distract him.

Webb stopped finally. 'Calm down, lad,' he said. He looked across the road, peering through the tree trunks, until his eyes saw what Jacob had seen. 'Bloody hell.' He marched over towards the tree, inspected the ground for a second, then said, 'Give me a leg up.'

He ordered Jacob to join his hands together, fingers inter-locked, then placed his boot on them and hoisted himself up until he was high enough to catch the loop of rope. A few seconds later he was sitting high on a branch above Jacob, experimenting with his body position. There was a second branch at chest height. 'Nice.'

'What?'

'This guy is a pro. If he sat here, he could have used this branch –' he tapped on the next one – 'to rest the hand guard on. Line of sight is perfect. He could have taken all the time in the world.'

'So someone shot from up there?' He tried to imagine Murphy perched in the tree, watching him.

'Someone with sniper training and a sophisticated weapon. No ordinary hunter with a rifle. Throw me the walkie-talkie.' Jacob did as he was told, reaching into the bag, finding the device and tossing it up to Webb.

'Tell Myroslav I think I've found the place the gunman used,' he said, talking into it. 'Jacob found it, as a matter of fact.'

Jacob wondered how long Murphy had been using this tree as an observation post, and how much of what went on in the compound he could see. But there were more important things to think about right now.

While Webb was talking to Iosef, Jacob backed across the road. He was still in Webb's line of sight, so he couldn't risk just bending down to pick up his message. He had to wait until Webb was distracted.

'I can't see any spent cartridges,' he was telling Iosef, 'but I've got a clear view right into the garden from here. We need to do a sweep of the woods around here. Whoever it was may still be near. Can you come and pick us up?'

He turned away to scan the woods in the other direction, giving Jacob the opportunity to swoop down, pick up the wrapped stone and slip it in his pocket.

'They're coming in the wagon,' Webb called down, lowering himself again on the loop, then dropping to the ground with a thump. 'Whoever did this would have come through the woods on foot. Probably from that direction.' He pointed out to the west. 'We're going to try and figure out where he left his vehicle.'

Jacob thought of Murphy and his anonymous-looking grey Audi, presumably chosen to look like any other car around here. Webb approached and began searching the ground around Jacob's feet. 'Thought I saw something here before you started shouting your head off.'

'What sort of thing?' asked Jacob, confident now that the evidence was safe in his pocket.

'Not sure.' Webb squatted lower to change his angle, then stood again. 'Maybe just a bit of litter or something, but given the location next to the tree, we better find it. Anything might give a clue as to who these guys are.'

'Right,' said Jacob, making a show of looking around. 'You think it's more than one person?'

'Might just be one person out here, but someone sent them, that's for sure.' They circled round the grass for a while. 'Weird,' said Webb. 'I could have sworn it was here.'

Jacob joined him, pretending to scan the ground, but stopped

188

and looked up when he heard the roaring of an engine from the top of the rise. The dark Mercedes SUV was bouncing along the track towards them, Iosef at the wheel, Fedor beside him.

Webb carried on his search even as they drove up. Jacob left him to it and waited for Iosef to jump out of the driver seat. 'Webb thinks he sat there. It gives a clear view of the lawns, apparently.'

'Let's go find him.' Iosef stomped back to the SUV. 'Come on,' he said. 'He may be close.' Jacob thought of the noise they had heard when they were searching.

Webb was still reluctant to get in. 'I could have sworn . . .' he said, looking down.

'I was standing a little further up,' suggested Jacob, thinking that if it had been Murphy watching them earlier, the longer he could delay the SUV the better. It would give Murphy time to conceal himself – or get away.

'Up here? Really?' Webb started kicking through the weeds higher up the slope.

'Come on. Hurry,' Iosef was beckoning. 'We are wasting time.'

'Just one minute.' And he leaned down. 'Got it.'

To Jacob's horror, he leaned down and he picked up a piece of white paper just like the one Jacob had in his pocket. Impossible, thought Jacob, as he watched Webb slowly unwrap the paper, letting the stone fall out onto the ground.

THIRTY

Webb held the paper in two hands, squinting at it, his back to the Mercedes.

'Get in,' shouted Iosef from his seat next to Fedor. 'Or we will leave without you.'

Webb stuffed the paper in his pocket, turned and glanced at Jacob, and in that look, Jacob knew that Webb had read it and understood everything completely.

Jacob was dead. He thought about making a run for it, but he wouldn't stand a chance against three armed men.

'In the wagon,' Webb said quietly, in English. He opened the back door and shoved Jacob inside, then got in afterwards.

Iosef slammed the vehicle into reverse and drove quickly back up the narrow track until he reached the larger lane that ran to the house's gate. He swung the car round and sped off west, turning off down another rutted unpaved track that ran along the contour of the hillside.

Jacob's brain was racing. He had assumed that Murphy would

have picked up yesterday's message by now, as arranged – but both had still been there. Yesterday's message and today's. He had not collected either. Jacob had been buoyed by the idea that he was passing on valuable information to the outside world, but instead it appeared that he had been talking to himself.

Jacob could sense that Webb was looking at him as they bounced down the uneven track, but he didn't dare turn to meet his questioning eye. The only good thing was that Webb hadn't told the others what he had found. Yet.

'Left,' said Fedor.

Iosef swung the wheel round and branches snapped at the windscreen. They hurtled downhill with the lake somewhere ahead of them for another couple of minutes, then Fedor braked and Jacob realised they were in a clearing and that everyone was jumping out of the vehicle, Iosef with his pistol in his right hand.

'Were they here?' Webb asked in Russian.

'Tyre tracks,' Iosef said, pointing. 'Not just one car. Two. Something heavy like a truck or a Range Rover.'

Fedor and Iosef stood for a second looking around the clearing, then Iosef started searching the perimeter more methodically. He stopped and looked at Webb, who was standing looking at Jacob.

'Hey,' said Iosef. 'What are you doing? Help us look for tracks.'

Webb finally tore his eyes off Jacob and joined Iosef to inspect the eastern side of the clearing, the side closest to the house.

'Here,' said Iosef. 'Boots.'

Jacob approached. In softer soil a pair of boot prints showed that someone had walked that way, and recently.

'They've run away, right?' Fedor looked around.

191

'Maybe one person. Maybe two. Maybe an hour ago. Maybe more. We need more cameras,' said Iosef.

Iosef insisted they spent another forty minutes looking around for any other signs of who might have fired the gun, but they found nothing. Jacob returned to the SUV and sat inside thinking. Murphy had promised that he would scan the perimeter for messages every morning, but it was possible that he had missed the first.

He had assumed that it was Murphy who had shot the dog, Murphy who had been watching with the drones. A few minutes ago he had felt a little safer, protected by a sophisticated operation watching after him with the most advanced equipment there was. But Murphy had failed to find a message, left exactly where he had told Jacob to leave it.

They rode back to the house in silence, pausing outside the white wall as the big metal gate slid back. Then they were in Myroslav's beautiful world again.

And still, Webb hadn't said anything about the note he had found. Jacob didn't understand.

Eloise was waiting on the driveway, still in her black-and-white swimsuit, hands on her hips. 'Hurry up. He wants to talk again.'

Jacob followed her through the house onto the terrace. Myroslav was walking up the slope from the helicopter pad. 'Nazim has messaged. He wants a conference call.'

'The Indian shithead?' said Myroslav.

'He says he wants to talk right away.'

'He can wait,' muttered Myroslav. 'Get me some water,' he said and wandered into the living room. When Vlada brought him a jug of ice-cold water with sliced lemon and sprigs of mint, he stood looking through the glass at the pile of earth on his lawn.

Myroslav took a sheet of paper and sat at the dining table with Iosef for a quarter of an hour, drawing a crude map of the land around the house discussing where they should put additional security cameras. Webb came and watched them for a while, in a chair pushed back from the table, occasionally glancing up at Jacob, who stood by the window. Myroslav kept Nazim waiting for over an hour while Eloise fretted.

Jacob was baffled. Webb had told no one about the note he had found.

Once they had finished drawing up the plan, Myroslav insisted that Vlada bring him a lunch of borscht and rye bread, which he ate calmly, sitting on the terrace, saying nothing. When he was finished, he stood up and beckoned to Eloise. 'Tell the Indian I'll be ready soon,' he said, though it was still another twenty minutes before he finally descended to the conference room.

Eloise had changed into a T-shirt and jeans. She placed her phone on the stand, like before. 'Ready?' she asked.

This time, when Nazim finally appeared on the screen, he was in a simpler room than the last one they had seen him in. It was a hotel, Jacob guessed. It looked like he was sitting up in bed somewhere, fully dressed, with daylight shining in a diagonal across his face. Instead of addressing Myroslav he talked directly to Jacob. 'Tell me, my friend, do they look worried now?' He smiled. 'Because they should.'

THIRTY-ONE

'It was you,' said Jacob to Nazim in Hindi. 'You shot the dog.'

It was not Murphy after all. Nazim blinked slowly and smiled. 'So they do look worried? Because they really, really should.'

'You had a marksman in the woods.'

Nazim's smile was fixed.

'What is he saying?' Myroslav demanded.

'They look worried to me.' Nazim's smile was fixed. 'What about you, Jacob? Are you worried?'

'Translate! Translate!' Myroslav ordered.

'I can keep you safe,' Nazim continued, ignoring Myroslav. 'Just remember that, will you? We are not enemies, you and me. You and me –' he leaned forward closer to his phone – 'we speak the same language.'

Jacob stared at the screen, trying to work out how to respond. If Nazim had killed Tamara, he was dangerous, but he was not just some hoodlum. As Webb had said, shooting the dog had been a professional operation. It hadn't been Murphy after all,

194

and – even more worryingly – Murphy hadn't even been there to pick up his messages.

'You have to make your mind up, which side you are on.'

He felt as if Murphy had abandoned him. In the end Jacob turned to Myroslav and Eloise and spoke in Russian. 'OK. He shot your dog. He pretty much admitted it to me.'

'Shitter,' said Myroslav in English – then he switched to his more familiar language. 'I have no time for this man.'

'Stay calm,' Eloise cautioned. 'This is business. You know that.'

Myroslav said simply, 'I don't bargain with people who don't respect me. This is my house. He has violated it. He has no class at all.'

'Ask him what he wants,' demanded Eloise.

'What is he paying you?' asked Nazim.

'Did he answer?' Eloise asked. 'Was that an answer?'

Jacob thought for a while. He had become a pawn in somebody else's game. He turned to her.

'He's been offering me more money if I act as a spy for him,' he said.

Myroslav banged the table. In the carafe of water, ripples circled.

'Stay calm,' said Eloise quietly in Russian.

'I am calm,' said Myroslav. 'I just want that man gone.'

'Find out what he wants next, at least,' pleaded Eloise.

Nazim was staring at the screen, intently. Jacob turned back to him. 'They are arguing, but they want to know your terms,' Jacob told Nazim.

'And I want to know yours,' Nazim continued smoothly. 'For you to start working for me.'

'My terms . . . ?' said Jacob in Hindi.

'How much money do you want? I will pay it if you help me. Meanwhile yesterday I offered them fifty per cent. The offer still stands. But they must hurry.'

'I am not interested in doing business with a dog killer,' responded Myroslav, when Jacob had told him what Nazim had said. 'It's our operation. We created it.'

'He advises you strongly to take it, he says.'

'He is a savage,' said Myroslav. 'We stop now, we have still made two-point-five million. Could have been better, but it's enough. We get out now.'

Jacob continued to speak Nazim's words. 'He says he can stop you from getting your hands on that money by exposing your shell company.'

Myroslav laughed abruptly. 'And what would be the point of that? If he trashes the company, he gets nothing at all. Does he think I'm stupid?'

Eloise was thinking aloud. 'Myroslav is right,' she said, thinking it through. 'Tell him we have already made enough money. If he won't work with us, we shut down the operation completely,' Eloise said. 'He can't operate without us either.'

'Tell him that,' Myroslav ordered.

Nothing seemed to dent Nazim's calm. He reached out for a bottle of mineral water that must have been sitting on a bedside table and cracked the seal on it. 'They're bluffing. Can you see that in their faces? Let me explain all this to you, Jacob. They have invested in this operation and they know perfectly well it could make ten, maybe twenty times as much money. They are both greedy. They want more, but I think that Myroslav is too arrogant and probably too racist to admit that a man from India has beaten him.'

'What is he saying?' muttered Eloise. Jacob felt like a tennis ball, being knocked one way and then the other.

'Tell me,' asked Nazim. 'Do you think I am right about Myroslav?'

'Yes. I think you are right,' said Jacob. 'Up to a point. He wants more money, but I think he's proud too. I don't think he will change his mind.'

Myroslav banged the table. 'Translator, translate.'

Nazim said, 'Interesting. Tell them that I can provide five thousand doses of Lutinol in twelve different shipments. We will be dispatching another five thousand next week.'

Jacob repeated the words.

'That's . . . fifty million dollars,' Eloise whispered to Myroslav.

Nazim was still talking. 'Every week we will ship five thousand more – for as long as we can. It won't last for ever, but why stop it now?'

Jacob boggled at the figures.

'You sell them through Singapore,' Nazim continued. 'We share the profits. In just two weeks you may get around twenty-five million instead of, what – two-point-five?'

'Tell him to go shit in his own trousers,' said Myroslav, when Jacob had translated Nazim's terms. 'I'm not doing business with a dog killer. And that is final.' And he stood.

'Myroslav. Think about it,' pleaded Eloise.

'He killed my dog.'

Jacob translated word for word. A flicker of annoyance crossed Nazim's face. 'You were right,' he said. 'He is proud. Now tell him this.' And again he lowered his voice and spoke quietly to Jacob and to Jacob alone, slowly enough for him to understand the importance of what he was saying.

And then, afterwards, he leaned forward to end the call, and then the screen was blank again.

'What?' demanded Eloise. 'What did he say?'

Jacob turned to her and said, 'He said that next time it won't be a dog.'

If the words weren't disturbing enough, as he spoke, something else occurred to Jacob as he walked back through the garden to his apartment. He had assumed that Nazim had been calling from Mumbai where it would already be evening and the sky already dark, yet the sunlight that played on his face was the warm sun of a late afternoon much like the one they were enjoying right now.

Tymko. You are my heart.

I adore you. Every night before I go to sleep, I wonder what you have done today. I miss you so much.

Today I prepared salo. *Pork lard is the most Ukrainian of all foods. We live in a country where the winters are long and cold. It's natural that we want food that lasts the winter, that comforts us on dark nights. If you are going to be a Ukrainian, you must profess to love it. It is a food for rich, fat men. I will tell you a secret, Tymko. I cannot stand it. Don't tell Baba. She used to feed me it on special occasions. Once, I threw it in the toilet. Don't try this yourself, my little treasure. It floats and is very, very hard to flush.*

I do not like salo, *but I can make it. I will tell you how. First, buy the best pork fat. The white must be around three or four fingers thick. Not your tiny little fingers, but the fingers of a grown woman. And make sure the butcher leaves the skin on it too. There are many ways to prepare it. Pickling is good but I prefer to dry-cure it. Cut it into big cubes, then bury it in salt for a few days until it is dry. The bigger the squares, the longer you have to leave it. Then add some flavour. I like to coat it with a paste of garlic and Hungarian paprika, but some people prefer black pepper, or hot pepper and bay leaf.*

199

Greedy people love the taste of fat. I am surrounded by greedy people here. I feed them salo *all the time. Soon their arteries clog and their hearts explode. I count the days.*

I am so tired, Tymko. I'm not sure I can live like this much longer. My time is running out, I think. I am sorry.

THIRTY-TWO

'If he wants a fight, let's give him a fight,' said Myroslav.

Myroslav had insisted everyone join him for drinks on the terrace in a show of defiance. If Nazim was watching, let him watch this.

Though the evening was warm, he had lit fires in stainless steel burners dotted around and ordered Vlada to mix Cosmopolitans. He was dressed head to foot in white.

'I just don't want anyone to get hurt,' said Eloise. She had dressed too, in a long red cocktail dress with spaghetti straps. 'That was never the plan. There is no need for violence.' Hollow cheeked, she sucked smoke hard from her cigarette.

'If you back down, you lose,' said Myroslav.

Jacob felt dowdy in his shirt and jeans. Draper appeared to have made no effort at all. He wore an old T-shirt with the words *Black T-shirt* on it, though washing had rendered the shirt more grey than black.

Webb and Iosef sat close by, watchfully, not drinking. A semi-automatic rifle was propped on a nearby chair.

'Do we need the guns?' asked Eloise.

'In my experience, guns make a good party a great party,' said Myroslav.

'What about some music?' demanded Eloise.

'Please,' said Draper. 'Not Ed Sheeran this time.'

'None of your crap,' said Eloise.

'Turn on the lights,' Myroslav ordered Vlada. 'If he is watching, I want him to see us.' And when the lights came on he stood at the edge of the terrace, looking out. If somebody wanted to shoot him, he would have made a perfect target.

Vlada brought dishes of blini with black caviar and soured cream, and plates of red mullet, served with dill and lemon, along with fresh cocktails. She brought dishes of pork fat which Myroslav pronounced delicious and made Jacob try.

Eloise sat next to Jacob and held up her cocktail glass. 'Know what this feels like? A party at the end of the world.' She leaned her head back and drained the glass.

After a while, Jacob stood up and walked down the steps into the dark garden and looked back at the house, illuminated in darkness like a ship at sea.

A voice next to him whispered, 'Did you send another note?'

He looked around. Vlada was sitting cross-legged on the grass, eating something. A sandwich, he realised. Vlada ran the whole house. She had to take her breaks when she could.

'I tried to,' he said. 'They didn't pick it up, though.'

'So much for the spies.'

'I'm trying, I promise. I'm not sure what's happening, though. They promised to come in a day or two at most, but they haven't done anything.' Up on the terrace, Draper and Eloise were arguing about something. Loudspeakers were playing Nina Simone.

'They?'

'Nothing,' muttered Jacob.

'I hate rich people,' Vlada said. 'The richer you are, the worse you behave. I knew that already. I worked in restaurants.'

Eloise was up there dancing on her own.

'Who is it? Who do you work for?' Vlada asked.

'I don't work for anyone. I just got dragged into this, like you. I was tricked. But there's an American out there, CIA.'

'Shit,' she said. 'Really? CIA?'

He watched her eyes widen.

'He's been watching Myroslav. He said the best thing was for me to stay in, to pass information.'

'The CIA are watching us? What the fuck are they waiting for?' she said, keeping her voice low.

'Evidence. They have evidence of crimes he has committed in the USA, but the Austrians refused to extradite him. So now they need proof of crimes that he committed here.'

'Evidence? I am evidence of crimes he is committing here.'

From the terrace Jacob heard Draper. 'Can I get another cocktail?'

'I know,' said Jacob. 'The guy I spoke to said he was worried that if they persuade the Austrians to raid before they had enough information, Myroslav will just get rid of the evidence. Like you.'

'Get rid of,' she repeated. 'It's true. He would do that. He has done it before.'

'Here?'

'No. Before he came here. He is a terrible man.'

'You know who he really is?'

'Sure. His real name is Melnyk. Vadym Melnyk.'

Jacob thought of the tattoo on Myroslav's chest: *VM*.

'People knew him from the bad days in Ukraine. He did all sorts of shit.'

'Did you recognise him when you were brought here?'

She shook her head. 'I recognised the name later, though. There were documents in his room one day. I found them in his desk drawer when I was looking for my passport. I never found it.'

Up on the terrace, Draper was calling for another drink.

'Fetch it yourself,' said Eloise.

'Twenty years ago Vadym Melnyk made a lot of money from natural gas contracts in Ukraine,' said Vlada. 'It was all corruption, corruption, corruption. He was close to the regime back then and the regime were just Russian puppets. He needed protection, so he made friends with the Donetsk mafia.'

'Like the Russian mafia?' asked Jacob.

Vlada wrinkled her nose. 'Same thing, pretty much. They were just gangsters, paid by the Russians. A lot of people died back then in the gang wars. People who got in Melnyk's way. Nobody was able to prove Melnyk was behind the killings because if you knew too much, you were dead. Anyone who could incriminate him. He doesn't care.' She lifted her fingers to her temple and made a gun shape. 'And Melnyk just kept getting richer. He bought property in London, in America. He was famous, those days. Famous for destroying my country.'

'Vadym Melnyk, right?'

'That is his name. The Russians protected him back then.

They let him make money. They let him create chaos. That's what the Russians wanted. And with the profits he made, he paid the politicians in Ukraine who supported the Russians, politicians in America who supported Trump. At least, he was supposed to pay them. I think mostly he kept the money for himself. Following this?'

Jacob nodded. 'So how did he end up here?'

'Don't rush me. You know in 2014 the Ukrainians revolted against their pro-Russian president – the Euromaidan? We were all there. We kicked the president out and moved much closer to Europe and NATO. He was suddenly *persona non grata* in Ukraine. Russia protected their own in Donetsk but Melnyk had been cheating his handlers. He had made too many enemies. Even the Russians didn't trust him. So Myroslav had to get out fast, taking as much of his money with him as he could. The Americans wanted to prosecute him for corruption, so they put an arrest warrant out on him, but Austria has refused to extradite him.'

'So he's stuck here?'

'Exactly. He steps outside of Austria and they will arrest him. So him and his mafia friends hang out here. Poor little rich kid, eh?'

'I promise you. I'll get you out of here.'

She laughed. 'What makes you think you're getting out of here?'

'Fair point.'

'I can't escape. They have my child and my mother.' She sucked in air, as if trying to hold on to her emotions. 'Even if I get away from here, they have them. Maybe in a year, if I've earned enough money, Myroslav says. But I don't think they will ever let us go. Why would they?'

'Where's the woman with the drinks?' Draper called.

'I sometimes think we have gone back a thousand years and all this is perfectly normal. The rich have no law.'

He reached out a hand towards her and, to his surprise, she took it.

'Fuck,' she said, looking at his hand. 'That's weird.' And she squeezed it back.

It was meant at first simply as a gesture of companionship, but seemed to become something else in no time at all.

'I hate them all so much,' she said. 'More than anything, I want to see him die.'

He squeezed her hand again.

'Sometimes I put my urine in the food.'

'What?'

'It's the only thing I can do. I put my urine in the food.' She was laughing now at the look of horror on his face. 'If I were you, I would avoid the soup.'

'Hey, Jacob? Where the hell did you go?' Eloise shouted.

Vlada pulled away. 'I must go.' She stood. 'Look. Lovely Eloise is calling for you. If you are a spy, she is the one you have to hold hands with, not me. She is the one who wants you.'

'You're not serious?'

'I am in hell, Jacob,' she said.

Myroslav was in the middle of the dance floor, dancing alone. He danced like a man who had spent a lot of his youth in nightclubs. He seemed totally caught up in the music. He rubbed his hands down his white shirt as he danced, as if he were caressing another dancer, only it was just himself he was holding.

Eloise was standing on the edge of the terrace in her red dress swaying slightly as she shouted, 'Jacob. Where are you? I want to fucking dance.' Jacob looked around. Vlada had disappeared.

In the middle of it all, Myroslav was suddenly still, staring out above their heads. Jacob realised something was wrong.

'Stop the music!' he shouted.

'Fuck sake, Myroslav. This is a party.'

'Stop the music!'

And there was suddenly silence. Now all of them were looking too, peering towards the north, above the house. 'Can you hear it?' demanded Myroslav.

Jacob listened. From above them, somewhere in the darkening sky, came the faint insect-like whirr. Now he joined them, looking up into the sky.

There it was. A single red LED blinked for a second against the violet sky, then disappeared again, leaving blackness. There was a drone somewhere, watching them.

'There,' shouted Myroslav, jumping up. 'You fuckers. Come and get me if you dare.' He grabbed a rifle, put it to his shoulder and fired up into the air.

The bang was deafening.

'What in hell's name are you doing?' shouted Eloise.

Myroslav handed the weapon back to Iosef with a sheepish grin.

Jacob looked up, half expecting to see fragments of the device falling, but there was nothing. A few seconds later, a red light blinked again, a little to the west of where it had been before.

'It's not funny, Slava. Shooting guns is just going to draw attention.'

'Music,' shouted Myroslav. 'Start the music again.'

Jacob returned to the balcony and picked up his drink, drained it, then danced.

The music became slower and gloomier. Eloise had put on Nick Cave records. Jacob tried to sit down but she grabbed him and put her arms around him and shuffled round the floor to the dark music, hip to hip, Eloise's hands running down his back.

'I should never drink cocktails,' she said. 'I always want to have sex after a couple. Do you want to have sex?'

She clung on to him. 'Are you OK?' he asked.

'You're a nice man, you know that? I know you're trying to just get on with your own life. I feel bad for dragging you into this.'

As they turned slowly on the paving stones, Jacob caught sight of Vlada standing in the darkened living room with a tray of empty glasses, but he couldn't quite make out the expression on her face.

'I'm scared,' said Eloise. 'I think something really bad is going to happen.'

Jacob thought of the sunlight in Nazim's video. 'I think you're right.'

'I got Myroslav all wrong,' she said. 'I realise that now. I thought he was a businessman. I thought all this house and art and decor was civilisation. But it's not. It's just a way to spend his money.'

'What do you mean?'

'If he was a businessman, he'd make a deal now, because if he doesn't, things are going to get pretty fucked up.'

Jacob looked around. 'What if we weren't here?' said Jacob. 'What if we could get out of this place?'

They danced a little longer until the record changed. 'You and me?' she asked.

They revolved slowly on the stone floor. As they turned, Vlada came into sight again, still standing with the tray in her hands.

'Why not?'

Far away on the other side of the lake, lights glittered. 'I'd like that,' she said. 'You and me.'

They danced for another few minutes. She pulled away from him and winked, slightly lopsidedly. 'I have to go somewhere.'

Jacob rejoined the others. Draper had stolen cigarettes from Eloise's handbag to roll a joint with. He was sitting cross-legged on the paving stones, surrounded by loose tobacco and paper.

'Eloise really likes you,' he said, a little sadly. 'I can't say I blame her. You're pretty cute and I'm as hetero as you get.'

It was hard to party when there were only a handful of you. Eloise had vanished. Draper was lying on his back, stoned, looking up at the stars. Myroslav was deep in conversation with Iosef. Jacob stood, and looked back towards the house once more but couldn't see Vlada any more, though the kitchen light was on.

He turned and made his way back to his apartment. It had been a disturbing day. There had to be a reason why Murphy had not been able to pick up his messages. There had been no sign of him, or his grey car, outside the walls. Something must have happened to him. He was on his own again.

Only when he opened the door to his living room did he notice the light from under the bedroom door.

Someone was waiting for him.

THIRTY-THREE

'Come in.' It was not Eloise.

Webb was lying on the double bed, a pistol in his right hand. The gun was pointing right at Jacob. In his left, he held the crumpled sheet of paper.

'I think you and me have some talking to do.' Webb twitched the pistol. 'Come in and close the door.'

Jacob did as he was told.

'Sit down.'

He pointed the gun at an armchair in the corner.

'Who were you trying to get this message to?' Webb's face was stony.

Jacob lowered himself into the chair. 'I don't know what you mean.'

'Don't treat me like an idiot, Jacob. I looked through your desk just now. This is your paper. This is your handwriting. Who were you trying to get the message to?'

'I can explain,' said Jacob.

'Please do so.'

Jacob took a breath. 'I just thought someone might find it. If I threw it over.'

Webb tilted his head slightly to one side, as if trying to see Jacob from a different angle.

'For the second time I'm telling you, don't treat me like an idiot, Jacob. You wrote the message in English. To me, that says you were addressing it to someone. If you were just chucking it over for someone to find, you would have written it in German. You do speak German, don't you?'

Jacob nodded.

'You have Myroslav and Eloise pretty convinced that you're on their side, apparently he's paying you all sorts of cash to stay, so why are you trying to tell this person – whoever it is – about what's going on in here?'

Jacob looked down at his own hands. They were shaking. 'Because really I just want to get out of here. I thought if someone found my message, they might want to help.'

Webb shook his head slowly. 'You're still taking me for an idiot. You had a chance to get away. You came back. Which means you came back for a reason. You have one more minute to tell me what that reason is, or I take you to Myroslav and show him this message, and I'm pretty sure what he will tell me to do once I've given him this.'

Jacob nodded.

'Who's out there, Jacob? Who were you trying to reach? You need to tell me what's going on. Right now it's the only thing that's going to save your life.'

Jacob's head was fuzzy from the cocktails, but that gun pointing at his head was sobering him up pretty fast. 'You haven't told Myroslav about the note?'

'Not yet.'

Jacob blinked. 'Why not?'

'Just answer the question.'

Jacob nodded, thinking this through. 'It's because you're worried, aren't you?'

'It's my job to worry. It's what I'm paid to do.'

'Yes. But this time you're really worried about what's going on here. About Nazim. About how Myroslav is going to get out of this. Otherwise you'd have taken that letter straight to him. You know something's off, don't you?'

'Tell me what you're up to.'

So Jacob took a breath and started to speak. 'OK. What if I was to tell you that there was a CIA agent outside the walls?'

Webb snorted. 'I'd say fuck off.'

'A CIA agent who I met when I tried to escape, who asked me to come back inside here. And I did. Against my better judgement.'

Webb lowered the pistol ten degrees. 'I don't believe you. I've checked that perimeter twenty times, maybe more. If there's a CIA agent, he's concealing himself pretty well.'

'Isn't that exactly what CIA agents do?'

There was a long pause, then Webb said, 'Fair point. You actually talked to this man?'

'I was trying to get away. He chased me down and persuaded me that the best thing I could do would be to stay.'

Webb seemed to think for a while. 'I don't get it. Why are the CIA watching the house?'

Jacob explained how the Americans had been after Myroslav for years but they didn't have enough to persuade the Austrians to allow them to extradite him. How they needed to prove to the Austrians that he was doing something illegal in their territory.

'And you agreed to come back in here and help them?'

'Yes. I did.'

Webb whistled. 'Jesus. You're more of an idiot than I thought. And this guy's out there now?'

'I hope he is. But he didn't pick up my notes, which is worrying.'

Webb reached out to the side of the bed and turned off the light. They sat in total darkness together for a while until Webb spoke again. 'Now what?'

'That's up to you.' Jacob was thinking fast. 'If the CIA get what they want, they will end up proving that Myroslav is involved in an international conspiracy to defraud. There will be one big unexplained wealth order put on every dollar he has, here and in Singapore. And more importantly, anyone who's been paid by him will have their money confiscated too. It doesn't matter whether you've got the money safely tucked away at home in your bank already. Your only chance is to get out now. Or to help me get a message to them.'

'I'm not a quitter,' said Webb. 'That's why I get work. And I'm paid to be loyal. It's what I do. It's my reputation.'

'So you're just going to wait until the Austrian police raid the place?'

'If need be.' It was strangely quiet outside. They had switched off the music on the terrace. The party was over.

'Tell me about your daughter.'

Webb was silent.

'You're doing this for her, right?'

Webb's voice came back in the darkness. 'Leave her out of this.'

'What's her name?'

'I don't talk about that kind of stuff, so leave it alone. This is just about me and you.'

'But you're doing this for her. To give her a chance, right? So she can be what she wants to be.'

'I'm warning you, Jacob.' Webb was the calmest of all of them, but there was tension in his voice now.

Jacob pressed on. 'What's the point of doing any of this if they take your money and lock you up? She'll never get a chance to know you.'

He could hear the sound of Webb's breathing.

'The Mumbai gang are already here. You know that don't you? That was them with the sniper rifle, killing Myroslav's dog.'

'It looks like it.'

'I've been thinking. Why hasn't Murphy picked up the messages I've been sending? Maybe it's become too risky out there now with Nazim's men, but if I can't get a letter out to him, somebody needs to get out there and tell Murphy and his colleagues.'

'Somebody,' said Webb.

The door to the flat below slammed. Music started playing below. Draper had left the party too.

'If you really want to help your daughter, you've got to get off the fence before it's too late. If you get out now, before the roof comes down on us, you can disappear and keep everything you've got in the bank so far.'

215

'Or I could just show Myroslav this letter.'

'But you haven't yet, so I don't think you're going to.' Jacob tried to make out Webb in the darkness. It was impossible. 'My parents died when I was twelve. Car crash. I've always wondered what it would have been like to have them in my life.'

'I know exactly what you're trying to do,' said Webb. They sat quietly for a long while as Draper's music rose up through the floor. In the end, Webb said, 'If I was to leave, why would I want to get a message to anyone? The best thing would be for this all just to disappear – you and me to walk out with the money we have in our pockets.'

'Did you know that the maid has a little boy too?'

No answer.

'His name is Tymko. Myroslav's people have him somewhere. Vlada hasn't heard from him since Myroslav forced her to work here. Trafficking. Slavery. Did you know that too?'

Webb didn't answer. In the darkness, Jacob heard him moving off the bed.

There was warm breath right next to his ear. The gun pressed against his cheek. Webb spoke in a quiet but menacing whisper. 'Don't you ever, ever try and tell me what I should and shouldn't do.'

The bedroom door opened and dim light from the living room flooded in. Webb left silently.

For the first time in what felt like a long time, Jacob took a lungful of air.

THIRTY-FOUR

When Webb was gone, Jacob walked to his desk and put the light on, and opened the book of Scottish love poetry he was supposed to have been translating. He had neglected it for days. He sat with a page open in front of him for an hour, making notes on paper until he had exhausted himself enough to sleep.

In the morning he took the book of poems with him again, walked past the freshly dug grave and sat down by the pool. Vlada brought coffee and orange juice. 'Good morning,' she said, and smiled.

Myroslav arrived soon afterwards in a white towelling gown, silent and brooding. Iosef joined them too. Today he carried a military-style rifle. Without speaking he sat in one of the dining chairs, gun propped at his side. Myroslav shucked off the gown and dived into the pool, swimming clumsy lengths while Jacob tried to work.

The whole house seemed slow to wake. It was the morning after the party, after all.

Vlada appeared with a breakfast of chicken breasts cooked in pork fat, onions and kale, with an egg broken over the top of it, and put the plate in front of him on top of the book of poems. After last night's bacchanalia, it looked too rich to touch. 'Is this a Ukrainian thing?'

'Maybe,' she said with a shrug. There was definitely something about her, this morning.

To Jacob, the food looked like a kind of revenge, but when Myroslav finally emerged from the pool he sat down at a table a little way off with Iosef and both of them worked their way through their plates, mopping the last of the fat up with bread.

It took Eloise a while longer to emerge. She wore a large T-shirt and her eyes were red from last night's drinking. 'Join you?' she said.

Vlada brought a coffee, but when she tried to put a plate of the fried chicken in front of her Eloise told her to take it away, and opted for a cigarette instead. To Jacob, it looked like Vlada actually winked at him as she removed the food and returned to the kitchen with it.

'About last night,' Eloise said.

'We were drunk.' Jacob smiled.

'Yeah. I was anyway.'

'You don't have to apologise.'

'Fuck you. I wasn't going to. I was just going to tell you that if I had been sober, I'd have maybe tried a bit harder. Does that scare you?'

'A little.'

She laughed, then winced. 'My mouth feels like it's gone

rusty.' She rubbed her forehead. 'Can I get some paracetamol?' she called after Vlada. 'All of this is weird,' she told Myroslav, speaking in Russian. 'The website just says, *New stock coming soon.* When the hell is soon?'

Myroslav ignored her.

Jacob pulled two sheets of handwritten paper out from under his coffee cup. 'Can you scan this and send it to my Portuguese publisher?' he asked.

'What is it?'

'It's a poem. He's been expecting me to send it to him. He needs it to complete the collection before he publishes it.'

Eloise looked over at Myroslav. 'A poem? I don't know.'

'It's just a poem. The address is at the bottom. That's my editor's name. You can look him up if you like. He's quite well-known in literary circles.'

She looked at the pages. Her tongue flicked over her lips as she tried to read it. 'This is Portuguese.'

'That's right.'

'I don't speak Portuguese. How do we know you're not sending a message – *help, I've been kidnapped*?'

'It's just poetry, Eloise. Put it into Google Translate. See for yourselves. You won't find anything in there.'

She squinted at it for a while, mouthing the words out loud, then looked up. 'Is it any good?'

'Yes. It's very good. I like it very much.'

She looked at the pages again. 'Tell me what it says.'

'OK. It's called "The First Lyric of Our Song".' He took the pages from her and started translating it back into English.

Away from you
Everything is grey
Empty
Arid.
Strange feeling
Deep longing
Such sadness
Your ambition is unattainable
Were I a millionaire,
You would be by my side . . .

He carried on translating it back into English for her.

She wrinkled her nose. 'Depressing as shit. I'm too hungover for poetry. So it's about a guy whose girlfriend is just into money, right?'

'That's right.'

She looked at the page and nodded. 'And it's good?'

'Yeah. I think so.'

She blew a soft raspberry. 'I would like to see the poem from the girl complaining that her boyfriend is an effete tight-ass who sits around all day writing poetry when he should be earning money.'

Jacob laughed. 'It's just that if I don't send it, my editor will start wondering where it is. There are probably a bunch of emails from him already. If you want me to stay out of sight until we're done here, it would be better if we send it.'

She looked over at Myroslav and said, 'I'll see what I can do.' She put it back down on the table. 'It's going to be another hot one. I wish we could go down to the lake and swim, but Iosef says it's not safe any more.'

'Where is the Englishman?' demanded Myroslav, looking around. 'Not him.' He pointed at Jacob. 'The other one.'

'Webb?'

'Has anyone seen him this morning?'

Jacob shook his head. Eloise did the same. She reached out and took the sheets of paper.

The morning dragged.

Jacob swam for a while. The effort helped get last night's booze out of his system. Eloise had taken the paper with her to the main house. She returned after half an hour dressed in another swimsuit. This one was blue and showed off how tanned she was.

'You sent it?'

'Of course,' she said. He wasn't sure if he believed her. If she hadn't sent the messages to Carla, she might not have sent the poem, either.

Putting a towel down, she held up some lotion. 'Could you?'

He joined her on the lounger, rubbing it into her exposed back and neck. She pushed back into him as he massaged it into her skin. 'I can do you after, if you want?'

'I'll stay in the shade,' he said, putting more lotion onto his hand. 'You definitely sent it?'

'Oh, for God's sake, Jacob.'

When Vlada returned with more coffee, Jacob was back under his own umbrella, trying to concentrate on his book of poetry.

'Webb has gone,' she said quietly, as she filled his cup. She said it as if it were some kind of personal achievement.

'What do you mean, gone?' Jacob whispered.

'Last night he came to my room. He woke me up.' She poured coffee into his cup. 'He wanted to talk to me. This morning he's gone. Completely.'

Iosef, Webb, Fedor and Vlada lived in servants' quarters above the garage. He must have gone there after he had left Jacob's apartment. 'Talked to you about what?'

'I made him cry,' she said. 'Big man. He cried.'

'You talked about his daughter?'

'And I told him about my son,' she said fiercely. 'He cried a great deal.' There was the ghost of a smile on her lips as she turned away.

On her sunbed, Eloise stirred, opening an eye and glaring at Vlada for disturbing her sleep. Jacob watched Vlada disappear down the path by the gym, trying to work out what she had meant when she said that Webb had gone.

'I prefer her when she's miserable and angry,' mumbled Eloise. 'What was she talking about?'

'Her son.'

'Does she have a son? Really? I didn't know that.' Eloise groaned and laid a towel over her head. Eventually that got too hot for her so she yanked it off and put on her dark glasses instead. Looking upwards, she asked, 'Do you fancy her?'

'Do I fancy who?'

'The maid, Jacob. You were whispering together like a pair of teenagers and she had this kind of smug smile on her face.'

'I wasn't.'

'Plus you were looking at her ass as she walked off down the path.' She propped herself up on the sunbed. 'I thought poor Carla was your true love?'

He ignored her, picked up a towel and wiped the oil off his hands with it.

'Some men go for that type. The waif. The helpless woman. It makes them feel big and strong.'

He remembered Vlada standing with the knife and wasn't sure she was exactly the helpless type at all. 'You know she's not here voluntarily, don't you?'

'I know she's getting paid, like the rest of us.' She lay back down again with a groan. 'None of my business. Do what you want with her, for all I care.'

A few minutes later she was snoring gently.

Jacob turned back to his poetry book and tried unsuccessfully to read. It was true, what Eloise had said. He had not thought about Carla for days. A shadow fell on the page.

'Where is Webb?'

When he opened his eyes he saw Iosef silhouetted against blue sky. 'Sorry?'

'He did not sleep in his room last night.'

'Webb?'

He noticed that Iosef had his shoulder holster on over a khaki T-shirt. 'I just checked the security footage. The camera at the front gate was switched off last night.'

'He switched off the camera?'

Iosef looked uncomfortable. 'Yes.'

'And then he left?'

'I also saw from the video that Webb left your room last night at around one a.m. Why did he visit you? What were you talking about?'

Jacob smiled. 'We're both English. I think he was homesick.

He just wanted to talk about . . . you know. The King. Football. Beer. Maybe he just missed it all too much.'

Iosef stared at him, disbelieving.

Jacob thought about what he had heard. 'So he just switched off a camera so you couldn't see him leave?'

Jacob turned his eyes back to the page, pretending to read. Webb had gone. He had left the house. His passport was, presumably, in Myroslav's safe along with his own. Without his passport Webb could not get that far. Maybe, thought Jacob, he had gone to find Murphy to try to put all of this straight. Or maybe he had just gone. If he had gone to Murphy, then he had done what Jacob had asked – and then surely it would only be a matter of time before the house was raided.

Iosef had begun walking away. Jacob jumped up and ran after him, catching him as he was about to ascend to the terrace. 'Wait,' called Jacob. 'Can I see the other camera footage?'

'Why?'

'You have cameras all around the place, yes? They were still on, yes?'

Iosef didn't answer.

'Webb didn't have a car, did he? How did he get away? Did he have someone waiting for him? Can I see the video? If we can see how he got away, maybe we can understand where he was going.'

'He's right.' Iosef spun around. Myroslav was standing at the big glass door at the back of the house. 'We need to check them all.' That's when he noticed Myroslav was wearing a shoulder holster too. He remembered Nazim's question: *Do they look worried?*

THIRTY-FIVE

Iosef had set up a MacBook on the dining-room table. The surveillance cameras were all wireless, accessed through an app. He clearly didn't like the idea of showing Jacob, but Myroslav had insisted. 'We need eyes,' Myroslav said. 'We need to know what's going on out there.'

'But we can't trust him.'

Myroslav shrugged. 'We trusted Webb.'

'Jesus. There are so many cameras,' said Jacob when he saw the screen. It looked like Myroslav had long had reason to be paranoid. The screen was full of little rectangles of live footage, outside and inside the compound. They seemed to point in every direction. There was one facing his front door. Another in the kitchen watching Vlada unload a dishwasher. Eloise was sound asleep again in the hot sun by the pool. Two more showed the boathouse. Others showed the walls themselves from inside and out. Jacob remembered the mental map of the garden he had drawn, walking around it. 'How would Webb have switched off the camera?'

'Easy,' said Iosef, and clicked on one of the rectangles to make it full screen. The controls were on the right. He simply toggled a switch and the camera feed went black.

'And this is how you found it when you logged on?'

'A few cameras had been switched off. Not just the pedestrian gate.'

'Can I see?'

Iosef sighed and showed him how to access the stored footage. Camera by camera, it was easy to scroll through the timeline of each one. 'These six cameras were off.' Iosef pointed to each of them on the screen.

'Weird,' said Jacob. The cameras that had gone off pointed in what appeared to be totally different directions. 'Kind of random which ones he turned off. What's that about?'

Iosef shook his head. 'I don't know.'

'There are cameras on my apartment, and on Draper's, but none on yours?' Jacob said to Iosef.

'We don't need cameras,' said Iosef tetchily.

'Naturally. So nothing shows where Webb went when he left your accommodation. If it was him who switched the cameras off, he'd have had to come to the main house, right?'

Iosef shook his head. 'No. He just needed a connection. He could have done it from his phone.'

'Where do you think Webb went?'

'I don't know. I checked his room. He took no clothes. No money as far as I could see. His wallet is still in his room.'

'His wallet?' That puzzled Jacob.

Jacob started going through the cameras one by one, Iosef watching him closely. 'How do I look at the old footage?'

Iosef showed him how to rewind and how to fast-forward through each recording.

'It's OK,' he said to Iosef. 'I can handle it from here.'

Reluctantly, Iosef left him to it.

At night, the cameras defaulted to infra red, which gave the images a ghostly feel. The place was utterly still. Jacob had been right about the dead spots on the lawn. There were places you could walk without being seen. On one screen he watched the fox emerge from the copse, light grey against the dark of the lawn, and trot across like it owned the place, its eyes like torches.

It stopped by the back of the garage and disappeared into the laurel bushes. A second later it emerged, carrying something in its mouth.

Out of curiosity, Jacob paused the video, zoomed in. What the fox was carrying looked very much like a leg of chicken.

Moving on, he examined the footage from the six cameras that had gone dark at just after 2 a.m. Two were at the front of the house, one on the inside, one on the outside, both aimed at the pedestrian door. The others were more random. It was hard to see why Webb would have turned them off. One was on the west side of the garden, showing the edge of the swimming pool. The other was right at the bottom, looking over the wall into dense forest. He could not have been in all of these places at once, so why had he turned off the cameras?

Odd.

And he had not taken his wallet. Presumably he had left with no means of buying even a bus ticket. So had he arranged to meet someone?

By moving the cursor under each frame he could scrub through them, minute by minute. He checked each one carefully.

He was looking enviously at the world outside. The images the cameras produced were astonishingly clear. He could zoom in on any detail to examine it, but in no frame was there any sign of Webb. He sighed, switched back to a live view of the world outside these walls.

In one of the live cameras, pointing towards the north, up the slope, crows were arguing with each other, circling over one of the trees. He watched them for a while, wondering why they had gathered there.

Then a larger bird swooped down into the woods and the crows scattered angrily. He had not had time to see it properly, but he wondered if it had been a vulture.

Iosef was sitting on a folding chair in the middle of the lawn, automatic rifle lying next to him, cleaning his pistol with a cloth.

'Where is Myroslav?'

'Why?'

'I think I figured out something,' Jacob said.

'Go on. Tell me.'

'It's best if I tell Myroslav.'

Iosef shrugged and led Jacob over to the gym, where Myroslav was exercising with dumb-bells, doing star jumps with them. 'English boy has a theory,' he shouted.

Myroslav put down the dumb-bells and pulled earbuds from his ears.

'He says he thinks he knows where Webb is,' said Iosef.

Sitting on a bench, he picked up a water bottle and poured

it over his head, drenching the basketball shirt he was wearing. 'Go on.'

'I think Webb was intending to come back,' said Jacob. 'He didn't take his wallet which he would have needed if he wanted to go far. He switched off several cameras to make it look like a glitch, as if the cameras were not working properly, but he was only really interested in the two at the pedestrian gate. So whatever he thought he was going to do, I think he was going to let himself back in and switch everything back on and hope that nobody noticed the missing footage. If they did, all they would find was several random cameras going offline. Nobody would have seen him leave or return but it would have looked like a fault.'

'Who was he seeing? Why didn't he come back?'

'I don't know. But I think I might know where he is.'

'What do you mean?'

'I need to show you something,' said Jacob. 'Something outside.'

'It might be a trick,' said Iosef.

Jacob shook his head and turned to go. 'OK. Do whatever you want. It was just a suggestion.'

Myroslav called out, 'Wait. Iosef, go with him. See what he finds.' Then he replaced his earbuds in his ear and picked up the dumb-bells again.

They walked a little way out of the door and up the hill through the woods, Iosef with a semi-automatic rifle over one shoulder, watching Jacob closely. The crows were still there, circling above the trees.

It only took a few minutes to find Webb. He was below the birds, sitting at the bottom of a fir tree, back to it, his legs splayed out in front of him, his dulled eyes half open.

There was a lot of blood, because the first crossbow bolt had hit him in the neck. Jacob guessed that must have been the first, at least. The others had hit him in the centre of his chest, but by then his time in this world was pretty much over. He must have fallen here after the first one hit and propped himself against the tree as the life drained out of him.

'Shit, shit, shit,' said Iosef, and he looked around him cautiously.

The bright pink fletching of the bolts protruded from his chest like flowers. Webb's right hand was bloody and torn. It lay on the ground, bone exposed. Repressing an urge to vomit, Jacob wondered whether that had been part of the struggle, or whether one of the birds circling above had done it.

Tymko. Tymko. Tymko.

I remember everything about you, but I know you are forgetting me, piece by piece. It breaks my heart to think of it.

You must be patient. Some things take time. Today I started to make kholodets. *This is a dish that requires patience and forethought. Pigs' legs are essential, because they are what produces the best meat jelly, but I like to use chicken as well. You have to soak the meats overnight first. If you don't, the blood in them will make the jelly dark. After soaking them, you must drain the meat well and boil it in fresh salted water. When it has cooked for a little while pour this water away and start again with a fresh brine, then finally boil it up a third time with an onion, a carrot and some celery for around ten hours. See? I told you it was not fast. Finally take out the meat, season it, put it in a glass bowl, and then filter the liquid. I use coffee filters to make sure that the jelly is pure and bright. Add bay leaves and redcurrants now and leave it overnight to set.*

I have learned patience. I hope I have also learned when to act. I think it will be over soon.

I adore you.

THIRTY-SIX

It was his fault, thought Jacob. He was the one who had cajoled Webb to leave and now Webb was never going to see his daughter. Jacob guessed he had gone to find out if Murphy was really there, to maybe make some kind of deal with him, but instead someone had killed him.

Iosef revolved slowly, gun at his shoulder, squinting down the barrel, but whoever had done this had either gone, or was watching them silently from a distance.

'We will have to get him inside,' he said. Leaving him outside was too risky, he must be reasoning. Though there weren't many hikers here, anyone might find him and they would wonder why a man had been shot with a crossbow and left to die in the woods.

'Carry him?'

'No.' Webb was a large man. He would be hard to drag through the forest. 'Come with me.' And, gun still raised, scanning the silent trees, Iosef retreated back, through the woods to the track.

Pausing to enter the code into the the keypad, he stepped back inside Myroslav's walls.

Jacob lingered at the open gate for a second as it rumbled shut. After Webb's death it felt just as dangerous to be outside the house's walls as within them.

Myroslav was waiting for them. 'Fuck,' Myroslav muttered when Iosef had explained what they found. His face was dark.

Iosef disappeared to the gardener's shed and returned on an olive green quad bike. 'Follow me,' he ordered as the big white gate rolled open again.

Webb was awkward to lift, already stiff from rigor mortis.

Iosef was in charge now, acting like a soldier behind enemy lines, looking round, gun at the ready. They worked fast, Jacob struggling to lift his legs while Iosef held his shoulders, putting him onto the back of the bike, belly down, until Webb lay humped grotesquely across the rack. Iosef tied him on with climbing rope, then got on and rode back the way they had come, driving round the trees towards the front gate while Jacob deliberately lingered behind, looking around.

The mystery remained. Where had Murphy disappeared to? There was no sign of him. He had not picked up the messages. Jacob had to wonder if he had been killed, just as Webb had been.

'Come on,' hissed Iosef at the open gate. 'Or do you want to be shot too?'

Jacob took one last glance into the trees, then stepped over into the pristine white driveway.

Myroslav was waiting for them. 'Not here,' he said. 'Take him up there.' He pointed towards the garage and the gardener's shed behind it. 'Get him out of sight.'

Jacob followed the quad bike. By the time he reached the shed, Iosef had already pulled the body off the bike onto the pale concrete floor and was wiping the bike down. Webb lay on his side, bent in the middle. It was a grotesque sight.

'Last night,' said Iosef, 'what did you say to him?'

Jacob kneeled down beside Webb. Up until this point, everything had been posturing and threats. Now Webb was dead. Nothing in his quiet, inconsequential life had prepared him for this.

'What did you talk about with him?'

'I told you what I said,' said Jacob, standing.

'Something you told him made him leave.'

'He didn't leave. I told you. He was intending to come back.' Jacob faced him, angry now. 'If you want to know, we talked about his daughter. Who he was desperate to see again. And that's not going to happen now, is it?'

Myroslav arrived and looked down at the body on the shed's floor. 'Take his clothes off. Cut away any tattoos. Anything that identifies him. We have to put his body somewhere far away.' He spoke in the kind of matter-of-fact voice that suggested he had done this before. 'The Englishman can do it. We need you on guard, Iosef.'

'No way,' said Jacob.

Myroslav gave that little crooked smile of his. 'You think you're too good for this work? You want my money, but you don't want to get your hands dirty. But your hands are dirty already.' He turned back to Iosef. 'If he won't do it, get the maid.'

234

It was an easy win for Myroslav. Jacob tried to imagine Vlady-slava being forced to do this. 'I'll do it,' he said, head down.

'Good,' said Myroslav and slapped him on the shoulder. 'After you have done it, burn his clothes.'

Iosef followed him out of the shed. For a while, Jacob looked down at Webb again, trying to find the stomach to carry out what Myroslav had ordered him to do, then turned away, gazing around the shed, looking for a tool he could use. There were various secateurs and shears hanging from hooks at the back. He chose the pair that looked most like scissors. Kneeling down, he began. The first time he touched the flesh of his leg, he recoiled. The coldness of Webb's skin was horrible. Taking a breath, he started by removing the dead man's running shoes. This was harder than he thought because Webb's sinews had become rigid. Only after pulling off the laces and cutting forward from the tongue, into the front of the shoe, was he able to pry them away.

The shirt was next. Jacob had been right about special forces. On his left arm Webb had a tattoo, *Per Mare, Per Terram*. He recognised it as the motto of the Royal Marine Commandos. He shuddered at the idea of cutting that skin away. He was not sure he could do that. On Webb's right forearm was a name, *Michelle*, written in florid italic. Jacob wondered if that was the daughter he had died for, or her mother, maybe. Removing a shirt from the dead weight of a man was not easy. Rolling him to one side to pull it off his back, he saw a large blue eagle spread across his shoulder blades and his heart sank again. If he was to survive here, he had to dissemble, to pretend he was one of them, to patiently record the evidence of what they were doing, but he could not do this. Each act was making him more complicit.

Murphy had persuaded him to return, then abandoned him.

He let Webb roll onto his back again and noticed his mouth had opened slightly.

Strange. There appeared to be something inside.

Jacob leaned forward and peered between Webb's teeth. It looked like a rolled-up ball of paper.

With the index finger of his right hand he poked inside and tried to scoop it out, but Webb's mouth was rigid. The teeth were only millimetres apart. Returning to the tool shelf, he found a rack of screwdrivers. Using two of them like pincers, he managed to force the ball of paper to the front of his mouth then hook it out with his finger.

Half of it was coated with blood from where the injuries in his chest had risen up and choked him, but the other half was clearly recognisable. On it was his own handwriting. It was the ball of paper Webb had recovered from the grass.

THIRTY-SEVEN

'What is that?' demanded Myroslav, turning away from the laptop. He was sitting at the dining-room table looking at the same screen Jacob had been using an hour ago. It was full of images of the perimeter of the house. He held out his hand towards Jacob.

'It's a message. I found it in Webb's mouth.'

'A message?'

Jacob had unrolled it and carefully torn away as much of the paper as he could, to remove evidence of his own handwriting. Only a scrap remained, on which was written a simple two-letter word in Devanagari script. *Ek.* 'It says, *One.*'

He handed it to Myroslav. 'One?'

'As in, one man down, I presume,' explained Jacob.

Myroslav screwed up the tiny ball of paper and tossed it aside. 'So it was the Indians,' he said.

'I think Nazim may be with them too.'

Myroslav slowly ran his hand over the top of his head. 'Changes

nothing,' he said. 'No one goes out. We stay here. Anyone suspicious outside, just kill them.' He turned back to the screen.

He lived for the fight, Jacob realised. He was probably even
enjoying it. This was his real world, not the fine house and furniture. All that was a world he pretended to. The real Myroslav
was still a street fighter and he was coming alive now. 'You want
a gun?' Myroslav asked.

'No. I don't.'

'We are going to need as many people as we can. And I
wouldn't trust Draper with one.'

'No. I wouldn't trust Draper with one. Or me.'

Myroslav nodded. 'I thought not. You will regret my offer,
though. In war, a man without a gun is worthless.'

'And this is war?'

'Of course. The Indians want to come and take over my business. So we fight.'

'What do you mean, fight?'

Myroslav leaned back in his chair. 'Did you not understand
what that Nazim is? He's a petty gangster who saw an opportunity. In my life, if I had given way to every petty gangster who
had tried to muscle in on me, I would never have all this. When
someone stands up to you, you have two choices. Negotiate or
fight. I'm not really much of a negotiator.'

'So you're going to fight?'

He gazed at the screen again. 'We all are, aren't we?'

'The maid, Vlada.' Myroslav stopped and looked up. 'You
should let her go,' Jacob continued. 'The rest of us chose to be
here in some way.'

Myroslav smiled. 'I've seen you talking to her.'

'Sure. I talk to her.'

The smile stiffened. 'I suppose she told you about her mother and her child then?'

Vladyslava had told him this in strict secrecy. He ignored the question. 'If Webb was number one, then they mean to kill again. There is a risk more of us will die. She is the only one who is not here of her own free will. She shouldn't have to be part of this.'

Myroslav nodded. 'She is here to repay a debt.'

'It's not her fault that she's here. You should let her go.'

Myroslav turned to him, examined him impassively, then returned to the computer screen. 'If I pay her debt off, will you fight?'

He found Vlada in the utility room behind the kitchen, ironing sheets.

'What is going on?' she asked. 'Something's wrong, isn't it?'

The room smelled of fresh clean cotton. It was orderly. Piles of white towels were neatly stacked. Jacob lowered his voice. 'Yes.'

'What?'

'Webb is dead. Somebody killed him last night after he came to talk to you.'

She put down the iron.

'Who killed him?'

Jacob sighed. 'Some people who want to take over Myroslav's business, I think. It's becoming too dangerous here.'

She nodded. 'I'm sorry. He was not the worst of them.'

'Bad things are going to happen, Vlada. You need to keep yourself safe.'

'Really? Is that so?' It was a taunt, as much as anything. She stood, sheet tucked under her chin, patiently folding it, adding it to the pile.

Myroslav was still peering at the computer when Jacob returned to the dining table. Iosef was with him, a gun strapped to a holster under his armpit. The bloody scrap of paper from Webb's mouth still sat next to the computer.

Myroslav acknowledged his presence with a grunt. 'Iosef says I shouldn't let you have a gun anyway. He still doesn't trust you – do you, Iosef?'

'What about Vladyslava? Will you let her go?'

Myroslav shrugged. 'We'll see.'

'There it is again,' said Iosef. 'Look.' He pointed towards the screen.

'Is it the same one?'

'Definitely. Let me rewind, I'll show you.'

They were both peering over the computer screen watching. 'Look. A silver Audi A3 saloon. It just passed the front gate, then turned round and came back again.'

'What do you think he's doing?' asked Myroslav.

Murphy drove an Audi. Jacob leaned closer.

'No. Not silver. It's grey,' said Iosef.

Jacob leaned in, trying not to look too interested or excited. It was definitely Murphy's car. Jacob could see his silhouette at the wheel. He was still alive. And he was back.

THIRTY-EIGHT

It was Jacob's sixth day in the mansion. Luxury wore thin fast.

At Myroslav's insistence they ate a late lunch at the dining table. Jacob and Draper joined him.

Vlada brought each a glass bowl, with pale jellied meat in it, with a bay leaf and a single bright red redcurrant. Beside it was a smaller dish full of what looked like a kind of beetroot pickle. It looked beautiful, a dish made with great care.

'Have you had this before?' asked Myroslav.

Draper made a gurgling noise. 'It's meat jello. Can I just get a burger or something?'

Myroslav sat at the end of the table, playing host, as if nothing out of the ordinary had happened today. The only thing out of place was the gun holster round his chest and the walkie-talkie lying on his side plate. 'It's *kholodets*. It's a traditional Ukrainian dish. It takes several days to prepare properly – a very special meal that they usually only serve on special occasions. Vladyslava makes it exceptionally well.'

'Is this a special occasion?' asked Draper.

'The maid obviously thinks so,' said Myroslav. 'Eat, eat, eat.'

Vlada came with a chilled Gerwürtztraminer and started pouring a glass for each of them, then turned to go. 'Wait, please,' said Myroslav.

She stopped, stood, hand on one hip.

'Jacob here says he thinks I should let you go. I would obviously be very reluctant to do so. You are a very talented cook. How would I ever find anyone who could cook as well as this?' He waved his hand over the beautiful dish in front of him.

'Is that what he thinks?' said Vlada.

'Did you tell him about your debt?' he said, looking at her.

She hung her head down. 'No.'

Myroslav turned to look at Jacob across the table. 'Vladyslava's mother borrowed money from a friend of mine. Quite a lot of money. The reason she is working here is to pay that money back. So I cannot just send her away.'

It was the money the people traffickers had snared her in with, guessed Jacob. 'How much money?' he asked. 'More than you're paying me?'

Myroslav's slow smile crept onto his lips. 'Maybe a little. Would you want to know the exact sum?'

'Yes.'

'And would you offer to pay this woman's debt if you could afford to do that?'

He looked up. Vladyslava gave him the tiniest shake of her head. Jacob sensed a trap but he was not sure what it was yet. 'Yes. I would.'

That slightly crooked smile again. 'So let me get this absolutely

242

straight. You would give all the money I'm going to pay you to this woman's family? Tens and tens of thousands of dollars maybe. And you would still stay here and work for us?'

Jacob hesitated. 'Yes.'

'Interesting.' Myroslav dug into the meat jelly. It wobbled on the fork. 'Then perhaps Iosef was right about you. I thought I understood you. I trust a man who wants to become rich because I understand him. But you're not a man I can trust at all.'

Myroslav put the fork in his mouth, swallowed, then laid it down again. 'If you are not on my side, Jacob, whose side are you on?' He faced Vlada and said gently, 'Go back to your work, my dear.'

'Fuck you,' muttered Vlada, turning to leave.

'You broke the terms of our agreement, Vladyslava. You talked to a guest. You know that will cost you, don't you?'

At the entrance to the hallway that led to the kitchen she turned again and said, 'Thanks, Jacob, you asshole.'

Jacob looked down at his untouched bowl. 'You're going to increase her debt because I asked if I could get her out of here?'

'She broke the terms of the arrangement,' said Myroslav, with the tiniest of shrugs. 'She talked about her terms of employment with a guest. That was forbidden. There are penalties.'

'You can't punish her for something I asked you to do.'

Myroslav scraped his bowl clean. 'Would you rather I punish you?'

'What for?'

'I don't know, Jacob. You tell me. When you came back here you said you were doing it for the money. Now it turns out you're not. So tell me, why are you here, exactly?'

Before he could answer, they were interrupted by Eloise bursting through from the terrace, a pool towel tied round her waist. 'What the actual fuck is going on? Where's Webb?' she demanded. 'Iosef said he's dead.'

'Your man Nazim killed him,' said Myroslav evenly. He put his fork down and picked up his napkin.

Eloise looked confused. 'Joke, right?'

'He went out last night,' said Jacob. 'Somebody caught him and killed him.'

'He's in the gardener's shed,' Myroslav told her. 'Take a look for yourself. He is definitely dead.'

'Don't go there,' blurted Jacob. He hadn't finished cutting off the clothes, nor had he started removing the tattoos – a job he wanted to avoid at all costs – but the body was grisly enough already.

She sat at the table, horrified. 'I didn't mean for anyone to get hurt,' she said. 'Honestly, I didn't. I didn't know any of this would happen.'

'Didn't you?' Myroslav looked surprised. Her eyes were pink.

The walkie-talkie at his side emitted a burst of white noise. Then a voice came from it. 'The car is back. It's coming our way.'

'What car?' Eloise rubbed her eyes.

'Cover the front of the house,' Myroslav said, standing.

'It's probably just a tourist,' Iosef answered.

'Do it,' ordered Myroslav. 'I'm coming.'

He looked down the table and sighed, then stood. 'Make yourself useful at least, Jacob. Take her away.'

Jacob led Eloise upstairs to her bedroom – on the same floor as Myroslav's. The master bedroom was at the rear of the house, looking over the lake. Hers faced out to the front, looking up the hillside to where Webb had been found. From above, he watched Iosef taking up position behind the gate, watching the cameras through his phone.

'Fuck,' she said, sitting heavily on the bed. 'Fuck. How was he killed?'

'With a crossbow. Just outside the gate. One hundred per cent it was Nazim's men.'

Eloise's eyes were wide. 'I don't believe it.'

He looked out over the woods. 'They must be out there.'

She leaned forward and put her head in her hands, her hair still damp from the swimming pool.

Jacob sat down beside her and looked around at her room, the make-up on the console desk, the thriller, half read on her bedside table. 'We've got to find a way out of here. It's too dangerous now. Nazim is somewhere outside.'

'Shit,' she said. 'Shit. Shit. Shit.' She looked down at herself, sitting in a damp swimsuit on her own bed. 'This is all too much.'

She stood and went into the bathroom, turned on the shower. Behind the half-open door, Jacob could hear her crying. And then, from downstairs came the sound of Iosef's voice, unnaturally loud, speaking through his walkie-talkie. 'The car has stopped outside the gate. There is a man getting out. What shall I do?'

'Watch him.'

'He's at the gate.'

'Ask him who he is, and what he wants.'

Downstairs, Jacob could hear Myroslav's voice talking to Iosef on the hand-held radio. Jacob closed the bedroom door behind him and started walking down the big wooden stairs.

245

Iosef's voice came from the walkie-talkie again. 'He says he wants to make a deal with us.'

'And who the fuck is he?'

There was another crackle of the radio, just as Myroslav came into view, holding the walkie-talkie close to his head.

'He says he is Eloise's husband.'

THIRTY-NINE

'Eloise's husband?' said Myroslav.

'That's what he says,' came Iosef's voice.

Jacob arrived at the bottom of the stairs just as Myroslav said, 'Tell him she is not here.' Jacob approached the laptop sitting at the end of the dining table and looked at the screen. It was showing the security footage from a camera high up on the door. Jacob could only see the top of the man's head.

'He says you need to talk to him.'

Behind the glass door, looking out, Myroslav cocked his head to one side. He spoke into the walkie-talkie. 'Do you think it's a trick?'

'I don't know.'

Myroslav walked back to the dining area, nudged Jacob aside, checked the other cameras, making sure the stranger was alone. With a sigh, he stood and unclipped his gun from his shoulder holster. Jacob followed him out to the front of the house again.

Taking up a position well to the left, Myroslav pulled a pistol from his holster and nodded. Iosef pressed the keypad. The outer door buzzed.

Murphy stepped inside the cage.

It was unmistakably him.

Jacob had to work hard not to look shocked, to not give himself away.

'Tell him to keep his arms in the air,' said Myroslav in Russian.

Jacob spoke to Murphy in English. Murphy raised his hands at a reassuring pace, a smile on his face.

'Are you alone?'

Murphy nodded.

'Let him in,' Myroslav ordered Iosef. The gate swung open and Murphy stepped forward, arms still in the air. Iosef patted him down carefully for almost a minute before he turned and nodded at Myroslav.

'Come inside,' said Myroslav.

Myroslav and Iosef waited until Murphy was ahead of them, then followed him back towards the house. For a brief second, Murphy caught Jacob's eye and gave him the tiniest of winks.

Jacob marvelled at the audacity. He had thought Murphy had abandoned him. Instead, the man from the CIA had tricked his way into Myroslav's house pretending to be Eloise's husband, calmly walking past him up the stairs and through the big glass door. He had stuck his head into the lion's mouth.

'You are Eloise's husband?' Myroslav said, speaking English.

'That's right. How is she?' Murphy stood and looked around. 'Wow. This place. It's incredible.'

'Thank you,' said Myroslav. 'Why have you come here?'

'I really love this place. I mean, I heard about it, but it's amazing.' He revolved slowly, looking at the space, just as Jacob had done the first time he stepped into it.

'Well?' demanded Myroslav. 'Why?'

'Uh, I just want to talk. I think I may be able to help you,' said Murphy.

'What is he saying?' Myroslav asked Jacob.

Jacob stepped forward. 'Would it be useful if I interpreted?'

Myroslav gave a small nod. 'Ask him what the hell he is doing here.'

'I'll explain,' said Murphy.

'OK. Sit.' Myroslav led him towards the sunken area, where the sofas faced the giant TV screen. 'Iosef. Tell the maid to bring coffee.'

'I would love coffee,' said Murphy.

Murphy seemed loud, confident. He would only be here, Jacob reasoned, if he was sure of his ground. There must be more officers out there. Perhaps the Austrian authorities were outside, ready to raid.

'So,' said Myroslav, sitting.

'I know everything about this operation,' Murphy declared.

'How?'

'We can come to that later. I know you are selling fertility drugs, mostly to America, using a false front in Brazil to conceal a shell company in a tax haven which is where all the cash goes. I'm thinking about this over the last couple of days and I figure the only way you're going to be doing that is if those drugs are counterfeit, right?'

Myroslav didn't answer.

'OK. If it's counterfeiting, then people are going to discover that those drugs aren't working. You've got a limited time period to make a great deal of money, but I believe you're currently having some problems. Right again?'

Jacob repeated this in Russian, taking great care to repeat exactly what was being said. If there was surveillance on the house, or if Murphy was wearing a hidden microphone of some kind, Murphy seemed to be deliberately getting Myroslav to admit to taking part in this fraud.

'I've seen your website. It's very cool but it currently says you're awaiting new supplies.'

Myroslav seemed to consider for a minute. 'First, I want to know where you get your information from. Did Eloise tell you this?'

Murphy laughed. 'Her tell me? God, no. She would never do that. You know she ran away from me, don't you?'

He was convincing, thought Jacob. He was good. Murphy was using what Jacob had told him the day they had met. Vlada arrived, bringing a tray of coffee and three white porcelain cups. She descended the steps into the sunken sitting area glaring coldly at Jacob. He couldn't help smiling. She couldn't know that in a little while they would all be saved. Everything was going to be OK.

'I'm the best person to help you right now,' Murphy was saying. 'Believe it or not, I know everything about your operation, and there's a reason for that. Do you want to know what it is?'

'Hey, boss,' interrupted Iosef. 'I think there's someone else out there.'

'You said you were on your own,' said Myroslav, standing.

Murphy just shrugged. There were others too, then, thought Jacob. In films, this was when smoke canisters came through windows and people were pinpointed with dots of red light. Presumably Murphy would give some kind of signal. Jacob looked around for an obvious hiding place. Mid-century modernism left few places to shelter.

Myroslav crossed the floor and looked at the screen over Iosef's shoulder. 'I thought I saw someone moving in the woods just there,' said Iosef.

Myroslav craned closer. 'I can't see anyone.'

'I don't know. I thought I saw someone else.'

Jacob wondered if they were special forces of some kind. Alone now with Murphy in the sunken seating, he leaned towards him, looking for some kind of explanation. 'What's going on?' he whispered.

To his surprise, Murphy muttered, 'Fuck should I know? Who are they expecting?'

'Are they your men out there?'

'What men?'

'But—'

'Ssh,' said Murphy.

Myroslav looked up from the screen, catching them whispering together. 'You said you came alone.'

'I did. Whoever is out there is nothing to do with me,' said Murphy. 'Honest to God. I just came to say, if you want to find another supplier for your fertility drug, I can help.'

Jacob was puzzled. Something was not right. 'Are there other people out there?' Myroslav turned back towards Murphy, unclipping his gun. 'If this is a trick, you are dead.'

'Not a fucking trick, man. Swear to God.'

Murphy looked confused, as if things were not playing out in the way he had intended.

'Murphy?'

Everybody turned. Eloise was standing at the bottom of the stairs that led up to the bedrooms, hair in a towel, staring.

'Murphy, is that you?'

'Hi, honey,' said the man next to Jacob. 'Just wanted to come by and see how you were doing, darling,' said Murphy.

Eloise crossed the floor. 'What the hell?'

Her con-man husband asked, his accent suddenly slipping into Australian, 'Do I get a kiss?'

FORTY

'Do you get a kiss? Murphy. You are fucking unbelievable.'

'Honey,' said Murphy. 'This scam was my idea. All this was my idea. You stole it from me. I've just come to get my share.'

Jacob had been taken in by a con man. There had never been any CIA. He had been persuaded to come back into this hellish place by a cheap crook, presumably because if he had gone to the police, the operation would have been busted and there wouldn't have been anything for Murphy to try to muscle in on.

'The hell it was your idea,' Eloise shouted. 'I'm the one who did all the research. I'm the one who found Myroslav. I'm the one who put it all together.'

'But I thought of it first. You stole it from me.'

Worse, he had persuaded Webb that there was an ally somewhere waiting for them on the outside. Webb had left the place trying to reach out to them, and now he was dead.

'I don't believe you came here. You are some creepy fucking stalker, Murphy.'

'Honey. Please. I just want what is mine.'

Myroslav said quietly, 'Tell them both to shut up.'

'I'm sorry, Murphy, but I wasn't going to wait around for another few years while you told me how rich you were going to make me. You are full of shit.'

Myroslav spoke louder. 'Tell them both to shut the hell up.' Jacob realised that Myroslav was addressing him. Myroslav turned to Murphy. 'So. What do you imagine you can do for me?'

Murphy lowered himself into a chair and steepled his fingers. 'I figured out that you are counterfeiting something called Lutinol, right?' The tiniest of conspiratorial glances towards Jacob. He was letting him know that he wasn't going to expose him, making out that they were somehow on the same side. 'Your supply of Lutinol has been compromised because of a gang war in India. I say fuck India. There are plenty of places in China that'll take our business. I've found contacts on the dark web—'

'Our business?' Eloise snorted. 'Excuse me.'

'Go on.' Myroslav stood, arms crossed.

'What's clever about this set-up is the marketing mechanism, set up by Eloise.'

'How kind,' said Eloise.

'That's where the power is. You have rich customers itching for it. You need to get back into business. There's only a few weeks left in this scam before someone blows the whistle. Waiting for the Indians to come back online is like burning money.'

'And what's in it for you?' demanded Myroslav.

Murphy smiled. 'Nothing at all. I'll just be happy with our share.'

'Our share?' Eloise raised her eyebrows.

'Yes, honey. You and me. Together.'

'Get lost,' said Eloise. 'Throw this loser out.'

'Well. If you throw me out, honey, I'll have to tell the local authorities what you're really doing in here.'

Eloise laid a hand on her husband's knee. 'Don't say that, Murphy. That's a really, really stupid thing to say.'

'I mean it,' Murphy said. 'I just came in here to negotiate for what's mine. You understand that – right, Myroslav? I spent a few days figuring out what you're doing in here, gathering intelligence you might say –' here he looked at Jacob again for just a fraction of a second – 'and a couple of days thinking of a way I could help you out. So what do you say?'

'And if I do as your wife said and throw you out?'

'Hey,' said Murphy. 'Don't be like that. I came here to help you.'

'Of course you did,' said Myroslav. 'But if we throw you out, what would you do with your . . . research?'

'Obviously I would have to let other people know what you're doing here.'

'Don't, Murphy. You don't know what you're doing,' said Eloise.

'You are trying to blackmail me?' Myroslav asked.

Murphy grinned. 'No. On the contrary. I'm just protecting you.'

'Protecting me.'

'Sure.'

But Myroslav was already standing. 'Do you box, Mr Murphy?'

Jacob said, 'Seriously? You want me to ask him that in English?'

'Yes.'

'I'm not taking part in this.'

But Myroslav's English was good enough for him to ask it himself. 'Do you box?'

'Sure. I used to box a little at college.'

'Very good. Would you like to have a fight with me?' Now Myroslav was unbuttoning the sleeves of his shirt.

'Why would I do that?'

'If you win, you'll get to share the money with your wife.'

'If I win, you'll cut me in?'

'No, Slava,' protested Eloise. 'Don't do this. Murphy's an idiot. There's no harm in him. He won't go to the authorities, I promise.'

'What if I lose?'

'Then I will probably kill you.'

Murphy was looking scared now. 'Hey, hey. I'm not really much of a fighter. I'm more of a cerebral guy.'

Myroslav had his shirt off.

'Maybe I should come back later. You obviously need to think about this for a while,' Murphy was saying.

He didn't have the chance. Myroslav grabbed Murphy by the shirt and pulled him outside.

'Where are we going?'

'I don't want blood on my furniture,' he said.

'Guys?' Murphy was pleading. 'Guys. Help me. Please.'

Iosef had already stood and was following with his gun.

'Don't, Myroslav,' Eloise pleaded. 'He's a fucking baby. He talks shit all the time.'

But Myroslav had already yanked him out onto the terrace.

Jacob stood with Eloise, knowing what would happen next.

They could hear Myroslav explaining the rules of Russian boxing. 'We take turns. First you hit me, then I hit you back.'

Murphy was screaming now. 'No. I'm not doing this.'

'He'll kill him,' said Eloise. 'You have to do something.'

'You first,' Myroslav was saying. 'No? OK. My turn.'

Murphy's screams stopped abruptly, then started up again, louder now and more desperate.

'Now yours.'

Jacob forced himself to watch. It only went on a few minutes. On the terrace, Iosef was behind Murphy, holding on to his waist, waiting for him to take his turn. Murphy's punch was feeble, barely touching Myroslav. Already Murphy was bleeding heavily down his shirt.

For his third turn, Myroslav pulled back his fist and smashed it into the side of his head. He was punching Murphy much harder than he had ever punched Jacob. There was real anger in the force of his punch. Jacob saw Murphy's legs start to fold, but Iosef was back, holding him again.

Myroslav waited to give Murphy a chance to reply with his fists, but as Murphy had nothing left in him, Myroslav pulled back his first for a fourth time, looking ready to kill.

Jacob stepped forward onto the terrace. 'Don't.'

Myroslav hesitated. 'Why not?'

'Because if you do, I'll have to break your nose, like I did last time.'

Myroslav looked at him for a second, then smiled. 'OK. Take the fucker away.'

★

They put Murphy in one of the rooms above the garage.

'You married that asshole?' asked Myroslav.

'When we met I really loved him, you know,' Eloise said. 'When I met him, I thought he was going to save me. What are you going to do with him?'

'You want to share your money with him?' Myroslav asked her.

'Hell, no.'

'He's a problem then.'

It was evening already. They were dining by the pool again, the four of them, Eloise, Myroslav, Draper and Jacob. Crickets buzzed in the grass. The surface of the golden pool was dotted with dead bugs, drawn by the underwater lights. The air was heavy and the night sky was cloudless. It felt like a storm was brewing. Jacob felt exhausted. Nobody was sleeping well any more. Iosef and Fedor were taking shifts on guard duty, keeping one eye on the security cameras, patrolling the walls.

'Since you won't let me kill him, I'll just have to keep him here until we are done,' he said.

He turned to Jacob. 'I noticed something, when we were talking. The man, Murphy . . . he kept looking at you. It was almost as if he knew you.'

Jacob hesitated. 'Me?'

'Yes.' Myroslav picked up a glass of wine. 'He smiled at you. As if he had seen you before. Earlier today I asked you why exactly you were here. You were willing to give up your own money to help a servant.'

'He what?' Eloise turned to look at him.

'Well?' Myroslav took a small, careful sip, put the glass down again. 'Why was he looking at you, Jacob? I want to ask you again, what are you really doing here, Jacob?'

There was nothing but the sound of crickets. The cloudless sky hung heavily overhead.

He was saved by the buzz of Eloise's phone, face down on the tablecloth. She turned it over and her shoulders shuddered, like a bug had landed somewhere on her skin. 'It's him. Nazim. He wants to talk to us. Tonight.'

'Ignore it,' said Myroslav. 'Fuck him.' He picked up his glass a second time and swirled the wine round in it.

A minute later the phone buzzed again.

'Ignore it,' ordered Myroslav again.

But Eloise was already looking at the message. Nazim had sent a jpeg. She held it up towards Jacob. 'What does it say?'

On the screen a finger and a thumb held a small rectangle of paper. On it was written a single word. '*Two*,' he said.

They all four looked at each other. 'Shit,' muttered Eloise. 'This is crazy.'

Then the photo vanished. Again Nazim had set it to disappear after a few seconds, to tantalise them.

'Psychological warfare,' said Draper. 'If he's trying to freak us out, it's working for me.'

'Relax,' said Myroslav. He picked up the walkie-talkie. 'Iosef?'

At first there was no answer.

'Iosef?' he said again. 'Where are you, Iosef?'

The sound of crickets seemed to get louder.

'Iosef. Answer me.'

Finally, the walkie-talkie crackled. 'Hey, boss.'

'All OK?'

'Sure. All quiet.'

'What about Fedor?'

'He's OK. I can see him on the surveillance cameras. He's checking the walls, like you asked.'

Everyone was fine. But after that no one felt like eating much more. Vladyslava came and collected the plates noisily, avoiding Jacob's eye. Jacob could feel the anger radiating from her.

FORTY-ONE

The night was muggy. Jacob slept with the windows open. At two he was woken by a wail.

He sat upright, hoping it was an owl, or some animal, hunted in the woods, but the next time it came the sound was undeniably human. 'Noooo.'

It was a woman's voice. Dressed in shorts and a T-shirt, Jacob jumped up and set off down the stairs and across the lawn towards the main house. As the lights clicked on, turning the lawn an unnaturally bright green, he realised the screams were not coming from the main house at all but from the staff quarters above the garage – where Vlada slept.

He broke into a run. The staircase up to the staff apartments was concealed behind laurel bushes. Jacob took the stairs in twos and reached the top just in time to see Eloise in jogging bottoms and T-shirt, backing out of one of the rooms, blood on her hands.

Then Iosef was pushing past him, into the corridor. 'What is going on?'

'He's dead,' Eloise cried.

'Who is dead?'

She was in shock, her face pale. 'Somebody killed him.'

Iosef had gone into the apartment now. Jacob stepped forward towards Eloise, who flopped into his arms. 'What happened?'

'I don't know.' She was pale. Jacob could fee her shaking. 'There's a knife.'

The wailing had woken Myroslav too. He arrived in his yellow silk dressing gown with a gun in one hand. '. . . fuck is going on?' he demanded.

'I came to talk to Murphy. To see how he was. The door was open . . . Did you do this?' She looked at Myroslav accusingly. 'You said he was a problem.'

'If I wanted to kill him, I could have done it with a punch. Why is there blood on your hands?'

She looked down at her own hands. 'I . . . I . . . Don't look at me like that. I didn't do it.'

It was a studio apartment. Jacob pushed past them and looked inside. Murphy lay in his bed on his back, naked except for pale yellow Y-front underpants. There was a black-handled knife sticking out of his throat, perpendicular to his body.

Murphy must have died quickly, Jacob reckoned. There was remarkably little blood on the pillow. Somebody had simply thrust a knife straight into his neck.

'Nobody got in from outside, I swear,' said Iosef.

'Tell Fedor to check the cameras again.'

Jacob stepped closer. The expression on Murphy's face was one of mild surprise. His lower lip was dark and swollen, Jacob noticed, but that must have been where Myroslav had punched him. The bruise on the side of his head, too.

Unceremoniously, Myroslav stepped forward and yanked out the knife. The body seemed to jerk as he did so and for a second Jacob thought that Murphy wasn't dead, after all. But Murphy had been stabbed so hard that the tip must have been embedded in his spinal column. Tugging the knife out had made his whole body move.

Jacob felt nauseous. Myroslav turned to him, holding the knife close to his face. The shine on the steel was crusted with dried blood. 'Do you recognise this?'

'It looks like one of yours.'

'I think it is.'

Knife in hand, Myroslav marched out of the apartment and made his way down the corridor to the door at the end. He banged on it hard with the other fist. 'Vladyslava. Open the door.'

There was no answer.

'Open the fucking door.'

She opened it eventually. She was dressed in what looked like children's Mickey Mouse pyjamas that hung off her thin frame. There were dark rings under her eyes. 'What? I am trying to sleep,' she complained. 'Only someone keeps screaming.'

'Show me your hands.'

She raised them for him. They were clean.

'She had plenty of time to wash them,' said Eloise.

Myroslav turned to Iosef. 'Check the knives. See if there is one missing.

'I don't suppose you know anything about this, do you?' He lifted up the kitchen knife with the blood on it. Vladyslava looked at it, puzzled. She shook her head slowly, then peered down the corridor. 'The American?'

'Was it that batshit crazy kitchen woman?' shouted Eloise. 'Was it?'

Vladyslava stood a little while longer at her doorway. 'Is he dead?'

'What do you know about it, Vlada?' Myroslav said.

'I was asleep. I know nothing.' She turned towards Eloise. 'I'm sorry for your loss,' she said. 'I really am. Can I go back to bed?'

She closed the door.

'It was her,' said Eloise. 'She's insane.'

Jacob was about to turn to go too when he thought of it. 'Have you looked in his mouth?' he asked.

'What?'

'The photograph,' he said.

Myroslav strode straight back into the apartment and returned a few seconds later holding a small, rolled-up piece of paper between his finger and thumb.

'Jesus, no,' Eloise gasped.

Myroslav unwrapped it, frowned, then held it out towards Jacob. On it, the Hindi word *Do*, just like the photograph on Eloise's phone. 'Two,' he translated.

Iosef returned from the kitchen. 'One of the knives is missing,' he said.

★

264

They convened in the living room of the main house where Fedor was patiently going over all the camera footage from last night.

Myroslav had given Eloise a tumbler of whisky. 'What's going to happen to him? He's still my husband. You can't bury him in the fucking garden like your dog.'

Myroslav was leaning back in his chair thinking. 'They sent us the photograph of the number yesterday. They sent it from outside, yes?'

'So someone came in last night and killed him?' Eloise said. 'I mean, why him?'

'But if they came from outside, why did they use my knife? Wouldn't they bring their own?'

Fedor rubbed his eyes, as if tired of staring at the screen. Myroslav turned to look at him.

Fedor shook his head. 'Nothing yet.'

'Show me the paper again,' said Jacob.

Myroslav squinted at him, then pulled the rolled-up paper from the pocket of his dressing gown and tossed it across the table towards him.

Jacob unfolded it again and examined it carefully. 'I don't think this is the same piece of paper that we saw in the photograph.'

'What?'

'It looks like it, but it's not. The other one, the photograph, was written by someone who is confident writing Devanagari script. This one –' he held up the paper – 'looks like someone who was copying from the photograph we saw.'

Myroslav said, 'I don't understand why that is important.'

'You're looking for an intruder. There wasn't one.'

Myroslav looked around the room. 'Yes. No one breached the wall. The note wasn't the one we saw in Nazim's photo. So it's one of us?'

'Fucking crazy maid,' muttered Eloise. 'I told you.'

FORTY-TWO

There were nine people within Myroslav's walls. Two of them were dead, laid out in the garden shed, which left seven. At least one of them was a killer.

Myroslav, Eloise and Jacob sat in the living room, waiting for dawn to come. On Myroslav's orders, Fedor was checking the computer trying to find footage that might help them discover who the murderer was. Iosef was patrolling the grounds. Vlada had gone back to bed, and Draper had never woken.

If Myroslav wanted someone dead, he didn't need to sneak around in the dead of night with a kitchen knife, so that left the others.

Eloise looked scared, but that didn't mean she wasn't the killer. Her estranged husband had arrived laying claim to the money she was making.

'What about Draper?' he asked.

'Draper can barely button a shirt,' said Myroslav.

'No. I mean, what *about* him? No one has seen him, have they?'

Myroslav nodded. He picked up his walkie-talkie. 'Iosef. Check on Draper. See if he's all right.'

Eloise looked wrecked. 'We should all stay together, right? In one room.'

'I need coffee,' said Jacob. 'Anyone else?'

Jacob went to the kitchen and switched on the coffee machine and waited for the water to warm. Iosef and Fedor had the run of the entire place. As employees, they were here because they were being paid. Though Iosef seemed loyal to Myroslav, anyone who worked for a fee could be tempted by a higher bidder. Nazim had tried to offer Jacob more money, so he could do the same to any of them. Unlike himself, he knew that Iosef and Fedor had access to the front gate. They could let themselves out at any time of day or night. They could have struck a deal with Nazim – or one of his men.

He realised that he was alone in the kitchen. If there was a killer picking them off, being on his own was not a good idea. And if the killer was picking off people who didn't matter – people who weren't directly involved in the conspiracy and who were dispensable – then maybe he himself was the next target.

Hurriedly he made three Americanos and then looked for milk. There was a small plate of chicken legs in the fridge. The milk bottle was next to it. He added it to the tray and carried it to the living room, relieved to be back in the presence of others.

He gave the first to Eloise and the next to Myroslav. 'I think I would prefer your cup,' Myroslav said, taking the third, instead of the one he had been offered.

'You think I tampered with it?'

'Like I said, I don't really know what you're doing here. So I'm keeping a close eye on you.'

Draper was right when he said this was psychological warfare. Just as he had the thought, Draper himself stumbled into the room in a grubby T-shirt and shorts, eyes bleary. 'Your husband is dead? Is that right?'

Jacob was oddly relieved to see him alive. Eloise nodded. 'Yes,' she said.

'So fucked up,' said Draper. 'That's a mess. I'm sorry, Eloise. Is that coffee? Is the maid awake?'

'Jacob made it,' Eloise said.

'Can I get one?'

'Make it yourself,' said Jacob, wary about returning to the kitchen alone.

'C'mon. I just got dragged out of bed and it's, like, half past three in the morning. I don't know how to make coffee on one of those doo-dahs.'

'Come with me and I'll show you.'

Reluctantly Draper followed Jacob to the kitchen. 'Someone stabbed the guy while everyone else was around? I'm losing it here,' said Draper. 'First Webb and now this.'

'It looks like it's someone on the inside too,' said Jacob as he knocked the grounds out of the filter holder into the bin.

Draper looked thoroughly shocked. 'How do they figure that out?'

Jacob filled the coffee filter again, then let the hot water pass through into the cup below, and went through the conversation he'd just had with Myroslav. No one had breached the perimeter

269

and the note was different from the one they'd been shown by Nazim. Someone had copied it.

'Iosef hates everyone's guts, that's for sure,' Draper said quietly. 'I'm scared, Jacob. I'm really frightened.'

'We have to get out,' said Jacob. 'If we stay here, we're all going to die.'

'Oh Jesus,' said Draper.

They returned to the living room. 'We should talk to him, that's all,' Eloise was saying.

'About what? About giving in?'

'People are dying, Myroslav.'

At around five Iosef returned from his patrol and swapped with Myroslav, who took his turn walking the grounds, while Fedor took a chance to get some sleep.

As dawn was finally starting to silhouette the mountains to the east, Eloise fell asleep on the couch, knees tucked up to her belly like a child. Jacob sat at the big window, watching the grey light turn pink and then creep down the side of the hillsides, turning them a rich green.

Not long afterwards Vlada appeared and started laying the table for breakfast. She hadn't even put on her proper uniform this morning. She was dressed in grey jogging bottoms and a T-shirt.

'Are you OK?' Jacob asked. She nodded, brought more coffee and orange juice, still saying nothing. In the dawn light they all looked as exhausted as she did now.

'I'm sorry I was angry. It's not your fault,' she said quietly, then sat down in one of the dining chairs.

'Tell me about your son. Are you married?'

She shook her head. 'His father was a DJ in Kyiv. It was a one-night thing. I don't even know where he is now, with the war. I was just unlucky to get pregnant.'

'Or lucky.'

'Yes. Lucky. It's true.' She picked up a table knife and squinted at it, then rubbed it with a napkin. 'How come you don't think I did it?'

'What?'

'Killed the man with the kitchen knife.'

Jacob looked at her. If anything, she looked thinner and more gaunt than when he'd first set eyes on her a week ago. 'I don't think you're that kind of person.'

'Anyone can be that kind of person,' she said. 'Trust me.' She stood and left the room, heading out towards the kitchen.

Draper had been lying on the floor. He stood up and stretched. 'This is too much. I'm going to go to my room. I'm going to play a game or something.'

'Don't,' said Jacob. 'You're vulnerable on your own. We should stick together.'

'If I play a game, I don't have to think about any of this shit. Seriously. I'll go insane if I don't.'

He pulled open the terrace door and made his way down the steps and across the big lawn. It was daylight now, at least. The world felt a little safer.

When Eloise finally woke, hair messy, red-eyed, the sunlight was disappearing behind thick cloud that was building around the mountain tops. It had started raining. She sat up and looked around. 'Where's Draper?'

'He went to his room.'

'And where's the psycho?'

'If you mean Vlada, she headed off to the kitchen.'

Eloise stood. 'What a night,' she said. She looked at the table. 'Did you have breakfast already?'

'I'm not exactly hungry.'

'Hey,' she shouted. 'Can I get some fresh coffee?'

Her voice seemed to echo in the big room. Nobody came.

'I don't understand why we can't just get in his helicopter and piss off,' said Eloise. 'It's not even about the money any more, is it?'

'Myroslav can't leave. He'll be arrested the moment he turns up anywhere else.'

'What do you mean?'

Jacob spoke in a low voice in English, hoping Iosef wouldn't understand. 'His name's not even Myroslav. He's wanted for all sorts of financial crimes.'

'How do you know that?'

'You seriously think he came by all this honestly? You never wondered why he's so cautious about leaving this place? Why he's built himself this castle here, miles away from anywhere? This is the only place he's safe.'

'Yeah,' she said. 'I suppose.'

'You knew that?'

'I knew he was no angel. So I guess we are stuck here with him, right?' She sat down and put her head in her hands. 'Sorry. I think I'm going to cry again.' She cupped her hands round her mouth and called out again, 'Can I please get some coffee?'

She crossed to the dining table, picked up a napkin and wiped her eyes with it.

'I know he was a dick, but, you know. He was my husband.'

In the end Eloise went and poured a cup of cold coffee from the jug on the table and drank it down. She looked more human for a second. And then came the clear bell-like ping of a phone notification. Her eyes dropped down to her phone and the colour left her face.

FORTY-THREE

'Don't look at it,' said Jacob.

'It's a photograph,' she said.

'You know what it'll be.'

She opened it. 'Shit,' she said. 'Shit, shit, shit.' She held it out to Jacob.

He was right. *Teen.* Three.

Iosef was already on the walkie-talkie checking on Myroslav. He answered. He was fine. 'I can see Fedor too,' Myroslav's voice came over the radio. 'He's just come out of the quarters.'

Eloise turned to Jacob. 'What about Draper?'

He had been alone, which meant he was vulnerable. 'I'll come with you,' Eloise said. She picked up her Burberry bag and followed him.

The rain started when they were on the terrace, darkening the grey stone. Eloise broke out into a trot as they crossed the lawn towards the apartments. Nazim had them dancing. 'Crazy psycho bitch,' she said. 'Where is she?'

The door was locked but they could hear an ominous soundtrack from the computer game he played. 'Draper?'

There was no answer, just the same loud drawn-out doomy synth notes.

'Draper. You OK?' called Iosef.

'Oh Christ.' Eloise put her face to the window but the curtains were closed – they always were. She slapped her hands on the glass. 'Draper!'

The music stopped. Jacob heard the door being unlocked. 'What the fuck has happened now?' Draper stood, game controller in one hand.

'He's OK,' said Eloise.

'You thought I was . . . ? What's happening?'

If Draper was OK, the only person who wasn't accounted for was Vlada. Jacob pushed past Draper and scanned the floor for his house phone.

'What the hell . . .'

He found the lead and followed it under the couch until he found what he was looking for. He dragged the phone out and dialled five.

It rang twice, three times, then Vlada finally picked up. She was abrupt. 'If you want a drink, you can fetch it yourself. I'm trying to get some sleep.'

'You're alive,' said Jacob, relieved.

'Jacob? What's wrong?'

'Stay in your room,' he told her. 'Lock the door.' He rang off and turned to Eloise. 'The note came before the last murder,' he said. 'It hasn't happened yet.'

'What are you talking about?' asked Draper, blinking in the dull light. 'What's going on?'

As Eloise explained, Jacob pulled back the blinds. The rain outside was falling steadily now from a thick grey sky. They made a space to sit on his sofa. 'So we have to get out of here,' said Jacob. 'Before it happens.'

Draper sat cross-legged on the floor in front of them.

'Christ,' said Eloise. 'My hands are shaking. Do you have any cigarettes, Draper? I need one.'

Draper shook his head. 'This place is driving me nuts. I'm with Jacob. I want out.'

'Wait. Wait. They want us to panic but they're not going to kill us,' said Eloise. 'They need us, right?' She looked around.

'Oh yeah, sure,' said Draper. 'And what do you actually do? Marketing?'

Eloise was indignant. 'It's not just marketing. All this was my idea.'

'That was exactly what your husband said and it didn't end well for –' Draper stopped. 'I mean ... I'm sorry. That was crass – even for me.'

'Quiet, please,' said Jacob. 'Let me think.'

'Let's face it, the only one with a unique skill set is Jacob here. He'll be the last one to die.'

'Thanks so much,' said Jacob. 'They don't need any of us. That's the point. They just need the system you have created. You're the only one who can get us out, Eloise. You can open the gate.'

Eloise was digging around in her bag. 'I can't think straight without a cigarette.'

Draper said, 'I mean, she could open the gate, yes. But you know what? She probably won't.'

She looked at him, half apologetic, half defiant. 'We can work with Nazim, like he wanted us to all along.'

Jacob looked at her. 'There are two dead men in the garden shed and a third on the way, and you want to stick around to find out what happens next?'

'She's not going to let go of the money,' Draper said. 'She's not going anywhere.'

'Money is that important to you?' Jacob asked her.

'What's wrong with that?'

Jacob addressed her. 'Well, let us out then. I don't want anything.'

Draper flopped back on the floor so he was looking up at the ceiling. 'Know what, Jacob? She doesn't want us to leave either. Because we're part of her grand design. She recruited both of us for this. She doesn't want to let us go.'

'I just think it's safer if you both stay, put it that way,' she said.

Draper groaned. The rain suddenly seemed to be coming down more heavily. 'I could do with a cigarette now, too.'

Jacob stood and looked out of the window. He could make out the lights of the house through the downpour.

'Where are your cigarettes?' Draper asked her, sitting up.

'I'm out. There are some in my room.'

He got up. 'I could run, right?'

Eloise wasn't going to say anything, so Jacob said it. 'There's an armed killer out there.'

'Yeah,' said Draper. 'Smoking kills, right?'

'Don't even think about it,' said Jacob.

The rain was coming down hard. The long dry spell was over. It seemed doubly dark until the lights suddenly blared.

Something had activated the motion sensors. In the blinding light, the pile of earth that marked Tamara's grave stood out. Rain was washing the loose soil down the slope of the hill.

Then the lights blinked off again.

'What was that?' Draper asked. 'Was it the fox? It does that all the time.'

'I think there's someone out there.'

The lights came on again. This time Jacob saw a dark figure running across the grass, out of the house, out across the lawn.

'Who was that?' Eloise was standing next to him, looking past his shoulder.

'I don't know.' Jacob stepped forward and checked that the door was locked.

'I'm losing it here,' said Draper.

There was a sudden bang on the door.

'Fuck!' Draper blurted.

'Who's that?' demanded Jacob.

'Stay away from the windows. Close the curtains,' shouted Fedor. 'Keep the door locked.' And then he was gone again.

Jacob pulled Draper's blinds closed.

'Well, that was reassuring,' said Draper laconically. 'I would really, really, really like a smoke now.'

'Tell me about it,' said Eloise. In the low light of Draper's room she looked pale and sunken-eyed. Draper walked over and picked up Eloise's bag and started taking things out of it. 'Hey. Leave that alone.'

'I was just checking to see if you hadn't left some in here.'

'Well, I haven't. Get your hands out of that.'

Draper dropped the bag onto the floor. 'Fedor smokes, right?'

'Yes.'

'I know where he keeps his stash. In that toolshed.'

Jacob crossed the room, took a glass from the cupboard in the kitchen area and filled it with tap water. 'Don't be stupid, Draper.'

'It's straight across the lawn. I can be back in two minutes.'

'Webb is in there,' Eloise said again. 'And my husband.'

'Yeah,' Draper replied. 'Webb doesn't smoke so much these days.'

'Don't be sick,' said Eloise.

'I can't help it. It's just nerves.' Draper was quiet for a while. As if he had suddenly made up his mind, he strode to the door, unlocked it and opened it. The rain was loud all of a sudden.

'Jesus,' said Eloise.

Draper pulled his T-shirt up over his head, exposing his skinny pale belly. 'Yeah. Well. If I'm not back in two minutes, send Lover Boy to get me.'

He set off into the darkness running. Eloise stepped forward, closed the door and locked it.

The pair of them waited, saying nothing, hearing nothing. A minute passed. Then another.

'What is Myroslav's real name then?' asked Eloise.

'His name is Vadym Melnyk. He was part of something called the Donetsk mafia before the Ukrainians kicked him out.'

'No shit,' she said. 'And how do you know all this?'

'Vlada told me.'

'And you believed her?'

'Don't you?'

Eloise wrinkled her nose. 'I mean, she would say it, wouldn't she? She hates his guts.'

Jacob went back to the window and looked out. The rain seemed to be easing.

'I don't see anything,' Jacob said. 'The lights didn't even come on. Do you think he's OK?'

Puddles had formed on the lawn. Outside everything looked still. Jacob looked at his watch. It was six in the morning now, but the low clouds made the sky dark.

'Where has he fucking gone?' Eloise asked, opening the door.

She stood by the door, Jacob by the window, peeping through a crack in the blinds, waiting for Draper to knock at the door to be let in. Outside, rain continued falling.

FORTY-FOUR

Draper had been gone ten minutes. There was still no sign of him.

'What if something happened?' asked Jacob.

'It's probably some sick stunt,' Eloise answered.

Another minute.

'Seriously, Jacob. What are you going to do when you get out of this? Are you really going to settle down in some little flat in Brighton with that woman?'

Jacob didn't answer.

'There's got to be more to life than just settling down and having babies and growing old.'

Jacob looked out of the window. It felt too long since Draper had left. Something was not right. 'I should go and check,' said Jacob. Draper had said: *If I'm not back in two minutes, send Lover Boy to get me.* He unlocked the door.

'Jesus, Jacob. Please. Don't leave me here on my own.'

He stepped out quickly. He heard Eloise turning the lock again. The air was humid and thick, the rain finally turning to drizzle.

Peering into the gloom, he took the first step cautiously, looking for any sign that there was someone hiding.

A hand dropped onto his shoulder. 'Boo!'

'What took you so long? I said two minutes. It's wet out here.'

'Shit.' When his heart finally stopped thumping he turned angrily to Draper and hissed, 'Why did you do that, Draper?'

Draper had been hiding behind the corner of the building all the time. He reached into his pocket. 'Because, this.' And he held out Eloise's wallet. 'I took it out of her handbag when I was pretending to look for cigarettes. You took long enough to come after me, you douche. I thought you understood what I was doing. Come on,' he said. 'Let's get out of here.'

'You have the code for the front gate?' whispered Jacob.

'No, the pedestrian gate. It has two sets of four numbers. Who's going to remember that? Especially as Eloise barely ever goes out on her own. I searched in her old phone but couldn't find it. So where is the other place people keep stuff they're going to forget?' He held up a small pink rectangle of paper. 'She wrote the numbers on a Post-it note which she put in her wallet.'

'Brilliant,' said Jacob, gazing at it. Written on the pink note were two sets of four numbers.

'Don't sound so surprised.'

'You sure that's it? Not just the numbers of her locker at the gym or something?'

'No, I'm not sure, actually, but it's all I have. Come on. We don't have much time.' He set off in a straight line towards the gardener's shed.

'Wait,' said Jacob, running after him and grabbing him by the shoulder so that he skidded on the wet grass. 'There's a camera aimed at the back of that building. Iosef is monitoring them. This way.' He led Draper on a route that circled well to the east of the main building, avoiding any of the sensors that he'd triggered on that first night walk, and dodging the cameras he'd seen on the laptop. The hours spent walking around the garden had finally paid off.

Eventually they stood by the sunken garage, below the staff apartments, peering across the white driveway.

'From here, we're going to be on camera,' explained Jacob. 'The moment we step out there we'll be seen. We will only have a few seconds to get to the gate, get it open, and get out, OK? You have the codes?'

Draper held up the pink note.

'Because you're only going to have one chance at this. Memorise them.'

'Jesus. Are you trying to make me more nervous than I am?'

'Memorise them. After we're out of the door, we need to run straight into the trees opposite the road. It's impossible to see into them. It's our best chance.'

They stood facing one another. Draper looked terrified. Jacob reckoned he probably looked just as bad. Draper stared at the piece of paper in his hand for a minute, lips moving.

'OK. Are you ready?'

Draper nodded.

Under his breath, Jacob counted, 'One, two, three . . .'

And they ran fast towards the pedestrian gate.

FORTY-FIVE

In the gloomy morning, the security lights blasted on, turning the driveway blinding white.

They made it to the pedestrian gate in seconds.

Jacob felt terrified – but exhilarated. He had been a prisoner here for a week. The world outside these gates had never seemed sweeter.

The keypad was illuminated and there was a small red LED showing at the top of it. 'The code,' hissed Jacob.

Draper punched four numbers. Nothing happened. The light stayed red.

'What if that's the order you need when you're coming in? Do the second number first.'

Jacob could hear someone running towards them.

'Someone at the gate. I can't see who they are. Should I shoot?' Fedor was out on the steps by the glass front door, speaking into his walkie-talkie.

This time the LED turned green and the gate buzzed, and

Jacob yanked it open and shoved Draper inside the cage, just as a shot rang out. Jacob ducked. 'Come on. Again,' he urged Draper. 'The next code.'

Another shot pinged against the metal of the gate. And then, as Draper entered the numbers, the light on the second panel turned green. The lock had opened. They were free.

The gate swung open without Jacob even touching it. A man, dressed from head to toe in black, grabbed him by the neck and was choking him.

It happened so fast, Jacob couldn't figure out what was going on. Another man already had Draper in the same hold. 'Fuck, fuck. Don't hurt me,' pleaded Draper.

There was a short, sudden burst of gunfire from close by and – from the corner of his eye – Jacob saw Fedor fall back on the wet gravel. Before Jacob could make sense of it, he was being pushed down hard. Draper was already on the ground next to him.

A third man was wrapping tape tight around their mouths. In the next seconds their captors had rolled them over onto their fronts and the same man was putting ties on their wrists.

Jacob could barely comprehend what had just occurred. In the darkness, someone was lifting him to his feet.

'*Go, go.*' The man who spoke lifted a single finger to his balaclava'd lips. *Quiet.*

Instead of escaping through the open gate, they had let the enemy inside. They must have been waiting there all this time, hoping someone would try and leave.

A gun in his back, Jacob was stumbling across the gravel

towards the front door, pushed by the same man who had tackled him to the floor in the first place.

Jacob looked to his right. Draper was being shoved forward too. It dawned on him that the men were intending to use them as shields. His heart was thumping. At his side, Draper seemed to be shaking with fear, whining gently.

Out in the open, in the middle of the driveway, the hands behind them tugged Jacob and Draper to a halt.

Jacob was conscious that the gun that had been at his back had been placed against the side of his head. He didn't dare move to check whether the same was being done to Draper, but he guessed it was.

It had been a blur. Jacob tried to piece it all together. There had been four men, Jacob calculated. Now he and Draper had been hauled onto the driveway, each with a man behind him. The other two seemed to have vanished into the gloom.

'Stop.' Jacob heard Iosef's voice, ahead of them, speaking in Russian.

From the shadows behind him out of sight came a voice he recognised, speaking in Hindi. 'Take the tape off that one's mouth.'

A hand reached forward and ripped. The gun at the back of his head moved far enough for Jacob to be able to turn and look in the direction of the voice. The speaker was completely hidden in the darkness behind them, tucked behind the cage of the entrance gate. 'What took you so long? We were about to blow the doors. Thank you for saving me the trouble. Tell Myroslav hello from me.'

'I'm not your interpreter,' said Jacob.

'As of right now, yes you are.'

'No,' said Jacob, teeth clenched. 'I am not.'

'If you're not going to translate, then I'll probably kill you because you're no use to me.'

Inside the house, behind the glass door, Iosef was calling out, 'Fedor is dead. I can see two intruders. Heavily armed.' He was standing half in view, gun raised. 'Shall I take them?'

Reluctantly, Jacob cleared his throat and spoke in English. 'Nazim is here. He says hello to Myroslav.'

Nazim laughed. 'See? It's not hard. Now tell them again, louder. Tell him to talk to me.'

Jacob shouted it this time. 'He says he wants to talk.'

There was silence.

'Tell him again.'

This time, Myroslav answered. 'Get out of my fucking house.' He was somewhere upstairs from the sound of it, behind one of the windows.

'Two intruders visible. Want me to take them?' Iosef shouted again from the floor below. He could only see two men. Nazim was still behind, lurking in the darkness by the gate, which left one unaccounted for. Jacob wondered where he had gone.

The man behind Jacob tightened his grip on him, holding him in place.

Jacob took a breath and said, 'Myroslav wants you to leave his house.'

'It's a very cool house,' acknowledged Nazim. 'You didn't talk to me when I was outside. So I had to come in. And now you want me to leave again so we can talk? I don't think so. We talk here and we talk now.'

'Tell him I'm going to count to five,' said Myroslav. 'And if he's not gone by then, we start shooting.'

Jacob hung his head. 'He says he is going to count to five.'

'One.'

Jacob looked around, desperately. He and Draper were directly in the firing line. If Iosef fired on Nazim's men, they were dead.

'Two.'

Where was the fourth man? Jacob looked around.

'Three . . .'

FORTY-SIX

Before Myroslav could say the next number, there was a loud crack.

Then a second.

Jacob flinched, trying to crouch, thinking he must have been hit, but there was no pain. What was strange to him was that the huge glass entrance door in front of them had suddenly frosted.

And then it was strangely quiet. 'Four' never came. When Jacob opened his eyes, he saw Draper had not been hurt either.

The huge glass door had a single hole in it. The entire panel had shattered around the hole. Spiderwebbed with fractures, it had remained intact.

The second door, behind it, was the same. Jacob finally figured out that a bullet had passed through both doors.

There was the sound of smashing glass from somewhere, then a figure in black appeared behind the second of the two doors. He lifted the butt of his gun and lunged at the shattered door.

Shards scattered onto the floor. He continued until there was a hole large enough for him to step through.

It was the fourth gunman, Jacob realised.

The front door that Jacob was standing in front of received the same treatment. Light shone from fragments as they fell. And then the gunman was standing in front of them beckoning them.

The men behind Jacob and Draper nudged the two of them forwards, pushing them up the steps, crunching over glass, ducking through the first ruined door and then the second.

Iosef lay on the dark wood floor, face down. A small red pool of blood was spreading in front of him.

Jacob looked up and saw that, beyond the dining table, the big window onto the garden had been shattered too. He finally understood what had happened. Glass houses were not easy to defend.

The fourth man had made it round to the back of the house and had shot Iosef from behind. That, presumably, had been the first bullet. The second had smashed the doors in front of them.

'Call for Myroslav,' said Nazim. He had emerged from his hiding place and was standing behind them. 'Tell him to come down. Nobody's going to harm him.'

It had taken maybe a minute, and it was already over. Nazim was here. Myroslav had lost. Five minutes ago Jacob had been about to escape, now he was a prisoner again.

'Maybe it's better if I go up and get him,' suggested Jacob. One of Nazim's men pulled a black-handled knife from a scabbard on his calf and motioned Jacob to turn around. Jacob felt the steel against his wrists and the cable tie that had bound them dropped to the gravel.

★

In the dawn light, Myroslav was standing in the middle of his bedroom floor, paunchy in a pair of white underpants, holding his pistol, pointing it at Jacob as he entered the room.

'They are in the house?' Myroslav asked.

'Yes,' answered Jacob. 'Iosef is dead. And Fedor too.'

Myroslav sat down on the bed heavily. 'Both of them? What about Eloise?'

'I haven't seen her. She was in Draper's apartment, so I think she must be OK.'

He nodded. 'How did they get in?'

'They came through the pedestrian gate.'

Putting the gun in the waistband of his underpants, Myroslav went and stood in front of a full-length mirror. He sucked in his chest a little and frowned. 'How?'

Before Jacob could attempt a lie, Nazim called up the stairs. 'What's happening up there? Tell him to come down.'

Jacob spoke to Myroslav. 'We should go downstairs, Mr Bondarenko. There's no point fighting. There are four of them and a lot of guns.'

Myroslav laid his hand on the holster of his gun and smiled. 'You think I should?'

'There are four of them, Myroslav. They are armed. If you die, we will all die.'

He shrugged.

'There's nothing wrong with losing, Myroslav.'

'You really think that?' he asked.

'I've a lifetime's experience.'

A small laugh. 'Exactly. You were born to lose. I was not. Those fucking NATO lovers threw me out of my own country.

291

The Americans tried to deport me. None of them have beaten me. Not yet. I never lose.'

Nazim called up the stairs. 'I can count to five too. Tell him I'll cut his balls off if he doesn't come down in a minute.'

'What did he say?'

Jacob paused and considered. 'He says he would like to talk to you. In your beautiful house.'

Myroslav thought for a minute, then nodded. 'Tell the maid to make coffee.'

Jacob approached the top of the stairs and called down. 'He wants to talk.'

FORTY-SEVEN

From below, Nazim called up, 'If he wants to talk, I want to see him. Face to face.'

Jacob turned to Myroslav, who was standing further down the corridor, his gun over his shoulder. 'Put the gun down. He promises he won't shoot.'

Myroslav said, 'Oh no. If he has a gun, I have to have a gun too. It's how this works.'

Jacob spoke to Nazim. 'He promises to come down without a gun if you put down your weapons.'

There was a short conversation in Hindi. 'Agreed.'

Jacob turned round again. 'They have put down their guns. They respectfully ask you to do the same.'

'Interesting,' said Myroslav, as if entirely pleased with the arrangement. But he came and stood in his underpants beside Jacob at the top of the stairs and laid his weapon down on the floor beside him. 'What now?'

Nazim stepped into view finally, appearing from the right.

He had removed his balaclava. He looked surprisingly young, but no less confident than he had on screen. 'Good morning, Mr Melnyk.'

'Good morning, shitbag.'

'Now we talk percentages.'

Myroslav sighed and walked downstairs, and saw the mess of glass on his floor. The two front doors were in pieces. There was a neat pair of holes in the rear sliding doors. 'You fucked my glass. You better pay for it before we talk about anything.'

Now Jacob finally had a chance to look around, he saw that Draper's skin was white. He was bleeding from the knees. It must have been where Nazim's men had forced him down onto the gravel.

Jacob explained what Myroslav had said. 'He wants you to pay for his doors.'

Nazim nodded. 'He's lucky we didn't just blow the whole gate off its hinges. That would have been really messy. We were about to do that when we heard you at the gate.'

The man who had shot Iosef appeared, dragging Eloise by her arm. She looked in horror at Iosef's body, prone on the floor, then up at the rest of the scene in the living room: Myroslav, still in his underpants; Draper, pale with shock, arms still bound, his legs bloody; the three other men in black military fatigues, semi-automatics on their shoulders.

'Come on,' said Myroslav, clapping his hands. 'Coffee.'

It was barely morning. They all sat in the living room. Eloise, Draper and Jacob sat together on one couch; Nazim perched on an armchair, Myroslav opposite him.

Two of Nazim's men had dragged Iosef's body out of the room into the garden, leaving a smear all the way down past the kitchen.

'You should probably mop the floor,' Myroslav told Vlada after she'd put the coffee on the table.

'Are you still my boss?' she muttered.

'Of course, my dear,' said Myroslav. 'And don't forget it. Clean the floor.'

Nazim took his coffee. 'I was offering you fifty-fifty. The offer still stands.'

Myroslav turned to Draper. 'Get some clean clothes on. I'm not having anyone bleeding on my Italian leather sofa. It's Poltrona Frau.'

Accompanied by one of Nazim's men, Draper disappeared down the hallway that Vlada was now slopping a mop over. The two others had sat down in the sunken area. One of them had found the remote and was flicking through the channels on the big TV. 'Tell him to switch off my fucking television,' said Myroslav. 'He is a guest.'

'Mr Bondarenko asks if you can switch off the TV,' said Jacob.

Nazim joined in the scolding. He was speaking what could be Marathi, Jacob registered, which meant his men were from Mumbai too. The men scrambled to switch off the television.

Nazim switched to Hindi again. 'Can you persuade him to make a deal with us, Jacob? He has lost. He has no choice.'

Jacob looked over at Myroslav. To Jacob's surprise, he seemed at ease, legs spread wide. Him still in his underpants, while everyone else in the room was dressed. 'Even if I wanted to, I don't think I can. He's a very stubborn man.'

'Yes. He is.' Nazim looked around. 'It really is an exceptional place. I would very much like to live in a house like this myself. I very much like the way he has decorated it.'

'What is he saying?' complained Myroslav.

'He's saying you live in a stunning house.'

'Yes, I do.'

Nazim drank his coffee to the clank of the mop in the bucket. 'Tell him I will fix his windows.'

Jacob repeated what Nazim had said.

'Of course he will,' said Myroslav, leaning forward and rubbing his hands. 'It will be a condition of doing business.'

Nazim spoke directly to Jacob again. 'It is hard for people sometimes to accept that their time is over. There is a new generation of people who understand the world in different ways. I don't want to disrespect a man who has built all this.' Nazim waved his arm around the room. 'Please tell him that I mean him no discourtesy and I would like to work with him if I can. That has been my only objective.'

'He has a hilarious way of showing his respect,' muttered Myroslav. He picked up his coffee and drank it in one gulp. 'Tell him if he wants to do business with me, he must first give me a gift.'

'A gift?' said Nazim, puzzled. 'What kind of gift?'

Myroslav shrugged and stood. He padded back up the stairs to his room, acting for all the world as if it had been him who had won the shoot-out, not Nazim.

'What kind of gift?' Nazim repeated, frustrated. 'What does he need? He has a boat, a helicopter, a Lamborghini in the garage. Is he mad?'

Nazim ordered his men to tidy up the place. He asked Vlada for a broom and spent a while sweeping the shattered glass from the floor himself.

He billeted the men in Iosef, Webb and Fedor's rooms, now that they were free.

'Ask Mr Melnyk if there is another room for me,' he told Jacob.

Myroslav returned to the living room in jeans and trainers. He went and inspected the floor where Iosef had been shot. 'His men are in the service apartments? Then tell him all the rooms are taken right now, but I can recommend a hotel.'

Nazim asked Jacob to fetch him a dustpan.

One of the men left through the gate and returned a few minutes later in a hired van. He unloaded their bags from the back of it and disappeared with them to their new quarters.

The afternoon passed uneasily.

That evening one of Nazim's men cooked chicken Makhani with delicately flavoured rice. Nazim insisted they all join him for dinner. He had changed from his black combat gear into jeans and a loose white shirt and his hair was gelled back neatly. He suddenly looked much more like a Silicon Valley executive than a Mumbai thug.

'I'm not sitting down to eat with that bastard.' Eloise refused to sit at the table. 'My husband is dead thanks to him. Who was it? Which one of you killed him?' She looked around the room accusingly.

'Please,' said Nazim. One of his men led her to a dining chair and put his hand on her shoulder, pressing until she finally lowered herself onto it.

'I do not like Indian food. Have Vlada make me something,' said Myroslav loudly.

'It's the first night off she's had,' said Draper. 'Let her have a break, for Christ's sake.'

Myroslav looked amused at being talked to like that. For a second, Jacob wondered if he was going to stand up and slap him, but instead he grunted and took a bowl of rice, and just ordered Vlada to fetch him a bottle of St-Émilion. None of Nazim's men drank, so he kept the bottle close to his own glass and refilled it the moment it was empty.

'I hope I can make you believe that I want to be your friend, Mr Melnyk,' said Nazim. 'You represent a type of business that I can learn a lot from. But you are living in the past, and we are living in the future.'

Myroslav grunted. 'Tell him his mother is a whore.'

Jacob said nothing.

Nazim continued. 'Our people are everywhere. We have connections that you can only dream of, the world over. But first I have to persuade you that we are on the same side.'

They finished the meal in awkward silence. Finally Nazim stood. 'I would like to suggest a toast,' he said, holding up a glass of water. 'To our new friendship.'

Myroslav ignored him. In the end, Nazim sat down again.

'I have been thinking what it is that I can give Mr Melnyk as a goodwill gift,' said Nazim. 'It's clear that he is a man who already has the best possessions. I am a man from the slums. He would probably think my own tastes vulgar. So instead, I want to give him something that he doesn't have.'

Hesitantly, unsure of how this was going, Jacob translated for Myroslav. For the first time Myroslav looked intrigued.

'I will give him the gift of information.'

Myroslav put his fork down, picked up the glass and took a small sip. 'What kind of information?'

'There is a traitor in his organisation. Here in this room.'

Jacob paused in his translation, waiting for Nazim to finish.

'Someone who has been in contact with the outside world. Someone who will jeopardise his chance of this operation running smoothly in whatever days it has left to run.'

When he spoke, he was looking directly at Jacob.

'You want me to tell him that?'

From his pocket he pulled out a pistol and aimed it at Jacob. 'I want you to tell him my words, exactly.'

Jacob spoke quietly, looking down at his own untouched plate. 'He is again saying that there is a spy in your organisation.'

The table was suddenly very quiet. 'What? Who?' Jacob raised his head. Myroslav looked from Eloise to Draper, and then to Jacob.

Nazim didn't take his eyes off Jacob.

Jacob thought of the poem he had persuaded Eloise to send to the publisher in Lisbon. It had been called 'The First Lyric of Our Song'.

FORTY-EIGHT

The gun was pointing directly at Jacob's head. He was going to die, now, because of the stupid poem. Nazim must have discovered the message he had concealed in it. It was not a real poem. He had made it up.

It began:

> *Away from you*
> *Everything is grey*
> *Empty*
> *Arid.*
> *Strange feeling*
> *Deep longing*
> *Such sadness*
> *Your ambition is unattainable*
> *Were I a millionaire,*
> *You would be by my side . . .*

It was a code, and one that was invisible to anyone who spoke English or Russian. In translation, the title of his poem, 'The First Lyric of Our Song', became '*Primeira letra da nossa cançao*'. In Portuguese *letra* meant 'lyric', but also 'letter'. That was the clue. The first letter . . . If they were smart, it pointed the reader towards an acrostic that would only reveal itself to someone who understood Portuguese:

> *Longe de ti*
> *É tudo cinza*
> *Vazio*
> *Arido.*
> *Estranho sentimento*
> *Saudade imensa*
> *Tanta tristeza*
> *Ambição desmedida, a tua.*
> *Milionário eu fosse*
> *Estarías junto de mim . . .*

L-E-V-A-E-S-T-A-M-E . . .

The first few letters spelled the words, *Leva esta mensagem para CIA*: 'Get this message to the CIA.' The rest of the long poem spelled out everything he had learned up to that point and urged the reader to track down Agent Murphy and get this message to him.

Except there was no Agent Murphy of the CIA and Murphy was dead now anyway. The message that he had been so clever to write had been pointless.

'A few days ago someone sent a message from your house.

301

They wanted to betray you,' said Nazim, still fixing the gun on Jacob. 'Mr Melnyk, I said I would give you a gift and I will. I will tell you who your traitor is. Who do you think has betrayed you?'

'Seriously?' said Jacob in Hindi. 'You want me to translate that?'

'If you don't, I will kill you.' Nazim pulled back the slide on the top of the pistol and let it spring back into place with a loud click.

Jacob looked into the barrel and did what he was told.

'It is him.' Myroslav pointed at Jacob. He shrugged. 'I never trusted him much.'

Sweat prickled on Jacob's forehead.

Nazim, however, seemed delighted by the answer. He lowered the gun. 'Sun Tzu said that the secret of a successful attack is to confuse your enemy. I believe I succeeded exceptionally well. No. It is not him.'

Jacob blinked. He looked around, heart thumping.

Nazim continued to speak. 'I started getting messages from one of your people several days ago. This person wanted to cut a deal with me behind your back. So I told them they had to complete some tasks for me. If it was not the interpreter, who else do you think it could have been?'

Eloise stood up. 'He's playing you, Myroslav. That's what he's been doing these last few days. You know that, don't you?'

Nazim's gun was on her now. 'Tell the lady to sit down.'

She sat back down in her dining chair. 'Jesus. It's not me, Myroslav. I swear it's not. I wouldn't do that.'

'Of course you would,' said Myroslav. 'Did you kill your own husband too, to stop him getting a share?'

'No. No. God, no.'

But Jacob knew who it was now. Out of the corner of his eye, Jacob looked towards him and knew he was right. Draper's pale face was whiter than usual.

The gun swung slowly round to aim at the American. 'Draper?' Myroslav looked puzzled.

'Eloise is right. Don't believe this bullshit,' said Draper. 'Check my email. I never sent anything. How would I know how to find him, anyway?'

'He had my number,' explained Nazim. 'I don't know how. I received a message from a friend of his – it came to my Signal. A friend who he talks with when he's playing his games online.'

Draper had used him to make it look like Nazim had burst in by chance when they were attempting an escape, when all along he had known Nazim was there. Draper had deliberately exploited him to hide his own complicity.

'I don't get it. How did he even know how to get in touch with Nazim?' demanded Eloise when Jacob had repeated what Nazim had said. 'I'm the only person with Nazim's contact details.'

'Your phone,' said Jacob quietly. He remembered what Draper had told him about looking for the door code in Eloise's iPhone. 'You gave it to him to fix, remember?'

The American looked terrified.

'You killed my fucking husband,' said Eloise, staring at Draper, horrified.

'Hey,' said Draper, becoming desperate. 'Don't believe him. Do I look like the kind of guy who would do that? Would I even be capable of it? I faint at the sight of blood.'

'I told him to open the gate this morning,' said Nazim. 'How else did I get in here? I told him to kill someone. I didn't really care who.'

Jacob didn't translate what Nazim said. He didn't have to. Myroslav was piecing it together by himself. 'He let those men in. He opened the gate deliberately.'

Draper said, 'Seriously?'

Eloise was shaking with anger. 'Stop pretending, Draper. Stop it! Stop all this *acting* you've been doing.'

Draper's shoulders slumped.

Eloise turned to Nazim and said, 'You ordered him to kill my husband?'

Nazim looked her in the eye. 'I didn't choose your husband. He did. So tell Mr Melnyk, that is my present to him.'

Myroslav poured himself another glass of St-Émilion, raised it and drained the whole glass. 'Do you box, Draper?' he asked, speaking in English.

'Oh, come *on*. You're not serious.'

'Don't,' warned Jacob.

'Do you box?'

'Of course I don't box.' Draper giggled anxiously. 'I'm a white guy from Upper New York State who spends his life playing games on the computer. I have bad eyesight and can barely run a mile without having a heart attack.'

'Fight me.'

Draper was scared. 'I can't.'

Myroslav stood up and began to unbutton his shirt.

Nazim may not have understood the conversation but he seemed to understand exactly what was happening. He nodded

304

at one of his men. Before Draper knew what was happening, that man was lifting him out of his chair.

Shirt off now, Myroslav strode out onto the terrace and started limbering up, throwing punches at nothing.

'We have to stop this,' said Jacob, looking around, standing.

'Do we?' Eloise remained seated, her face dark.

Jacob strode out to the terrace. Nazim's man had his arms under Draper's armpits and was dragging him out of the room, to where Myroslav was waiting.

'You understand Russian boxing? First you punch me, then I punch you.'

'Fuck. He's going to kill me.'

'Myroslav. Don't,' shouted Jacob. He was inches from Myroslav's face. Myroslav stopped.

'Don't?' Myroslav frowned at him.

Jacob shouted. 'Please! Please don't do this.'

Myroslav cocked his head to one side, ran his hand through his greying hair. 'No. You're right,' he said finally, with a smile. 'Thank you, Jacob. I was getting carried away.'

He walked back into the house, picked his shirt back off the chair and started buttoning it again.

Jacob looked back at Draper, standing, still terrified on the terrace, unsure what to do.

'Jesus, man. Thank you. He would have fucking slaughtered me.'

When Myroslav had completed his buttons he walked around the table to Nazim's chair. 'You are welcome to stay here, of course,' he said. 'A room has just become free.' He held out his hand. 'May I?'

'What is he saying?' Nazim demanded, puzzled, looking at Myroslav's out-held hand.

Slow to understand what was happening, Jacob told him, 'He says a room has just become free and you are welcome to stay in it.'

'Oh,' said Nazim, as if he finally understood something. Jacob got it now too, as he watched Nazim reach into his pocket and pull out the pistol which he had been aiming at Jacob only a few minutes ago, and give it to Myroslav.

Myroslav nodded thanks and, before anyone could say another word, strode straight back out of the room through the shattered glass doors again.

There was a single shot.

Myroslav handed the gun back to Nazim.

'So do we have a deal?'

'For now,' said Myroslav. He held out his hand again.

Nazim took it, and they shook rather formally. 'Don't worry about software developers. I can find another. In India they're like rats.'

Through the cracked glass, Jacob watched as one of the men arrived with a wheelbarrow from the shed. They lifted Draper's body, dropped him into it and wheeled him out into the darkness, limbs flopping over the side of it as he bumped down the stone staircase.

FORTY-NINE

'A man is coming to fix the windows,' said Nazim. 'All is arranged. At least we didn't have to use the explosives. That would have made a real mess.'

'What explosives?' Myroslav poured himself more wine. 'Are you crazy?'

'Show him.'

One of the men disappeared and returned a short while later with a small grey package.

For the first time today, there was a note of admiration in Myroslav's voice. 'Let me have it.'

Nazim nodded and the man stood and approached Myroslav with the small rectangular pack. The explosive was wrapped in cloth, strapped around with black rubber. A couple of yellow wires ran from a simple circuit board with a calculator-style read-out to what must have been the detonator.

Myroslav reached a hand out to touch it, but the man pulled it away before he could. 'What is it? C-4?'

307

'RDX,' said one of the men.

'It's the same,' said Myroslav grudgingly. 'We used it in the army. I love it.'

'You're monsters. I never wanted anything to do with this,' said Jacob in Hindi.

'I wanted to be born a prince,' said Nazim. 'I grew up in shit. Life is hard,' he said, looking around. 'It has been a long day. And then, in the morning, the real work begins. Because we are a team now.' He beamed. 'Together, yes?'

Jacob locked his door behind him and ran a shower.

He was about to undress and step in when he heard someone letting themselves into the apartment below, then the sound of a vacuum cleaner. It would be Vlada, preparing the room for Nazim.

Switching off the shower, he went downstairs.

He opened the door and watched her for a minute, pulling the nozzle over Draper's dirty carpet. She had already packed much of Draper's stuff into bin bags.

Turning to move an armchair, she stopped, turned off the machine and looked at him.

'I'm sorry. I tried to help. Now everything's worse.'

'Is it? I hadn't noticed.' She gave him a small smile. 'We are living among degenerates and savages,' she said. 'Sometimes I think it will make me a monster myself.'

He looked around the room. 'I don't know what to do any more.'

'You can strip the bed for a start,' she said.

When he'd bundled up the sheets, she joined him in the bedroom, running the vacuum around the floor. Then they both made the bed with clean sheets, standing on each side of it.

By the time the room was ready it was after midnight.

'Thank you,' he said. 'It's the first normal thing I've done since I got here.'

She laughed hollowly. 'You are welcome. Any time you like.'

Taking his hand, she squeezed it and said, 'You mustn't lose hope. You lose that and everything is over.' She held his hand for what felt like a very long time.

When he went upstairs, Eloise was in his room. 'Where were you?' she said. 'I let myself in. I didn't want to be alone.'

He remembered the tough, smart-looking executive who had stood outside his flat in Brighton. She looked puffy-faced and scared.

That night they lay together side by side in his double bed, neither of them sleeping. At some point she got up. 'Mind if I put the air con on?'

He told her he didn't.

The low hum was reassuring. Before dawn, he heard Eloise crying, but kept his back to her.

In the morning he woke from something close to sleep and realised he was in bed alone. Eloise had showered and was standing by the bed in a T-shirt. 'All this will be over soon. It'll be like a dream.'

'Really? You think?' He got up, shaved and dressed with her watching. Standing in his living room, he looked over towards the shed, hidden behind the acacia tree. 'What are they going to do with the bodies?' Jacob asked.

'Bury them with Tamara, I guess,' she said. There were four now. Jacob doubted they would bury them on the grounds. That would be too risky. They would have to dispose of them somewhere, though.

'So what now? We wait until Nazim and Myroslav decide that they have made enough money?'

'I don't know,' Eloise answered. She sat down on the couch.

'And you think they'll just pay us and let us go after that?'

'I don't know,' she repeated tetchily.

'Seriously?'

A little before nine there was a light knock on the door, and when Jacob answered it, Vlada was standing at the door in her jogging bottoms, her hair as much of a mess as she could make it. She looked past Jacob and saw Eloise sitting there in just a T-shirt.

'It's not what you think,' said Jacob.

'You don't know what I think,' replied Vlada stonily.

'Can you fetch another coffee for me, honey?' Eloise said, and she rose, approached Jacob and put her hand round his waist. 'An Americano, with hot milk on the side? And can you fetch me a packet of my cigarettes? They're in my dressing table.'

Vlada left and returned ten minutes later with a tray with coffee on it, with warm milk on the side and a single packet of Marlboro Lites, without saying a single word.

'Is this some special blend?' asked Eloise after she'd drunk half a cup. 'I don't know. It tastes kind of different. I can't put my finger on it.'

★

Later that morning one of Nazim's men came by. 'They want you to write some things for the website,' he said in English.

'OK,' said Eloise.

'No. Not you. The man.'

'Me?' Jacob asked.

'But I do the marketing. I should be there.' Eloise looked puzzled.

'They just want him.' The man pointed at Jacob.

'I think you'll find they'll need me,' she said.

But the man blocked the door. 'Nazim said you have to stay here.'

Jacob looked back as he crossed the lawn. She was standing looking over the first-floor balcony, a cigarette in her hand.

Nazim and Myroslav were at the dining table, an open laptop and cups of half-drunk coffee in front of them.

'Did you sleep well?' Nazim asked.

'Not really.'

'You and the Australian woman. You are friends?'

'You had her husband murdered. She was upset.'

'Of course,' said Nazim. 'I'm sure you were able to comfort her.' He pushed the laptop he had been working on across the table. 'Write this in Portuguese,' he said, handing him a piece of paper torn from a notebook.

Jacob read it: *Due to high demand, only limited supplies of Lutinol are available. We recommend ordering the full course of treatment as we cannot ensure supply over the coming weeks.*

Jacob read it and looked up. 'I'm not doing that.'

Nazim seemed to have expected this. He nodded. 'You don't think it is right?'

'No, I don't.'

He picked up a biro from the table. 'You think the world needs more babies?'

'I don't think that should be up to me.'

Nazim flicked the pen round in his hand. It spun a hundred and eighty degrees and came back to rest in the dip between his forefinger and his thumb, the kind of movement that he must have practised over and over to get it perfect. He did it again, and again. 'You worry about rich women who can afford to put off having babies until they are old more than you worry about yourself?'

'I'm not doing it,' said Jacob. 'That's the end of it. Can I go now?'

'I'm sorry to have to do this,' said Nazim. 'Fetch the Australian woman, the one you slept with last night.'

Eloise arrived two minutes later, looking vindicated. 'So? What does he want me to do?' she asked Jacob.

Instead of addressing her, Nazim spoke directly to Jacob. 'It's simple. If you don't cooperate, I will hurt her.'

Back in Jacob's apartment, Eloise said, 'He didn't mean it. He just wanted to make sure you did the work. All this was my idea. Nazim was just messing with your head.'

She was scared, though. Arms crossed, she scratched at the skin of her upper arms with her painted fingernails.

FIFTY

By evening, the website was functioning again and money was flowing into the account in Singapore.

The next day Jacob woke early. Eloise had stayed over again. She had brought pyjamas this time. 'I don't want to be alone,' she had said.

Jacob stood looking out of the window as dawn broke over the mountains behind them. At seven in the morning the lawn sprinklers came on, as if they too were pretending that the world was perfectly normal. But Fedor was dead and after only two days the grass was already starting to look unkempt.

There was a pile of cigarette butts outside his door, left there by Eloise. Nobody came to clean up after her any more.

When Eloise woke he made coffee himself rather than disturb Vlada. 'They're going to kill us both, you know,' he said.

'I don't believe it. I'm smart. They need me,' she said again. 'This isn't the only scheme I've thought of. There's a shit load of potential in the luxury food and beauty market right now.

Did you know that there's only, like, seventeen hundred tonnes of Manuka honey produced each year, and about ten times as much as that is actually sold?'

She took her coffee outside and lit another cigarette.

He joined her. 'If you don't want to get out, are you going to help me escape?'

She held the burning cigarette in one hand, the coffee cup in the other. 'I would love to do that,' she said, 'but it's not that simple. I want to help you, I promise. But if you get out of here, you'll go straight to the police, won't you?'

'Obviously.'

'See?'

One of Nazim's men had emerged from the shed carrying a blue barrel with a black lid, the kind of thing people use to store chemicals in. Jacob watched him, curious.

Nazim appeared from below, making his way across the lawn. 'Hey!' Eloise called out to him. 'I would like to talk to you.'

He stopped and looked back up at her.

'Ask him if I can review the sales figures. I could maybe suggest some marketing angles.'

'What does she want?' Nazim spoke to him in Hindi.

'She wants to help you.'

Nazim turned away. 'Tell her we do not need her right now.'

'Sexist little fucker,' she said, when he told her what Nazim had said. 'He doesn't believe all this is me, does he?'

Next time Jacob looked, there were four blue plastic barrels at the back of the shed.

★

'Where is your girlfriend?' Vlada asked when she came over with two bowls of vichyssoise for lunch.

'She's not my girlfriend,' said Jacob, looking at the soup suspiciously.

'Don't worry. I didn't wee in that one,' Vlada said.

'She's gone to talk to Myroslav' he said. 'She's worried that Nazim is going to cut her out of her share, worried that she isn't getting the credit for all this.'

'How do people become so greedy?' She flopped down across the couch, legs up on the arm of it.

'There has to be a way out of here,' he said.

She didn't say anything, just stared up at the ceiling for a long time.

'They'll kill us all in the end, won't they? They can't afford for us to tell the authorities what they do. They'll never let us go.'

When he looked at her again, her eyes were closed. He tiptoed over to the window and pulled down the blinds.

She had only been asleep for ten minutes when Eloise came back, furious. 'Basically, they told me to bog off. I could be helping. I could be streamlining this operation. And you're no help.' She looked down at Vlada, lying on the couch, blinking back at her. 'What's she doing here?'

'She was resting. You just woke her up.'

'I didn't know,' Eloise protested. 'Is that my soup?' she asked.

'Yes,' said Vlada, sitting up and rubbing her eyes. 'If you like, I can warm it.' She heated the bowl in the microwave in Jacob's kitchen, then sat watching Eloise eat it.

'Nazim is just an arrogant little man. He doesn't believe a

woman could have come up with all this.' She took another spoonful. 'You should give me the recipe,' Eloise said.

'It's a secret,' said Vladyslava.

'I don't cook much anyway,' said Eloise. 'When I'm a millionaire, I'll employ you to work for me. That would be cool, wouldn't it? You're amazing, you know that?'

'I would sooner kill you than work for you.'

Eloise laughed, as if she believed Vlada was joking.

'You think you're actually going to get your money when all this is done?' asked Jacob.

'Why wouldn't I? It's what I'm owed.' She looked out of the window. 'Hey. What's that guy doing out there?'

A man was kneeling by one of the barrels with an electric hand drill, making holes in the side of it with what looked like a keyhole bit. He drilled about a dozen large holes in the barrel, then moved on to the next one.

'Have you finished?' Vlada stacked the bowls. 'I should get back.'

'We need to get out of here. All three of us,' said Jacob.

'I'm not going anywhere,' said Eloise. 'Not until I get my money.'

Vlada looked at Jacob, then spoke. 'Nazim betrayed Draper because he had no use for him. What happens when they've got no more use for you?'

'You don't understand. This is my operation. It was my idea. I understand how it works. Nazim's not that stupid. Look.' She pointed towards the lawn. 'What the hell are they doing out there?'

Nazim's man was carrying weights from the gym across the lawn. He dropped them by the four blue barrels.

'Nazim wouldn't just kill me.'

'Tell me about Rakesh Garg,' Jacob said.

She frowned. 'Why are you asking about him?'

'He was your business partner, yes?'

She nodded. 'I came across him on the dark web when I was researching this project. He had a friend who worked in pharmaceuticals. Rakesh paid him to use his factory after hours. That's why our stuff looked so good. It was made in the same place as the real thing.'

'What happened to him, Eloise?'

'He sold the business to Nazim.'

'Have you heard from him since?'

She lowered her head a little.

'I bet he thought he was indispensable too.'

'Shut up, why don't you now? You're being a pain in the ass.' She picked at the skin around her nails.

Vlada looked from Jacob to Eloise. 'He was killed?'

'Yes, he was. Wasn't he, Eloise? You saw the photograph. It was him.'

'I couldn't see it properly.'

'It was a man's head, wasn't it?'

Eloise stared at him. 'How did you know?'

Jacob thought of the photograph of the body in the Norwegian newspaper. They had found it in the Thames but they had not found the head, the police had told journalists. The time frame fitted.

'Was it?'

She smiled tightly. 'It was a prop or something. Some photo off the web. And then it was gone and I couldn't be sure.'

'Everyone lies in this house, right?' Jacob said quietly. 'You knew, the moment you saw it, it was Rakesh Garg. You've known all along. You just choose to pretend not to. You lied from day one and now it's going to bite you in the arse.'

Eloise lowered her head again.

'These people don't care about shit,' Vlada said. 'Each of them thinks they are the genius behind everything.' She put the bowls on the tray and walked to the door. Jacob went to open it for her. 'Promise me,' she said quietly, 'if you get out, you will look for my mother and son.'

'You'll come with me, won't you?' asked Jacob, puzzled.

He watched her walking across the lawn with the tray. She paused halfway across to look at the barrels.

Jacob knew what they were for. There was one for each body. They had put weights in each barrel. Myroslav was planning to seal them and sink them to the bottom of the Milstätter See.

It wasn't until later, when they were trying to watch some awful film with Hugh Grant on Netflix, that he looked over at Eloise and realised she was crying again.

'Really?' he said. 'I didn't take you for someone who cried at romantic comedy.'

She punched him hard on the arm. 'It's not the stupid film.'

He paused the film. Hugh Grant and Drew Barrymore stopped mid-song. 'You get it now, don't you?' he said. 'Vlada is right. Unless we do something, they're going to kill us all.'

FIFTY-ONE

With nothing to do, the afternoon passed achingly slowly. Jacob tried to go for a walk around the grounds, thinking of a way to get out of here, but one of Nazim's men came after him and told him to go back to his rooms.

Back in the apartment, Eloise was lying on the bed.

'Have you been smoking in here?' he asked.

'Call the police,' she said.

He lay on the bed next to her, exhausted, trying to think. Eloise rolled over, took his arm.

At eight that night, Vlada banged on the door. 'Dinner,' she said. She had brought two steaks.

Eloise got up and answered the door. 'I didn't ask for steak.'

'Tough,' said Vlada, barging in with the tray. 'Tonight I cooked steak.'

'You didn't bring any wine,' Eloise complained.

Jacob emerged from the bedroom and joined them.

'You drink too much,' said Vlada. She pulled out a chair at

the dining table and sat down alongside them. 'You two want to get out of here?'

Eloise and Jacob exchanged a look. 'Yes. We do,' said Eloise.

'Then shut up for a minute and listen to me,' said Vlada, lowering her voice. She turned the TV on, switched the volume up loud. They joined her, sitting at the table. Vlada looked at Jacob. 'I have a way in which you can escape. It's dangerous, but I think it can be done.'

'You?' Eloise sounded surprised.

'Every day I think about escaping. I have thought of every possible way out of here. Every vehicle that goes in and out. At night I ask the foxes how they come in and out, but they would never tell me.'

Jacob said, 'How do we do it?'

Vlada reached across the table and took his hand. 'First, you have to promise me. You must find out what happened to my son and my mother.'

He was shocked. 'You're not coming?'

'I can't. I don't trust Myroslav not to punish them if I run away. He would do it.'

She was silent a while to let that sink in. 'Yes. He probably would. But if you don't come with us, they'll know I will have gone to the police. They'll be expecting a raid. They may feel they have to get rid of you, just like they're going to get rid of those bodies.'

She tightened her grip on his hand. 'I will look after myself.'

'Hold on,' said Eloise. 'So if you come with us, your child may die. If you don't come with us, you may die. I mean, fuck.'

'I've thought it through,' said Vlada. 'Believe me. This is the best chance I have. You go, and I stay. You must find my family. He may kill me, he may not. But he will definitely do something to my mother and son if I go. Their best chance is for me to stay.'

'Jesus,' said Eloise.

'OK,' said Vlada, sitting up straight. 'Are you agreed?'

Jacob shook his head. 'We can't do that. We can't just leave you here.'

'She's right, though,' said Eloise. 'We have to.'

'There's one chance to get away and it's tonight.' And she explained the plan. 'We take two of the bodies out of the barrels . . .'

It took her about a minute to explain the plan.

'That is clever,' said Jacob. 'Go through it again.'

She did so. This time, Jacob added a few details. Vlada considered them, nodded vigorously. 'Good,' she said. 'Good.'

'I'm in,' he said. 'Eloise?'

Eloise looked at each of them in turn. 'Before I agree to it, I have a condition.'

They both turned towards her.

'We don't have much time.' Vlada glowered. 'It's now or not at all. We have to be quick.'

'I'll do it,' Eloise announced. 'But only if you agree to what I say . . .'

Ten minutes later Vlada left the apartment, heading back to the kitchen again. Both plates were empty. She left the door half open behind her. A few minutes later another person emerged from the the half-open door, stooping low, working round the edge of the apartment block, sticking to the routes no cameras could see.

FIFTY-TWO

At around three in the morning, the big metal front gate slid back.

With only its sidelights on, a minivan drove out of the main entrance, turning left to head slowly down the track towards the lakeside. It drove slowly, as if the driver was doing his best to attract no attention.

It was a warm, clear night. The storm had cleared the air. A half-moon cast pale shadows beneath the acacia trees.

Half an hour later the security lights at the rear of the house came on. In the glare, the garden looked unnaturally green, the shadows unnaturally dark. Roused by an alarm, one of Nazim's men came out of the main house, gun over his shoulder, and looked wearily around.

The lights went off and he turned to go back inside, but immediately they came straight back on again.

Fully awake now, the man unclipped a pistol, took a torch

from his utility belt and put it alongside the barrel of the gun. He shone it across the garden, swinging it slowly left and right, cautiously shining the torch across the undulating lawn.

Something moved.

The man tensed. He raised his gun – then relaxed as he caught sight of the fox. Just a fox, staring back at him, two eyes glowing in the torchlight. It must have been the fox that had triggered the motion sensor, he decided.

He looked a while longer and the smile left his face.

Something was wrong. In the beam, the fox's muzzle shone red.

Curious now, the guard walked forward again, then stopped, staring at something in the light of his torch.

He spun around. Running back to the house, he was shouting, 'Wake up!'

Soon lights were coming on all over the mansion. Nazim appeared from the apartment block in a pair of Myroslav's white silk pyjamas.

'What the hell is it?'

'Look,' said the guard, pointing.

Two bodies lay on the ground just behind the garage, tucked just a little way into the shelter of the laurel bushes. One was Iosef, the other Draper. The fox had been eating Draper's face, pulling the already loose flesh from around his mouth, leaving his white teeth exposed.

Two bodies that were supposed to be on their way into the lake by now, driven to the boathouse in the minivan, along with Webb and Fedor, to be dropped down into the deep water in the blue containers.

It took Nazim a beat to figure out what must have happened. He shouted across the garden to the guard who had been stationed outside the apartment block. 'Check the Englishman's rooms.'

The guard emerged from the flat. 'Gone. Both gone. The Australian gone too.'

'Call the boat,' said Nazim, sounding angry for the first time. 'Tell them not to drop the bodies.'

The guard pulled out a mobile phone. The call was short.

'They dropped them in the water ten minutes ago,' the man said. 'They are almost back at the shore now.'

'Tell them to go back and look for two people swimming to the shore.' Nazim swore.

'What?'

'Jacob and the woman were in those barrels. They used them to escape in.'

The house was alive now. Lights on everywhere. 'Who can fly the helicopter?' shouted Nazim, then turned around.

Myroslav, in yellow silk boxer shorts, a black sleep mask perched on the top of his head, was leaning out of the bedroom window in the apartment block. 'What the fuck is going on?'

The two remaining guards jumped into the SUV and disappeared out of the gates. A few seconds later the lights came on at the helicopter pad. Myroslav turned on the engines and by the time Nazim came to join him they were ready to lift off up into the night sky.

The roar of the engine became quieter as the helicopter rose into the night air. It switched a beam on, illuminating the pad it hovered over. Soon it was heading out over the lake.

The house became oddly quiet. The fox re-emerged, heading for where the bodies were, to recommence its work.

The next time the security light came on, there was nobody there to worry about what was happening. Two figures emerged from their hiding place behind the trees, and made their way to the garage.

A minute later the garage doors slid open and a low yellow car rolled slowly out onto the gravel. As it approached the front gate, the gate began to roll slowly back again, until there was a big enough gap for it to pass through. About 100 metres down the narrow lane to the right of the gate, the driver sped up. The quiet of the early hours was broken by the deafening roar of an expensive car engine.

Loose stones spat from its wheels as it wound its way up the steep track.

Above the garage, silhouetted at a window, a lone woman watched as the headlights disappeared over the hill.

Tymko

I hope you get this letter one day. I am not sure how you will.

I did what I could to get back to you, but I'm afraid it was never enough. I hope you grow up into a good man. Good men are rare but they are worth a thousand of the other kind.

There is a man who has gone to find you and Baba. His name is Jacob. I hope he does what he says he is going to do, and that he takes you and Baba somewhere safe.

I loved you so much. That's all I have time to say.

Your mother V xxx

FIFTY-THREE

The bargain Jacob and Vlada had made with Eloise was a simple one. Instead of going straight to the police or the British Embassy, he would give her a couple of hours to escape. The borders to Italy and Slovenia were close. Once she was safely away, then Jacob could speak to the authorities. She just needed a head start, she said.

Acceleration pushed Jacob backwards in his seat. 'Jesus.'

'Slow down,' shouted Eloise, sitting in the passenger seat beside him. 'You'll get us noticed.'

'How are we not going to get noticed?' They were driving a yellow Lamborghini.

'We can't get stopped by the police.'

'Right now I would bloody love to be stopped by the police,' Jacob said, looking in the rear-view mirror.

'Fuck you. I agreed to escape with you on the condition I would be given a fair chance to get away.'

It had been Vlada's plan to remove two of the bodies from

328

the blue containers and to replace them with bags of sand, taken from Fedor's shed.

She had guessed rightly that when they found the bodies still at the house they would assume that Jacob and Eloise had taken their places.

Villach was still half an hour away down the A10. Now they were on the main road, he slowed to keep the speed below 130 km/h. Dawn was breaking over the peaks of the Nockberge – clean, summer light, pink on the mountain tops. The interior of the car was tiny, the dashboard black, littered with digital symbols he didn't understand. It wasn't like any vehicle he had driven before.

Clutching the small steering wheel, he drove, windows half open, breathing free air for what felt like the first time in an age, listening to the roar of the engine behind them. Soon they would part ways. She would disappear somewhere.

'Vlada's plan.'

Eloise grinned. 'Pretty fucking good.'

'The steak to attract the fox. She knew that if she put steaks out, she would attract the foxes and they would find the bodies and trigger the lights.'

Following Jacob's map of the dead zones where the alarms would not be triggered, they had taken both bodies from the barrels and dragged them into the darkness beneath the laurel bushes. After the van had left, Jacob sneaked out a second time to heave them out to where they could not be missed when the foxes, lured by a trail of meat, would trigger the lights.

Eloise looked out of the window, then reached forward to the shoulder bag that she had stowed between her feet, pulled out a bottle of water and offered him some. He shook his head.

Driving below the speed limit, a motorbiker passed them, giving them a wave. Coming in the opposite direction, a trucker flashed his lights.

'What's wrong?' Jacob asked.

Eloise pulled the water bottle from her lips and laughed. 'Nothing's wrong. You're the man driving the Lamborghini Huracán. That makes you the guy. You are the fucking guy!'

'Do you think Nazim has noticed we've gone yet?'

'Relax,' she said. 'He's probably still looking for us in the lake.'

The car was almost certainly fitted with a tracker. That's why they had to ditch it as soon as they were in a town, somewhere they could disappear into the crowd.

He checked in the rear-view mirror to see if there was anything following them, but the road behind was empty. That's when he noticed the light, low in the dark western sky.

'It could take them ages to search the lake, especially at night.' Eloise sounded excited. 'Or maybe they think we never got out of the barrels and drowned. You're paranoid. We made it.'

When he looked a second time, the light seemed a little closer. It was definitely not a star. It was an aircraft of some kind, flying above the road. Turning a bend, it disappeared behind the hillside, but when the highway straightened again, there it was, still behind them.

'What's wrong?' asked Eloise.

'Is that a helicopter?' He took a hand off the wheel and pointed at the the light in the rear-view mirror.

Eloise undid her seatbelt and turned in the small seat. She didn't answer.

'Myroslav?' Jacob asked.

'Shit.' She dropped back into her chair. 'It's getting closer. How did he catch on so bloody fast? He must have some kind of motion alarm on the car.'

Jacob pressed his foot onto the accelerator. The digital readout shot up towards 200 km/h.

'Jesus,' she said. 'It must have triggered something on his phone.'

He swung into the outside lane to overtake the biker who had waved at them minutes before. The car ate up the road.

'Slow down. You'll draw attention to us,' she hissed.

A road sign told him Villach was still twenty kilometres away. 'We need to get to cover.'

At this speed, Villach would be less than ten minutes away now. Ahead, traffic slowed for a tunnel. When they emerged, Eloise said, 'Stop here. There's a *Rastplatz*.' A rest place.

This time of night it would be deserted, so it wouldn't be a good idea. He needed to be with people, among crowds. 'No. We need somewhere safer.'

The turning for the town finally came and he screeched right, off the Bundestrasse, and put his foot down again. It seemed to take an age to reach the outskirts, Jacob looking up for any sign of the helicopter above them. As he approached the town centre, roundabouts slowed him but he roared through the red lights.

Finally he found a wide street lined with supermarkets, restaurants and car showrooms.

'There,' shouted Eloise.

A few cars had parked at a disused petrol station under the dark of the canopy.

Myroslav would be following a GPS tracker. They had to get

out of the car and get as far as they could away from it before he was overhead.

Jacob braked and skidded into the disused petrol station, then turned off the engine.

Eloise was rummaging inside the glove compartment.

'What are you looking for?'

'Get out,' she said. 'They might land.'

He did as he was told. She followed a second later, slinging her bag over her shoulder.

He ran back onto the main road.

'Do you hear that?' she said as he caught up with her.

He listened. The sound of rotor blades. It was still much too early for any shops to be open so there was no obvious shelter, but on the opposite side of the street there was a fast food cafe. It was closed but it had an awning outside. Grabbing Eloise's hand, he ran across the street to shelter beneath it, out of sight, just as the dark shape of the helicopter crossed the suburban road, roaring above them.

FIFTY-FOUR

As the noise of the rotors subsided, Jacob and Eloise emerged onto the pavement and headed for the town centre on foot. After the horror show of the house, Jacob felt out of place on this neatly clipped Austrian street. A thin light was starting to seep into the sky. Bulbs blinking on in the small houses. Birds already singing in suburban trees.

At the sound of an approaching vehicle, Jacob tugged Eloise into the driveway of a small block of flats. It turned out it was only a delivery van.

'Come on.' Silhouetted against the dull sky, he could see the spire of an Austrian church, one that looked like several onions balanced on top of each other. Assuming that would mark the town centre, he marched towards it.

'Do you think they're here?' she asked.

'We keep off the main road.' They walked, ducking into shadows when they could.

A priest in a black suit came hurrying towards them, leaning into his gait. 'Ask this man the way to a hotel,' muttered Eloise.

'Why do we need a hotel?'

'Just ask him. Please, Jacob.'

Jacob did so, speaking German. Unaccustomed to being accosted so early in the day, the priest was ill-tempered, but he pointed them north and scurried on in the opposite direction.

Avoiding main roads, it took them twenty minutes to reach the chalky-green river that divided the centre of town. The hotel was on the other side. On the bare concrete bridge out in the open, Jacob felt exposed and scanned the horizon for Myroslav's helicopter, but couldn't see – or hear – it.

On the other side, just where the priest had said, they found a big white tourist hotel, orderly and rectangular.

They waited, anxious, looking around for any sign that they were being watched.

'Your identity, please,' demanded the sleepy desk clerk who emerged when they rang the bell.

'I don't understand why we need a room,' asked Jacob quietly.

'It's still an hour before the shops open. I need a shower. We need to be off the streets.'

'Your identity,' repeated the desk clerk.

'Mine's in my luggage,' said Jacob. 'I'll fetch it in a minute.'

'Sure, sure,' answered the clerk, who Jacob guessed would forget all about it the moment they had gone. 'One room?'

'Yes. One room,' said Eloise.

The desk clerk peered over the desk. 'Your bags?'

'They're in the car,' Jacob lied. 'We'll fetch them later.'

It felt so ridiculous to be here in this cheap place after the life they had been living, to be safe after the horror of the last week.

The banality of it was thrilling. The freedom of being far away from Myroslav's house.

The hotel room was small and functional, with a view out over the Alps to the north. There was a small grey house telephone on the table between the two single beds. Jacob looked at it longingly.

'I'm going to have a shower, OK?' Eloise said. She must have noticed him looking at the phone. She reached down and tugged the cord from the wall. 'Remember?'

'I know.'

'You won't, will you? Please? I just need to clean up a little.' She picked up a towel and disappeared.

He lay on the bed and listened to the noise of the shower, wondering if it was loud enough for him to be able to plug in the phone to call the embassy before she was finished, but she re-emerged in just a couple of minutes anyway, with the ungenerously small towel around her.

She dressed in front of him in the same clothes she had escaped from the mansion in. When she was finished, she looked in the mirror and checked her hair, then grunted in displeasure. 'Aren't you having a shower?'

'No. I just want to get this done.'

She checked her watch. 'Twenty minutes and the shops will be open. We can go out, buy a phone and hire a car.'

'Hire a car? But you can't drive.'

'You can, though.'

'No.' He sat up, alarm bells ringing. 'No, no. That's not part of the agreement. We got out. I let you get away. Then I'm free to do what I want. That's the end of it.'

She seemed to ignore what he had just said completely. 'Can you pass me my bag, Jacob?' She asked, nodding at the bag beside him.

She reached inside it and pulled out a small black gun. 'You do exactly what I say from now on, OK?'

'You played me. You cried.'

'I'm just a poor vulnerable girl.' She pretended to sob as she had yesterday, watching the TV. 'And you, being the kind of man you are, lapped it all up.' She stepped forward with the gun and placed it right against his skull. He felt the hard metal against his skin. 'You're so predictable.' She jabbed the gun in harder. 'Fuck sake, Jacob. You seriously thought I was going to walk away from this without a penny? I'm sick of being underestimated.' Looking up, he could see her finger, taut on the trigger.

FIFTY-FIVE

'Where did you get the gun?' he asked.

She finally pulled it away from him, looked down at it. 'Myroslav keeps it in the glove compartment of his car. I guess it's an old habit of his.'

She stepped forward and rifled through the drawers on her side of the bed, pulled out a couple of envelopes.

'Inside the house, you pretty much told me I had no power at all. Nazim didn't respect who I was. But here, outside, you see, I have you. They know I won't dob them in. It's hardly in my interest. To them, you are the threat. They want to know you're not blabbing to the cops. That's my power.'

Jacob said, 'You're the one who didn't want anyone to get hurt.'

'You want tears again? I can cry to order if you want. I've a lifetime's experience. Your weird maid's not the only one who thinks up clever ideas. Is there any paper in the drawer on your side? I've only got envelopes on mine.' She waved the gun at him. 'Chop-chop. Look in the drawer.'

He got up, opened the drawer of the flimsy table. There was old-fashioned lilac writing paper and a pencil in it.

'OK. Write everything you want to tell the police.'

He blinked. 'Why?'

'Just do it, please. Tell them anything you need to. You're the one who wants to expose them, right? Go for it. Go crazy. Tell them about Kolophant Ltd, the account in Singapore, Lutinol, everything you know. Tell them about your maid and about how you so desperately want to save her.'

'Why?' he asked again. 'Why can't I tell them myself?'

'Don't ask questions, Jacob. We're in a hurry. If we want to save your precious Vladyslava, you need to act quickly, and there is still a lot more to do.'

So he picked up the pencil from the drawer and wrote. On sheet after sheet he scribbled everything he knew about Eloise and Myroslav's conspiracy to defraud people, about the names of people who had been killed. He wrote the names of Vlada's son and mother, and the real name of the man who was keeping Vlada captive.

'Finished?' she demanded.

He looked at the pages spread out across the desk. 'I think so.' It was not everything, but it was enough.

'Write at the top, *Take this to the police immediately. Urgent.*'

He hesitated. 'So I take it I don't even have to be alive to make your plan work?'

'Just do it . . . Good. Now take this.' She gave him an American five-dollar note. 'Put it with the letter into one of those envelopes.'

'Why?'

'Stop asking questions. Just do it.' So he did, folding the sheets and cramming them into the envelope which she slipped into her bag.

'I don't understand.'

'You don't have to.'

He did as she asked. She slung her bag over her shoulder, holding the gun inside it, still pointing at him. 'And now we get out of this dump,' she said.

They walked through the wide, quiet streets, her keeping one step behind. 'If you run, I swear I will shoot you,' she said. 'Your best chance of saving the maid is to do exactly what I say.'

'How?'

'Just shut up and do it.'

They were walking towards the station, he realised. Close to the big, bland square at the station's entrance, down a small alleyway, she found a mobile phone shop that was just opening its shutters. She told Jacob to buy a used smartphone and a new SIM, and handed him her credit card.

They emerged back into the square. The day was warming up already. She had started the phone and was opening up a maps app. 'Ahead,' she said. 'Now left.'

They crossed the river again and reached the old town. 'You have a phone,' he said. 'You can call Myroslav. Tell him your plans. That way, at least he'll know that I'm not running to the police.' If he knew that, he would have no reason to harm Vlada.

'When we've got a car, I'll call him.'

They walked to the other side of the small old town towards an industrial estate.

'Right. Now next left. There.' She pointed towards a unit called Austria Rent and pulled another card out of her bag. 'Here. Now. Rent us a car. Anything they have. As quick as you can. Don't even think of talking to them about anything else because I'll kill you if you do.'

He looked at the card and examined it. It was an Australian driving licence. 'This is your husband's,' he said.

'I took his wallet from his pocket. He carries all sorts of phoney IDs. That's real, though.'

'I don't look anything like him.'

'Well, you better hope they don't notice that when you rent the car, then. Now go. Remember, I'm right behind you.'

It was a small local rental service, staffed by a young woman with thick make-up and a big friendly smile. Renting a car seemed to take for ever. There were so many questions. Did he want a two-door or a four-door? Manual or automatic? Would he be travelling outside the country? Would he like to take out insurance? Would he also like a Collision Damage Waiver?

He tried to answer the questions as calmly as he could. She tapped each answer into the computer, peering forward each time to check the screen.

Before they would let him have the BMW, she insisted he walk carefully around it, noting the small ding above the right wheel arch, the scratches on the hubcap. Then there were documents to sign. He had not had a chance to inspect the signature on Murphy's licence, so he did the best he could to scrawl a name. The woman didn't even look to check.

And then, finally, when they were sitting in the car together, him in the driving seat, her next to him with the bag with the gun on it in her lap, her hand still inside the bag, the woman leaned in the window to explain all the controls for a second time.

'Drive out of town,' said Eloise, when they were finally finished.

'Aren't you going to call him?'

'You're getting boring now.'

'Please.'

'Drive.'

It was a short journey to the edge of town. He stopped on an unmarked road leading up to farmland.

She handed him a piece of paper – one of the envelopes from the hotel. On it were the words *Zmajski most*. 'Put that into the satnav,' she said.

The map on the screen showed a blue dot on a bridge crossing a river. It told them it would take one hour and twenty minutes to reach their destination via toll roads. There was a warning triangle on the screen: *This route crosses a border.*

'Slovenia?' Jacob asked.

But she was ignoring him, holding the phone to one ear. 'Hello, Myroslav. It's me,' she said.

The call was short and to the point. She said she would exchange Jacob for three million dollars in cash. 'Then I'm out. Call me back fast and I'll tell you where and when the exchange takes place. If I don't hear back in ten minutes, the deal is off.'

'Ask him about Vlada. Is she still alive?' But she had already ended the call.

Afterwards Jacob said, 'So this was your plan all along? To take me back?'

'Inside the compound, you were not worth much to me. Outside, it's a different story.'

She reached in her bag and rewarded herself with a cigarette, fumbling with one hand to get it out of the packet. Jacob wound down his window.

'Three million is not as much as I would have earned if this hadn't gone to hell, but I know Myroslav has that much in his safe. It's his escape money. That's why he's based here, I guess, so he can make it over the border to Italy or somewhere. The point is, at least I get to walk away from this shit show with something.'

'I'm worth that much?'

'I don't know. Are you? We'll find out in a few minutes, won't we?'

They were surrounded by lush countryside. To their right, brown stalks of maize waited to be harvested. To the left was open pasture. Less than fifteen minutes after she'd made the call, the phone buzzed.

'I knew you'd do it,' she said. She checked the clock on the dashboard. It was just after nine thirty in the morning. 'Exactly midday on the Dragon Bridge in Ljubljana. Meet me there with the money. I'll have Jacob. We do the swap there. That gives you a couple of hours to get across the Slovenian border and get into the city. If you get your shit together and drive fast, you can do it in half that.'

From the passenger seat, Jacob could hear the anger in Myroslav's voice.

'A word of warning,' Eloise continued. 'If the exchange doesn't happen at midday today, you're toast. The whole operation comes down. Don't ask how, it just will. Understood?'

'Wait,' Jacob called. 'One more condition. You set Vladyslava free.'

'Is that the Englishman?'

'You get me, but she goes free. That's the deal.'

Eloise ended the call abruptly, then turned to him. 'Fuck you. Never do that to me again,' she said angrily, thrusting the gun hard into his ribs. For a second he thought she was going to shoot.

Then she sat back. With her free hand she pulled out a pair of reflective dark glasses and put them on. 'Drive,' she said.

FIFTY-SIX

The Dragon Bridge was in the heart of the old Slovenian town, just an hour from where they had phoned Myroslav. According to a brass sign on the south side, it had once been known as the Butchers' Bridge.

Tourists queued to photograph themselves against the big green dragons that guarded both entrances to the river crossing. Four of them, one perched on each corner, mouths wide, copper bat-wings streaked black by corrosion.

The journey had been easy. The roads were beautiful. The traffic had been light.

Eloise and Jacob were sitting at an outside table in the market-place that stretched along the bank of the Ljubljanica River, drinking coffee beside the granite colonnade.

The server had recognised them as English speakers. 'Would you like another coffee?' she called above the hubbub of the market.

'Thank you,' answered Jacob. 'Americano. And maybe a pastry?'

'My friend is fine,' muttered Eloise. 'Just the bill, please. As soon as you can.' She kept one hand inside her bag, still holding the gun.

'So what now? We wait? You really don't think they're going to bring money in exchange for me, do you?' He looked around. 'This is a public space. It's too risky.'

'Shut up.'

'You know they'll kill me, don't you, if you do hand me over?'

She didn't answer.

'All that *I never wanted anyone to get hurt* – all bullshit, then?'

She had chosen the location deliberately. Nobody would notice them here. It was Friday morning and the market was packed with locals buying fruit and vegetables and loaves of freshly baked bread; backpackers taking photographs for Tripadvisor.

Eloise had made him sit with his back to the bridge so she could keep the gun on him at the same time as watching out for Nazim's men arriving. Families were having a day out. Children thronged round a street entertainer dressed in a green dragon suit, a loose approximation of the fiercer-looking monsters that guarded the bridge.

'I could run,' he said.

'And I would shoot you.' She raised the bag and put it on the table. 'I'd scream, obviously. Point at those lads over there on scooters. In this chaos, no one would know. What would be the point? What's the time?'

Jacob checked his watch. 'Ten to twelve. What if no one shows up?'

'Oh, he will,' she said, scanning the crowd behind him. 'I know him. He does not like being beaten by anyone, least of all a woman. He'll do something. What exactly, I don't know. Excuse me.' She hailed the waitress again. 'I asked for the bill.'

'Yes, madam. I'm just coming.'

Eventually the young woman approached. She was round-faced and young, with a small piercing in the side of her nose.

Eloise paid her by credit card. 'You're busy. What time do you finish?'

'What?' The woman's head went back.

'Just answer me, please.' Eloise stared her down.

'Not till four.'

'Excellent. Now I am going to give you a hell of a tip,' said Eloise. Out of the bag, she pulled the letter Jacob had written. 'A tip like you've never had in your life. But only if you keep this safe for me.' She held it out.

'I'm sorry?' The waitress looked confused.

'If you keep it for me, for one hour, which is one o'clock, I will give you one hundred dollars. As a tip. That's the biggest tip you've ever had, right?'

The waitress looked nonplussed. 'A hundred dollars?' She held the letter up to the light. 'What is it, drugs or some shit?'

'Not at all. It's just a letter,' Eloise said. 'If I come back within one hour and the letter is untouched, unopened, untampered with, you can have a hundred-dollar tip.' Letting go of the gun for a second, she took five twenties from her wallet, showed them to the woman, then put them back. 'But if I don't come back, then you can open the letter and there is just a five-dollar tip inside. Not a bad tip, but not a great one. Your choice. Five dollars or one hundred. Which will you get?'

'Is this some kind of TikTok thing?' the young woman asked, looking around.

Her hand was back inside the bag now, clutching the pistol. 'Just remember. If I'm back in an hour, you get the full hundred. If not, you can open it. Agreed? One thing, though. It has to be me who comes for it. Don't give it to anyone else, however much they ask. OK?'

'You're crazy.'

'Like batshit,' said Eloise. 'But you'll do it, won't you?'

'I guess.' The waitress walked away, stuffing the letter into her apron.

Another minute passed.

To their right, the dragon was high-fiving a crowd of children, unaware that a woman sitting close had a gun in her hand. A girl, maybe six years old, ran screaming to the dragon, hugged him. Jacob scowled at her in the hope of driving her and the other kids away, to encourage them to play somewhere safer, but they were enjoying themselves too much to notice.

'There,' said Eloise, looking over his shoulder, triumphantly. 'I told you.'

A woman in a black hooded rain mac and dark glasses was approaching the northern end of the bridge. In one hand she held a yellow leather briefcase. It wasn't just the mackintosh that made her look out of place in the summer sunshine. She paused under one of the plinths, pushed back the hood and stood beneath the dragon, exposing her badly cut hair.

Eloise's phone chimed.

'Are they exchanging her for me?' demanded Jacob.

'*The maid has your money*,' she read. 'Get up,' she ordered, standing.

As if on cue, and in full view of the tourists around her, Vlada lifted the briefcase and held it horizontally in front of her, handle facing out. Jacob peered through the crowd at her. She looked nervous. One hand reached around and flipped both clips open. Then she opened the case, lowering it slightly at the front so that everyone around could see what was inside. Even from here Jacob could hear the gasps. Visible to everyone who had gathered around her, there were bundles of green notes inside. One of the tourists took out her phone and started filming, as if assuming Vlada was some kind of busker act. Somebody laughed.

'What the hell . . . ?' Eloise scanned the crowd, looking for any accomplices, but Vlada seemed to be there on her own. By now Vlada had snapped the case shut again, turned on her heels and was setting off onto the bridge.

Eloise walked behind Jacob through the crowd, prodding the bag with the gun in it into his back. 'Follow her,' she ordered.

Pushing through, past the rows of parked bicycles at the edge of the square, they turned left onto the bridge. Vlada was standing in the middle of it, her back to the grey balustrade, holding the briefcase in both hands in front of her.

'I don't trust this,' he said. 'Something's wrong.'

Eloise checked the crowd around her. 'She has the money, for pity's sake. Come on,' she urged. 'Hurry.' And she prodded Jacob forwards.

FIFTY-SEVEN

They walked slowly up the pavement towards her.

'What's going on, Vlada?' Jacob asked as they approached. 'What is happening?'

People pushed past them. Vlada looked down at the pavement. 'They told me to come here. To show the money.'

Jacob saw them first. Two of Nazim's men had stepped out from behind the concrete plinth that supported the dragon at the far end of the bridge.

Jacob asked, 'Have they come to collect me?'

'I didn't want this,' said Vlada. 'You should leave. Go now. Run away. He's going to trick you.'

One of the men was wearing a light blue bomber jacket. As Jacob watched him, he tapped his jacket just at the belt-line and nodded. Jacob understood. He was carrying a gun under there.

'Look ahead,' Jacob told Eloise, raising his hands in surrender. 'There's a man with a gun coming towards us.'

Eloise saw both men too. 'Give me the money,' she ordered Vlada urgently. 'Give me the briefcase. That's the deal.'

'I can't.' Vladyslava held up the briefcase. For the first time they saw that the sleeve of the mackintosh she was wearing hid a pair of handcuffs. One end was round her wrist, the other was attached to the case.

'Shit,' said Eloise, grabbing her. 'Shit. Come with me then.'

One of the men approaching from the south had broken into a trot, his hand unzipping the bomber jacket that covered his gun.

Jacob held his hands up, chest height, to indicate that he was not intending to go anywhere. He was giving himself up so Eloise could escape with Vlada. But instead of stopping to take him, the man ran past Jacob, on towards Eloise.

Clutching Vlada's arm, Eloise couldn't move fast. A mother was leaning against the bridge balustrade, taking a selfie, ignoring her small child who dawdled on the pavement. Dragging Vlada with her, Eloise barged into him. The boy fell backwards onto the pavement with a loud wail.

Before they reached the end of the bridge, Jacob heard a car horn blaring behind them. He turned just in time to see a black Mercedes minivan racing over the bridge towards them, forcing oncoming cars out of the way.

'Get into the market,' he shouted.

The van roared past Eloise and Vlada, dodged an oncoming taxi, then mounted the pavement right in front of them, narrowly missing pedestrians. Brakes screeching, it halted just at the bridge's edge, blocking Eloise's path.

To anyone watching, it looked like the van driver had lost

control, but Jacob could see that he knew exactly what he was doing.

The front door opened. The driver jumped out and, in one swift movement, flung open the side door. Eloise and Vlada were trapped between the van in front and the man behind them.

The second man had reached Jacob now. 'Don't move,' he whispered in Hindi, grabbing both his arms from behind.

Jacob watched helplessly as Vlada was bundled into the van. Eloise was pushed in behind her. It happened so fast that bystanders were not sure what they were looking at. No one intervened. No one came to help.

'No,' screamed Eloise from inside the van. 'No. No. No!'

'Now you,' said the man, pushing Jacob towards the Mercedes.

Jacob swung round, punched the man hard. The man had one hand on his gun, still tucked in his trousers.

Jacob took his chance. Moving fast, he reached out, grabbed a lamp on the edge of the bridge, and swung himself up over the parapet. The last thing he saw before he dropped into the milky green water beneath was the look of horror on Eloise's face, pressed up against the glass of the van window.

FIFTY-EIGHT

It was a longer drop than he had expected. He landed on his back, feeling the sting on his neck as he hit the water, sinking deep beneath the surface.

The river was much colder than the Milstätter See. The rain had swollen it. It was deep enough. By the time he surfaced, looking up to see if Nazim's man was still there above him, he had figured it out. The money had been bait for Eloise. Vlada was bait for him.

Somewhere, bizarrely, applause broke out as he surfaced. He straightened, swimming against the sluggish current, looking around. A small crowd had gathered at the bottom of the stairs that led down from the bridge. They seemed to think it had all been great entertainment.

Looking up again, he could no longer see the van up against the balustrade. It must have driven away with Eloise and Vlada in it. They had them both.

As he approached the steps, he noticed that the street-performing dragon was in amongst the crowd, jumping comically from one clawed foot to the next.

'Help!' shouted Jacob. 'Help!' But the cheering was still too loud. It was as if they all assumed this had been some drunken stunt. He was some Englishman from a stag party – a fool who'd overdone it.

A big man reached out his hand towards Jacob as he approached the steps. 'You shouldn't do that. It is dangerous. People get hurt.'

'I need to speak to the police.' He spoke in English first, then German. 'Something terrible is happening.'

'Of course,' said the big man, pulling him out. 'Don't worry. We will get you dry first and take you there. It's not a problem.'

'It's urgent. People are going to be killed unless I talk to the police.'

Nobody seemed to be listening to him. 'He's had too much Laško,' someone said. More laughter.

Instead, the dragon pushed his way forward through the crowd and put his arm around him as he emerged from the water. More cheers. Someone snapped a photograph of the two together.

'You don't understand.'

The dragon placed one hand on his hip, posed for the cameras. People laughed louder.

'Let go.' Jacob struggled. 'I need to get to the police station.'

'Disgusting,' said one woman. 'Tourists are like animals. They are ruining the place.'

'I need the police. Help me.'

The dragon leaned closer and said in a loud voice, 'Shut up.'

Jacob looked round at the dragon's big, friendly yellow eyes and the comical green horn at the end of his nose.

'Not another word. I'm pointing a gun at you.' He poked a three-clawed hand at Jacob. 'Smile or I will kill you and start killing everyone else around here too.'

The dragon swept his right claw across the front of him, aiming it at the smiling people. It looked innocuous, as if he were about to take a bow. And the crowd carried on laughing and taking photographs. It was hilarious. Of all the people there, only Jacob understood what he said because the dragon was speaking Hindi.

They stood for a minute, posing for photographs, the green dragon hamming it up.

'When we're done, I'm going to walk you to our car. You're not going to shout for help. You're not going to try and run away. If you do, it will be carnage, OK?'

Jacob stopped struggling.

'That's better.'

'Are they taking Vlada back to the house?'

'Shut up. Just smile.'

The applause was dying down. The show was over and people were turning away. The dragon poked his clawed hand into Jacob's gut. 'Move. Now.'

Jacob put his own arm around the dragon, pretended to pose some more, though the crowd had all but disappeared.

'Enough,' the dragon growled. 'We need to go.'

The dragon suit was cumbersome. It had a long tail with felted scales along the ridge. Instead of moving up, Jacob stepped back, down one step, tugging the creature back towards the river edge.

In big green slippers, three claws on each, the dragon was finding it hard to keep his footing.

'I'll kill you,' roared the dragon, furious.

'Look out,' shouted someone from above. 'He'll fall.'

By the water's edge, the steps became slippery. Jacob was already sliding backwards, tilting towards the water.

He grabbed the tail. And, with a huge splash, they were both in.

In the water, it became an unequal fight. The soft suit, padded with foam, took on water fast. The man thrashed his dragon limbs underwater.

Beneath the milky green surface it was impossible to see. Jacob was behind the man, clutching on, dragging him deep down into the water. On land, the man might have been stronger than Jacob; here it was a more equal contest. It was a question of who would give out first. The man's arms and legs flailed and kicked, but that only pushed them further away from the air above. Even Jacob was surprised at how heavy the suit became when it was waterlogged.

They sank until Jacob's ears rang and his arteries cramped for air. The struggling got worse, fiercer, more desperate, then weakened.

Jacob knew he was close to passing out himself, but he was better at this, panicking less than the man he was clinging on to. Lungs bursting, Jacob stayed down as long as he could, then released his grip. Weighted by the gun it held, the man's right arm flopped lower than the rest of him.

Kicking away from his victim, Jacob floated downriver, before breaking the surface as slowly as he could.

He gasped for air. He tried to do it silently, but the need for oxygen was too great.

'There!' somebody shouted.

Jacob looked.

They weren't pointing at him, they were trying to draw attention to something that had floated up to the surface.

Somebody jumped in to try and save the dead man. Then another.

Being so close to death brought a strange lucidity. As Jacob floated into the shadow of the river edge, he knew what he had to do now, and hoped he still had the strength to do it.

Beneath the pedestrian bridge, a little further downriver, there was another set of steps.

He tried to emerge from the river inconspicuously, but too many people were looking over the built-up banks now.

'There. He killed the dragon,' someone was shouting. 'That man there. He killed the dragon.'

FIFTY-NINE

Jacob ran.

'There!' somebody shouted.

He made his way onto the walkway along the north side of the river, then broke into a trot along the thin street that ran parallel. It was full of dawdling shoppers, people sitting outside at cafes, teenagers loitering.

The streets here were crowded and narrow. He stopped, looked round. He might be able to conceal himself in the crowd, but he was leaving a trail of wet footprints on the cobbles. No one seemed to be chasing him yet, but he would not be hard to find.

He slowed to a less conspicuous walk. He didn't want to be caught yet. There were things to do first.

Working his way back in a loop around the middle of the city, he came to the road they had arrived on, the road the Dragon Bridge was on. Looking south, towards the river, he saw the flashing blue of police lights. They were already taping off the centre of the town.

Head down, he crossed the road, staying parallel to the river, making his way along a narrower street, where the walls were thick with graffiti. There was no point trying to run. The path ahead was packed with bars and cheap burger restaurants. Chairs and tables filled the pavement. When he had gone far enough to the east, he found an alley that headed towards the river again.

The town centre was full of the noise of sirens now. People would be trying to explain what had just happened to the police.

He crossed over the footbridge, heading towards the side street where they had left the rented BMW, hoping that the electronic key still worked after its soaking in the Ljubljanica River.

The closer to Myroslav's house he came, the darker Jacob's mood. He hadn't wanted to come back, but the way he saw it, he had had no option. He had just killed a man. Even if he could persuade the police he had done so for a reason, that would take too long. He would have to do this alone. There was not enough time to do this any other way.

The drive had been strangely smooth. There were no customs checks between the two countries, no police to flag them down. He drove as fast as he could, knowing that cameras would be watching him, but not so fast that anyone would pull him over.

The motorway was busier at it approached Villach. Lorries slowed his way as he passed through the small hamlets on the plains before he rose up into the steep hills around the lake, but finally he turned off the paved road, onto one of the tracks.

It took him a while to find the house again. These woods were criss-crossed with small tracks, hugging the contours of the hill. He had to get out twice, stand, and try and orientate himself against the mountains opposite. Time was running out.

And then he caught a glimpse of white, through the dark trees.

Jacob checked the clock on the dashboard. It was a quarter to two.

He approached the doorbell and pressed it. There was a long wait before he heard Myroslav's voice. 'I'm surprised,' he said. 'You're alive.'

'I don't think you were expecting me,' Jacob said.

'No,' said Myroslav. 'We were not.'

The big white gate rolled open. He returned to the BMW and drove it slowly into the white driveway. Nazim's two men were there with guns aimed at him.

'On your own?' Nazim was standing by the fountain, looking past him at the open gate. 'No one following you?'

He stepped out of the BMW, arms in the air.

'Why? Why did you come back?'

It had been less than a day since he'd last been here, but Myroslav's house already looked shabbier. Leaves had fallen among the white gravel. The broken glass in the doorway had been roughly boarded up with plywood.

One of Nazim's people approached, made him turn round and put his hands on the roof while he patted him down.

'What happened to our man?' Nazim asked. 'We have not heard from him.'

Jacob noticed that the Mercedes van that had picked Eloise and Vlada off the street was there, parked close to the garage, its door wide open still.

'The dragon thing was clever,' Jacob said. 'Did he rent the suit, or borrow it off whoever was using it?'

Nazim grunted. 'Sometimes you have to improvise. I don't understand what you're doing here. You are here by yourself?'

'What about Eloise? Did you kill her already?' Jacob asked.

Nazim looked at him for a minute. 'Not yet. She has been trying to tell us some kind of story though. I wasn't sure I understood it properly. As you are here, I think you'd better come in.' Nazim held open the boarded-up door. 'Perhaps you can help. Since you vanished we've been trying to talk on our mobiles. Half the time you're wondering if it's you that's talking shit or them.' He led Jacob through the living room. That was different too. There were boxes of half-eaten pizza lying on Myroslav's pristine Noguchi table. Nobody had cleared the place up. Jacob's stomach tightened.

Outside, Myroslav was standing on the terrace with a belt in his hand.

Eloise was sitting in a garden chair, her arms and legs tied with the kind of nylon straps builders used. There was blood on her lips and a sharp bruise reddening beneath her left eye. She looked pale, exhausted. She had been crying. Her eyes flickered when she saw him. 'They caught you?'

'I came back on my own.'

'Have you come to save me? I'm just a poor vulnerable girl,' she said, with a weak laugh. 'God. I'm grateful, though. I'm sorry I was such a bastard. Really I am. You have to tell them, Jacob. They think I'm bluffing.'

'What does she mean?' demanded Myroslav.

Jacob knelt beside her. 'I was worried they *would* believe you,' he said. 'And scarper before the police had a chance to arrive. Fortunately they know you're not trustworthy.'

'You have to get them to let me go. There may still be time for me to get the note. Tell them, Jacob.'

'It took me a while, but I realised why you made me write the note – when you could have written it yourself,' he said. 'I was your witness. You needed me there to tell these people that what you were saying was genuine. That you *had* left a note telling the police what was really going on here.'

'It's true then?' Myroslav said. 'She left a message exposing us. Fuck.' He stamped angrily on the paving stones. 'Shit.'

'Only we got separated, which left you here, tied to a chair. And why would they believe anything you say?'

'I told them. If they don't give me the money and let me go, everything stops. I tried telling Nazim that I had to get away. Myroslav doesn't believe me. Nazim doesn't understand.' She blinked, clearly in a lot of pain. 'You ever tried talking through Google Translate when you're being tortured? The bastards didn't trust me.' She started crying for real now.

'I never know when to believe you myself,' said Jacob.

'Stop it. Help me, Jacob, please. They're going to kill me.'

'I was the one who you were planning to send back here to die, remember?'

'I'm sorry. I'm sorry. I'm sorry,' she pleaded. 'Tell them the truth. Tell them that if they don't let me go, the police will find out everything.'

Nazim had joined them. 'So it's true. There is a message for the police?'

'All this is his fault,' Myroslav muttered, eyeing Nazim. 'He came here and he fucked everything.'

'Can you please tell him to be quiet?' Nazim shouted.

They talked angrily, but without Jacob translating, neither understood the other.

'Will somebody untie me here? Please. Untie me. There's not a lot of time. I can still do it.'

'Fuck. Fuck. Fuck!' Myroslav raged. 'Tell us where the message is.'

He reached behind the chair and tugged the strap off Eloise's hands. They had been tightly bound and she had to hold them in front of her, flexing her fingers to get the blood moving again, before she reached down to loosen the ones around her ankles.

Jacob left them to it. The place was descending into chaos.

He crossed back through the ruined terrace door into the living room and into the kitchen. There were piles of dirty plates in the sink. Maybe he was too late already.

SIXTY

Whatever Eloise was telling them, to try and save her own life, it was too late to stop things now. The waitress would have given the letter to the police shortly after one. There had been police everywhere around the market. It wouldn't have taken long. The Slovenians would be in contact with the Austrians by now, he guessed.

It was guesswork, but it could be another twenty-four hours before they raided. They might be cautious. There would be warrants needed and plans to make. They might need to call in SWAT teams. The only way to make sure that Myroslav didn't try and get rid of Vlada was to be here himself, so he had come back.

By the time he got back to the terrace, Eloise was standing shakily, trying to wipe the blood from her lips with a paper handkerchief.

Jacob stepped forward. 'They are letting you go?'

'Yeah. One of Nazim's men is going to drive me back there,' she said. 'I will give him the letter. They give me the briefcase.

That's the deal.' She was full of shit. The letter wouldn't even be there. But the story gave her the chance to get away.

'Where is she?' Jacob asked, looking round. 'Where is Vlada, the maid?'

Myroslav looked down uncomfortably.

'Have you seen her?' Jacob asked Eloise, scared now. The untidied rooms. The fast-food containers.

'Relax,' said Eloise. 'I heard the weird harpy tried to poison everyone. They locked her in her room.'

He smiled to himself. 'What if you insist she drives you?' he said, looking at her meaningfully. That would get her away from here.

'Myroslav?' She turned to him. 'What do you say?'

'Out of the question,' he snapped. 'Hurry. It's time for you to go. The car is ready.' He clapped his hands. 'Where's the fucking Indian?'

He stormed into the living room. Nazim's man was sitting on a couch, attaching the yellow briefcase to his own wrist.

'That's the money?' said Eloise, following him inside.

'He'll give it to you when he gets the letter. Now go!' He pushed her to the front door where the van was waiting.

'Wait. Wait. My bag,' she said, pushing back. 'I have to have it.'

'Jesus Christ. Go.'

'I need it,' she protested.

Jacob saw it first. Her big Burberry bag. It was sitting in the Arne Jacobsen chair. He strode over, picked it up and was about to hand it over, when he paused. He flipped back the flap and peered inside, and knew why she needed it so badly.

'Give it to me,' she screamed.

Closing the bag again, he stepped forward and held it out to her. She tugged at it, but he didn't let go of the strap until she looked directly into his eyes. When he did, he gazed at her with pure loathing.

'Please,' she whispered.

He let it go and she ran to the car.

'What the shit was that all about?' demanded Myroslav as the gate rolled shut.

'Nothing,' said Jacob. 'Nothing at all.'

She had tricked him. Again. The envelope into which he had put the sheets of paper he had written had been lying at the bottom of her bag. She had never given it to anyone. He guessed it was just an envelope stuffed with blank paper that the waitress would have opened.

There would be no police. No one was coming to save him and Vlada.

When she got to whatever location she chose, she would hand Nazim's man the real envelope, the one in her bag, and he would hand over the briefcase containing three million dollars. Or kill her. One of the two.

He sat down heavily in the Jacobsen chair and spun himself slowly around.

'What shall we do with him?' asked Nazim, pointing towards Jacob.

'What is he saying? I don't understand a word,' Myroslav complained.

Jacob circled slowly, using his feet to push him round. The police knew nothing. He was alone.

Frustrated, Nazim was punching phrases into his phone. He held it up to Myroslav.

'*What do we do with it?*' read Myroslav. 'What the fuck does he mean?' he asked Jacob.

'It,' said Nazim, pointing. 'It.'

'Oh, him?' Myroslav looked tired. He was not the man he used to be. He waved his hand. 'You can kill him. He's no use to us any more.'

Automatically Nazim looked to Jacob for a translation. Jacob said nothing.

From somewhere outside came a woman's voice, screaming.

SIXTY-ONE

'Look!' the voice shouted. 'They're coming for you!'

Jacob blinked to clear his head.

'Look, you bastards!'

He stepped out onto the terrace. Standing in the middle of the big green lawn, Vlada was pointing at the sky.

Vlada was dancing, spinning around in the middle of the lawn, waving. She jumped up and down on the grass.

Finally Jacob looked to where she was pointing. A helicopter floated in the sky looking down. It was silver, with a blue stripe on the side, and close enough for Jacob to be able to make out a single white word against the blue: POLIZEI.

Jacob stared. It made no sense. The letter hadn't been delivered to the police and yet they were here. Eloise had lied, yet it was as if somehow he had willed the police into being. It was a curious kind of magic. They were here, just as he had prayed they would be.

The helicopter circled slowly over the garden.

'Fuck,' said Myroslav.

Jacob looked around at the shock on the men's faces.

'What now?' asked one of Nazim's men.

And now Eloise was running towards them across the living-room floor, her face pure panic.

'Eloise?' Jacob couldn't figure out what was happening. Eloise had not escaped; she had come back.

'What are you doing here?' Myroslav demanded. 'Look.' He pointed up to the sky.

'The main road is blocked. There are police at the top,' she shouted. 'They're armed.'

Myroslav was screaming at her. 'You idiot. You told them about us.'

She produced the letter from her bag. 'I never told them. The letter is here.' She pulled out the pages. Every one of Jacob's handwritten sheets was in there.

'What is going on?' demanded Nazim. 'I don't understand.'

'The police. They've come for you,' Jacob enjoyed explaining. 'The roads are blocked.'

Now Eloise was staring at her phone. 'Myroslav?'

'We have to leave,' said Nazim calmly. 'Get your stuff, fast.'

'Wait, Myroslav,' said Eloise in a dazed voice, phone in her hand. 'I've just had a message from Cheong Young Zu in Singapore.'

'There is no time for this. We need to get to the helicopter.'

'They've blocked our account. There are police at his office already. They have a warrant.'

'What?'

'I don't understand it. It can't be happening,' Eloise cried.

Jacob could not believe it any more than Myroslav seemed to be able to.

The police helicopter seemed dangerously close. They could see a man with binoculars, or maybe a camera, looking at them.

'They will be here any minute,' said Eloise. 'I have to get out of here.'

Nazim's men were running to gather their weapons and belongings. Myroslav alone seemed suddenly calm. 'We will take the helicopter,' he said.

One of Nazim's men was standing in the room with the yellow briefcase, looking around, unsure what to do.

'OK. We go,' declared Myroslav.

'What about me?' said Eloise.

Myroslav seemed to pause for a second. 'Take the boat. The keys are in the garage.'

'You're letting me go?'

'Wait. One moment.'

He took the yellow briefcase from Nazim's man and calmly handed it to her. 'Here,' he said.

'What?' Standing in the middle of his living room, Eloise's mouth opened wide. 'You're letting me take the money? When you're getting nothing?'

'Fuck you,' Myroslav boomed. 'You played. You won. It was good. Now go.'

Jacob too watched in a daze, unable to keep up with the way events were unfolding.

From a distance came the sound of sirens.

'Come on,' shouted Eloise, running towards him on the terrace. 'What are we waiting for? The police will be here any second.'

Jacob was transfixed.

Myroslav too had a briefcase in his hand as he jogged across the lawn, past Vlada who was swearing at them, giving them the finger, laughing. He ran on down the slope towards the helicopter. With his free hand he was pulling Nazim with him, towards the waiting aircraft. He pushed Nazim in first. Nazim seemed dazed, unsure what was happening, but he scrambled into a seat. The two remaining men squeezed into the back.

Just before Myroslav finally got in, he turned, looked around, spotted Jacob up on the terrace, and gave a wave. It was weird. He was smiling as he switched on the helicopter engine. Popping open the side window, he shouted something.

'What?' Jacob shouted back.

Myroslav cupped his hands and shouted again. 'Fuck you.' Jacob wasn't sure whether that was directed at him or at Eloise, who was standing next to him. The rotors began to turn. There were Russian mafia in Italy. The border was not far. Maybe they would make it across before the police caught up with them. He watched as the helicopter finally rose slowly into the pure blue sky. It took a second before the police helicopter saw it, speeding in pursuit.

When Jacob looked back at Eloise, she was pointing a semi-automatic rifle at him, one hand on the trigger, the other on the barrel. 'We need to go. You have to drive me down to the boat. You have to do it for me.'

'No. I'm staying here. The police will be coming soon.' He looked over at Vladyslava. She was still on the lawn, laughing.

'Drive me away from here.'

He looked at the gun that was pointing at him again. 'No.'

'I'm warning you.'

'No. You don't have any hold over me now. Don't you understand? It's over. The police will be here.'

'Don't I?' In one swift motion Eloise turned and shot at Vlada. Vlada screamed, clutched her arm, fell back onto the grass.

Eloise shot a second time, this time at the lawn in front of Vlada.

'No!' shouted Jacob.

'Want me to shoot again?' she said. Somewhere up the hill, the sirens were getting louder. 'Or are you going to try and save her? Drive me or I'll kill her. I swear I will.'

Jacob ran down the steps to the lawn, where Vlada was lying. 'She shot me,' she said angrily. 'She fucking shot me.'

Blood was streaming from a wound in Vlada's forearm. Jacob tried to cup it with his hand. A lot of blood.

'Come on!' screamed Eloise, spitting blood. 'Both of you. With me.' The gun was pointing at Vlada's head now.

SIXTY-TWO

They ran to the BMW, Jacob supporting Vlada, whose face was white, her legs already weak from blood loss.

'Check the boot,' shouted Eloise.

'What?'

'I don't trust him.'

Jacob dropped Vlada into the back seat of the BMW and told her to hold her wounded arm up. Then he did as he was told while Eloise stood back. 'It's empty,' Jacob called.

'Now the glove compartments. And under the bonnet. Look under the car. Hurry. Hurry.'

'I can't see anything there. What are you looking for?'

'Then get in and drive.'

Eloise pushed Vlada over and got in beside her. 'You think there's a bomb?'

'I don't understand why he was so fucking eager to let us go. Drive. Drive, or I shoot her again.'

Jacob switched on the engine, half expecting an explosion himself now, but there was nothing, just the familiar grumble of an engine. He put the car into gear and headed left, around the building and down to the boathouse. Stones crackled under the tyres. The road was pitted and bumpy. He heard the sump hit the ground and in the rear-view mirror he saw Vlada wince from the jolt. Eloise was holding the gun in both hands, pointing towards her.

'Faster,' said Eloise. 'Drive faster.'

'How are you doing?' Jacob asked Vlada, glancing into the mirror. She looked weary, her eyes half shut. 'Stay awake,' he said. 'We will get you to hospital soon, I promise.'

'Concentrate on the road,' Eloise ordered.

'Talk to me, Vlada. I thought you were dead when I couldn't see you at the house.'

She smiled weakly. 'They locked me in my room. They thought I was trying to poison them with a salad.'

'Were you?'

'Maybe. You remember that plant with the yellow flowers on the lawn? The one my mother told me never to touch. I asked you its name. It's datura. Very poisonous. Unfortunately, they refused to eat it and locked me in my room.' Her voice was quiet. He had to strain to hear her. 'I smashed the window with the sink from my bathroom when I saw the helicopter.'

'The sink?'

'Why not?'

He was keeping her conscious, at least.

The journey took only a minute or two. 'We're here. Now get out.'

One arm around Vlada, they hobbled to the boathouse door. Eloise threw the keys at Jacob. 'Open it.'

Inside, lake water slapped against the hull of the white boat. Jacob lowered Vlada carefully onto the back. 'Hurry,' urged Eloise.

He unwound the mooring lines at the stern and stepped forward into the driver's seat. Switching the engine on, he experimented with the silver handle at his right. The boat lurched forward.

'Go, go.'

The lake was bright and clear. They were away from the bank in no time.

'Stop. Look,' cried Eloise. He looked, but at first he wasn't sure what he was supposed to be seeing. 'They got away.'

Jacob eased off the throttle.

Eloise was pointing past the back of the boat, past Vlada. Jacob turned his head towards the mountain top. Myroslav's helicopter was already a green speck far above them. The police helicopter was close, but once Myroslav was over the summit, he would be at the Slovenian border. Maybe they would make it over.

Everything felt suddenly still. Above the noise of the idling engine he could hear Vlada's rasping breath. He tried to make sense of the last few frantic minutes. The smile Myroslav had given him had been the strangest thing.

It dawned on him for the first time that the bag Myroslav had been holding as he had run across the lawn had been a yellow briefcase, just like the one he had given Eloise, the one she was clutching to her belly, next to her gun.

He turned in the driving seat and asked, 'Eloise. Did you check the briefcase?'

'What?'

'What if Myroslav swapped it?'

374

She looked down, puzzled. 'I don't know what you mean.'

The smile. That shout of 'Fuck you'. He realised that Myroslav hadn't given them the money after all.

'He got into the helicopter holding a briefcase just like that one,' he said slowly. 'When he took the bag he swapped it. Nazim had one, which you saw. He had another. There were two briefcases.'

'I saw the money. It was in the case.' Eloise laid the gun across her lap, put the case on top of it.

'But you don't know if it was that case.'

She went to open the clasps on either side.

'Don't!' he shouted.

She looked at him, pale.

Lunging round, he snatched the case off her, and with all his force swung it out into the air. He hunched, watching it arc upwards until it splashed down. He saw it again briefly, zigzagging its way down through the lake water on its way to the bottom. Crouching, he waited for the explosion – the massive plume of water.

There was quiet, interrupted only by the distant police sirens from the road to the east of them and the sound of helicopters far above.

Eloise looked over the side of the boat. 'You stupid bloody idiot. What the hell did you do?'

'There is a bomb. Nazim's RDX. Myroslav wouldn't have let us get away with the money so easily. They didn't put the bomb in the car, they put it in the briefcase.'

They waited, tense, for the air to be filled with noise. But there was no explosion.

Jacob stood there blinking. 'At least . . . I thought it was a bomb,' he said.

Jacob looked at Eloise. She was furious.

'I thought Myroslav switched the cases. That's why he was so keen to give you the money,' he explained. 'Why else did they want you to have it?' It sounded so stupid now, he realised.

'You absolute fucking—'

It sounded like the faintest of pops. They turned in time to see the streak of yellow flame descending from the sky onto the Alps behind them.

'Oh . . .' Eloise held one hand to her mouth.

Fuck you, Myroslav had said as he had carried the bomb onto the waiting helicopter.

In mid-air, the helicopter had exploded into a fiery ball, taking Myroslav, Nazim and both of Nazim's men with it.

'Shit,' said Jacob. 'There *was* a bomb.'

'He took the wrong briefcase,' said Eloise with a high, nervous scrape of a laugh. 'Nazim put a bomb in it and the stupid wanker Myroslav took the wrong bloody briefcase. Nazim meant to kill me.' Her laughter seemed to echo around the lake. It became gleeful.

Jacob considered this. The boat was stationary in the lake now. 'You're wrong,' said a voice from the back of the boat. 'The Russian did it deliberately. I wanted so much to kill him myself, but the arrogant bastard saved me the trouble.'

Eloise stared at the distant smudge of black smoke rising into the crisp blue air. 'Shit,' she said.

Jacob looked around the lake. He could hear police cars

all around it now. Two more helicopters were passing low overhead.

'So pretty here,' Vlada said. 'I would like to come back one day.'

Eloise made them ditch the boat on the rocky shoreline under the shade of trees.

'Now what?'

'We walk.'

'Vlada is in no state for that,' he said.

There was a first-aid kit in a seat compartment. Jacob insisted on dressing Vlada's wound before abandoning her. She winced each time he wound the bandage around her arm. He found painkillers too, and gave them to her.

'I'll send for help,' he promised.

Then, gun at his back, he stepped off the boat onto one of the rocks. His foot slipped and he fell forwards into the grass bank.

'Vlada was right, you know,' he said. 'The bomb was meant for you. Nazim was going to switch it for the one with the money in. Myroslav knew that. He didn't make the switch. He deliberately kept the bomb. He just saved your life.'

Eloise considered this. 'The bastard. He didn't do it for me. He did it because he didn't want Nazim to get a single cent of his money. He would rather kill himself.'

Jacob realised that was true too. Myroslav had done it because it was the only way he could win.

She jumped down, landing awkwardly next to him.

She had chosen a bad spot to bring the boat in. After twenty minutes struggling through the undergrowth, a thin rain started to fall. The weather had turned again. Soon the rain became harder. The steep ground became treacherous, the mossy rocks slippery. Eloise was wearing court shoes. When she lost one between two rocks she cut her foot on a broken pine branch, and started crying.

When they finally emerged onto the road above, weary and wet, the police were there waiting for them, guns drawn.

They waited there while the rescue team brought Vlada up on a stretcher.

'My son's name is Tymko,' she was telling them, over and over. 'My mother's name is Iryna Yershova. My son's name is Tymko.'

The police had handcuffed Jacob, arms behind his back, so he couldn't give her a last wave as they drove her away.

SIXTY-THREE

The Brighton flat was perfect.

It was in Phase 2 of the development and it had been recently completed. It smelled of new paint. The balcony looked out over the rooftops towards the sea. The light here, when the sun set over the Channel, was almost as beautiful as the estate agent had said it would be.

Jacob had bought the flat with the money that had appeared in his bank account. He had been surprised to find so much in there. Myroslav had paid him, after all.

'Good work on the poem,' the Austrian police had said.

'The poem?'

'That's what did it. We got a phone call from the CIA in America,' the softly spoken officer told him. 'A Portuguese poetry publisher had been in touch with them a few days ago with a cryptic message addressed to them – more specifically one of their officers called Murphy.'

He couldn't believe it. 'They got the poem?'

'Obviously they had quite a few officers with that name, Murphy – it's pretty common – so it pinged around until someone decided to look at the content and discovered that the message was exposing a massive counterfeit drugs fraud based out of Austria. The message had all the information they needed for us to raid the place. What's so funny?'

'Nothing,' Jacob said. 'Nothing at all.'

'It was clever. First time a crime gang has been brought down by poetry.'

Though he had been interrogated several times, both in Vienna and in London, by British, Austrian, Brazilian and American officers, the police had accepted that Jacob had been trafficked illegally and forced to work for an organised crime syndicate. The Austrian police had found Jacob's passport and phone in Myroslav's safe.

After extensive searches, police divers had found the bodies of two men concealed in barrels at the bottom of the Mill-stätter See. Two other bodies had been discovered hidden in the grounds of Vadym Melnyk's house.

Eloise, awaiting extradition to the USA to face multiple charges of fraud and several charges of people trafficking, had denied everything. However, Vladyslava's evidence was particularly damning, and corroborated everything Jacob had told the police. Jacob was a free man.

The authorities were tracking down women who had bought the counterfeit drugs, many heartbroken they had wasted their time and money.

They had frozen Kolophant's assets. For a while, Jacob was expecting that someone would ask for the money that had appeared in his bank account, but so far no one had. It was not much, in the scheme of things. There was talk that they had already recovered over eighty million dollars from the Kolophant accounts.

Investigations into financial fraud were complex and took a long time, one officer had told him. Maybe they would ask for it one day.

He had bought the flat and decorated it. It was Myroslav's money. He figured he had earned it. The furniture he had chosen was old, mostly Victorian. He was less interested in mid-century modern furniture than he had been.

Though he had intended to put a desk in the small spare room, he had made that his bedroom instead. The roll-top desk faced the balcony. His books filled an entire wall. He was working on the translation of a Hindi poem on it, and was proud of the result for its simplicity.

The bed said to the carpenter, don't make me,
Because if you do, some day soon they will carry you on me to
   your grave.
And there will be no one to save you.

The sun was starting to set over Shoreham-by-Sea, lighting up the Channel. He heard the key in the door just as he posted the translation off by email.

Tymko ran down the hallway, stopping to grin at Jacob. 'Hello,' he said brightly in perfect English, then lapsed into Ukrainian. 'Can I please have some cake?'

★

Iryna and Tymko Yershova had been picked up by police in Hungary, wandering the streets in a small town close to the Serbian border. They had been held by a gang elsewhere – nobody was sure where because Iryna and Tymko were never allowed out of the house itself. When the gang had heard of Myroslav's death, fearing arrest, they had put them in the back of a van and driven them somewhere far away, and then pushed them out of the doors to fend for themselves. They were reunited with Vlada by an Austrian refugee agency, and the three spent a few weeks together getting over the trauma they had been through.

Iryna had insisted on moving back to Ukraine, so Jacob had offered to host Vlada and Tymko as refugees. The refugee charity helped them expedite the application, and Jacob met them at Gatwick Airport. He and Vlada hugged for a long time as other passengers pushed past them. Then disengaged awkwardly and made their way to the train station.

Vladyslava found work helping in a restaurant in Hove. She was quietly scathing about the chef there, and the Brighton customers who insisted on vegan options, but she was allowed to add one or two Ukrainian dishes onto the menu.

'No special ingredients,' Jacob said.

'Only for irritating customers,' she answered.

Jacob didn't mind looking after Tymko in the evenings when Vlada was at work. He had never imagined himself in the role of a father – if that's what it was – but he found himself enjoying it very much. Vlada liked to go out and dance sometimes too. It wasn't really Jacob's scene, so he was happy to stay in with Tymko.

Just once, in early December, Carla came to visit Jacob in

his new flat. She had started going out with a man who wrote logistics software and who, she said, was going to be worth millions. 'It's nice.' She looked around. 'But smaller than I thought it would be, now you've filled it with this old junk,' she said, pointing at his desk. 'You should buy something more modern. Some mid-century modern would be nice.'

Carla looked puzzled when he laughed at her.

'I think it's great,' said Vlada. 'I love the place.'

'You have a very beautiful boy,' said Carla stiffly. She and her boyfriend were trying for a child themselves, she said, but without any luck so far.

'I'm happy for you. I did send you messages,' Jacob told Carla. 'Or at least I tried to. But Eloise never passed them on.'

'No – she did,' answered Carla. 'I got them.'

'Really? Oh. In that case, Eloise never gave me your replies.'

Carla stood and looked out through the window over the balcony towards the sea. 'I didn't answer them, actually. At the time, I thought it best not to. I wanted to make a break. I feel bad, but I didn't know what you were going through.'

'Well, she was very pretty,' said Vlada, when she had finally gone, which seemed to be the only nice thing she could find to say about her.

Vlada and Tymko shared the main bedroom. Jacob said he was fine in the second bedroom.

At Christmas, Vlada and Jacob drank too much wine together, sitting wrapped in blankets on his balcony. It was nice. The winter light was low, and the sunsets, when they happened, really were incredible. That night they held hands under the blanket, remembering the times that they had done that in Myroslav's house.

Tymko had been given a place at an infants' school in Brighton, where he seemed to make friends easily. His English was excellent. So much so that Jacob was learning Ukrainian to make sure that they spoke it when he was at home, but Vlada was not a patient teacher. Jacob insisted that it was important that Tymko spoke at least two languages.

Sometimes Vlada talked about going home, but Tymko was happy, so she stayed a bit longer. In April she announced that Tymko was old enough to have a room on his own and that Jacob should give up his spare room.

'Where shall I sleep?'

'With me, of course,' she said.

By summer, when Tymko's school holidays began, the lake water was warm again. Jacob had not been convinced that it was a good idea for Vlada to return with him. 'Are you sure you want to go back?'

'Oh yes,' she had said. 'Quite sure.'

They bought swimming gear.

They drove by the house first, in their rented car, then got out and stood by the entrance.

The white paint on the walls was flaking. There was a notice on the gate announcing that the property had been seized by the Federal Anti-Corruption Bureau.

'Seems like a dream now,' he said.

She didn't say anything. Jacob reached out and took her hand again as they stood in front of the monstrous place. She leaned into him.

*

They rented a boat and spent their days on the lake. Jacob had brought a fishing road, which he dangled over the side of the boat, but most of the time, he and Vlada took turns to swim.

'What are you looking for?' Tymko asked.

'Magic fish,' said Jacob.

They had already discussed what they would do with the money if they found the briefcase – the trust fund they would set up for Webb's daughter, the house they would buy for Iryna.

In the summer of 2023 they are both back in Brighton and still living together. Eloise's trial is about to start.

Vlada has set up her own restaurant in the North Laine. She serves borsch and *kholodets*. She has even put some vegan items on the menu, and has stopped looking annoyed when they are ordered.

When people ask her where she found the money to set a place this good up, she tells them she found it at the bottom of a lake, and nobody believes her.

Jacob is running a publishing house. It specialises in poetry in translation. It is doing surprisingly well, and in time will publish books that are nominated for – and win – prestigious awards. Nobody expects him to get rich from it, because as everyone knows, there is no money in poetry, but for some reason, he doesn't seem to mind that at all.

THANKS

Firstly, thanks to Vladyslava Bondar for lending her name and her advice. Vlada has been a powerhouse in the Ukrainian refugee community in the Brighton area and her optimism and courage in these shitty times are inspiring. Thanks too to Marek Kohn for making the introduction. It was Marek's fascinating book about bilingualism, *Five Words for Friend*, that inspired me to write a book in which the hero's real superpower was language.

Thanks to my bilingual friends who helped with the book. Andrew Packett and Maria Amélia Tellechea wrote the poem. Thanks Kristina Quintano who is, like Vlada, something of an inspiration. Kristina was my interpreter on a book tour in Norway, during which I learned of her own amazing work helping and defending the rights of refugees attempting to cross to Malta. Vaseem Khan and Anna Cartwright also set me straight on important details.

Others whose input was extremely helpful include Susi Holliday, Fiona Erskine and Elly Griffiths.

Thanks too for comments, friendship and support, Ruth Ware, Brian Ogilvie, Lesley Thomson, Ann Cleeves, Samantha Brownley, Caroline Maston and all at UK Crime Book Club, Fiona Sharp, Jane Casey, Colin Scott and many more. I'm really grateful for the brilliant work done on the book by Jasmine Palmer and Nick de Somogyi.

It's ten years since I started working with my agent Karolina Sutton and she continues to be a brilliant colleague and ally. It's also ten years since I started working with my editor Jon Riley. I owe him a lot. Without him, this novel would have missed its mark by a country mile.

Finally, Jane McMorrow: x.